The Bee keepers' magazine

Charles C. Miller Memorial Apicultural Library WU

The Bee keepers' magazine

ISBN/EAN: 9783741190087

Manufactured in Europe, USA, Canada, Australia, Japa

Cover: Foto ©Andreas Hilbeck / pixelio.de

Manufactured and distributed by brebook publishing software
(www.brebook.com)

The Bee keepers' magazine

<u>This Volume contains :— Extracts.</u>

1.
(a) "A method of constructing Bee hives of wood" &c. by the
Rev. Andrew <u>Jamieson</u>. (in. Ed. Philos. journal)

6.
(b) "On sounds inaudible by certain Ears" by Wm Hyde
<u>Wollaston</u> M.D. (Ed Philos. Journal)

11.
(c) "Observations on Bees made by means of the Mirror Hive"
by Rev. W^m <u>Dunbar</u> (Ed. Philos. journal)

17.
(d) "Some Observations on the Instinct and Operations of Bees" &c.
by Rev. W^m <u>Dunbar</u>. (Ed. Philos. journal)

p. 23. (e) "Altägyptisches Bienenwesen" &c. von Dr Alexander
<u>Dedekind</u>   Berlin 1901.

p. 59. (f) "Wasps ancient and modern" by Ed. Latham <u>Ormerod</u>
M.D.   &c.

p. 80. (g) "On the Anatomy and Functions of the Tongue of the
Honey-Bee (Worker)," by Travers James <u>Briant</u>. Read
3rd April 1884.   Linn. Soc. Journ. Zool. Vol. XVII.

p. 90. (h) "Lincolnshire Pseudoscorpions" &c. by H. Wallis <u>Kew</u> F.Z.S
from the "Naturalist". July 2nd 1901.

p. 114. (i) "Introduction or Early History of Bees and Honey". By
Wm Carr. Newton Heath. Shears. Manchester.   1880.

p. 130

j) "The Habits and Intelligence of Bees" by Benjamin Kidd.
          Longman's Mag. Vol. VI.   1885.

p. 143.

k) "Scientific Bee Culture", by S. Hopkins, Apiarist,
   — Matamata.   Brett's Colonist's Encyclopædia, 1883.

p. 155.

l) "Experiments relating to the management of Bees". by
   Mr. George Hubbard.   Trans. Soc. of Arts. 1770.

p. 159.

m) "Relation of a case of poisoning caused by the Honey of the
   Lecheguana Wasp". By Auguste de St. Hilaire.
   Trans. from Mémoires du Museum. Paris, 1825.

p. 164.

n) "On the great advantage of giving premiums to farmers ....
   with a proposal for the increase of apiaries in Ireland" &c.
   by Sir James Caldwell, Bart. F.R.S. Ann. Reg. 1765.

p. 169.   (followed by)

o) "Description of a very curious and useful bee-hive invented
   by Mr. Thorsley (Thorley)   Ann. Reg. 1765

p. 171.

p) "Account of a petrified bee-hive, discovered by Mr. Lippi,
                              Ann. Reg. 1767.

p. 173.

q) "A curious and interesting account of a substance" &c. viz.
   "Honey-dew, from the Mémoire of the Abbé Boissier de
   Sauvages 1763.   Ann. Reg. 1768.

p. 182.

(t) "An Account of the Manner of rearing Bees in Portugal"; from <u>Murphy</u>'s Travels in Portugal. Univ.ᵉ Mag. 1795.

p. 184.

(u) "<u>Owen</u>'s Translation of Geoponica - (Review of) 1806

p. 189

(v) A review of <u>Huish</u>'s Treatise on Bees. London 1815. from the Critical Review, Jan, 1816.

p. 216.

(w) "Of Bees" from "A Compleat Body of Husbandry". by Thomas <u>Hale</u> Esq. London, 1759.

p 228.

(x) A Treatise on Bees from "Rural Recreations or the Gardener's Instructor" by a <u>Society</u> of <u>Practical Gardeners</u> London 1802.

p.281.

(y) The Bee-keepers. Mag. New York. May, 1868.

p. 299.

(y) "The Blind philosopher of Geneva" (<u>Huber</u>) - from the Sixpenny Mag. Oct 1862

p. 306.

(a.a) A review of <u>Huber</u>'s "Nouvelles Observations sur les Abeilles" - Paris 1814. Edinburgh Rev. Oct 1815

p 331.

(b.b)"Industry" a moral Song, by R. S. <u>Brough</u>. from Part I. "Shadow & Substance" London 1858.

p.336.

(c.c.)"Apis Indica" by (Capt.ⁿ) A.P. <u>Beresford</u> (R.N.) Badminton Mag. Dec. 1900.

p. 343.

(d.d.) "The Honey Bee" a Lecture by the Rev. S. Kevan, Poulton.
i. Fylde, Lancashire   Feb. 14th 1891.

p. 352.

(e.e.) "The Honey Bee" from Murray's Mag. Vol II. 1887

p. 367.

(f.f.) "Bees" from "On the Beauties, Harmonies, and Sublimities
of Nature", by Charles Bucke.   London   1837.

p. 391.

(g.g.) Profitable Bee Culture by Herbert S. Shorthouse F.C.S.
a Lecture delivered Nov. 1902.   Birmingham 1903.

Edinburgh
PHILOSOPHICAL JOURN.

EXHIBITING A VIEW OF

THE PROGRESS OF DISCOVERY

IN NATURAL PHILOSOPHY, CHEMISTRY, NATURAL HISTORY,
PRACTICAL MECHANICS, GEOGRAPHY, NAVIGATION,
STATISTICS, AND THE FINE AND USEFUL ARTS.

No. V.

JULY 1820.

TO BE CONTINUED QUARTERLY.

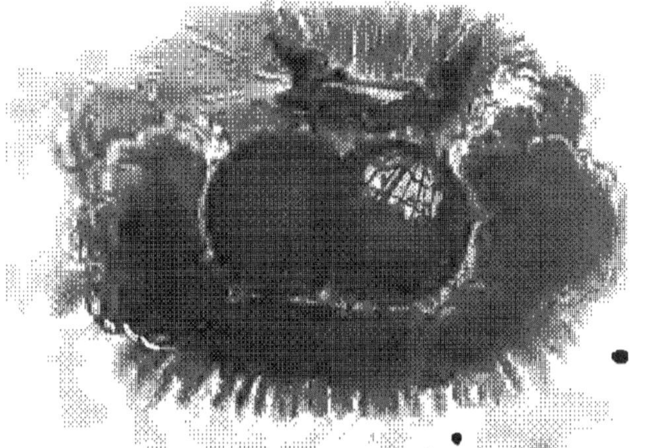

EDINBURGH:

PRINTED FOR ARCHIBALD CONSTABLE AND COMPANY.

1820.

ART. XV.—*A Method of constructing Bee-Hives of Wood, so as to resist the Cold of the severest Winter.* By the Reverend ANDREW JAMESON. In a Letter to Professor JAMESON.

SO many are the inconveniences connected with using bee-hives of straw, that apiarians have had recourse to wood in constructing them, and with considerable advantage. Straw-hives must be thatched during winter to protect the swarm from the cold ;—they must be thatched and screens must be put up before them during the hot summer months, to protect the wax and honey from the fatal effects of the heat ; and this thatching, so useful at both seasons, is at all times an evil, as it serves to harbour many insects hurtful to the hive, becomes a lurking place for mice, and in general retains a quantity of moisture, very prejudicial to the health of the bees. Another serious evil

---

* In many countries, remains of marine animals, sometimes of great magnitude, are found in alluvial strata, considerably above the present level of the sea, while in others, terrestrial productions appear under the surface of the waters of the ocean. In some cases, these phenomena are to be explained by a reference to the agency of earthquakes, and the action of volcanoes, as stated in the text.—ED.

connected with straw-hives, is the impossibility of securing them from *human* depredators.   M. Huish has proposed one of the most useful methods of securing the straw-hives from thieves, but still there is no great difficulty of very quietly robbing his secured hive.

To remedy these evils, wooden-hives have been proposed, and could they be so constructed as to resist the cold during winter, and heat of summer, without thatching, a very important end would be gained.   To attain this object, wooden-hives have been made of deal plank very thick, even as thick as two inches; still, should the winter be very *hard*, thatching must be resorted to,—one of the evils connected with the old straw-hive.   By the application of a good non-conductor of heat, secured from the action of the weather, this evil may be completely cured.   Let us suppose a hive made of wood, of whatever shape, is 12 inches diameter; then, let another hive of the same material be made 2 or 2½ inches larger; place the one within the other, and fill up the space left by the difference of size with powdered charcoal, hard rammed down; nail a fillet of wood at the bottom, to connect the two hives and to prevent any of the charcoal falling out, or damp ascending through the coating, which would destroy in some measure its non-conducting power.   The bee-door edges must be secured in the same manner.   By this plan, you have (out of sight) a non-conductor more powerful than straw, at all times possessing its non-conducting property, which the straw only has when *dry;* and no harbour made for vermin of any kind.   It is proper here to state, that great care must be taken to have the charcoal put into its place in as dry a state as possible.   Should charcoal not be to be had, any other non-conductor of heat may be used, as dry saw-dust, chopped straw, feathers, &c., but the charcoal is to be preferred, not only as better suited from its most powerfully resisting the transmission of heat, but as less liable to absorb moisture, and so destroying that power.

As the coating prevents the transmission of the internal heat of the insects in summer, this will tend to raise the temperature too high for the health of the bees.   This inconvenience may be obviated by a small perforation made through the entire hive at one of the corners, immediately under the projecting part of the roof.   To prevent any of the charcoal being moved, a tube must be inserted as long as the thickness of the entire hive, a plug made to fit it of the same length; and when the ventilation is used, care must be taken that no light be perceptible by the insects, which may be effected either by partially withdrawing the plug, or hanging over the hole, at a *little distance* from the outside of the hive, a piece of black cloth. Perhaps two such ventilating holes may be required; but experience must determine this.

The double hives I now recommend, may be used by those who think them *too heavy*, merely as *cases for the hives* which may be in use; removing the covers or cases when any operation is to be performed on the hive.

Since writing the above, I have seen a contrivance for securing bee-hives from being stolen superior to that recommended by M. Huish, but only applicable to *wooden hives*. The hive is so attached to a stone pedestal, as to render it necessary either to knock the hive in pieces, or carry off *nearly 200 lb. weight* before the thief can secure his prey. By this simple contrivance, all the hives in the extensive apiary at Applegarth-Manse, belonging to the Reverend William Dunbar, are secured.

MANSE OF ST MUNGO, }
   June 4. 1820. }

ears. I remarked, that when the mouth and nose are shut, the tympanum may be so exhausted by a forcible attempt to take breath by expansion of the chest, that the pressure of the exter-. nal air is strongly felt upon the membrana tympani, and that, in this state of tension from external pressure, the ear becomes insensible to grave tones, without losing in any degree the perception of sharper sounds.

The state to which the ear is thus reduced by exhaustion, may even be preserved for a certain time, without the continued effort of inspiration, and without even stopping the breath, since, by sudden cessation of the effort, the internal passage to the ear becomes closed by the flexibility of the Eustachian tube, which acts as a valve, and prevents the return of air into the tympanum. As the defect thus occasioned is voluntary, so also is the remedy ; for the unpleasant sensation of pressure on the drum, and the partial deafness which accompanies it, may at any instant be removed by the act of swallowing, which opens the tube, and by allowing the air to enter, restores the equilibrium of pressure necessary to the due performance of the functions of the ear.

In my endeavours to ascertain the extent to which this kind of deafness may be carried, some doubt has arisen, from the difficulty of finding sounds sufficiently pure for the purpose. The sounds of stringed instruments are in this respect defective ; for unless the notes produced are free from any intermixture of their sharper chords, some degree of deception is very liable to occur in the estimate of the lowest note really heard. I can, nevertheless, with considerable confidence, say, that my own ears may be rendered insensible to all sounds below F marked by the base cliff. But as I have been in the habit of making the experiment frequently, it is probable that other persons who may be inclined to repeat it, will not with equal facility effect so high a degree of exhaustion as I have done. To a moderate extent the experiment is not difficult, and well worth making. The effect is singularly striking, and may aptly be compared to the mechanical separation of larger and smaller bodies by a sieve. If I strike the table before me with the end of my finger, the whole board sounds with a deep dull note. If I strike it with my nail, there is also at the same time a sharp sound produced

by quicker vibrations of parts around the point of contact.
When the ear is exhausted it hears only the latter sound, without perceiving in any degree the deeper note of the whole table.
In the same manner, in listening to the sound of a carriage, the
deeper rumbling noise of the body is no longer heard by an exhausted ear; but the rattle of a chain or loose screw remains at
least as audible as before exhaustion.

Although I cannot propose such an experiment as a means of
improving the effect of good music, yet, as a source of amusement even from a defective performance, I have occasionally
tried it at a concert with singular effect; since none of the sharper sounds are lost, but by the suppression of a great mass of
louder sounds, the shriller ones are so much the more distinctly
perceived, even to the rattling of the keys of a bad instrument,
or scraping of catgut unskilfully touched.

Those who attempt exhaustion of the ear for the first time,
rarely have any difficulty in making themselves sensible of external pressure on the tympanum; but it is not easy at first to
relax the effort of inspiration with sufficient suddenness to close
the Eustachian tube, and thus maintain the exhaustion; neither
is it very easy to refrain long together from swallowing the saliva, which instantly puts an end to the experiment.

I may here remark, that this state of excessive tension of the
tympanum is sometimes produced by sudden increase of external pressure, as well as by decrease of that within, as is often felt
in the diving-bell as soon as it touches the water; the pressure
of which upon the included air closes the Eustachian tube, and,
in proportion to the descent, occasions a degree of tension on
the tympanum, that becomes distressing to persons who have
not learned to obviate this inconvenience. Those who are accustomed to descend, probably acquire the art of opening the
Eustachian tube by swallowing, or incipient yawning, as soon as
the diving-bell touches the water.

It seems highly probable, that in the state of artificial tension
thus produced, a corresponding deafness to low tones is occasioned; but, as I never have been in that situation, I have not
had an opportunity of ascertaining this point by direct experiment.

In the natural healthy state of the human ear, there does not seem to be any strict limit to our power of discerning low sounds. In listening to those pulsatory vibrations of the air of which sound consists, if they become less and less frequent, we may doubt at what point tones suited to produce any musical effect terminate; yet all persons but those whose organs are palpably defective, continue sensible of vibratory motion, until it becomes a mere tremor, which may be felt and even almost counted.

On the contrary, if we turn our attention to the opposite extremity of the scale of audible sounds, and, with a series of pipes exceeding each other in sharpness, if we examine the effects of them successively upon the ears of any considerable number of persons, we shall find (even within the range of those tones which are produced for their musical effects) a very distinct and striking difference between the powers of different individuals, whose organs of hearing are in other respects perfect, and shall have reason to infer, that human hearing in general is more confined than has been supposed with regard to its perception of very acute sounds, and has probably, in every instance, some definite limit, at no great distance beyond the sounds ordinarily heard.

It is now some years since I first had occasion to notice this species of partial deafness, which I at that time supposed to be peculiar to the individual in whom I observed it. While I was endeavouring to estimate the pitch of certain sharp sounds, I remarked in one of my friends a total insensibility to the sound of a small organ pipe, which, in respect to acuteness, was far within the limits of my own hearing, as well as of others of our acquaintance. By subsequent examination, we found that his sense of hearing terminated at a note four octaves above the middle E of the piano-forte. This note he seemed to hear rather imperfectly, but he could not hear the F next above it, although his hearing is in other respects as perfect, and his perception of musical pitch as correct as that of any ordinary ears.

The casual observation of this peculiarity in the organ of hearing, soon brought to my recollection a similar incapacity in a near relation of my own, whom I very well remember to have said, when I was a boy, that she never could hear the chirping that commonly occurs in hedges during a summer's evening, which I believe to be that of the gryllus campestris.

I have reason to think, that a sister of the person last alluded to had the same peculiarity of hearing, although neither of them were in any degree deaf to common sounds.

The next case which came to my knowledge was in some degree more remarkable, in as much as the deafness in all probability extended a note or two lower than in the first instance. This information is derived from two ladies of my acquaintance, who agree that their father could never hear the chirping of the common house-sparrow. This is the lowest limit to acute hearing that I have met with, and I believe it to be extremely rare. Deafness even to the chirping of the house-cricket, which is several notes higher, is not common. Inability to hear the piercing squeak of the bat seems not very rare, as I have met with several instances of persons not aware of such a sound. The chirping which I suppose to be that of the gryllus campestris, appears to be rather higher than that of the bat, and accordingly will approach the limit of a greater number of ears; for, as far as I am yet able to estimate, human hearing in general extends but a few notes above this pitch. I cannot, however, measure these sounds with precision; for it is difficult to make a pipe to sound such notes, and still more difficult to appreciate the degree of their acuteness.

The chirping of the sparrow will vary somewhat in its pitch, but seems to be about four octaves above E in the middle of the piano-forte.

The note of the bat may be stated at a full octave higher than the sparrow, and I believe that some insects may reach as far as one octave more; for there are sounds decidedly higher than that of a small pipe one-fourth of an inch in length, which cannot be far from six octaves above the middle E. But since this pipe is at the limit of my own hearing, I cannot judge how much the note to which I allude might exceed it in acuteness, as my knowledge of the existence of this sound is derived wholly from some young friends who were present, and heard a chirping, when I was not aware of any sound. I suppose it to have been the cry of some species of gryllus, and I imagine it to dif-

fer from the gryllus campestris, because I have often heard the
cry of that insect perfectly.

From the numerous instances in which I have now witnessed
the limit to acuteness of hearing, and from the distinct succession of steps that I might enumerate in the hearing of different
friends, as the result of various trials that I have made among
them, I am inclined to think, that at the limit of hearing, the
interval of a single note between two sounds, may be sufficient
to render the higher note inaudible, although the lower note is
heard distinctly.

The suddenness of the transition from perfect hearing to total
want of perception, occasions a degree of surprise, which renders
an experiment on this subject with a series of small pipes among
several persons rather amusing. It is curious to observe the
change of feeling manifested by various individuals of a party
in succession, as the sounds approach and pass the limits of their
hearing. Those who enjoy a temporary triumph, are often
compelled in their turn to acknowledge to how short a distance
their little superiority extends.

Though it has not yet occurred to me to observe a limit to
the hearing of sharp sound in any person under twenty years of
age, I am persuaded, by the account that I have received from
others, that the youngest ears are liable to the same kind of insensibility. I have conversed with more than one person who
never heard the cricket or the bat, and it appears far more likely
that such sounds were always beyond their powers of perception, than that they never had been uttered in their presence.

The range of human hearing comprised between the lowest
notes of the organ and the highest known cry of insects, includes
more than nine octaves, the whole of which are distinctly perceptible by most ears, although the vibrations of a note at the
higher extreme are six or seven hundred fold more frequent
than those which constitute the gravest audible sound.

Since there is nothing in the constitution of the atmosphere
to prevent the existence of vibrations incomparably more frequent than any of which we are conscious, we may imagine that
animals like the grylli, whose powers appear to commence nearly where ours terminate, may have the faculty of hearing still
sharper sounds, which at present we do not know to exist; and

that there may be other insects hearing nothing in common with us, but endued with a power of exciting, and a sense that perceives vibrations of the same nature indeed as those which constitute our ordinary sounds, but so remote, that the animals who perceive them may be said to possess another sense, agreeing with our own solely in the medium by which it is excited, and possibly wholly unaffected by those slower vibrations of which we are sensible.

DEAR SIR,

BEING desirous of ascertaining the consequence of introducing a stranger queen into a hive, without removing the reigning one, I procured from my neighbour, the Minister of Tundergarth, a small second swarm, and added it, with its queen, to the swarm already in the hive. I had no doubt that one of the queens would be sacrificed for the public good; but I wished to ascertain, whether, as Huber states, these great personages decide the matter by single combat, or whether the bees themselves destroy the supernumerary ruler. I noted down at the moment, by way of journal, the circumstances as they occurred, and I transcribe them in the same form.

July 28.—10 o'clock A. M. Put into the mirror-hive a swarm from Tundergarth Manse. During the bustle of the entry, the old queen has hid herself; the new queen is seized by a few of the old bees, the rightful inhabitants, and is in imminent danger; is rescued by a crowd of her own subjects, who treat her with much respect, and form an open circle round her, as if to defend her. A partial engagement between the swarms.

Afternoon. The battle has ceased, and the bees seem united. One queen, which I believe to be the young one, is surrounded closely by about 100 bees; no appearance of the other.

29th.—Morning. One queen on the opposite side of the comb from where the stranger one was yesterday, and closely confined; the other walking among the bees at perfect liberty; cannot ascertain which is the old one, and which the stranger; should have marked the latter before introducing her. Opened the hive, in order to bring the queens into view of each other: both escape to the other side of the comb, and *both* closely encircled by dense crowds of bees.

12 o'clock. Both still remain encircled. Opened the hive again, and seized a queen from amongst a great number of bees, not one of which attempted to sting, though, in my eagerness, I had neglected to cover my face and hands; put the prisoner into a glass tumbler, and clapped it above the circle where the other queen was; from the inequality of the comb's surface, one escaped, and was instantly surrounded; took off the tumbler, and the other instantly received the same treatment.

Afternoon. One queen close prisoner, the other at liberty, and sometimes within two inches of her rival, but without any appearance of anxiety to get at her. The crowd is pressing so very closely round the captive queen, that in all probability she will be suffocated or starved.

Evening. Matters remain in the same state.

30th. The prisoner queen on the same spot; the other at large.

Afternoon. The captive removed to the distance of twelve inches from her former station, but still vigorously confined; dispersed the cluster, and set her at liberty; but, alas! her liberty was of short date; she ran about six inches, hotly pursued by her jailors, and was again seized and surrounded as before. During her confinement, she emits almost unceasing cries, resembling the *peep, peep,* emitted by a queen previously to her leading off a second swarm, but wanting its regularity. The reigning queen does not seem to notice that she has a rival; shews none of those symptoms of rage and jealousy which Huber speaks of, but walks about very composedly, and shews no desire to break through the inclosure, to attack her rival. I observe, however, she is not laying eggs; probably her instinct is affected by the convulsed state of her empire.

31st. 9 o'clock A. M. The captive queen in the same situation, hemmed in by her cruel persecutors; opened the hive again, and dispersed the cluster of jailors, but in vain; the poor prisoner made a strong and desperate effort to escape, but had not fled two inches, when she was again arrested, and every limb held hard and fast. Resolve to remove her in the afternoon; the reigning queen has begun to lay eggs.

Afternoon. The captive queen is dead. On surveying the state of matters this afternoon, I saw her still imprisoned; opened the hive, with the intention of taking her away; dispersed the crowd, which almost totally concealed her, and found her quite dead,—a victim to my own curiosity, in the first instance, and to the jealousy of a prudent people, who seemed to know that a divided empire would not conduce to the public interest.

It appears from this experiment, that in some instances, at least, the bees themselves, contrary to the opinion of Huber, take upon them the task of dispatching a supernumerary queen; not, indeed by their stings, for I never saw one made use of on the occasion, but by suffocation or hunger. On the closest examination, I could not discern the slightest inclination on the part of either queen to decide the matter by single combat. They seemed, in fact, to be totally unconscious of each other's presence, for the reigning queen walked past the crowd which guarded her rival with great composure, seeming neither to court nor to shun the mortal strife.

A singular circumstance has taken place in this hive since the introduction of the stranger swarm, which, while it has given me much pleasure, as verifying an extraordinary fact in the natural history of this wonderful insect, presents, at the same time, a difficulty which I am unable to solve. The fact to which I allude is, that bees have the power, when deprived of their queen, of rearing an artificial one from a common worm, provided it be under three days old. In this process, they enlarge the original cell which contains the selected worm, by demolishing the three which surround it, and supply the larva with food in greater quantity, and probably of a different quality, from that which nourishes the common brood. By this treatment, naturalists say that the ovaries,—for all the working bees are females,—are expanded and developed, and the insect comes forth in due time, not as originally intended, to earn her bread by the sweat of her brow, but to assume all the honours of majesty, and to become the mother of a numerous race. This extraordinary fact I have had an opportunity unexpectedly of realizing.

When I introduced the stranger swarm with their queen into the mirror-hive, I expected, agreeably to the experiments detailed by Huber, that the two rivals, each of whom can " bear, like the Turk, no rival near her throne," would decide by duel which should retain the honours and privileges of royalty. I contemplated also the possibility of both falling in the conflict, —an instance of such a calamity having come to my knowledge, —and therefore, with the view of remedying this calamity, if it should occur, and thus of preventing the total destruction of the hive, I took a piece of comb from another hive, containing eggs and common worms of the proper age, and fixed it in the comb of the mirror, that the bees might, by proper treatment, convert a common worm into a royal one, and thus supply the vacant throne.

To my astonishment, as both queens were alive on the morning of the 29th, I saw the workers commence building a royal cell in this piece of comb, demolishing several cells around the one they had pitched upon, and enlarging this last, giving it a cylindrical instead of an hexagonal shape, and bestowing the most eager attention on the worm it contained. During the day, the royal abode made considerable progress; and on the 30th, in the afternoon, it extended above half an inch in perpendicular length. On the 31st, the royal cell advanced rapidly: saw the larva at the bottom of it, of a great size, and differing in appearance from a common worm, the bees very attentive in feeding her; the reigning queen passing her frequently, but taking no notice of what was going on. On this day, 1st of August, I observe the royal cell is sealed, of course eight days have elapsed since the egg was laid, and in eight days more the young queen should come forth.

Thus Schirach's famous discovery of bees having the power of converting common into royal worms, and which has never yet gained general belief, is completely verified. But here is the difficulty: All this time there were two queens in the hive. There was no want of a ruler, which has been supposed the only case in which the bees have recourse to this expedient. There is not a sufficient number of inhabitants in the hive to render emigration necessary; and if there were, it was never known that an artificial queen either led off a swarm, or was the cause of another doing so. I merely state the fact; let those who can, account for this anomalous proceeding. I shall of course watch the progress of this coming stranger, and should not be surprised if the reigning queen should make an attempt to destroy her on her coming into light. In that case, I may yet have an opportunity of witnessing a personal combat between two queens.

August 8. 8 o'clock A. M. The young queen is hatched; but short-lived has been her enjoyment of liberty, and, from all appearances, as short-lived will be her existence. Like her predecessor, she is already in " durance vile," about six inches distant from her cradle. A cluster of bees has hemmed her in as closely as possible, and only the lower half of her body is visible. She is making painful struggles to extricate her head and shoulders, and emitting the same dolorous sound as the former captive. In all probability she will experience the same fate. The reigning queen is very busy laying eggs, within an inch or two of the prisoner, but goes about her business with as much unconcern as if she knew that her subjects would of themselves soon rid her of this puny rival.

10 o'clock.   As I anticipated, the fate of the young queen is decided.   Her body had dropped lifeless from the surrounding circle to the bottom of the hive.   It is considerably smaller in girth than the reigning queen, but as long.   Her belly, which in a full grown one is of a dusky yellow, is in this rather of a pale reddish cast.   Her legs, like those of the rest of the royal race, are of a dark orange colour, and her whole figure bears the unequivocal stamp of royalty, though originally destined for a plebeian station.

From this experiment, I am warranted in drawing two conclusions.   The *first* is, That those naturalists are correct, who have asserted that the queen or mother-bee lays only two kinds of eggs, those of drones and of workers; that the egg which she lays in a royal cell, would, if deposited in a common one, produce a working bee; and that the egg she lays in a common cell, when hatched, can, by a peculiar mode of treatment, be converted by the bees into a queen.   This fact, though to this day a matter of doubt, was ascertained years ago by our countryman Bonnar, whose acuteness led him to the very verge of the greatest discoveries that have yet been made in the natural history of bees.

The second conclusion I am authorised to draw from this experiment, militates strongly against the opinion and observations of Huber, on the combats of queens.   Here were two cases, in which one, at least, of these great personages had an opportunity of shewing her prowess; but she seemed to be not at all blood-thirsty, and we must allow, that it is not consistent with the welfare of an empire, for the occupier of the throne to risk her personal safety in combating the enemies of the state.

I have great confidence in the veracity of Huber, and am satisfied he saw what he affirms, and that he saw it oftener than once; for otherwise he would not have spoken so decidedly on the subject.   My experiment, however, establishes the fact, that, in some cases at least, the reigning queen leaves it entirely to the working bees to despatch her rivals.

APPLEGARTH MANSE, }
  21st August 1820. }

AGREEABLY to your request, I send you the few observations
I made last summer on the instinct and operations of my bees.
I attach but little value to them, as they are all of minor moment, and shrink into nothing compared with the astonishing
discoveries of Huber. Unimportant, however, as they are, comparatively speaking, they add something to the general stock of
our knowledge respecting these interesting insects; and they
strengthen, in a certain degree, the evidences adduced by Huber of their wonderful instinct in more important operations.
They were made by means of a hive containing only one comb,
and glazed on each side; the whole swarm, therefore, half on

144 Rev. Mr Dunbar *on the Instinct and Operations of Bees,*

each side of the comb, was exposed to my view; not a single bee could escape my notice, nor could even Majesty itself be secure from my observation. This unicomb-hive was set to work only last summer, and its ill-fated inhabitants perished in the intense cold of the 1st of January,—facts which will account for the observations being confined to what passed during the warm season. I was much disappointed at this catastrophe, as I anticipated no small amusement from observing their operations during spring, the commencement of the laying season,—the period at which the queen lays the eggs of working bees,—of drones,—and of young queens;—the preparations for swarming,—the appearance of the interior of the hive at and after that interesting crisis,—in short, the whole process *ab ovo* till the final emigration of the superfluous population. To repair the misfortune, however, I introduced, on the 25th current, a swarm from another hive into the unicomb; and this morning, the 27th, I had the satisfaction to see her majesty very busy laying the eggs of workers. · As the hive contains plenty of honey and farina, stored up during last summer, I have no doubt the breeding will go on rapidly; and I shall perhaps have the pleasure of realising all my former expectations, and of transmitting to you, in the course of the season, observations more worthy of your notice than those I send at present.

Observation 1.—When the bees were put into the unicomb-hive in June last, they of course instantly began building comb. But the narrow limits of their new abode being only one inch and two-thirds between the glasses, prevented any considerable number of them from working at the top. A large portion of them, therefore, began a comb on the stick which crosses the hive in the middle, see Plate VI. Fig. 6. and thus two combs were going on at once, which eventually became one when the upper half reached down to the stick. It appeared, however, that there was still a want of room and of employment for these willing and industrious labourers; for, to my surprise, a portion of them began a comb on the upper side of the cross stick, and, contrary to their natural mode of proceeding, *wrought upwards*; so that in four days or less, the upper comb and this middle piece met, and the whole separate parts were joined, and became one square, see Fig. 7.

2. When the queen is about to lay an egg, she puts her head into a cell, and remains in that position a second or two, to ascertain whether it be fit to receive the deposit. She then withdraws her head, curves her body downwards, inserts her tail into the cell, and having kept this position for a few seconds, turns half round on herself, and, after laying the egg, withdraws her body.

3. When the queen lays a cluster of eggs, to the number of thirty or forty, more or less, on one side of the comb, instead of laying in all the empty cells in the same quarter, she leaves it and goes to the other side, and lays in the cells which are directly opposite to those she has just supplied with eggs, and in none else. In this order she seems to be scrupulously exact, and probably it is to ascertain whether there be an egg in the opposite cell that she keeps her head inserted, previous to laying, longer than would be necessary merely to find whether the one she is inspecting be empty. This mode of proceeding is of a piece with that wise arrangement which runs through all the operations of the bees, and is another effect of that remarkable instinct by which they are guided. For as they cluster closely in those parts of the comb which are filled with brood, in order to hatch them, the heat will penetrate to the other side, and some part of it would be wasted, if the cells on that side were altogether empty, or filled with honey. But when both sides are filled with brood, and covered with live bees, the heat is confined to the spot where it is necessary, and is turned to full account in hatching the young, see Fig. 7. ABC represents that part of the comb which was filled with brood, the rest of the square being all sealed honey. On the opposite side, the brood-comb was exactly of the same shape; insomuch, that on the narrowest inspection, I could not discern one cell where there was brood in the one, and honey in the opposite.

4. The shade round the brood-comb ABC in Fig. 7. is designed to represent cells filled with a mixture of farina and honey for nourishing the young, and which I often saw carried to them by the older bees. Where the brood cells covered a considerable surface, these store-cells were in three rows, as represented in the figure; where they were of less extent, there were two rows; and, at the neck of the figure, only one,—thus preserv-

ving a due proportion between the quantity of the food, and the extent of the brood-cells.

5. When a bee arrives loaded with farina, which is now known to constitute the principal ingredient in the food of the young bees while in the maggot state, she searches for a cell in which she may deposit her burden; and, having found one, she fixes her two middle and two hind legs on the edge of it, and, curving her body, seizes the farina with her fore legs, and makes it drop into the cell; after which she instantly hurries away to renew the labours, while another bee inserts her head into the cell and packs it properly, probably mixing, as may be judged from the moist state in which it appears on her retiring, a little honey with it.

6. It was ascertained by Huber, that wax is the produce of the saccharine part of the honey, and that it exudes from the bodies of the bees, between the rings of their bellies, in the form of small thin scales. In confirmation of this fact, I saw one bee, and only one, in the very act of squeezing out thin scales of very pure wax from the rings of her belly. She retreated from my view before I could discern her after-proceedings.

7. I observed the queen at one time hard pressed to get quit of her egg, and not being able to find a cell readily, she dropped it on the edge of one, when half a dozen bees, like so many dogs after a bone, instantly ran to it and devoured it.

8. In the honey months of July and August, when the weather is very fine, the bees form comb intended for containing honey alone, and different from that which is in the first instance destined for brood. The texture of this is much thinner, the cells considerably larger and deeper; and as the honey is then, in the hot season, of a rarer and more fluid quality, these cells are wisely made with a much greater dip or inclination than the ordinary ones, that there may be less risk of the liquid running over before it is sealed.

9. It has been often said, that the queen is attended in her progress through the hive by a number of her subjects, formed in a circle round her, and these have, of course, been called the guards of royalty. The truth is, her majesty has no attendants, strictly speaking, but wherever she moves, the bees she meets with in her progress instantly clear the way for her, and all

turning their heads towards her, fawn upon her, if I may use
the expression, lavish their caresses upon her, touching her softly with their antennæ; and this appearance has given rise to
the idea that she is attended by guards. The moment she has
passed a circle of her admiring subjects, they instantly resume
their labours, and she passes on, receiving from every cluster in
her way the homage due to a mother and queen.

Such are the few observations I made during the first season
my hive was at work. You have the simple facts as they were
noticed at the time, without any embellishment; for if they add
little of importance to what is already known of the nature and
habits of the bee, they owe nothing to the colourings of fancy. If
you think them worth sending to the *Edinburgh Philosophical
Journal,* you are at perfect liberty to do so; and I hope one
good effect of their publication will be, to induce others also to
contribute their mite of information. I am myself an enthusiast
in the cause; nobody can study them closely without becoming
so. " Beaucoup de gens," says a good old clerical bee-master
of Switzerland, " aiment les abeilles; je n'ai vu personne qui
les aimat mediocrement; on se *passionne* pour elles." Fortunately, I have a reverend brother in my neighbourhood whose
enthusiasm equals mine, and whose experience is much greater.
I allude to the gentleman whose humane method of saving the
lives of these amusing insects has been made honourable mention of in a recent Number of that Journal. If he, and such as
he, could be prevailed on to communicate the result of their experience to the public, the natural history of the bee would be
better understood, and its cultivation much more profitable.

APPLEGARTH MANSE, ⎱
   March 27. 1820. ⎰

Explanation of Figures 3, 4, 5, *of Plate VI.*

Fig. 3. is the external appearance of the hive, mounted on its
     stool, and having the shutters closed on the glass; front
     view.

Fig. 4. is a profile of the same, shewing the edges of the three
     frames of which the hive is composed, joined on the

one side by hinges, on the other by hooks and eyes; the centre one contains the comb, and the outer ones the glass, which is placed one-third of an inch from the inner edge of the frame, to afford a passage for the bees between the comb and the glass. *a a* are two lighting boards to the two entrances, either of which may be opened at pleasure.

Fig. 5. is the stool, fixed upon a square block *a*, and made to turn upon a pivot *b*, which is driven into the ground. The entrances, *c*, are cut, one in each side, in the thickness of the stool, sloping upwards to the floor. When the observer has viewed the bees on one side, and wishes to see the other also, instead of sitting in front where they are busy in coming out and going in, and thus exposing himself to their stings, he has only to shut the front entrance, wheel round the hive on its pivot, and open the other entrance. *d d* are two iron rods fixed on the stool, and which support the hive by two staples in the centre frame.

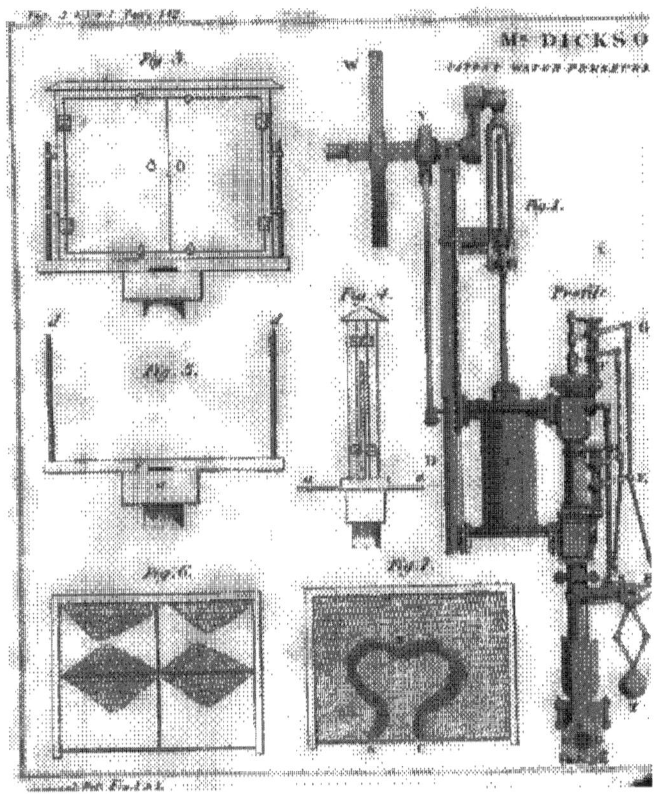

Mr DICKSO
Fig. 3
Fig. 5
Fig. 6
Fig. 4
Fig. 1
Profile

one side by hinges, on the other by hooks and eyes; the centre one contains the comb, and the outer one the slider, which is placed one-third of an inch from the

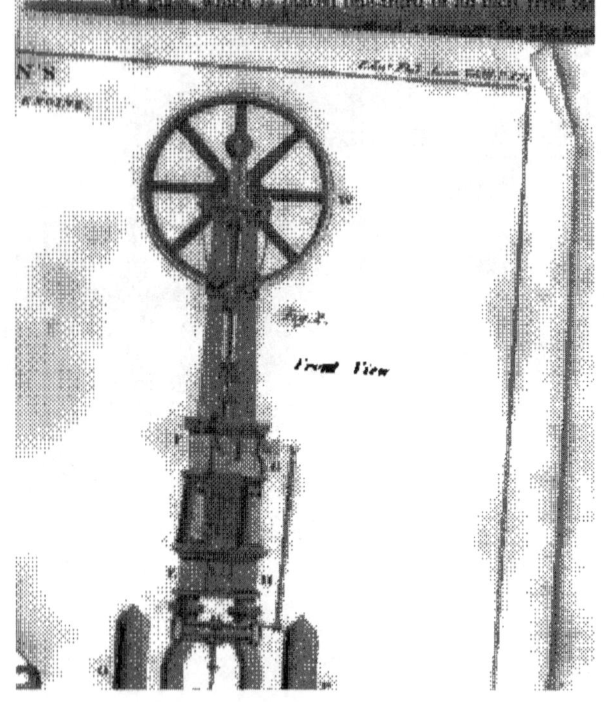

ALTÄGYPTISCHES

BIENENWESEN

IM LICHTE

DER

MODERNEN WELT-BIENENWIRTHSCHAFT.

VON

DR. ALEXANDER DEDEKIND,

K. UND K. CUSTOS DER SAMMLUNG AGYPTISCHER ALTERTHÜMER
DES ÖSTERREICHISCHEN KAISERHAUSES.

— — —◆—◄—❦—►—◆— — —

BERLIN.

MAYER & MÜLLER.

1901.

Druck von Adolf Holzhausen,
k. und k. Hof- und Universitäts-Buchdrucker in Wien.

DEDICATED TO

DR. JAMES HENRY BREASTED,

PROFESSOR OF EGYPTOLOGY IN THE UNIVERSITY OF CHICAGO

A MARK OF GRATITUDE AND REGARD.

1.

Der derzeitigen Vertreter für historische Bienenkunde unzulänglicher Kenntnissstand, betreffend altägyptisches Bienenwesen. Mittel zur Abhilfe.

Die Begriffe ‚Bienen‘ und ‚Bienenwirthschaft‘ erwecken bei den am tiefsten Gebildeten der ganzen Welt die sympathischsten Vorstellungen, hauptsächlich bei Denjenigen, welche das Bienenwesen von einem höheren Standpunkte aus selber zu kennen das Glück haben.

Angesichts dieser notorischen Thatsache ist es in hohem Grade überraschend, dass — während die civilisirten Völker dieses Erdensternes in rastlosem Fortschritte auf zahllosen Gebieten historischer Darstellung begriffen sind — die historische Bienenkunde, sofern sie um Bienen und Bienenwirthschaft im alten Aegypten gravitirt, recht stiefmütterlich bearbeitet erscheint. Während die gewaltige Culturarbeit Englands, Frankreichs, Deutschlands eine ganze Reihe der verschiedenartigsten literarischen Specialgebiete aufzuweisen hat, vermöge deren jedwedes dieser rastlosen Völker von der Donau, Seine, Themse, sei es auf diesem, sei es auf jenem Zweige der Wissenschaft weit voraus vor den übrigen Völkern der Erde sich befindet, liegt bei allen diesen Trägern der Pflege historischer Wissenschaften die auf das altägyptische Bienenwesen bezügliche historische Bienenkunde absolut brach.

An ausgezeichneten Werken der Aegyptologie, in welchen wundersam gediegene Rückblicke auf die älteste geschichtliche Vergangenheit des interessanten Landes am Nil krystallisirt sind, und welche an einer stupenden Fülle wichtiger verstreuter bienenwirthschaftlicher Notizen weitaus die früheren Publicationen übertreffen, ist kein Mangel.

Und angesichts dessen soll es keine speciellen Fachbücher geben, welche uns einen Einblick in altägyptisches Bienenwesen böten?

Allerdings existiren derlei Werke. Sie entrollen aber keineswegs in trefflicher, zuverlässiger Weise die Geschichte des altägyptischen Bienenwesens, bieten nichts weniger als eine höchst lehrreiche Lectüre und können von keinem Aegyptologen gelesen werden, welcher nicht für jene Autoren erröthet.

Es liegt mir ferne, das gesammte, von namenloser Naivetät schriftstellernder Imker zusammengetragene und hier in Betracht kommende Material Revue passiren zu lassen. Nur einige Seiten des in Rede stehenden Themas sollen im Nachstehenden besonders hervorgehoben werden. Bei allen jenen Arbeiten, welche über altägyptisches Bienenwesen Licht zu streuen versucht haben, vermisst man jene Reife wissenschaftlichen Geistes und fachgemässer Ausbildung, welche bei der Darstellung dieser Dinge von einem höheren Standpunkte aus unerlässlich ist.

Mehr als traurige Bilder von Halbbildung[1] bieten zahlreiche einschlägige Arbeiten, wie die eines TONY KELLEN[2] und ALBERT GMELIN,[3] lauter Schriftsteller über altägyptisches Bienenwesen, welche

---

[1] Ausdrücklich sei bemerkt, dass hier das Wort ,Halbbildung‘ in einer ganz speciellen Bedeutung gemeint ist, also keineswegs in dem landläufigen, ohne Weiteres wegwerfenden Sinne, sondern, wie gesagt, in dem ganz specifischen, hier in Betracht kommenden Sinne, wie noch des Näheren erörtert werden soll.

[2] Cf. ,Bienenpflege‘ 1892, S. 197, Kritik über KELLEN.

[3] Cf. ,Die Biene von der Urwelt bis zur Neuzeit‘. Eine kurze Darstellung der Entwicklung der Bienenzucht. Von ALBERT GMELIN, Pfarrer in Schwabbach (Württemberg). Sonderabdruck aus: ,JOHANN WITZGALL, Das Buch von der Biene‘. Stuttgart 1899. Verlag von Eugen Ulmer. S. 6f. — Auf Seite 6 und 7 steht unter Anderem folgendes Verblüffende: ,Aegyptische Schriftsteller mag es in einem so geeigneten Culturlande wohl gegeben haben, aber leider ist uns von ihren Werken nichts mehr überliefert, denn schon 312 v. Chr. verbrannte die grosse Bibliothek zu Alexandrien sammt allen reichen Schätzen und Urkunden.‘ —

leider nicht zu den Wenigen gehören, welche wissen, wie viel man wissen muss, um zu wissen, wie wenig man weiss.

Glücklicherweise bietet sich reichliche Gelegenheit zur Vertiefung und zur sonstigen Fortentwicklung der Einblicke in die Lehre von Bienen und Bienenwirthschaft im alten Aegypten. Dabei muss aber vor allem Anderen ein einziges grosses Uebel in

---

Bereits diese Ungeheuerlichkeit einer grellen Stichprobe von flagranter Unkenntniss in der Geschichte lässt tief blicken. Die grosse alexandrinische Bibliothek war in Flammen aufgegangen, als Cäsar die im Hafen liegende ägyptische Flotte in Brand steckte (Sen. de tr. an. 9. Dio XLII, 38. Gell. VI, 15. Oros. VI, 15). Irrig nennt Ammianus Marcellinus (XXII, 17) die Bibliothek des Serapeion als die vom Unglück betroffene. Vgl. PAULY's Realencyklopädie der classischen Alterthumswissenschaft. I. Bd., 2. Hälfte, zweite Aufl. Stuttgart 1866, S. 2375, s. v. ‚Bibliotheca‘. — Den Rath zur Gründung einer Bibliothek in Alexandrien hatte der Phalereer Demetrius dem Könige Ptolemäus Soter gegeben. Ptolemäus Euergetes (247—221) liess systematisch Handschriften in ganz Griechenland sammeln, brachte den ganzen Bücherschatz des Aristoteles und Theophrast in seinen Besitz, erborgte sich gegen ein Pfand von 15 Talenten von den Athenern das authentische Exemplar der drei grossen Tragiker, ohne es ihnen zurückzuerstatten. Cf. l. c., I. Bd., 1. Hälfte. Stuttgart 1864, S. 746. Diesen historischen Schnitzer, dass jene Bibliothek von Alexandrien bereits 312 v. Chr. verbrannt sei, hat GMELIN — sein Separatabdruck ist, wie bemerkt, 1899 erschienen — vollständig kritiklos aus J. G. HISSLER, Reallehrer in Ludwigsburg (Geschichte der Bienenzucht. Ein Beitrag zur Culturgeschichte. Stuttgart 1886. Verlag von W. Kohlhammer, S. 9) herübergenommen, wo in dem Abschnitte ‚Aegypten‘ nachstehender Passus vorkommt: ‚Die meisten historischen Notizen sind wohl mit dem Brande der Bibliothek in Alexandrien (312 v. Chr.) zu Grunde gegangen.‘ — In demselben Werke von J. G. HISSLER kommt auf S. 10 folgender Passus vor: ‚Die Biene selbst galt den Aegyptern als Symbol der Monarchie, des königlichen Amtes und des höchsten Gottes, und da diese die Repräsentanten des höchsten Wesens darstellten, als Sinnbild der Gottheit selbst.‘ !!! — Ibid.: ‚Es stimmen viele Archäologen darin überein, dass der Name Apis, des heiligen Stieres der Aegypter, welcher mit der späteren römischen Benennung der Biene identisch ist, die Heiligkeit der letzteren andeute.‘ !!! — Ibid.: ‚Wegen des vermeintlichen Entstehens aus Stierleichen wurde die Biene bei den Aegyptern zugleich als Symbol der Unsterblichkeit betrachtet.‘ !!! Blüthenreicher und erhabener haben sich die Phantasien eines Milton und des unsterblichen dänischen Märchendichters Andersen auch nicht angelassen. Und derlei Producte bodenloser einschlägiger Ignoranz eines CREEK (‚Symbolik‘), J. G. HISSLER, GMELIN und wissenschaftlicher Compileen sind in der historischen Bienenkunde, betreffend altägyptisches Bienenwesen, bis jetzt unbeanstandet geblieben.

Wegfall kommen, nämlich die wechselseitige Geringschätzung der
in Rede stehenden Fachgebiete und das vollständige Ignoriren
der wechselseitigen stupenden Fortschritte, welche die
Aegyptologie sowohl als die **Bienenwirthschaft** in der letzten
Hälfte des 19. Jahrhunderts in bewundernswürdigster Weise zu
verzeichnen haben. Durch diesen Mangel einer strengen Evidenzhaltung der gegenseitigen Fortschritte ist gerade die Entwicklung
dieser beiden Wissenszweige selber in mancher Hinsicht gehemmt
worden, während die wechselseitige Befruchtung der beregten Disci-
plinen reciproke Fortschritte inaugurirt haben würde.

Soll auf dem Gebiete der historischen Bienenkunde, soweit sie
das alte Aegypten betrifft, etwas geleistet werden, bezüglich dessen
Klio wünschen müsste, dass dasselbe zu dem dauernden Besitzstande
dieser Wissenschaft gehöre, so muss die Liebe zum Fortschritt unbedingt diese beiden Bildungsgruppen, die Aegyptologie und die
Lehre von der Bienenwirthschaft, durchschreiten. Das ist die
conditio sine qua non zum bleibenden Werthe einer Arbeit über
altägyptisches Bienenwesen. Das in Rede stehende Wissensgebiet
gehört decidirt zu jenen zahlreichen Wissenschaften, angesichts deren
Beherrschung die wenn auch noch so ausgezeichnete Kenntniss von
nur einer einzigen Disciplin genau so bekümmernd sich anliesse
wie bei einem Zugvogel angesichts des bevorstehenden Wanderfluges
der Besitz von nur Einem Flügel. Wohl existiren, wie bereits
bemerkt, summarische Belehrungen über altägyptisches Bienenwesen.
J. G. Bessler in seiner ‚Geschichte der Bienenzucht‘ (Stuttgart 1886)
und Albert Gruen, Pfarrer in Schwabbach in Württemberg (‚Die
Biene von der Urwelt bis zur Neuzeit‘, Stuttgart 1899) und viele
andere, lediglich in der Disciplin der Bienenwirthschaft geschulte
und weit bekannte Imkerhistoriker haben über dieses Thema geschrieben und gesprochen; doch sind diese Arbeiten und Reden von
dichterisch-phantasievollem Aufputze nicht frei, welcher dort die Rolle
eines vermeintlichen Surrogates für ganz specifisch ägyptologisches
Fachwissen in waghalsigster Weise spielt. Andererseits lässt sich
aber auch constatiren, dass von den Herren des Wissens des Morgen-

landes, welche dem Thema Bienen und Bienenwirthschaft im alten
Aegypten ihren ausgezeichneten Fleiss und Scharfsinn zugewandt
haben, auch nicht ein einziger Draht in den organischen grossen, ganz
specifischen Lehrencomplex über Bienenkunde und Bienenwirthschaft hinüberläuft. In dieser Beziehung steht die Aegyptologie
vollkommen auf einem Isolirschemel und hat daher nicht die auch
nur allergeringste Idee von dem, was die Geschichte der Bienencultur
weiss, was sie bis zu diesem Augenblicke vom ägyptologischen
Standpunkte aus noch nicht weiss (aber mit Leichtigkeit wissen
könnte), was der historischen Bienenkunde aus der reichen Schatz-
kammer des derzeitigen unglaublich hohen Standes der Aegyptologie
zu gute kommen könnte, und was gar die Aegyptologie — sofern
sie das einschlägige historische Material tiefer würdigen und im Bilde
der gewaltigen Continuität dieses wichtigen Culturzweiges von einem
höheren Standpunkte aus auffassen will — ganz gut für sich selber
aus dem specifischen Fachgebiete der Bienenwirthschaft verwerthen
könnte, oder anders gesagt: was die Aegyptologie für ihr Ressort
der auf Bienenwesen bezüglichen Klarlegungen selber von
der Disciplin der Bienencultur profitiren könnte. Es fehlt den Aegyptologen, um es kurz zu sagen, der Zug ins Grosse angesichts der
Lehre vom Bienenwesen. Von den in den letzten Jahrzehnten statt-
gehabten kolossalen praktischen Umwälzungen in der Bienenwirthschaft (Mobilbau, künstliche Mittelwände, Honigschleuder) und gar
erst von der Welt-Bienenwirthschaft wissen die Aegyptologen nicht
das Geringste. Sie selber ahnen gar nicht, dass die im Hieroglyphischen, Hieratischen, Demotischen, Koptischen zerstreuten Notizen
über Bienenwesen kostbare Edelsteine in der Krone der historischen
Bienenwirthschaft bilden. Der Zusammenhang, die Würdigung
der gewaltigen historischen Continuität ist es ja doch aber,
was dem Vereinzelten erst seine rechte Weihe verleiht.

Der Werth der zahlreichen altägyptischen, auf Bienenwesen
bezüglichen Notizen geht weit über die Grenzen der Philologie, betreffend altägyptische Sprache, hinaus. Es gibt aber dermalen eine
Menge Aegyptologen, welche ohne Kenntniss des für die historische

Bienenkunde hohen Werthes der beregten zerstreuten Notizen dieselben als nur zu ihrem ganz specifisch philologischen oder
metrologischen und sonstigen lediglich an eine Alterthums-
wissenschaftsbranche accrochirten Studienkreis gehörend er-
achten. Doch hier gilt das Wort der Dichterin:

,Für Dich allein nicht — lebe für das Ganze!‘[1]

Thatsache ist es, dass bei den obgedachten Philologen der Sinn
für die Würdigung der einschlägigen gewaltigen historischen Continuität noch sehr entwicklungsbedürftig ist. Es wäre zu wünschen,
dass von der historischen Grossartigkeit des in seiner Reichhaltigkeit
tausendfach verästelten Bienenwesens die derzeitigen und späteren
Aegyptologen sich ausreichender Kenntnisse erfreuten. Nach einer
guten bienenwirthschaftlichen Schulung vermöchte dermalen gerade
ein Aegyptolog sehr Erspriessliches für die Geschichte der Bienenkunde zu leisten. Wem an dem Fortschritte jeder der beiden in
Rede stehenden Wissenschaften gelegen ist, dem kann das Studium
dieser beiden Wissensgebiete zur Kreuzung und der dadurch er-
zielten wissenschaftlichen Blutauffrischung nicht dringend genug
empfohlen werden.

Warum hat denn eine Arbeit, aus welcher ernste Freunde antiker Bienenwirthschaft eine sowohl dem derzeitigen Stande der
Bienencultur, als auch dem dermaligen Stande der ägyptologischen Wissenschaft gerecht werdende Belehrung über, wenn auch
nur einen einzigen Theil des altägyptischen Bienenwesens mitsammt
dem einschlägigen Sprachgute hätten schöpfen können — warum,
sage ich, hat denn eine solche Arbeit bis zu diesem Augenblicke
nicht existirt? Aus dem Grunde, weil die einschlägigen fachlichen
Kenntnisse, welche eben mehreren ganz specifischen Fachgebieten
zugehören, in Niemandem vereinigt gewesen waren.

---

[1] Aus den Gedichten ,Der Göttin Eigenthum‘, von Marie von Najmájer.
Wien 1901, C. Konegen. Vorstehende Zeile ist aus dem ,Gruss der Invaliden an
das neue Jahrhundert‘.

Bis auf meine Epoche hatte kein einziger aus Bienenwirthschaft Geprüfter jemals auch aus Aegyptologie eine Prüfung abgelegt — und umgekehrt hatte bis jetzt niemals Jemand, welcher sich aus der Aegyptologie seinen Doctorhut erworben hatte, auch Curse über Bienencultur frequentirt, sich am Schlusse dieses nicht minder wie die Aegyptologie sehr interessanten Studienganges vor einer Prüfungs-commission einer strengen Prüfung aus der Theorie und Praxis der Bienencultur unterzogen und nach bestandenem Examen sein Diplom als geprüfter Apiolog entgegengenommen.

Das war eben der grosse Fehler, dass zwischen den beiden in Rede stehenden Wissenschaften eine chinesische Mauer bestand. Die aus dieser wechselseitigen Absperrung resultirenden Unzu-kömmlichkeiten und schweren Schäden müssen unbedingt näher beleuchtet werden. Je besser ein Arzt den Grad einer Verletzung kennt, desto wirksamer kann der sanirende, operirende Eingriff er-folgen. Und nichts sehnlicher kann die Wissenschaft wünschen, als dass die Nachwelt auf dem in Rede stehenden Wissenschaftszweige kenntnissreicher sein möge, als das Ende des 19. Jahrhunders war.

Noch in diesem Augenblicke haben die Imker — selbst die-jenigen, welche über Bienenwesen bei den alten Aegyptern ge-schrieben haben — nicht die geringste Spur eines absolut fach-gemässen Beurtheilungsvermögens, betreffend die zahllosen eingehen-den, die interessantesten Gesichtspunkte aufrollenden Arbeiten von Aegyptologen über hieher gehörige Punkte. Die Folge hievon hat keine andere sein können, als dass diese schriftstellernden Imker denn auch mit einer bodenlos dilettantischen Naivetät über das in Rede stehende Thema geschrieben haben.

Schön und rückhaltslos anerkennenswerth ist ja unbestreitbar der Drang der tiefer denkenden Imker, auch in die Geschichte des Bienenwesens bei den alten Aegyptern einzudringen; aber der — Dilettantismus! Und was für ein Veitstanz von Dilettantismus und splitternackter Naivetät gegenüber dem derzeitigen Stande der nach jedweder Richtung hin von dem Scharfsinn der ersten Meister durch-gearbeiteten Aegyptologie! Von der Kenntniss feinerer einschlägiger

Details aus dem Hieroglyphischen und Hieratischen ist bei den
dermaligen Imkern, sogar denjenigen, welche über Bienenwirthschaft
bei den alten Aegyptern geschrieben haben, gar nichts zu finden.
So weiss kein Vertreter der historischen Bienenkunde, dass das
Wort für ‚Wachs‘ im Hieroglyphischen ⳡ geschrieben worden
ist und wohl, wie im Koptischen, ⲙⲟⲩⲗⲁϧ. ⲛ (oder auch nur ⲙⲟⲩⲗϧ
geschrieben) geheissen hat.[1]

Unter den im k. k. kunsthistorischen Hofmuseum zu Wien ex-
ponirten Objecten der Sammlung ägyptischer Alterthümer des österreichischen Kaiserhauses befinden sich im Hochparterre (Saal IV, in
der bei einem Fenster stehenden Horizontalvitrine IV, sub Nr. 46
bis 89 und von Nr. 91—98) sehr interessante Amulete aus Wachs,
welche Munienbeigaben gebildet haben. Mit Ausnahme von Nr. 87
bestehen alle jene Amulete aus vergoldetem Wachs, z. B. 46
(3418) Schildchen aus Wachs mit Vergoldung, 49 (3457) Wachs-
schüsselchen vergoldet, 51 (3409) Geier mit ausgespannten Flügeln,

---

[1] McCauly transscribirt ⳡ durch ‚merk‘ (wax). Man vergleiche bezüglich des Wechsels von r und l im Altägyptischen auch die analoge Erscheinung
im Indogermanischen (Barbier und Balbier, Amsterdam und Amstelodamum und
zahllose sonstige Beispiele). Es ist der Aegyptologie bis zu diesem Augenblicke
absolut unbekannt geblieben, dass sich die Manierirtheit von Aristoteles darin
gefallen hat, beim Sprechen den altägyptischen Wechsel zwischen r und l zu
imitiren. Cf. Pauli’s Realencyklopädie der classischen Alterthumswissenschaft,
1. Bd., 2. Hälfte. Zweite Aufl. Stuttgart 1800, S. 1645: ‚Ausserdem geschieht (betreffend Aristoteles anlässlich der Schilderung seiner Persönlichkeit) eines Fehlers
in der Aussprache Erwähnung, welche in einer zu weichen, in den Laut L über-
gehenden Aussprache des R besteht (Timotheus bei Diog. La. 1. Anonym. Menag.
Suidas), welche Eigenthümlichkeit manche seiner Schüler nachzuahmen die
Schwachheit hatten (Plut. aud. poet. S. adul. 9). Ueber diesen Fehler der Aussprache
(τραυλότης, unterschieden von ψελλότης und ἰσχνοφωνία) handelt Aristoteles selbst,
Problem. XI, 30. p. 902b.‘ — Vgl. Transactions of the American Philosophical
Society, held at Philadelphia, for promoting useful knowledge. Vol. XVI. — New
series. Part 1. Dictionary of Egyptian Hieroglyphics. By Edward J.
McCauly, U. S. N. Philadelphia 1883, S. 97, oben links, die zweite Vocabel. —
Ferner: Vocabularium coptico-latinum et latino-copticum e Peyroni et Tattami lexicis
concinnavit G. Parthey, Dr., Berolini 1844, p. 300. — Das Wort ⳡ findet
sich z. B. bei Reinisch. Die ägyptischen Denkmäler in Miramar, Taf. III A 2.

Wachs vergoldet. Besonders auffallend sorgfältig gearbeitet ist Nr. 87, ein nicht vergoldeter, daumenlanger Adler oder Geier aus Wachs, dunkeldrapfarben. Alle diese höchst interessanten alt-ägyptischen Mumienbeigaben aus Wachs verdienten durch getreue colorirte Abbildungen in Originalgrösse weiteren Kreisen zur näheren Kenntniss gebracht zu werden. Es könnten diese aus dem genannten wichtigen Bienenproducte im alten Aegypten angefertigten reizenden Proben antiker Kleinkunst auch auf die dermalen an neuen Ideen vielfach Mangel leidende Kunstindustrie befruchtend wirken und durch glückliche Anregungen geschickten Meistern in der modernen Kleinkunst lohnenden Verdienst sichern. Man sehe sich nur einmal auf den Bienenproducten-Ausstellungen unserer Tage um, und man wird wahrnehmen, dass der Kreis an Motiven zu Darstellungen aus Wachs ein verhältnissmässig sehr kleiner ist. Gewiss würden viele Meister der so unendlich sympathischen Kleinkunst die vermöge getreuer Reproductionen der genannten Amulete aus

Taf. IV, Zeile 3. Reinisch übersetzt das Wort irrthümlich durch ‚Öl' (vgl. ibid., S. 88, 93). Dass die Bezeichnung für ‚Wachs' auch vermöge des Ideogrammes [Hieroglyphe] dann und wann im Hieroglyphischen erscheint (vgl. Leo Reinisch, ‚Aegyptische Chrestomanthie', I. Lieferung, Wien 1873. Taf. 6, oberste Zeile der Inschrift aus dem Grabe des Admirals Ahmes in El Kab; XVII. Dynastie) deutet Pfarrer A. Gmelin in ganz deplacirt mystischer Weise an. Betreffend [Hieroglyphen] Wachs, cera, μοτλαϧ, vgl. Gmelin's (‚Die Biene von der Urwelt bis zur Neuzeit.' Stuttgart 1899, S. 8) einschlägige, der Illustrirung vermöge der betreffenden hieroglyphischen Gruppen [Hieroglyphen] (Honig, εβιω) und [Hieroglyphe] oder [Hieroglyphen] (Wachs, μοτλαϧ) dringend bedürftig gewesene Worte, welche auf Schritt und Tritt den grünsten Dilettanten markiren: ‚Schwieriger (nämlich als die Darstellung des Begriffes für ‚Honig' im Hieroglyphischen) war es schon, die Begriffe Honigwabe und Wachs in der hieroglyphischen Sprache (Gmelin meint augenscheinlich nicht die Sprache, sondern die Schrift. A. D.) zur Darstellung zu bringen. Letzteres wurde auf Grabsteinen durch Abbildung eines Wachsgefässes angedeutet.' — Gmelin ahnt offenbar nicht, dass gerade umgekehrt (so dass Gmelin's Ausdruck ‚schwieriger' absolut deplacirt ist) im Hieroglyphischen für ‚Wachs' die phonetischen Elemente sehr häufig erscheinen, dagegen niemals complet für ‚Honig'. Gmelin hat sämmtliche einschlägigen Momente viel zu sehr auf die leichte Achsel genommen. Hat Gmelin ja doch sogar Humor genug gehabt, einen Tony Kellen als vermeintlichen Fachmann auf dem Gebiete des altägyptischen Bienenwesens unaufhörlich zu citiren!

10

vergoldetem Wachs sich bietenden Anregungen auf das Freudigste begrüssen; und es würde sich da sohin auch auf kunstindustriellem Gebiete einmal wieder der Segen zeigen, welchen der Anblick der gedachten stummen Zeugen antiker künstlerischer Formvollendung und antiker Versatilität auf dem so anziehend sich anlassenden Gebiete der Kleinkunst spendet.

Bereits in meinen Vorträgen über Geschichte der Bienencultur habe ich dieser genannten, meinem Schutze als Custos der gedachten Sammlung anvertrauten altägyptischen kleinen reizenden Kunstwerke aus Wachs immer gerne gedacht, und es sind meine damaligen Hinweise auf diese beachtenswerthen Proben altägyptischer Verwendung von jenem nützlichen Bienenproducte auch weiteren Kreisen bekannt geworden.[1]

Doch wie kann man von den derzeitigen Imkern, welche über altägyptisches Bienenwesen geschrieben haben, Kenntnisse feinerer Details auf dem beregten Gebiete erwarten, wenn diesen Schriftstellern sogar nur die Namen der hervorragendsten ägyptischen Rollen, in welchen zerstreute Notizen über Bienenproducte und über sonstig Einschlägiges vorkommen, noch niemals zu Gehör gekommen sind! Kein einziger über altägyptische Bienenproducte schriftstellernder Imker weiss etwas von dem ‚Papyrus Ebers' genannten medicinischen Sammelwerke oder gar von dem grossen Papyrus

---

[1] Vgl. „Neue Freie Presse' (Morgenblatt), Wien, Freitag, 26. Mai 1899, Nr. 12.483, S. 6: „Antikes Wachs. Am Pfingstmontag (22. Mai 1899) hielt Dr. Alexander Dedekind einen sehr anziehenden Vortrag über die Geschichte der Bienenkunde. Die Ausführungen leiteten einen Curs über Bienenzucht ein, welcher gegenwärtig in der von dem bekannten Imker Raimund Friedrich geleiteten Fachschule für Bienencultur zu Währing, Gersthoferstrasse Nr. 31, von den Herren Friedrich und Wistawel abgehalten wird. Der Vortragende skizzirte den Entwicklungsgang des Bienenwesens seit den ältesten Zeiten bis zur Gegenwart. Namentlich wurde die altägyptische Literatur sehr eingehend vom bienenwirthschaftlichen Standpunkte aus behandelt. Aus dem grossen Papyrus Harris wurden zahlreiche Textstellen über genaue Gewichtsmengen von Honig und Wachs angeführt, welche bienenwirthschaftlichen Producte Ramses III. während seiner 31jährigen Regierungszeit den Tempeln Aegyptens hatte zukommen lassen. Auch der Purpurindustrie der Alten wurde, weil dieselbe mit dem Honigmarkte eng zusammenhing,

Harris Nr. 1, dem Juwel antiker genauer Evidenzhaltung betreffend Honig- und Wachsquantitäten, welche während der 31 Regierungsjahre von Ramses dem Dritten an die hervorragendsten Tempel von Aegypten verabfolgt worden waren (circa 1200 v. Chr.).

Gewiss ist ja alles Wissen auf dieser grossen Erde mit ihrer Legion von Wissenschaften und deren Verästelungen relativ. Das bringt absolut das Gesetz der Theilung der Arbeit mit sich. Und dass ein Aristoteles und Baco de Verulam das Gesammtwissen ihrer Zeit repräsentirt haben sollen, ist als die denkbar grösste Geringschätzung des Meeres voll Civilisation jener Epochen zu nehmen. Aber das muss die Wissenschaft denn doch wohl aussprechen, dass die Unbekanntschaft mit dem grossen Papyrus Harris Nr. 1 seitens eines Imkers, welcher sich nicht nur für Geschichte der Bienenwirthschaft interessirt, sondern welcher diesbezüglich auch schriftstellerisch, betreffend das alte Aegypten, thätig gewesen ist, genau auf die nämliche Stufe zu stellen ist, wie wenn Jemand einen Grundriss der griechischen Literatur geschrieben hat, aber absolut nichts von der ‚Odyssee‘ oder von Aeschylos‘ ‚Oresteia‘ weiss.

Dafür bietet Gmelin guten Ersatz, indem in Gmelin's Abhandlung über altägyptische Bienenkunde 3, sage drei! Seiten von der Entstehung oder angeblichen Entstehung der Bienen aus Stiercadavern schwatzen. Schade, dass Gmelin seine hohen geistigen

----

eingehend gedacht. Dies wenig bekannte Capitel illustrirte Dr. Dessung unter Verweisung zahlreicher köstlicher Purpurproben, welche ihm von dem 78jährigen französischen Naturforscher Professor Henri de Lacaze-Duthiers überlassen worden waren. Lebhaftes Interesse bot der vom Vortragenden auf Grund zahlreicher Experimente erbrachte Nachweis der Richtigkeit der Bemerkungen Vitruv's und Plutarch's, dass vermöge Verwendung von Honig die Frische von Purpur gewahrt werde und die Purpurtöne lebhafter zur Geltung kommen. Die im Alterthum reiche Verwendung des Wachses zur enkaustischen Malerei wurde gleichfalls betont. Dr. Dessung wies ferner auf zahlreiche altägyptische Amulete aus vergoldetem Wachs hin, welche im Kunsthistorischen Hofmuseum ausgelegt sind. Mit warmen Worten gedachte der Vortragende des für die Hebung der österreichischen Bienenzucht hochwichtigen Patentes der Kaiserin Maria Theresia vom 8. April 1775. Am Schlusse seiner Ausführungen wurde Dr. Dessung auf das Herzlichste beglückwünscht u. s. w.

Fähigkeiten und seine reiche Lust zu bienenwirthschaftlich-historischen Arbeiten nicht würdigeren Zielen zugewendet hat und auf keinen würdigeren Punkt der historischen Bienenkunde, betreffend die altägyptische Bienenwirthschaft, gerichtet gehabt hat, als die Erörterung über die sich durch Jahrhunderte fortziehende Irrlehre von der Bugonie ist.

Wer als ernster Forscher solche Arbeiten und derart bienenwirthschaftlich alberne Erörterungen mit Unbefangenheit und einschlägiger Sachkenntniss Revue passiren lässt — und um zu reformiren, muss man ja doch die Schriften seiner Vorgänger auf das genaueste kennen —, der fühlt sich da beinahe einem Reiche von Humbug gegenübergestellt. Und all dieses Unzulängliche wird von der nach Belehrung lechzenden Imkergemeinde für baare Münze des angeblich derzeitigen Standes der Wissenschaft gehalten, verschlungen, als neuester Fortschritt der tausendfältigen Forschungen auf dem Gebiete der historischen Bienenkunde begrüsst.

Und wenn es nur mit jenen drei Seiten über Stierleichen — als Pförtner zukünftiger Bienen — abgethan wäre! Aber GMELIN kommt in seinem Werke auch noch später wiederholt auf dieses Thema mit implicite absolut deplacirter Ironisirung der altägyptischen Bienenwirthschaft zu sprechen. Freilich lächelt GMELIN mit Recht über die durch Jahrhunderte sich hinziehenden beregten unsinnigen Anschauungen über Bienenzucht, welche Verkehrtheiten aber denn doch schliesslich auf angebliche Anschauungen ägyptischer Bienenzüchter zurückfallen. Verschlagen sind die Aegypter, wie auch zahlreiche andere Culturvölker des Alterthums das waren, freilich reichlich gewesen; doch darf deshalb aus irgend einem Aufsitzer, den ein ägyptischer Bienenwirth sich, betreffend die Bugonie, irgend einem Naivetätskrösus gegenüber gestattet hat, kein Rückschluss auf die altägyptischen Anschauungen überhaupt, betreffend die Entstehung der Bienen, gezogen werden. Sich über die Anschauungen der alten Aegypter bezüglich ihrer angeblichen Maxime, wonach man sich Bienen verschaffen könnte, aufzuhalten, möchte wohl kaum anders sich anlassen, wie wenn man sich über eine

Krone lustig machte, aus welcher alle Edelsteine ausgebrochen waren.

Mit der humorvollen Erwähnung des Scherzes der Bugonie — trotz des Ernstes wissenschaftlicher Erörterungen brauchte es überhaupt niemals an der launigen Wiedergabe heiterer Episoden zu fehlen — hätte GMELIN der einschlägig guten Laune der bienenwirthschaftlichen Klio vollauf Genüge gethan und gegenüber dem wiederholten Auftauchen des in Rede stehenden Spasses von der Bugonie wohl ein Auge zudrücken können. Statt dessen aber nimmt da diese überdies mit einem verblüffenden Citatenschatz garnirte Erörterung über den Hintritt von Stieren und über Rinderwänste — als Mutterschooss von ‚Kindern der Sonne‘ und folglich als Grossmütter von Honig — schier gar kein Ende. Statt uns etwa Interessantes aus dem grossen Papyrus Harris Nr. 1 über genau überlieferte Quantitäten von Wachs und Honig aus den Zeiten Ramses des Dritten mitzutheilen, kommt GMELIN in einemfort und stets und immer wieder auf sein todtes Rindvieh zurück, wie ein Muhammedaner auf sein ‚la ilaha‘ u. s. w. und wie ein Jude auf sein vielgeliebtes Geschäft. Und das Köstlichste ist, dass GMELIN — der offenbar niemals im Stande gewesen ist, auch nur den einfachsten Hieroglyphentext oder den leichtesten Papyrustext vom Blatt zu lesen — das beregte Capitel über altägyptisches Bienenwesen mit dem grossen Vorwurfe gegenüber den Alten abschliesst, der aber wie ein rückschnellender Pfeil gerade den Autor ALBERT GMELIN selber trifft, dass das Alterthum ‚blindlings copirte, offenbar aber deshalb sich auch nicht ernstlich bemühte, den wahren Sachverhalt zu erforschen‘.

Eigentlich sollte man dem Autor für seine gedachte Darstellung zürnen, aber der Humor des Ganzen trägt den Sieg davon; denn hier gibt es eben keinen Zwang zum Heitersein, wie in ‚Emilia Galotti‘, wo (im vierten Aufzuge, gegen Ende des dritten Auftrittes) die Gräfin Orsina ‚ernsthaft und befehlend‘ — so schreibt Lessing das vor — zu Marinelli sagt: ‚So lachen Sie doch!‘, und Marinelli devot entgegnet: ‚Gleich, gnädige Gräfin, gleich!‘

Allen Halbheiten und Verkehrtheiten von Anschauungen der
derzeitigen Imkerhistoriker gegenüber den vermöge der Aegyptologie
sichergestellten Ergebnissen, betreffend die Kunde des altägyptischen
Bienenwesens, muss auf das strengste und unnachsichtigste gesteuert
werden. Solche Arbeiten wie von ALBERT GMELIN und J. G. BESSLER
(„Geschichte der Bienenzucht‘, Stuttgart 1886) sollten bezüglich der
in Rede stehenden Partie der historischen Bienenkunde ja doch eine
Paradeausstellung dessen, was die Wissenschaft bislang erforscht
hat, bilden, aber keine Kette von Märchen. — Doch hier muss
auch die Exclusivität der Thätigkeit der Herren des Wissens
vom Morgenlande wenigstens in gewissem Grade getadelt werden;
denn die während der letzten Hälfte des 19. Jahrhunderts statt-
gehabten verblüffenden Fortschritte in der Aegyptologie haben ihr
Licht viel zu sehr unter den Scheffel gestellt. Infolge dessen hat
absolut kein rechter Gedankenaustausch platzgreifen können. Nur
spärlich ist von dem gedachten Meere von Licht stellenweise ein
Strahl durch die chinesische, rings umschliessende Mauer in die
Aussenwelt gedrungen. Nur kümmerlich ist in weitere Kreise etwas
von den ausgezeichneten Forschungen der grossen Meister der
Aegyptologie hinübergesickert. Zögernd hat die Imkerwelt hie und
da, wo etwas durch die Ritzen gedrungen war, ein Bröckchen von
den Entzifferungen hieroglyphischer, hieratischer, demotischer u. s. w.
Texte aufgegriffen. Aber damit war auch schon wieder dem Fortschritte von Jahren auf dem Gebiete der historischen Bienenkunde
vermeintlich reichlich Genüge geleistet.

Man sieht thatsächlich vielfach Spuren redlichen Strebens
schriftstellernder Imker, hie und da Resultate gedachter Entzifferungen
der Darstellung über altägyptisches Bienenwesen einzufügen. Bei
BESSLER und GMELIN und bei anderen hier in Frage kommenden
Schriftstellern, welche jedoch von der Aegyptologie nichts verstanden
haben, ist das rühmend und rückhaltslos anzuerkennen. Das muss
absolut betont werden. Unthätig sind die Imker, welche der Geschichte ihrer Wissenschaft sich nützlich zu machen versucht haben,
auf diesem in Rede stehenden Gebiete der Erweiterung ihrer Kennt-

nisse, betreffend das alte Aegypten und dessen Bienenkunde, mithin durchaus nicht gewesen. Nach meiner bisherigen Darstellung könnte man leicht versucht sein, die ernster forschenden Imker der Saumseligkeit im Sammeln ägyptologisch einschlägigen Materiales zu zeihen. Man wäre auf dem Holzwege, wollte man tadeln, dass die gedachten Schriftsteller eben gar nichts in dem in Rede stehenden Streben nach Fortschritt gethan hätten. Nein, das kann man nicht sagen. Das wäre entschieden ungerecht — genau so ungerecht, wie wenn die zeitgenössische Culturgeschichte behaupten wollte, dass gewisse Herrscher der afrikanischen Küste oder von Haïti, welche Monarchen mit Vorliebe auf dem ansonsten ganz nackten Körper irgend einen goldstrotzenden Waffenrock tragen, nicht mit Spuren der Civilisation in Annäherung gekommen wären, in welcher Beziehung das Höchste bekanntlich der König Soulouque erreicht hatte, welcher seinen Generalstab summarisch mit Epaulettes, mit nichts Anderem als Epaulettes bekleidete. Und was für Epauletten! Sie bestanden aus leeren Sardinenschachteln.[1]

Auch gefallen sich die über altägyptisches Bienenwesen schriftstellernden und bei Festen redenden Imker darin, dass sie sich direct aus dem immer grünenden Walde der Idylle, im Knopfloch die blaue Blume der Romantik, an den Schreibtisch setzen oder auf die Festtribüne steigen und (wie der Ehrenpräsident des ‚Centralvereines für Bienenzucht in Oesterreich‘, Herr Sectionschef und Präsident des k. k. Patentamtes Dr. Paul Ritter Beck von Mannagetta, im Juni 1900 solches vor der andächtig lauschenden Festversammlung gethan hat) zu singen und zu sagen anheben von altägyptischen Prinzessinnen in ‚nilgrünen Gewändern‘.

Wo anlässlich der Festrede zu Ehren der Eröffnung einer staatlich subventionirten Imkerschule (die in Rede stehende Fachschule befindet sich seit Juni 1900 im Prater zu Wien) statt historisch feststehender Facten auf Befehl der Phantasie sogar grüngekleidete

ägyptische Prinzessinnen lustwandeln müssen, damit deren Grazie
ein Surrogat für wissenschaftlich gesunde Kost abgebe, da muss sehr
viel Ueberfluss an Grünem sein.

Ja, sogar auch von den Haaren altägyptischer Prinzessinnen
hat Herr Sectionschef Dr. Ritter Beck von Mannagetta in jener
Festrede zu Preis und Ehr' der Geschichte der Bienenwirthschaft
geredet. In welcher auch nur geringsten Weise ist der tieferen
Erkenntniss von der so vielfältigen Bedeutung der Hieroglyphe
vermöge einer derartig romantischen ‚Belastung‘ gedient?

Solch rhetorischer Aufputz ist für die Geschichte der Bienenkunde, wo es viel Wichtigeres zu vermelden gibt, ich will nicht
gerade sagen völlig unbrauchbar (auch der grosse Menschenkenner
Dr. Heinrich Laube — er starb 1884 in Wien — hat ‚leichte
Reizungen‘ für unentbehrlich gehalten, um für den selbst erhabensten
Idealismus Menschen einzufangen), aber denn doch wohl etwas deplacirt -- wie hier von dem Ernste der Wissenschaft überhaupt
jedwedes mit fadenscheiniger ägyptologischer Sachkenntniss flun-
kernde, sei es gedruckte, sei es gesprochene Geschwätz der Imkerhistoriker unter Anklage gestellt wird.

Unzweifelhaft hätte bei einer solchen grossen Gelegenheit der
Festrede anlässlich der Eröffnung der ersten österreichischen
Imkerschule gerade ein Mann von Geist, wie Herr Sectionschef
Dr. Paul Ritter Beck von Mannagetta ein solcher ist, hin-
sichtlich einer sinnreichen Verschlingung bienenwirthschaftlicher
Weisheit mit der um das alte Aegypten gravitirenden Geschichte
der Bienenkunde leicht in Wettbewerb mit den geistreichsten und
tiefsinnigsten Arbeiten der Aegyptologen auf dem beregten Gebiete
treten können, wenn es bezüglich des ganz specifischen Sachver-
ständnisses bezüglich dieses Theiles der historischen Bienenkunde
nur nicht gar so öde in sämmtlichen Imkerkreisen aussähe.

Die wichtigsten und detaillirtesten Untersuchungen über altägyptische Bienenkunde, über die Räthsel, welche die Hieroglyphe
bislang geboten hat, über Bienenwirthschaft und Bienenproducte im
alten Aegypten sind während der rührigen letztverflossenen Jahr-

zehnte von hervorragenden Aegyptologen angestellt worden, schöne
Fortschritte sind von der Aegyptologie in der zweiten Hälfte des
19. Jahrhunderts auf dem Gebiete des altägyptischen Bienenwesens
gemacht worden, das Verständniss der Aegyptologie für einschlägiges
Fachgut hat sich von Jahr zu Jahr geläutert und der Scharfsinn der
Aegyptologen für in Rede stehende Punkte zusehends verfeinert,
ohne dass die Imkerhistoriker der damit Schritt gehaltenen Kenntniss
von diesen bedeutsamen Arbeiten sich erfreuen, während diese
imkernden Schätzer historischer Bienenkunde selber aller einschlägigen persönlichen Initiative bar sind. Wohl wird uns die Aegyptologie über zahlreiche in Frage kommende Momente niemals eine
Antwort zu ertheilen vermögen, doch ist nicht zu verkennen, dass
zahllose Schleier, welche über dem Wesen der altägyptischen Bienenkunde geruht hatten, definitiv gefallen sind; aber die einschlägigen
klargestellten Punkte sind den Imkern noch in viel höherem Grade
unbekannt, als der derzeitige Stand der Aegyptologie glauben sollte.
An dieser Thatsache lässt sich nicht rütteln. Und es kann gar keine
Frage sein, dass die beregte Nichtversirtheit in den dermalen vor-
liegenden Entzifferungen der Aegyptologie, welche bedeutsamen Er-
folge ebenso sehr den unermüdlichen Bestrebungen der Aegyptologie,
als dem Fortschritte der historischen Bienenkunde zur Ehre und
zum Vortheile gereichen, in allererster Linie auf Conto der Saumseligkeit der Imker zu setzen ist, welche gegenüber der Aegyptologie
ja doch die Ehre des Louvre haben.[1]

Ueberhaupt werden historische Arbeiten, welche eine Menge
sehr interessanter bienenwirthschaftlicher Notizen enthalten, von den
derzeitigen Imkern, welche Sinn für historische Bienenkunde aus-
zeichnet, viel zu wenig gelesen. Dahin gehört z. B. auch das meister-
hafte zweibändige Werk des im December 1889 in Wien (Döbling)
verblichenen ehemaligen österreichischen Handelsministers Alfred
Freiherrn von Kremer, meines edlen Wohlthäters ‚Culturgeschichte

---

[1] ‚Die Ehre des Louvre haben‘ hiess früher: in allen königlichen Schlössern
freien Zutritt haben.

des Orients unter den Chalifen'. Dieses ausgezeichnete Werk enthält höchst interessante eingestreute Notizen über mohammedanische Bienenwirthschaft der genannten Epoche.

Es muss eben bei den Imkern der ganz specifisch historische Sinn für Imkerwesen noch viel mehr entwickelt werden, als er es bislang erst ist. Einschlägige Lectüre etwas abseits liegender musterhafter Werke macht nun einmal die stille Keimarbeit der historischen Bienenkunde aus.

Wie es dermalen keinen einzigen Aegyptologen gibt, welchem die mit der Geschichte der Bienenwirthschaft für alle Ewigkeit verknüpften Namen eines Dr. Dzierzon, Major v. Hruschka, Baron Berlepsch, Mehring, des amerikanischen Imkerfürsten Langstroth,[1] eines Dadant, Alberti, Weygandt, Gerstung, Theodor Weippl in Klosterneuburg bei Wien[2] und zahlreicher anderer hervorragender Imker geläufig sind, so existirt auch kein einziger Imker, welcher auch nur die Namen eines W. Pleyte, Johannes Dümichen, C. W. Goodwin, F. Chabas, Le Page Renouf, Carl Piehl, W. Max Müller, Georg Müller, E. Lefébure, Kurt Sethe und einer Unmenge anderer ausgezeichneter Aegyptologen kennt, geschweige deren in die Lehre vom altägyptischen Bienenwesen einschlägige wichtige und sehr interessante Publicationen zu würdigen vermöchte,[3] welche sich ein-

---

[1] Langstroth starb in Amerika 1895 in einem Alter von 85 Jahren. Ausgezeichnet ist sein berühmtes Werk 'The hive and honey-bee'. Cf. Elsass-Lothringische Bienenzeitung 1883, Nr. 1.

[2] Der höchst verdienstvolle Herausgeber der ausgezeichneten, mit sehr interessanten Abbildungen reich ausgestatteten bienenwirthschaftlichen Zeitschrift 'Illustrirte Monatsblätter für Bienenzucht', Zeitschrift für die Gesammtinteressen der Bienenwirthe Oesterreichs. Herausgegeben und redigirt von Theodor Weippl. Redaction und Administration in Klosterneuburg bei Wien, Leopoldstrasse 68.

Auf Seite 9 der Nummer vom 1. Jänner 1901 befindet sich eine sehr hübsche Federzeichnung von Fr. Wttopiz, welche 'Dr. Dzierzon's Wohnhaus in Lowkowitz' darstellt. Auf den Seiten 6 und 7 ibid. befinden sich vorzügliche Porträts von Dr. Dzierzon, und zwar aus den Jahren 1856 und 1893. — Am 10. Januar 1901 ist Dr. Dzierzon neunzig Jahre alt geworden.

[3] Vgl. zur Frage:

1. La guêpe ☙. Von W. Pleyte. (Zeitschrift für ägyptische Sprache und Alterthumskunde, Jänner 1866, 4. Jahrgang, S. 14 und 16)

gehend mit den um ⬡ gravitirenden Fragen befasst haben. Und wie bewundernswürdig, wie schön und wie vornehm nehmen sich alle diese Arbeiten der verschiedensten Aufklärer einschlägiger, dunkel gebliebener Punkte als Symbole wissenschaftlichen Friedens und — bei aller Verschiedenheit und Divergenz der zur Rede kommenden Anschauungen — als Symbole wissenschaftlicher Eintracht aus!

Namentlich mein hochverehrter und lieber Mitforscher Kurt Sethe hat sich um die ausgezeichnete Ventilirung einer grossen Reihe von hiehergehörigen schwierigen Fragen namhafte Verdienste erworben. Sethe's werthvolle Untersuchungen über die beregte lehrreiche Materie der Honigfliege ⬡ (welche so oft von den Aegyptologen als Studienmaterial benützt und im Dienste der Wissenschaft gequält worden ist, dass man ihr wohlwollend mit Hamletscher Beschwichtigung zurufen möchte: ‚Ruh, Ruh! gestörte Hieroglyphe!‘) werden dauernd mit Aufmerksamkeit gelesen werden müssen.

Ueberhaupt sind alle die von Aegyptologen verfassten Abhandlungen, welche um das Thema Bienen und Einschlägiges gravitiren, sehr bedeutende Arbeiten von grossem Ernste, welche die

---

2. Einige Beobachtungen über die Silbe ‚men‘ in dem hieroglyphischen Schriftsystem. Von Johannes Dümichen. (Ibid. 1866, August und September, S. 60 bis 62. — Ibid. 1866, October und November, S. 81—85. — Ibid. 1867, Jänner; 5. Jahrgang, S. 4—6.) Am Schlusse des Aufsatzes steht ‚Fortsetzung folgt‘.

3. Notes on Egyptian Numerals. By C. W. Goodwin. (Ibid. 1867, December, S. 99, sub Nr. 4.)

4. Miscellanea III. By P. Le Page Renouf. (Ibid. November 1867, S. 90.) — Dazu die Notiz ibid. Jänner 1868. 6. Jahrgang, S. 9. — Ferner dazu die Notiz ebenfalls von Le Page Renouf in ‚Miscellanea IV‘; ibid. April 1868, S. 48. — Ferner in ‚Proceed. XIV‘, wo Le Page Renouf gegen Sethe's Ausführungen Einwände erhebt.

5. Der Name des Königs von Unterägypten. Von Kurt Sethe. (Zeitschrift für ägyptische Sprache und Alterthumskunde, XXVIII. Bd., Leipzig 1890, S. 125—128.)

6. Der Name des Königs von Unterägypten. Von W. Max Müller. (Zeitschrift für ägyptische Sprache und Alterthumskunde XXX. Bd., Leipzig 1892, S. 56 bis 59.)

Resultate tiefgehender und gründlicher Untersuchungen darlegen, ohne übrigens darum auch immer von Irrthümern frei zu sein.

Doch alle diese genannten und sonstigen ausgezeichneten Aegyptologen, welche sich Stufe um Stufe zu immer klarerem Erkennen emporgerungen haben, indem sie sich in ihren Arbeiten mit altägyptischem Bienenwesen in Berührung gesetzt haben, sind den ganz specifischen Fachkenntnissen aus der sehr interessanten und reichen Wissenschaft der Bienenwirthschaft absolut fern geblieben, z. B. Heinrich Brugsch, welchen bei seinen Erörterungen betreffs Berechnung der Gewichtsmengen bienenwirthschaftlicher Producte, welche im grossen Papyrus Harris Nr. 1 aufgezählt erscheinen, lediglich das metrologische Interesse geleitet hat.[1]

Es ist überhaupt sehr schwierig, dass sich Gelehrte finden, welchen in beiden beregten Wissenschaften eine vollständige Fachbildung zur Verfügung steht, um der Bearbeitung der in Rede stehenden Punkte in allseitig befriedigender Weise gerecht werden zu können. Allerdings muss in gewissem Sinne auch eine Neigung gerade für diese Dinge disponirt sein. Das ist zwar freilich in beiden in Rede stehenden Lagern wohl der erfreuliche Fall. Aber diese Neigung kann einer ganz specifisch fachmännischen Doppelschulung absolut nicht entrathen; und diesbezüglich fehlt es eben wechselseitig an den reciproken Fachkenntnissen. Das ist hier dermalen der grosse wunde Punkt, welcher unverzüglich Sanirung erheischt.

---

7. Ueber einen vermeintlichen Lautwerth des Zeichens der Biene. Von Kurt Sethe. (Ibid., Leipzig 1892, S. 113—119.)

8. Un des noms de la royauté septentrionale. Par E. Lefébure. (Zeitschrift für ägyptische Sprache und Alterthumskunde, XXXI. Bd., Leipzig 1893, S. 114 bis 117.)

9. Aufsatz von Georg Müller in der Zeitschrift für ägyptische Sprache und Alterthumskunde, XXXV. Bd., Leipzig 1897, S. 166.

10. La lecture du signe 𓆤. Par Karl Piehl. (Ibid., XXXVI. Bd., Leipzig 1898, S. 85.)

[1] Heinrich Brugsch, ‚Die Aegyptologie‘. Leipzig 1891, S. 377 ff.

Der Mangel an wechselseitig einschlägigen Kenntnissen manifestirt sich in erheblicher, ja vielfach sogar in geradezu empörend störender Weise in den betreffenden Arbeiten, z. B. in denjenigen von Tony Kellen. Ja, wenn es nur so wäre wie mit den Flecken in der Sonne! Tony Kellen[1] gehabt sich unglaublich naiv auf dem Gebiete der vielen Fragen betreffend Bienen und Bienenwirthschaft bei den alten Aegyptern. Trotzdem ist Kellen für den bekannten und auch bereits erwähnten Schriftsteller über die Geschichte der Bienenzucht Albert Gmelin (Pfarrer in Schwabbach in Württemberg)[2] der massgebende Meister in der Aegyptologie; und jedwede einschlägige Naivetät, welcher Tony Kellen, betreffend altägyptisches Bienenwesen, so schwer wie noch Niemand vor Kellen und mehr als genug zum Opfer gefallen ist, hält Gmelin für die reinste Offenbarung und schätzt sie hoch, wie wenn sich ein Orakel für Schwabbach kund gethan hätte. So vermeldet Gmelin, wie oft nach Kellen's genauer Zählung die Hieroglyphe der Biene auf dem Obelisken von Luxor auf der Place de la Concorde in Paris vorkommt!!!![3] Das ist auch ein Standpunkt. Und nun gar erst Glock's „Symbolik!" Oh . . . .

Alle diese letztgenannten Forscher haben ihre Arbeiten mit allzu grosser Leichtgläubigkeit eingerichtet und ihre Empfänglichkeit bei einschlägig unzureichenden Bildungsgraden zu hoch geschraubt gehabt.

---

[1] Er ist am 24. Jänner 1869 in Luxemburg geboren worden und hat auch mit geschlossenem Visier als „Jan van der Elt" geschrieben.

[2] Albert Gmelin, l. c., S. 7, 77. — Vgl. Adolphsons „Bienenzeitung", S. 28, 110.

[3] Gmelin, l. c, S. 7: „Auf dem Obelisken von Luxor, der sich (seit) 1836 in der Mitte des Concordienplatzes zwischen den elysäischen Gefilden und den Tuileriengärten einerseits, dem Tempel der Madeleine und der Concordienbrücke, sowie dem Palaste der Deputirtenkammer in Paris erhebt, hat Tony Kellen nicht weniger als 17 Bienen entdeckt." — Die Aegyptologie gratulirt Herrn Kellen zu dieser „Entdeckung", und Fiesco mahnt den Naivetätskrösus und Addierer der „17 Bienen" leise daran, dass der Humor seine Schuldigkeit gethan hat u. s. w. Muley Hassan, der Mohr von Tunis, sagt in der „Verschwörung des Fiesco zu Genua": „Der Mohr hat seine Arbeit gethan" (Dritter Aufzug, Ende des vierten Auftrittes).

Unhaltbare Behauptungen haben auf dem in Rede stehenden Gebiete der historischen Bienenkunde zwar auch hervorragende Aegyptologen, deren Arbeiten mit zu den bleibenden Besitzthümern der Aegyptologie gehören, aufgestellt; aber das rangirt nur in die Kategorie des unvermeidlichen Uebels allgemein menschlichen Irrens und hat mit der facies hypokritica der Gelahrtheit jener im Uebrigen höchst ehrenwerthen schriftstellernden Imkerhistoriker nicht das Mindeste gemeinsam. Zwischen tauben Nüssen und einem lediglichen lapsus ingenii ist eben ein erheblicher Unterschied. Ein solcher Lapsus darf die Pforte der Pflege der historischen Bienenkunde zu jedweder Stunde passiren, aber noch niemals, so alt die Welt ist, hat der geheiligte Genius des Fortschrittes bei der Entgegennahme des Zehents des Intellects sich mit Windeiern abspeisen lassen.

Wer auf dem in Rede stehenden sehr interessanten Gebiete der historischen Bienenkunde auf gutem, solidem Boden stehen will, muss vor allen Dingen trachten, sich sowohl auf dem grossen Wissenszweige der Bienencultur, als auch auf dem nicht minder wichtigen und ausgedehnten Reiche der Aegyptologie eine zweckmässige Ausbildung zu erwerben und muss sich in jedem dieser beiden Fächer möglichst gründliche Kenntnisse zu Eigen machen. Einzig und allein angesichts einer derart ernsten, gediegenen und zielbewussten Doppelforschung vermag die beregte Wissenschaft auf tüchtige Belebung zu hoffen. Elemente ohne Tiefe und Grund sind principiell auszuscheiden, was übrigens ebenso selbstverständlich sein sollte, als dass eine Disciplin nicht aus zwei Hälften bestehen darf, von welchen wechselseitig eine von der anderen nichts weiss. Darf ja doch nach Abraham **Lincoln's** Grundsätzen auch eine Republik nicht zur Hälfte frei, zur Hälfte geknechtet sein.

2.

Die Biene im Hieroglyphischen.

In dem 36. Bande der Leipziger Zeitschrift für ägyptische Sprache und Alterthumskunde (1898, S. 85) kommt KARL PIEHL zu der, bezüglich ihrer Richtigkeit aber doch wohl anzuzweifelnden Schlussfolgerung: ‚Ils (nämlich die beiden Gruppen   ) donnent un fort appui à la théorie qui veut conférer au groupe   ‚Roi de la basse Égypte‘ la lecture bāt.‘ Meine Kenntnissnahme von dieser Schlussfolgerung ist der Anlass zu nachstehenden Seiten gewesen.

1. Nicht nur die Imker, sondern auch die Aegyptologen selber sind über das altägyptische Bienenwesen derzeit noch nicht derart ausreichend orientirt wie Solches wohl zu wünschen wäre. Die im Nachstehenden versuchte Zusammenfassung einiger einschlägigen markanten Punkte bietet vielleicht die Anbahnung zu einer eingehenderen Beschäftigung mit dem altägyptischen Bienenwesen, nachdem sowohl in der umfangreichen Fachliteratur der Imker — wo nirgends der grosse Papyrus Harris Nr. 1 auch nur erwähnt ist[1] — als auch im Kreise der Aegyptologen durchgängig zu Discussionen einladende einschlägige Anschauungen zu constatiren sind, wie aus

---

[1] Cf. J. G. Bessler, Illustrirtes Lehrbuch der Bienenzucht. 2. Auflage. Stuttgart 1896. — Bessler, Geschichte der Bienenzucht, Stuttgart 1886. — Albert Gmelin, Die Biene von der Urwelt bis zur Neuzeit (Sonderabdruck aus: Joh. Witzgall, Das Buch von der Biene'). Stuttgart 1899.

zahlreichen Stellen der ÄZ., aus Samuel Birch's irreführender Note 3
in Wilkinson[1] II, 416 und sonst hervorgeht.

Es dürfte sogar anzuzweifeln sein, ob die allbekannte hieroglyphische Gruppe [Hieroglyphe] bis jetzt von der Aegyptologie richtig aufgefasst worden ist. Während nach meinem Dafürhalten die beregte
Gruppe nur corren auszusprechen ist — wie auch die von Piehl
angeführte ideographische Gruppe [Hieroglyphen] lediglich corren, beziehungsweise [Hieroglyphen], ausführlich geschrieben: [Hieroglyphen], ausgesprochen zu werden hat — ist meines Erachtens bis jetzt immer
gänzlich misskannt worden, dass das Bild der Biene in Verbindung
mit Königsnamen nur ein Sinndeterminativ ist und daher gar nicht
ausgesprochen werden darf.

Was für hochpolitische Schlussfolgerungen sind nun aber an
die Gruppe [Hieroglyphe] geknüpft worden, indem Amélineau und Kurt Sethe[2]
meinen, dass diese Gruppe schon eine gewisse Zeitbestimmung mar-
kire ‚da sie auf die Vereinigung der beiden Reiche, in die Aegypten in vorgeschichtlicher Zeit zerfallen war, Bezug nehme‘.

Nicht auf politische Geschichte, wie Amélineau und Sethe
gemeint haben, sondern auf einen sehr hohen Stand der Einblicke
der alten Aegypter in die Bienenwirthschaft, also auf landwirth-
schaftliche Geschichte, wirft die Gruppe [Hieroglyphe] — die nur corren
auszusprechen ist — ein ausserordentlich helles Licht. Diess Bild
der Bienenkönigin (daher das ⌂) ist ein Bild der Herrschaft
und ist für die Geschichte der Landwirthschaft dessbalb hochwich-
tig, weil die bereits in den ältesten uns bekannten Zeiten der ägyptischen Geschichte stattgehabte völlig richtige Einsicht in den
bewundernswürdigen Staat eines Bienenvolkes, welcher eben
eine Königin an der Spitze hat, der Aufmerksamkeit jener alten
Aegypter für die Bienenwirthschaft ein glänzendes Zeugnis ausstellt.

---

[1] The manners and customs of the ancient Egyptians. A new edition, revised
and corrected by Samuel Birch. London 1878, II, 416: ‚The bee is not represented
on the monuments: the insect, the emblem for king so often repeated, being the
hornet or wasp; honey, however, is often mentioned. — S. B.‘

[2] ÄZ. XXXV (Leipzig 1897), S. 1.

Für die Richtigkeit dieser Auffassung zeugt in gewissem Sinne — weil nämlich die **Bienenkönigin** und die **Arbeitsbienen** im Hieroglyphischen und Hieratischen vermöge des **nämlichen** Bildes dargestellt wurden — Ammianus Marcellinus.[1] Die Biene **markirt** in Verbindung mit Pharaonen-Namen oder auch in Gruppen wie [Hieroglyphen] den Grossherrn von Aegypten; und da dieser Staat eben in dem Pharao verkörpert ist, so markirt jenes wunderbare Insect in derlei Gruppen zugleich Aegypten. Und in diesem Sinne wird [Hieroglyphen] in hochpoetischer Auffassung von Jesaias (z. B. 7, 18) als die „Macht des Aegypterlandes‘ aufgefasst und in Jesaias’ schwungvollen Gesängen direct genannt: Die „Fliegen und Bienen‘ (Parallelismus der Glieder! Denn ⲁϥ ⲛ̀ ⲉⲃⲓⲱ „Fliege von Honig‘ ist ja eben: *apis mellifica*) bedeuten dort die Fürsten (resp. Kleinkönige) der betreffenden Länder Aegypten und Assyrien. Recapituliren wir das Gesagte kurz:

Die Bienenkönigin in ihrem Staate ist ein Spiegelbild, ein Symbol des Staatslenkers auf ägyptischem Boden. Eine sehr naive, echt kindliche Auffassung, wie derlei schlichte, ungekünstelte Parallelen **überhaupt** den alten Aegyptern so häufig zu Eigen waren.[2]

Wolle sich die Wissenschaft nun aber erinnern, wie die beregte Gruppe [Hieroglyphen] (welche also **synonym** mit [Hieroglyphen] oder [Hieroglyphen], beziehungsweise [Hieroglyphen], ist) bisher — von Kurt Sethe,[3]

---

[1] Im 17. Buche, 4. Capitel: „Unter dem Bilde einer honigbereitenden Biene (cf. „apis mellifica‘. — A. D.) wollen die Aegypter einen König verstanden wissen, zum Zeichen, dass ein Regent neben einem ansprechenden Benehmen auch mit einem Stachel versehen sein müsse.‘ — Vgl. Franz Olck's Aufsatz über „Biene‘ in Pauly-Wissowa, Realencyklopädie der class. Alterthumswissenschaft, S. 447: „In Aegypten wurde das Bild der Biene als Hieroglyphe für den König gebraucht (Amm. Marc. XVII, 4, 11).‘

[2] Cf. Édouard Naville, Additions et corrections aux trois inscriptions de la reine Hatshepsou, Rec. de travaux, XIX. — Nouv. sér., III, p. 212: . . . . seulement au lieu de [Hieroglyphen], on lit [Hieroglyphen]. — Cf. Chabas, Mél. égypt. 3ᵉ série, t. I, Paris, Septembre 1870, p. 200, wo Goodwin sagt: „The phrase [Hieroglyphen] and [Hieroglyphen] are written in the inscription parallel to one another.‘

[3] Loc. cit.

26

Heinrich Brugsch,[1] Édouard Naville,[2] Gaston Maspero[3] und Anderen
— gelesen und übersetzt worden ist!

II. Das Bild der Biene ist in allen Stellen, wo sie die Biene
selber (nicht den König) bedeutet, als ‚ab‘ (oder ‚af‘) zu lesen,[4]
beziehungsweise (da ⟨hierogl.⟩ oder ⟨hierogl.⟩ für sich allein nur ‚Fliege‘
heisst) als *ab en ebio* oder *af en ebio* (Fliege von Honig). Das ist
z. B. der Fall in dem Passus des Papyrus Sallier II, Tafel 5, 5, wo
es heisst:[5] ‚Der Barbier rasirt bis tief in die Nacht u. s. w., er muss
von Haus zu Haus eilen, seine Kunden aufzusuchen; er muss seine
Hände abarbeiten, um seinen Magen zu füllen, gleich den Bienen,
welche die Frucht ihrer Arbeit verzehren‘; ⟨hierogl.⟩
⟨hierogl.⟩ (*ma abu en ebio* [Honig-Fliegen] *im er kot set*)
‚gleichwie Bienen (wörtlich: Fliegen von Honig), welche essen in
Bezug auf ihren Bau‘, d. h. welche von dem in ihrem Wachsgebäude
(in den Zellen) aufgespeicherten Honig zehren, welchen sie sich
(analog zu den vorsorglichen Barbieren) für die Zeiten der Noth
gesammelt haben.[6] Die erschöpfende Erklärung dieser Gruppe
möchte ich mir aber bis nach Erledigung der Frage vorbehalten, wie
‚Honig‘ im Hieroglyphischen, resp. Hieratischen geschrieben wurde.

Chabas (Réponse à la critique. Paris 1868, S. 42) spricht anlässlich dieses Passus auch sehr richtig darüber, dass der Name
der Biene weiblichen Geschlechtes sei: ‚en copte ⲧ.ⲁϥ, ⲧ ⲁⲃ, apis‘.
E. de Rougé lässt l. c. (planche VIII) den Lautwerth ⟨hierogl.⟩ für die
Biene gelten, Sethe die Phonetik ⟨hierogl.⟩. Vgl. ÄZ. XXXV. Bd., 1897,

[1] Die Aegyptologie, Leipzig 1891, S. 499.

[2] La succession des Thoutmès d'après un mémoire récent; S. 32 des Separat-
abdruckes aus der ÄZ. XXXV.

[3] Une enquête judiciaire à Thèbes au temps de la XX⁰ dyn. — Paris 1871, p. 52.

[4] Le Vicomte E. de Rougé, Chrestomathie égypt. I. Paris 1867, Pl. VIII.

[5] Cf. Wiener Zeitschr. f. d. Kunde d. Morgenl. VIII. Bd., S. 80.

[6] Vgl. Lucius Junius Moderatus Columella, 12 Bücher von der Landwirthschaft; übersetzt von Michael Conrad Curtius. Hamburg und Bremen, 1769, S. 121:
(Col. 9. Buch, 14. Abschnitt): ‚Vom Untergange des Siebengestirns bis zum kürzesten
Tage, welcher ungefähr auf den 25. December, in den achten Theil des Steinbocks
fällt, zehren die Bienen von dem eingesammelten Honig, und erhalten
sich davon bis zum Aufgang des Fuhrmanns.‘

S. 166, wo Georg Möller bemerkt: ‚Sethe hat vor einigen Jahren für das Zeichen [Hieroglyphe] den Lautwerth [Hieroglyphen] (ÄZ. XXVIII, S. 125) ermittelt, und in der Folgezeit ist durch ihn und Andere (M. Müller, ÄZ. XXX, 56 ff. Sethe, ibid. 113 ff. Lefébure, ÄZ. XXXI, 114 ff.) ferneres Beweismaterial gesammelt. Vgl. auch ÄZ. XXXVI (1898), S. 85, Karl Piehl's Aufsatz: La lecture du signe [Hieroglyphe].

III. Das Bild der Biene dient aber auch zur Bezeichnung des Wortes für Honig und correspondirt in diesen Fällen dem koptischen ἐβιω, m. Im Falle, wo die Biene den Begriff für Honig markirt, wird die Gruppe [Hieroglyphen] oder [Hieroglyphen] (de Rochemonteix, Temple d'Edfou, p. 495) und in anderen interessanten Weisen geschrieben. Piehl irrt sohin, wenn er meint, dass die Phonetik für ‚Honig' einen wesentlichen Stützpunkt biete für die Theorie, nach welcher der Gruppe [Hieroglyphen] die Lesung bît zukomme. Mit der Phonetik von [Hieroglyphen] als [Hieroglyphen] hat die Phonetik von [Hieroglyphen] oder [Hieroglyphen] nur rein zufälliger Weise eine Art verwandtschaftlichen Klanges. Indem mein verehrter Mitforscher (ÄZ. 1898, S. 85) betont, dass die Gruppen [Hieroglyphen] donnent un fort appui à la théorie qui veut conférer au groupe [Hieroglyphen] Roi de la basse Égypte ‚la lecture bât', verwechselt Piehl das Ideogramm der Biene für König (corren oder [Hieroglyphen] — ausführlich geschrieben [Hieroglyphen] — was nämlich, wie Kurt Sethe nachgewiesen hat und durch W. Max Müller[1] eingehend dargethan worden ist, gleichfalls ein Titel des Königs des Aegypterlandes gewesen ist) mit der Phonetik des Ideogramms für Biene selber (aâ) und mit der Phonetik des Ideogramms für Honig (ἐβιω).

Fassen wir das vorgeführte Raisonnement kurz zusammen, so ergiebt sich Folgendes:

1. Das Bild der Biene ist entweder Sinndeterminativ zu [Hieroglyphen] oder steht ideographisch für corren oder [Hieroglyphen], respective [Hieroglyphen], wie in dem Falle [Hieroglyphen].

---

[1] ‚Der Name des Königs von Unterägypten.' Von W. Max Müller. Zeitschrift für Ägyptische Sprache und Alterthumskunde. XXX. Band. Leipzig 1892, S. 68—69.

28

2. Das Bild der Biene ist, falls es für die Biene selber (ideographisch) steht, *ab en ebio* oder *af en ebio* zu lesen.

3. Das Bild der Biene zur Bezeichnung des Begriffes ‚Honig‘ ist ‚ebio‘ zu sprechen, wie in den Fällen c oder 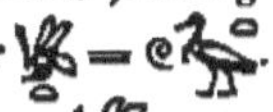 .

Darauf dass — wie DÜMICHEN nachgewiesen hat — mitunter auch als Träger der Silbe steht, und auf eine Menge anderer, um die Hieroglyphe gravitirenden Fälle soll in meinem Buche ‚**Raimund Friedrich, ein Wiener Imkerfürst**‘ näher eingegangen werden.

DÜMICHEN's **Generalisirung**, dass in **sämmtlichen** neun von ihm vorgeführten Beispielen (ÄZ. IV. Jahrg., Leipzig 1866, S. 61 und ÄZ. V. Jahrg., Leipzig 1867, S. 6) die Phonetik repräsentire, ist absolut unrichtig. Häufig ist die Biene, respective Fliege  nur ein Sinn-Determinativ zu dem Wort für ‚Ruhebett‘, ähnlich wie  ja auch sehr häufig sonst — aber in einem ganz anderen Sinne — als Sinn-Determinativ steht. Die Hierogrammaten sind sehr sinnreich bei all diesen Schreibungen verfahren; und es bildet eben einen sehr grossen Reiz, sich hiebei in den Gedankengang der Alten wieder zurückzuversenken. Es ist also gänzlich unrichtig, wenn viele Imker-Historiker glauben, dass die Hieroglyphe  immer nur das **Königthum** markirt habe. Man sieht, wie einseitig bei den Imkern, welche über altägyptische Bienenkunde geschrieben haben, die Einsicht in diese ganze Materie sich bis zu diesem Augenblicke angelassen hat.

Bereits zu Beginn des vorstehenden Raisonnements und auch anlässlich der Besprechung des Passus im Papyrus Sallier Nr. 2 Seite 5, Zeile 5 ward angedeutet, dass die ‚Biene‘ im Aegyptischen ‚Fliege (*ab*) von Honig (*ebio*)‘ hiess. Daher denn auch bei Jesaias der Parallelismus der Glieder (7, 18): ‚Die **Fliegen** und **Bienen** von Aegypten und Assyrien.‘ Dieses ägyptische ‚*ab-en-ebio*‘ entspricht genau dem wissenschaftlichen Namen der Bienen ‚*apis mellifica*‘. Das *b* und *p* ägyptischer Worte zeigt sich in den betreffenden in's Griechische und Lateinische übergegangenen Worten sehr häufig vertauscht. So ist auch [⸻] zu *Anub-is* geworden. Ebenso ist das ägyptische Wort [⸻] in das Lateinische übergegangen und zeigt sich hier in der Form *ap-is*. Nun bedeutet aber [⸻] in Wirklichkeit nur Fliege, so dass denn auch in dem erwähnten Passus des Papyrus Sallier Nr. 2 diese Lesung — und Chabas hat seiner Zeit diesen Punkt eben noch nicht ganz klar erkannt gehabt — keineswegs ausreicht.

Obige dreifache vorläufige Auseinandersetzung habe ich des besseren Verständnisses halber vorausschicken zu sollen geglaubt, um erst jetzt die vollständige Klarstellung des zweiten Punktes durchzuführen, bei welchem nämlich in jener Gruppe des Papyrus Sallier Nr. 2 in Wirklichkeit die combinirte Schreibweise von ‚Biene (*ab*)‘ und ‚Honig (*ebio*)‘ vorkommt. In diesem Passus erscheint mithin das Wort ‚*abu (en) ebio*‘ (Fliegen von Honig = Honigfliegen). Auch im Koptischen heisst Biene ⲁϧ ⲛ ⲉⲃⲓⲱ oder ⲁⲁⲛⲉⲃⲓⲱ. Die volle hieroglyphische Schreibweise für ‚Bienen‘ wäre sohin eigentlich [⸻]. Statt dessen wird vermöge Contraction das Wort ‚Honigfliegen‘ kurz [⸻] geschrieben; und diess wird ‚*abu en ebio*‘ gelesen. Das bedeutet ‚Bienen‘.

Wie überaus sinnreich das hieroglyphische Schriftwesen ist, zeigt auch in dem hieroglyphischen Worte für ‚Wabe‘ oder ‚Wachsgebände‘ [⸻] das Determinativ der — ich möchte sagen, gebundenen Marschroute. Es ist nämlich der Raum zwischen den einzelnen Waben so eng, dass zwar über jede Wabe zu gleicher Zeit die Bienen dahin laufen können; aber auch nur bis zu dieser äussersten Grenze geht im Bienenstock die Freiheit der Bewegung.

Der grosse Papyrus Harris Nr. 1 hat die sehr interessante Mittheilung zu unserer Kenntniss gebracht, dass Pharao Ramses III. während seiner 31jährigen Regierungszeit[1] den Haupttempeln Aegyptens auch Honig und Wachs in namhaften Quantitäten gespendet

---

[1] Professor Hermann Guthe in Leipzig kommt in seinem neuesten Werke ‚Geschichte des Volkes Israel‘ zu ganz anderen Resultaten.

30

hat. Diese Mengen wirthschaftlicher Producte sind vermöge Hin-
Bemessungen auf das genaueste ausgewiesen.

An der Hand von Samuel Birch's Ausgabe des grossen Papyrus Harris Nr. 1 habe ich nachstehende Stellen über die von Ramses III. an die Tempel Aegyptens verabreichten Quantitäten bienenwirthschaftlicher Producte herausgehoben:

15 a, line 3: honey, jars 1,065;

18 b, line 7: honey, amphorae 310;

Ibid., line 14: wax, pounds 3,100 (bei Birch irrig: 310);

39, line 6: honey, puka 21 (Unterabtheilung von hin) 20,800, various
jars, each 1/4-hin, making 5,200 hins;

Ibid., line 7: honey, jars ([Hieroglyphen])[1] 1,400, each a hin, making
1,400 hins;

Ibid., line 8: honey for food (also die Aegypter unterschieden bereits die als mindere Qualität bekannte Honigsorte ,Futter-
honig'), hins 7,050, 1/8-hins 15 [That is, 15 additional pots
holding 1/8-hins);

55 b, line 2: honey for food hins 66;

Ibid., line 3: honey, ark 164;

Ibid., line 4: honey, puka 3,260;

57, line 9: wax, pounds 3,100.

Bei der Transcription ist Samuel Birch hier bei den Zahlen
mehrfachen Irrthümern anheimgefallen, welche bei der Umrechnung
in Kilogramm erheblich in die Waagschale fallen. Im hieratischen
Originaltexte erscheint nämlich wesentlich weniger Honig (XXXIX, 7,
muss es 1040 statt ,1400' heissen, und in LV b, 4 muss es statt
,3260' in Wirklichkeit 3280 heissen) und erheblich mehr Wachs,
denn in XVIII b, 14 muss 3100 stehen, statt Birch's irriger Zahl 310.

---

[1] Diese total verfehlte Transcription von Birch [Hieroglyphen] muss durch
[Hieroglyphen] ersetzt werden. Vgl. H. Brugsch, l. c., S. 377: „. . . . . Es geht daraus
hervor, dass das für die Messung von Honig bestimmte Hin die Bezeichnung
[Hieroglyphen], seine Hälfte den Namen [Hieroglyphen] führte und sein Viertel
[Hieroglyphen] hiess.'

Hält man diesen Birch'schen irrigen Angaben nun Brugsch's Worte[1] gegenüber: ‚Nach den Kyphi-Recepten (aus der ptolemäischen Epoche) besass ein Hin Honig das Gewicht von 7½ ägyptischen Pfunden, oder von 682 Gramm (das Hin hatte einen cubischen Inhalt von 0·455 Liter)‘ — so ergiebt sich, dass Ramses III. den Tempeln Aegyptens während seiner 31 Regierungsjahre[2] zusammen 10.964 Kilogramm 855 Gramm Honig hätte zukommen lassen, wenn Birch's Transcription richtig wäre. Sie ist aber fehlerhaft. Es kommt also wesentlich weniger Honig heraus.

Die Wachsmenge ist entsprechend geringer, denn die Wachsbereitung stellt nicht nur grosse Anforderungen an die Lebenskraft der Bienen, sondern kostet dieselben, und mithin auch die Züchter, viel Honig. Man hat berechnet, dass zur Production von ½ Kilogramm Wachs 5—7½ Kilogramm Honig nöthig sind, den Verlust der durch das Bauen versäumten Zeit ganz ungerechnet.[3] Aus diesem Grunde hat man nämlich gegenwärtig vielfach künstliche Waben, und nach dem Ausschleudern des Honigs vermöge der von dem österreichischen Major v. Hruschka erfundenen Honigschleudermaschine kann man die völlig unversehrt gebliebenen Waben dann sofort wieder in den Bienenstock (Mobilständer) zurückgeben. Grossartig sind diessbezüglich die Leistungen von Otto Schulz in Bukow, welcher gegenwärtig durchschnittlich im Jahre über 50.000 Kilogramm Kunstwaben fabricirt und in alle Welt versendet. Dass hiedurch die moderne Honigproduction gegenüber der altägyptischen enorm erhöht wird, liegt auf der Hand.

Wie verschwindend gering jene Mengen von Honig und Wachs, welche der grosse Papyrus Harris Nr. 1 aufweist, gegenüber der

---

[1] Aegyptologie, S. 377. Vgl. ibid. S. 378: ‚Ein Pogi-Mann (cfr. S. 377: [hieroglyphs]) besass allerdings die Fassung des Hin-Masses, aber an dasselbe knüpfte sich die Vorstellung des Gewichtes von 7½ (ägyptischen) Pfund, wie es dem Honig (-Hin) eigen war.‘

[2] Professor Hermann Guthe in Leipzig (‚Geschichte des Volkes Israel‘, 14. Abtheilung des ‚Grundriss der theologischen Wissenschaften‘. Freiburg im B., 1899, S. 37, 64, 65) dagegen lässt Ramses den Dritten nur 28 Jahre regieren und weist ihm die Zeit 1209—1180 zu.   [3] Hermann l. c., S. 262.

32

dermaligen colossalen Menge von Bienenproducten sind, möge aus Folgendem ersehen werden, angesichts welcher statistischen Ausweise man staunen muss, welche ganz unglaubliche Mengen von Honig und Wachs jährlich in Europa allein von den so fleissigen Bienen producirt werden. Die Bienen Europas geben nämlich jährlich 15.000 Tonnen (zu 1000 Kilogramm) Wachs, die einen Werth von 33 Millionen Mark darstellen, wogegen an Honig 80.000 Tonnen, gegen 50 Millionen Mark Werth, erzeugt werden. Die einzelnen Länder betheiligten sich zu Anfang der Neunzigerjahre des 19. Jahrhunderts jährlich an der Production wie folgt: Obenan steht Deutschland mit 1,910.000 Stück Bienenkörben und 20.000 Tonnen Honig; dann kommt Spanien mit 1,690.000 Bienenkörben und 19.000 Tonnen Honig; Oesterreich besitzt 1,550.000 Körbe und liefert 18.000 Tonnen Honig; Frankreich hat 950.000 Stücke und producirt 10.000 Tonnen, Holland mit 240.000 Stöcken, 2500 Tonnen; Belgien kommt alsdann mit 200.000 Körben und 2000 Tonnen Honig, hierauf erst Griechenland mit nur 30.000 Stöcken und der geringen Ausbeute von 1400 Tonnen; Russland hat 110.000 Stände, liefert aber nur 900 Tonnen Honig, Dänemark dieselbe Menge mit nur 90.000 Stöcken.[1] In den Vereinigten Staaten von Nordamerika gibt es 2 Millionen Bienenstöcke. Der Durchschnittspreis des Honigs beträgt 25 Cents per Pfund und das Land wird von den Bienen jährlich mit einer Einnahme von über 8,800.000 Dollars beschenkt.[2]

Angesichts dieser statistischen Ausweise ist es interessant zu ersehen, wie gering jene im Papyrus Harris Nr. 1 aufgezählten, sich überdies auf den langen Zeitraum von 31 Jahren vertheilenden scheinbar riesigen Mengen von Honig und Wachs sind gegenüber den jährlichen Quantitäten gleicher Bienenproducte in der jetzigen Welt-Bienenwirthschaft.

----

[1] Vgl. „Fremdenblatt" (Abendblatt), Wien, Freitag 5. April 1895 (49. Jahrgang, Nr. 93), S. 4 unter „Bienenfleiss".

[2] Bessler, Geschichte der Bienenzucht (Stuttgart 1886), S. 230.

WASPS ANCIENT AND MODERN.

BY EDWARD LATHAM ORMEROD, M.D., F.R.C.P.,

Physician to the Sussex County Hospital.

Wasps were the first paper-makers, but, unfortunately for their reputation, they never had the use of pen and ink to put their own good qualities on record. So they have been the silent suffering victims of an unjust judgment ever since their younger fellow-citizen of the world, Man, could read and write, and transmit his opinions. I am not going to inculcate sentimental zoology and to try to set them right in the world's estimation; but rather, I fear, while retaining my own conviction, to confirm this ill-feeling towards wasps by showing that they have always held the same hateful position as is assigned to them now-a-days: as far, at least, as the occasional notices of wasps, which have occurred to me in my reading, have allowed me to trace their family history.

Wasps have a long, though perhaps somewhat of a Welsh pedigree. The Pyramids of Egypt, the occupation of Canaan by the Israelites, the siege of Troy, and the fall of the Roman Empire, are all land-marks in their history. And the wasps over whom these great events passed were probably either identical with the present wasps of Western Europe, or so nearly resembling them as to be undistinguishable from them except by a practised eye. Their story, as presented in these pages, is written quite from a British point of view, to culminate in our own wasps, as we see and feel them now.

The storms of the world have not hurt wasps in their insignificance, they have reappeared like the barnacles on the rocks when the waves retired, to take and give, to be trampled on and wound in return, feared and yet despised through all ages, their bright redeeming quality being their intense domestic affection.

The insect which appears so often engraved on Egyptian monuments may be taken, from its form, either for a bee, a wasp, or an ichneumon fly, which last it most nearly resembles. Horapollo[*] distinguishes between the hieroglyphic representations of wasps and bees, and says, among other things, that a wasp on the wing denotes a murderer. But Mr. Sharpe, so well known for his successful studies of Egyptian hieroglyphics,[†] and whose kind assistance I

---

[*] "The Hieroglyphics of Horapollo Nilous," translated by A. T. Cory. Small 8vo.

have great pleasure in acknowledging, tells me that Horapollo is not quite a safe guide, that his interpretations are not to be unreservedly adopted; and, with regard to the point under consideration, that there are no sufficient grounds for asserting that any distinction of bees or wasps was intended. In one figure,* indeed, the coincident emblems—honey-pots—make it most probable that a bee was intended. But such a coincident explanation is exceptional, and, as the rule, there is no allusion to the habits of the insect, whatever it may be, nor is any moral implied. The figure of the insect is a symbol or letter, not a picture; it is simply the prefix to the name of a king, and, as such, is placed over the oval ring which surrounds the royal name. Expressed in phonetic characters it is NOU; or, with the semicircular T beneath it, NOUT, as the hieroglyph to the left is so, or, with the suffix, SOT. Here the com-

Name of an Egyptian king, with the usual prefix. Copied from Mr. Sharpe's work.

bination of a plant and a winged insect represents a king. In a North American tribe, Max Muller† tells us that the conjunction of somewhat similar emblems is employed in a different sense. To the Red Indian mind the figure of a man with a plant for a head, and with two wings, denotes a doctor, skilled in medicine, and endowed with the power of ubiquity.

After Mr. Sharpe's observations it is unnecessary to follow Horapollo any farther. Though it is with some regret that one turns away from all that Aldrovandus ‡ says on the subject, in elucidation of the good qualities of wasps, and of the high appreciation of those qualities by the ancient Egyptians. Horapollo's text, however, it must be acknowledged, does not quite bear out all that his genial commentator builds upon it.

From the Hieroglyphs, in which wasps have only a contingent and divided interest, we turn to the Bible, where these insects are mentioned by name, and a distinct duty § is assigned to them.

* Fig. 288, op. cit.
† "Chips from a German Workshop." Vol. i., p. 318. 1867.
‡ De Animalibus Insectis. Folio. Bononiæ, 1638, p. 220.

The hornet is expressly indicated as a means for slowly driving out the Canaanites before the advance of the Israelites, who were as yet too few in numbers to take full possession of the promised land. The allusions to hornets and wasps, though no more than four altogether, are all to the same effect, and very precise.

There can be no doubt that the hornet was quite equal to the task assigned to her. Whether the expulsion was effected by direct attacks on the people themselves, or by destruction of their cattle or their other means of livelihood, there need be no difficulty in accepting the Scripture statement literally. A much more insignificant insect might have accomplished this quite as effectually; a much less powerful instrument might conceivably have rooted up folks whose ties to house and home were much stronger and more material than were those of the devoted nations.

Apart, however, from the question of whether the insects intended were capable of the task assigned to them, another question arises as to whether hornets were intended at all, whether the word *tsirah* does not mean something different to a hornet. In favour of the correctness of the received text it may be urged that, as hornets were, and still are, very common in Palestine, the authors of the Septuagint translation had every opportunity of being familiar with what they were writing about. So, if they rendered *tsirah* as we read it in our own translation, and selected the hornet as the particular one of all noxious insects to which the word might most properly be applied, we may contentedly acquiesce in their decision. Should any one, however, demur to this conclusion, and wish to exercise his right of private judgment, he will find much further information on the subject in Bochart's "Hierozoicon," * where the question is discussed with great impartiality, and, I may add, at great length. Bochart mentions other interpretations of the word, such as a leprosy or a plague, bodily or mental, but concludes that there is no sufficient reason to doubt the literal accuracy of the received text, and that *tsirah* meant a hornet. It must shake the confidence of any one in Bochart's conclusion to observe that throughout his pages, replete with book-learning and curious items of wasp-lore, the distinctions of natural history are very lightly regarded. It would be too much to expect any distinction to be drawn between different kinds of wasps; but one is scarcely prepared to find wasps and bees confused together, and to see that both alike are supposed to collect honey in their cells. Such, however, and so loose, were the ideas on these matters of many

* Bochart, "Hierozoicon." Ed., Rosenmüller, 4to, Lipsiæ, 1796. Tom. III., cap. xiii.

of the authors from whom he quotes; and of these ideas he cannot wholly divest himself.

For those who may not care or may not have the opportunity to examine Bochart for themselves, and probably most of my readers would fall under this category, I will, in illustration of this point, reproduce one of his allusions in detail. Later in point of time than the hieroglyphical or Scriptural references, this story is curious as presenting our clients under another, which we will call a mythological, point of view. I do not know of any book in the English language above the range of nursery tales which corresponds to Ovid's " Fasti," by which to measure the amount of authority and credibility which may have been formerly allowed to the narrative. So Ovid shall tell the story, and himself vouch for the accuracy of the facts, both of mythology and of natural history. *

Once upon a time, Bacchus, so the story goes, was returning from his triumphant progress into the East, with his camp-followers, who constituted the greater part of his army, in attendance. Just under Mount Rhodope a swarm of bees were attracted by the cymbals of the Satyrs, and were adroitly hived by Bacchus, who was equal to the occasion, in a hollow tree. The progress must have been quite in the ancient style, for there was time for the bees to build cells and fill them with honey, and for the motley following to learn the taste of honey. The flavour set them all honey-hunting on their own account, and Silenus, the master of the revels, was lucky enough to find a swarm of bees, all to himself, in a hollow tree, where he heard them humming.

We are cautioned by the poet that, though these are in a certain sense serious things,—*Fasti*—we may laugh.

Non habet ingratos fabula nostra jocos.

And he goes on to tell us how Silenus brought his jackass alongside the tree, and, standing on its back, held on by one hand to a branch while he put the other hand in to reach the prize. The result needs no oracle to foretell it. The insects which fly out by thousands are now called *crabrones*, no longer *apes*; but bees or wasps, it is all the same to poor Silenus, whose bald head and shining face are made a pincushion for their stings. The ass, too, gets his share, and, lashing out, deals his astonished master a kick on the knee as he falls headforemost to the ground. The action of the drama now becomes very rapid. The curtain falls amid shrieks of laughter of the Satyrs at the plight of their master, thus punished for his greediness; while

Silenus is limping and roaring for pain ; and Bacchus appears at last, the *Deus ex machinâ*, to prescribe Nature's ointment, a good plaster of mud, for his aide-de-camp's face, and a ration of honey all round for the Satyrs. All compressed, as can only be done in Latin verse, into a few lines. Strange that so much nonsense should have clustered round and obscured a few simple facts ; that the moral intended in Bacchus, if we take Bacon's* explanation should be actually perverted by the copiousness of illustration, or that the introduction of religious rites from the East, according to modern views,† should be turned into a peg on which to hang stories of how men learned to hive bees and eat honey.

I have already remarked that it is not clear that the insects intended in these early notices were all of them really wasps. The ancients, as a rule, at least those who read and wrote, were not good naturalists. A point of character took their fancy, and dwelt in their memory, more than a point of colour or structure. And they bestowed their names on insects with no more precision than Juliet did on her roses. It is not that the Greeks, to whom I am more particularly alluding just now, were indifferent or incompetent observers of nature, like the modern Brazilians, who call all flowers alike *flores*, and all animals from a fly up to a mule, or an elephant, *bixos*,‡ or that they thought the study of natural history beneath them ; but that the knowledge necessary for accurate distinction was not yet in existence. And their thoughts ran in quite another direction. They did not compare trees with trees, and stones with stones, seeking for differences where all seemed alike ; but they clothed inanimate objects with life and feeling, and peopled the earth, sea, and sky with beings like themselves. They classed insects, not by their structure, but by their habits, and endowed their familiar animals, in imagination, with the mental characters of their acquaintances. So it is not to be wondered at that there was a special antipathy to our little black and yellow friends, who had no economic properties, like the bees, to recommend them. In the immediate presence of the enemy, probably, then as now, there was no opportunity for discrimination between wasps and bees. But when the danger was over, and became a matter of history or poetry, the stings were put down to the account of the *crabrones*, while the bees got the credit of the music, and the wax and honey.

Bacchus claimed something more than a royalty, the perpetual

---

* " Wisdom of the Ancients," XXIV. Dionysus, or Bacchus, explained of the Passions.
† Cox, " Tales of Ancient Greece." Introduction, p. xxxii.

gratitude of mankind, for having discovered the use of the frying-pan, which has been, from that date, a domestic institution in hiving a swarm of bees. But it does not appear that he improved the occasion, by inculcating any rules of caution in handling his favourite insects, nor does any such caution seem to have been habitually observed. Instance the way in which Samson just stepped aside to take some honey from the swarm in the lion's carcase,* and went on eating as if he had done nothing out of the way. The mode of taking wasps' nests, however, was reduced to regular strategic rules by the Greeks. Timolaus† was not above taking an illustration from wasps, when he advised the allies to attack the Lacedæmonians in their own country, on the same principle as they would put a torch to a wasp's nest, before the enemy could get out. Unfortunately his advice was not followed, or the wasp might have become to the Corinthians, what the cicada was to the Athenians, at once their pride and their annoyance.

Euripides ‡ alludes to the same mode of taking wasps' nests in the curious Satyric drama of the Cyclops, suggestively, and as a piece of comic by-play on the part of the Chorus. Homer makes no mention of this use of the blazing torch, in the original draft of the story,§ but the antiquity of the method appears from an indirect allusion in the Psalms.‖

The fact of a swarm of bees alighting on the lips of the infant Pindar was hailed as a sign, perhaps a cause, of his future powers. What would a British mamma have thought under the circumstances? Certainly the bees made the most of their time, for cells were run up and filled with honey, actually under Pindar's nose. The omen was certainly auspicious, as it turned out, and no harm happened. But it contrasts with what the Augurs thought of wasps; for the appearance of a swarm of this unpopular insect in the temple of Mars at Capua was regarded as a most alarming occurrence. However, all was done that could be, for not only were the wasps burned, but the magistrates were had out, and a regular form of sacrifice and supplication was gone through to avert the impending calamity.¶

So much for the religious significance of wasps. The bees per-

* Judges xiv. 8, 9.
† Xenophon, "Historia Græca," Lib. IV., § 2, p. 116. Dindorf.
‡ Cyclops, v. 475.
§ Odyssey, IX., v. 382.
‖ "They compassed me about like bees; they are quenched as the fire of thorns." Ps. cxviii. 12.

haps had as little reason to congratulate themselves personally on their more dignified position, for when the wax and honey were wanted their crown of honour equally ended in smoke. Still they lived afterwards in grateful memory, while quite another epitaph was inscribed upon the tomb of the wasps. They are appointed the guardians of the grave of the ungentle poet Archilochus* by Gætulicus.

> ἠρέμα δή παράμειψον ὁδοιπόρε, μὴ ποτέ τοῦδε
> κινήσῃς τύμβῳ σφῆκας ἐφεζομένους.
> Good traveller beware not to rattle these stones,
> Lest you stir up the hornets that swarm round his bones.

And, worse still, Hipponax, another of the *genus irritabile vatum*, was himself poetically transformed into a wasp by Leonidas,† for a similar offence of having stung his rivals to death by his caustic verses.

> ἀτρέμα τὸν τύμβον παρτμείβετε, μὴ τὸν ἐν ὕπνῳ
> πικρὸν ἐγείρητε σφῆκἀναπαυόμενον.
> Tread light as you journey, and, mind, give his nest
> A wide berth, lest you wake the cross wasp from his rest.

If wasps had no fame, they had plenty of notoriety. Aristophanes stigmatizes them in the title of one of his Comedies. There is little in the play bearing on their natural history. They are only brought forwards as apt images of the litigious Dicasts, who lived by bullying and plunder committed under cover of the law. He was indeed aware of the fact that the drones had no sting,‡ but the argument which this fact is made to point is unsound, as the food which drones consume is very small in amount. And the comparison of Philocleon creeping into his house, like a bee or humble-bee with wax—from the tablets—under his nails,§ probably involves an erroneous notion as to the mode of formation of wax.

Aristophanes, in all that he said, did but express the popular notions concerning wasps, and availed himself of an illustration which his hearers could readily appreciate. Why should we blame him in particular for this poetic injustice? The modern wasp was to Shakespere what her ancestor was to the Greek muse, quick and irritable, stinging and making to sting, a robber by taste as well as by trade. It was just the thing for Katharine and Petruchio

* Anthologia Græca, Thackeray. London, 1867, p. 340.
† Quoted from Bochart, "Hierozoicon," Tom. III., p. 414.

to bandy words about.* But Shakespere had a deeper feeling than this about our clients, and the thought which his mention of a wasp suggests, on more than one occasion, is expressed in Julia's outburst of pettish anger against her own mischief-making fingers—

> Injurious wasps, to feed on such sweet honey,
> And kill the bees that yield it with your stings.†

Cowper, again, who warmed, like the Ancient Mariner, in his love for animals, caps his opinion of sour old Miss Bridget and her ἔπεα πτερόεντα, by an illustration drawn from the same source‡—

> Censorious, and her every word a wasp.

To point a satire or to furnish the sting of a proverb has been the literary use of wasps in all ages. *Quod semper, quod ubique, quod ab omnibus*, must be true; still there is something to be said on the other side of the question.

The wasps which lived before Agamemnon, as we have seen, have no reason to complain of neglect and oblivion. Agamemnon's contemporaries are still better off, embalmed as they are in Homer. Here are no prejudices, nothing to detract from the simple beauty of the comparison; one of Homer's touches of nature sets them before us in all their native restlessness, and their recklessness of danger in defence of their brood, hid, then as now, in holes dug out by the rugged way-side :—

> ὥς τε σφῆκες μέσον αἰόλοι, ἠὲ μέλισσαι,
> οἰκία ποιήσωνται ὁδῷ ἔπι παιπαλοέσσῃ,
> οὐδ' ἀπολείπουσιν κοῖλόν δόμον, ἀλλὰ μένοντες
> ἄνδρας θηρητῆρας, ἀμύνονται περὶ τέκνων.
>
> "Iliad," xii. 167.

> They're like the many-coloured wasps, or bees by the wayside,
> Making their nests by the dusty road, nor will they relinquish
> Their deep-hollowed hall, but await the assault of their foemen,
> Combating well to the last, for the sake of their home and their offspring.
>
> Simcox's Translation, 8vo, London, 1865.

It is fine to hear the grand old man, as we fancy him, for whose observation nothing was too small. With his harp tuned in the halls of princes, he was not too proud to tell, and to tell exactly, of the ways of Nature's lowliest creatures. He could feel for aught that was noble, and speak of it in the same words, whether it dwelt in the breast of his mighty Hector or in the little body of a wasp. And he had a heart to love all things, both

* "Taming of the Shrew." Act II., Sc. 1.
† "Two Gentlemen of Verona." Act I., Sc. 3.
‡ Table-talk. Truth.

great and small, all, save only the irrepressible small-boys, the
Bedouins of all ages, to whom, probably, Homer was then in
the body, as now still in the book, a natural enemy.

> ἀυτίκα δὲ σφήκεσσιν ἐοικότες ἐξεχέοντο
> ἐινοδίοις, οὓς παῖδες ἐριδμαίνωσιν ἔθοντες,
> αἰεὶ κερτομέοντες, ὁδῷ ἔπι οἰκί᾽ ἔχοντας,
> νηπίαχοι· ξυνὸν δὲ κακὸν πολέεσσι τιθεῖσι.
> τοὺς δ᾽ ἅπερ παρὰ τίς τε κιὼν ἄνθρωπος ὁδίτης
> κινήσῃ ἀέκων, οἱ δ ἄλκιμον ἦτορ ἔχοντες
> πρόσσω πᾶς πέτεται, καὶ ἀμύνει οἷσι τέκεσσι.
>
> "Iliad," xvi. 259.

Instantly they poured forth like the wasps which dwell by the wayside,
Which, as their custom is, by boys are ever tormented,
For still they vex them as they dwell in their nests by the roadway,
Fools that they are, and a common ill they bring upon many.
Then if some wayfaring man unwittingly move them,
Having, their puny breasts within, a vehement spirit,
One and all, they fly forth enraged, in defence of their young ones.

Simcox's Translation.

The poetry of wasps begins and ends with Homer. However,
it is something to have been sung of by the Father of Poetry, and
it is still more to have engrossed so much of the attention of the
Father of Natural History. Aristotle's knowledge of the habits
of wasps was considerable, and contrasts favourably with that of
other more familiar animals. Speaking, apparently, from his
own observation, he traces the nests from their small beginnings
to the point when the mother wasp ceases to build, and confines
herself to her strictly maternal duties inside the nest. He describes accurately the position of the egg at one side of the cell,
and notices how the grubs at the end of the season are developed
into larger wasps—mothers, as he calls them. And following
their history through the complete cycle, he tells how, at the
end of the season, all the wasps perish, except the females, which
are to continue the race during the ensuing year. Mixed with
these apparently original observations are various statements,
which he thinks it right to reproduce at second-hand without vouch-
ing for their accuracy.

The deficiencies in Aristotle's information, are obvious enough
to us now, but scarcely more so than they were to himself. He
expressly indicates many of the Hymenoptera as forming a natural
order, which much needed a name, under which so many insects,

he instances bees, wasps, and ἀνθρῆναι, as having their natural home
here. He keeps the bee family distinct, but the ἀνθρῆναι are
mixed with the wasps; and though the word is translated *hornets*,
it is not certain that these insects were always intended by the
term. Not species only, but genera, were involved in a confusion
from which it needed years of patient accumulation of observation
to extricate them. And he, whose work was so sadly marred by
the want of the knowledge which he did so much to supply, felt its
need more keenly than any one else.*

Pliny, to whom I must confess that I refer more as a matter of
natural history etiquette, than from any respectful consideration of
what he has to say on this subject, has a short chapter on wasps and
hornets.† But he adds nothing of value to what he adapts, or adopts
from Aristotle. He retains, and indeed, rather increases, the confusion about the drones, and he repeats the story of the ichneumon
fly, carrying away spiders to lay her eggs in them, with the farther
improvement that she sits on these spiders to hatch her young.

Doubtless, by a little more irregular reading and hunting in
indices, and a little more canvassing of my literary friends, I might
be able to lengthen this list of authors, and produce a few more who
had something of their own, or of some one else's to say about
wasps. But I think that I can claim my reader's willing forgive-
ness for abstaining from these researches. Passing, therefore, over
this period, we come to another, lasting many centuries, during
which wasps, like so much else, were trodden under foot unnoticed.
Perhaps, the representative men of those ages, who have left their
mark so indelibly for good or for bad on that dark period, might
have found their own chief characteristics, as great robbers, great
melodists, and great builders, reflected in a wasp's nest. It was
many centuries before books were written about wasps, such as we
write and read, now-a-days. Meanwhile the wasps themselves had
been modernized. With the decline of the Roman Empire, a
gradual change, though only in name, came over our little friends.
The ancient *crabro*, of uncertain etymology, and of the masculine
gender, disappeared, to be replaced by the feminine *vespa* of
Greek origin. Curiously, *chheka*, the Sanscrit word corresponding

---

* See Cresswell's translation of " Aristotle's History of Animals." Bohn, London,
1862. The most important passages are p. 127, Book V., chap. 17, § 15; p. 262 Book
IX., Chap. 27, § 1, and Chap. 28, §§ 1, et seqq. I have quoted from this as more
accessible and more inviting than the original text.

† "Natural History," Book XI., chap. 24 (21). Vol. III., p. 24. Bohn, London,

to the Greek σφήξ, does not mean a wasp, but a bee; a wasp being represented in Sanscrit by *varatd*, or *varald*.* Vespa now appears in one or other guise, in all the chief languages of western Europe, though the Celtic dialects have their separate names for this insect.

With the revival of learning, wasps came in for their share of attention. One or two of these we may notice, commencing with Olaus Magnus,† Bishop of Upsala, who in his retirement from Rome, much like our own Izaak Walton, found a safer occupation in natural history, than in politics, briefly alludes to them in the history of his native country. The description has a special interest to us as probably relating to the species with which we in the north have to do, and it is quite as minute as any one might now-a-days find room for in an account of the Fauna of a country in which he had ceased to reside.

But the type of mediæval naturalists is Aldrovandus,‡ who, like Réaumur, devoted his wealth and leisure to the study of natural history, and in a portion of whose voluminous works the lover of wasp-lore will find some most amusing reading. A first glance at these venerable pages—I quote from quite a typical copy in the library of the College of Physicians, frilled with marginal references, and crowded with quotations—might lead to the conclusion that wasps were a very popular subject with the older writers, and that here was a mine of information on this branch of entomology. But further observation corrects this impression; for the references are numerous rather than various, chiefly to Aristotle and Pliny, with allusions to Nicander and the classic poets, pointed by quotations from Ariosto. And the original observations are few, and so circumstantial, as to suggest the suspicion that the writer was not very practically familiar with his subject. But it would be ungracious to dismiss in these terms a book to which I would confess my obligations, if not as a repertory of original observation, at least as an index where I have re-found all my own references, and found many more besides. Useful on this account, the work is curious also as illustrating a phase in the history of physical science when men played,

* I have the greatest pleasure in acknowledging my obligations here, as on many other occasions, to my learned friend Dr. Greenhill, of Hastings, for an introduction to sources of wasp-lore, which, but for his kind and able assistance, would have been closed to me.

† Historia de Gentibus Septentrionalibus, etc. Folio, Basiliæ, 1567. Lib. XXII capp. 3, 4.

‡ Ulysses Aldrovandus de Animalibus Insectis. Libri, VII. Folio, Bononiæ, 1638. Lib. I., capp. 6, 7, de Vespis et Crabronibus. The entire work runs to 13 folio volumes.

as it were, with the statements of the older writers instead of confirming or correcting them by recurring to the observation of Nature. It was not the *Hippocrates ait—Galenus negat* of the schools, but Galen and Hippocrates were jumbled up together, and everything that everybody had said was reproduced till the fact was quite put out of sight by the multitude of the authorities, the wood by the trees.

One more author of this period, though scarcely a typical one, claims attention here. The versatile genius of Porta,* to whom we owe the invention of the camera-obscura, was for a passing moment turned to natural history, but only to add the weight of his name to the statement of half-a-dozen older authors that wasps were generated from the carcase of a horse. This belief of former ages neatly expressed by Nicander†—

$$\text{Ἵπποι γὰρ σφήκων γένεσις ταῦροι δὲ μελισσῶν}$$

he reduces to a formula, by the aid of which any one may produce a swarm of bees, within a given number of days. Had Porta interrogated Nature herself in this matter, the asserted origin of such perfect creatures as bees and wasps in the decomposition of animal substances would scarcely have been recognized as a fact of natural magic.

In a few years' time a change came over the study of natural history. The book of Nature now took precedence of all others. The scholastic incrustation which incumbered every topic which had been mentioned, however casually, by any writer of note, was swept away, and the path was re-opened by which all subsequent observers have travelled.

I cannot be far wrong in selecting Swammerdam as a representative of the class of naturalists who took up the work where Aristotle had left it. There is something in the title of his work suggestive of the spirit in which it was written.‡ Wasps, however, it must be owned, obtain but scant notice from him, and the descriptions are almost exclusively comparative, in illustration of the habits and structure of his favourite bees. The longest and most particular description is of the tongue of the wasp, and the

---

* Porta, J. B., "Magia Naturalis," 24mo. Lugd., Batav., 1650, p. 52. Contrast with this book its modern representative, "Letters on Natural Magic," by Sir D. Brewster. Small 8vo. London, 1833.

† Quoted from Aldrovandus, op. cit., p. 228. Nicander is cited by Cicero, De Oratore, Lib. I. Cap 16, as having written on agriculture, as Aratus did on astronomy *præclare*, though both alike were practically unacquainted with what they were writing about.

occasion of introducing it is characteristic. He scarcely thinks that the lapping mechanism of the tongue, which he denies the existence of in the bee, would be sufficient to satisfy the requirements of wasps,* "Cum rapaces admodum, truculentæ, atque avidissimæ sint Bestiolæ," and concludes that they must employ some other method of taking in food besides that which the form of the tongue suggests. The poor wasps have no share in the note of general pious admiration which the mention of the honey-bee evokes in every page.

Limited in the choice of authors to a few well-known and accessible volumes, still I have no doubt in adopting Réaumur † as the representative of a still later and more advanced stage of modern Natural history as applied to our particular subject. A wider choice might supplement, but could scarcely replace these interesting volumes. We feel at once among our friends—the wasps—of this season. There is nothing in the pages of Réaumur to indicate that he wrote so many years ago. The descriptions and figures are true to Nature now as then, and we need the old-fashioned vignettes of the quarto to remind us that these observations were not made by one who lived and dressed like us, but in the fresh recollection of the times of the Grand Monarque.

The honey-bee had the foremost place in Réaumur's as in Swammerdam's affections, and the wasp is introduced with an almost apologetic preface, as the natural enemy of the bees which have been just before described. Two memoirs are then devoted to a systematic account of wasps and their works,‡ in which the chief features of their natural history are sketched with great care and skill. The distinction between wasps and bees is drawn from the old classical character of the narrow waist, the black and yellow or orange livery, the short and square tongue, and the habit of folding the wings during rest, peculiar to the family of wasps both solitary and social. He describes from personal observation, both on wild and imprisoned swarms, the mode of making and laying on the paper of which the nest is composed, and, with some doubt as to the correctness of the results, from the difficulty of observing all the circumstances accurately, he calculates the time required to develope an egg into a perfect wasp. A nest of *Polistes* and a small hornet's nest, which last he transferred to a situation

* Op. cit., vol. i., p. 451. Gaubius, in his Latin translation, fully conveys the animus of the original, but less generally intelligible, Dutch.

† "Mémoires pour servir à l'Histoire des Insectes." 6 Tomes, 4to, Paris, 1734—42.

‡ Op. cit. Tome vi. Mémoires 6 et 7.

convenient for observation, supplied more accurate data for his inquiry, but the same accident befell his tame hornets as subsequently both Pastor Muller's * and Mr. Newport's,† the swarm languished and failed after the loss of the queen.

Each page of this narrative tells of the exercise of the most constant varied observation. The habit of the insects, their gentleness to those who would handle them properly, their mode of feeding their young, and the difficulty of bringing wasps up by hand, with many little points of difference in the arrangement of various nests, all are duly noted. The nocturnal habits of hornets, which cost him his queen, the symmetry of their comb depending from a larger central column, and the coarseness of the paper, are set before us as freshly as if only written yesterday; though an economist might deem the suggestion of importing from Cayenne the materials of which the card-board wasps make their nest, a little out of date, and not a little visionary.

The distinction of sex, as far as was then known, is clearly laid down and illustrated by careful microscopic drawings; and if the microscopic anatomy of wasps occupies so small a space in their history, we can hardly be surprised when we consider with what difficulties this branch of inquiry was beset in Réaumur's time. But the want of proper optical appliances was scarcely so great a stumbling-block as the want of proper distinctions of species. Seeing farther than Aristotle, Réaumur demurred to his opinion, that the cause of wasps building in high places, was the loss of their ruler. But he does not explicitly refer this habit to a difference of species, nor does he describe what really does happen when the wasps have lost their rulers.

De Geer closely follows on the track of Réaumur, in a work of the same title,‡ and on a similar plan. As Réaumur had made his observations on ground-wasps, so De Geer turned his attention to the species which build in trees or under eaves. His descriptions lack the fresh interest which we find in Réaumur, but this is due, in a great measure, to the care with which De Geer has constructed his narrative, supplementing, not reiterating the observations which had as great a charm for him as they have had for all other naturalists since his time. Here are more or less exact descriptions of three kinds of wasps. The small wasp needs little more to

* Magazin der Entomologie. Germar. Halle, 1817. Band III., s. 50; Band III., s. 56.
† Trans. Entomological Society of London. Vol. III., 1841-43, p. 183.
‡ "Mémoires pour servir à l'histoire des Insectes." 4to. Stockholm, 1752—1778.

be said to establish it as *V. Britannica*; and the importance of the form of the male sexual organs is insisted on, as at once showing that we are dealing with a different species to Réaumur's ground-wasps. His middle-sized hornet appears distinctly to be *V. media*, a species not known in these islands. And the third species is the familiar ubiquitous hornet, drawn with unmistakable accuracy.

If the mode in which De Geer tells his story, and the generous way in which he limits his subject, detract from the interest of his work, they add much to its usefulness. Omitting all such topics as he deems to have been fully illustrated, he never fails to throw the light of his better knowledge on any point to which he addresses himself. If Réaumur was the first truly modern writer on this subject, De Geer was the first to show how to profit by such a master.

He dwells on the notched outline of the compound eyes, as a character distinguishing wasps from bees; he describes the locking of the wings in action, and their folding in repose, and while he improves on Réaumur's account of the teeth, he denies the accuracy of his description of the form of the opening of the mouth. Speaking from his own experience, he evidently thinks, and all will probably agree with him, that Réaumur greatly overestimated the number of wasps in a swarm.

Though our knowledge of the natural history of wasps has been much advanced since Réaumur wrote, there can scarcely be said to be any work which constitutes an epoch in the subject, since his time. Perhaps Kirby and Spence's work, which has done more than any other work to popularize entomology, may seem an exception to this statement. But it is not really so. They stand on the same ground as Réaumur, the popularity of their work is due to the same fresh truthful observation of Nature, and the form in which their work is cast, to which, indeed, a good deal of its popularity is owing, tends to keep out of sight much of the direct advance of entomology since Réaumur's time. How all this knowledge grew up and was put together, it would exceed my present limits to say, and I would not willingly deter any one from the study of a most interesting subject by a display of names, which he could easily procure for himself, whenever he may need the information.*

* Westwood "On the Modern Classification of Insects," vol. ii. p. 236, gives a list of authors on the Diplopteryga, to which may be added the foot notes and textual references in the particular description of the Vespidæ, p. 244. It might be thought superfluous to mention other books to any one who has Hagen's admirable Bibliotheca Entomologica, 8vo, Leipzic, 1862, to refer to. But De Saussure's "Etudes sur la Famille des Vespides," 3 Tomes, 8vo, Paris, 1852—58, has claims to the student of this

The natural history of wasps, it is needless to say, is not co-extensive with entomology generally, and I fear lest I should seem to have given them a longer notice than they can fairly claim. Yet I must plead that much entomological knowledge has been obtained by the study of the structure and habits of the Hymenoptera, and that the hornet—in her own way—deserves as well of science as the frog. And if wasps have always stood in the cold shade of the bee, at least there is a stamp of earnestness on all that has been written about them, and an entire want of that gasconading which occupies so much of bee-literature. And yet another recommendation to busy men who take up entomology as a pastime, the literature of wasps, however fragmentary, is much more compendious than that of their popular cousins.

The history which began with a few scarcely intelligible scratches on an Egyptian monument, has expanded, at the present time, into an account as circumstantial as many animals standing much higher in general esteem than wasps can boast of. We recognize now in the wasps a large well-defined family of the Hymenoptera. They shade on one hand into the bees, from which they are chiefly distinguished by the arrangement of the nervures of the wings, the narrow tibia, the form of the tongue, and of the compound eyes. On the other hand they are separated from the sand-wasps by less distinct characters, both of habit and structure. Though we do not feel this indistinctness in our British classification, the only intruder among our *Vespidæ*, breaking the sharp outlines by which the *Vespæ* are defined, being our harmless unnoticed *Odyneri*. The mention of a wasp to us in England, recalls the idea of a smooth yellow or orange-insect striped with black, with a square short tongue, thin legs, a pinched-in waist, and a sharp sting. And the narrow space into which its wings are folded in repose, must have struck many of those who were unaware of the distinctive importance of this habit.

The *Vespæ*, the typical family, make their nests of paper, with the case separate from the horizontal combs. Though, on this point, there is considerable difference in the different families of Vespidæ, yet, for each, its rule is so strictly maintained, that the relation of the case to the comb, the direction of the central axis of the nest, the form and material, to the minutest detail, have been made the basis of a method of classification of social wasps. But, however much the general form of the comb or case may differ, the cells are always

substance, we must take their form as a result of the instinct of
the individual, not as an incidental effect of the combined work of
many labourers.

They are divided, like bees, into males, females, and neuters,
which last, since Réaumur wrote, have been shown to be abortive
females. Their nest is the work of a single season, the colony
beginning with the queen, who is impregnated in the previous
autumn, and survives the winter to lay the foundation of the paper-
city. The whole well-being of the community turns on the queen-
mother, and her loss is absolutely irreparable. Unlike the queen-
bee, who can be reproduced, not by a breath exactly, but by good
feeding. The singular law of Parthenogenesis, by which abortive
or unimpregnated females can lay male eggs, obtains among wasps,
as among bees.

Wasps are no respecters of persons, it is only our knowledge of
them and their habits, that gives us power over them. Much as I
have handled them, I never venture to approach them without
caution, or to neglect such means of defence as are adapted to the
probable amount of disturbance I am about to cause. At least,
however, they are not capricious, and they only give blow for blow.
The happy owner of an active wasps' nest, may extract much
scientific interest out of it, but no sentiment, and no honey worth
the having. Wax of course is out of the question, and the honey
which some wasps are said to collect, is, judging from the production of *Nectarinia*, a nasty mixture of pollen granules and honey
which they have stolen from the bees and put away, for a more
convenient season, in their cells. The scientific interest of a wasps'
nest, however, is far greater than that of a bee-hive; as the movements of wasps are more easily directed, and more readily intelligible, than those of honey-bees.

The title of this paper suggests a question, which it seems most
convenient to discuss here, namely, whether the species of wasps
which we see, and sometimes feel, now-a-days, are identical with
those of ancient times? whether Homer and Aristophanes took
their ideas from the same wasps as supply images to modern
poets? This is a question to which perhaps no positive answer can
be given. However, in the absence of any direct information, we
may reasonably infer that the species of wasps have not changed
within the period of Man's knowledge. For, during these few hundred or thousand years, there have been no considerable changes
in the external conditions on which the well-being of wasps

depend, by which such mutation of species could have been
effected, or to which wasps might have adapted themselves. For
rugged ground, rotten trees, garbage, fruit, and insects, all the
ways and means of wasps, have certainly been available for them
ever since Man could describe what he saw around him. The
varieties, indeed, which we notice in collecting the Fauna of
different countries, show that the laws of mutation which have
affected the species of other animals, have equally affected those of
wasps; but within human knowledge, in the cycles counted by the
historian, not by the geologist, there is no reason for asserting that
any change has taken place. And all that has been said of the
classical wasps of ancient times, may be applied to our own, saving
always the difference between Monmouth and Macedon, between
Greek and English wasps.

There are seven kinds of wasps indigenous to these islands
which seem fairly established as distinct species. The varieties
within the limits of some of these species are, however, considerable
in Great Britain, and the variation is still greater in some Continen-
tal specimens. At the risk of being tedious I must notice some of
these more particularly.

V. sylvestris, so variable in her habits that it is questionable
whether she should be regarded as a tree or a ground wasp, is
singularly uniform in her markings. But *V. rufa* presents such
various forms and tints in different broods, that none but close observers could be sure of the identity of the species in them all. Only
by such careful observation is *V. arborea* to be discriminated from
V. rufa. The difficulty is greater still in the case of *V. germanica*
and *V. vulgaris*, which vary into each other's markings, the variation
of the former being chiefly by increase, that of the latter species
by diminution of the markings. As a matter of fact the exact distinction between these two rests not on any outward markings but
on differences of the internal structure of the males of the two
species respectively. A very large nest of *V. germanica*, which a
friend kindly brought me from Madeira in 1865, had all the wasps
marked in a very peculiar manner, the type of the markings tending strongly to that of *V. vulgaris* in both sexes, in the abortive as
well as in the perfect females.

But the occurrence of the same markings in specimens of
V. germanica from Mentone, prevents the inference that the Madeira
wasps were in process of development into a species peculiar to
that island. Again *V. britannica* varies very much in different
broods, the lateral orange spots being well marked in one, while

they are scarcely to be seen in another. But the nearest approach
to a fixed variety seems to occur in *V. Crabro* where there are two
distinct types of external marking, one kind cloudy, very exactly
resembling the markings of *V. vulgaris*, the other with hard outlines
and narrower. Still as these distinctions of colour are unconnected
with difference of habit, and, as far as 1 have seen, difference of
internal structure, they cannot claim the importance of specific
distinctions.

To the question how far are these 'distinctions hereditary? I
can return no answer. A season devoted to the study of wasps,
in a demesne from which all animals injurious to wasps, and
especially little boys, were rigidly excluded, might probably show
how far the characters of the mother were impressed on her brood.
But, such as wasps are, I could scarcely anticipate any satisfactory
results, even with all these advantages, from an attempt to carry
this inquiry over a second year, into the next generation. Wasps
are manageable enough when they have given hostages to fortune
in the form of houses and children, but it is as impracticable to
make a wild wasp build, as to make a polypody grow in confinement,
and when once a wasp has left the nest, she is lost to observation.

I suppose that it will be generally conceded, by those who have
considered the subject, that the various species of animals and plants
which occupy different countries are fixed varieties, which have grown
up in the lapse of ages, adapted to the various circumstances of the
countries in which these animals and plants have been placed. But
how they grew up, whether the mutation of species was under
the guidance of natural selection, or of some other influence for
which we have no name, and of which we have no precise idea,
observers are by no means so universally agreed. And a great deal
of feeling, which has nothing whatever to do with the question, has
been introduced into the discussion.

I have neither the knowledge or the leisure to enter into the
question here, nor do the social Hymenoptera furnish the ground
which an advocate of the mutation of species by external influences
would willingly take his stand on. Their history, indeed, supplies
some of the most formidable objections to this theory, and one of
these is notably the relation of the workers to the rest of the
swarm. The workers do all or nearly all the work; all the qualities
which are beneficial to the race are centred in them, all the
capacities of the race are tested in them. Yet these workers are
only the barren recipients of excellences which their own good

mitting. Again; the adaptation of a common larva to the condition
of a queen-bee by change of position and nourishment, while it
shows what can be done by external influences in this direction,
shows how very limited the effects are. For when the results
of these preparations are to be worked out, at the very moment of
projection, the embryo is most carefully sealed up, in order that the
powers which it has within itself may work without any hindrance
from external interference. What happens to the embryo of the bee
happens to the embryo of all animals; the materials may be
supplied from without, but the directing power which disposes of
all these materials comes from within. And beyond the external
supply of materials, and the internal force which disposes of
them, there is another influence, for which we have not a name,
which adapts the progressive changes of the embryo to conditions
with which it is wholly unconnected. Under such guidance are the
preparations of the embryo for extra-uterine life. Such, more
remotely, are the adaptations of the chrysalis for its evolutions
exactly at the time when the series of arrangements for the sustenance and reproduction of the perfect insect are completed. And
such a relation, though it be less obvious, I believe to exist between
all created beings in process of development and the places they are
to occupy in creation. Else, considering the long period that is
required for the development of a new, or the modification of an
established form, by the time that the zoological changes were
completed, the external conditions to which they were adapted
might have passed away, and the change would have been all in
vain, hopelessly futile after countless ages.

It is quite as consistent with all that we know of the
attributes of our Creator to suppose that He endowed all creatures
in the first instance, with a power of adapting themselves to all the
varying circumstances of the world in which He placed them, as
that He created them in all their different varieties in each different
place, and still creates them anew as may be required. We are at
liberty to suppose either case, for we know nothing about it; they
are both equally possible, equally consistent; but Science shows the
former to be the most probable. On the farther question, whether
the power of adaptation has been left entirely to the creatures
themselves, or whether a constant directing influence is exercised
over them, Science has nothing to say, and we must be guided by
the analogy of God's government of the world, as far as we can
trace it, in drawing our inference.

Only one word more in conclusion. The most probable result

of all the living occupants of the world striving independently after their individual advantage, seems to me illustrated in the result ot the mutual attrition of the pebbles on the beach. I see no sufficient reason to discard such phrases as a place in the Scheme of Nature or in the Scale of Creation. Admitting fully the existence and action of faculties in all the different living creatures by which to adapt themselves to their several places, I cannot but recognize in all this the Hand which made both them and their places, and draws them there. And holding the one opinion to be just as tenable as the other, from a scientific point of view, I prefer the belief in a constant superintending benevolence to that which is expressed in the terms of the Battle of Life and the Struggle for Existence.

On the Anatomy and Functions of the Tongue of the Honey-
Bee (Worker). By TRAVERS JAMES BRIANT. (Communicated by B. DAYDON JACKSON, Sec.L.S.)

[Read 3rd April, 1884.]

(PLATES XVIII. & XIX.)

IN order to arrive at a just appreciation of the relationship of
the tongue of the Bee to the rest of the head, it will be necessary
to refer to the more conspicuous parts of the endo-skeleton to
which it is related.

From the lower half of the ring which surrounds the occipital
foramen arise two pillars (*a*, fig. 1, longitudinal section of head,
without muscles; fig. 2, horizontal section, with muscles), which
pass obliquely downwards to the front wall of the head, and there

blend with two ridges that correspond inwardly with the furrows, which, on the outer surface, mark off the clypeus. From the lower side of the base of each of these pillars spring second pillars (*b*, figs. 1 & 2), running parallel with those first mentioned until they approach the outer wall of the head, where they terminate in a bifurcation; they cannot, however, in strictness be considered pillars, as they each unite with and form part of the chitinous wall bounding the oral chamber.

This bifurcation receives the end of the cardo (*d*, figs. 1, 2, & 5, details of the base of maxilla, with adjacent parts). The cardo is channelled on the medial side and terminates at each end in two unequal processes, those at the forward end receiving the muscle *cx m*, those at the other being hinged to the base of the maxilla (see fig. 5); in the centre of this fork is placed the end of one of the wings of the lora (*c*, fig. 8, longitudinal section of head, with muscles; figs. 5 & 6, tongue of queen from above). The central portion or body of the lora is triangular in shape and is hinged to the base of the mentum.

The mentum is a semitubular body, bearing at its anterior end the labial palpi, the tongue, and the other organs connected with it. It contains the muscles acting directly on the tongue, and the salivary valve; and into it is withdrawn a large portion of the basal end of the tongue in the manner hereafter to be described. The anterior end (fig. 15, from above) is cut by two longitudinal notches; the central portion bears the paraglossae, the hyaline rod which traverses the tongue (*l*); and the lateral parts bear the palpi. These latter organs (fig. 7) consist of one long and three succeeding shorter joints. The long joint contains a muscle which acts upon the remaining joints. The whole organ is kept in its place adpressed to the tongue by a muscle which arises from the walls of the mentum (*p*).

The maxilla (fig. 9) consists of a stipe and a blade. When the maxillæ are closed together, they cover the tongue on the upper or forward side, and, together with the labial palpi, completely surround it. When folded back the blades carry with them the tongue and palpi; the lower edge of the blade fits into the space between the base of the maxilla and the mentum, and thus the whole apparatus is neatly tucked away and safely protected. The lower side of the blade is plaited at its anterior end (fig. 14), the extreme edge is fringed with hairs (*d*), and between these hairs are smaller hairs or bristles (*b* and *c*) seated on papillæ; alternately a shorter and weaker hair on a longer papilla and a longer and stouter hair on a shorter papilla. There is nothing in the appearance of the end to support the assertion frequently made, that it is used for cutting purposes. The harder the chitine, the darker it is; but the end of the blade is very transparent and delicate.

The movements of the organs before mentioned are controlled by the following muscles. A pair of muscles (*ex m*[1], figs. 2 & 5) which spring from the outer base of the cranial pillar (*a*) are inserted into the end of the cardo (*d*), together with a second pair, which spring from the back wall of the head, *ex m*[2]. The contraction of these moves the cardo on the fulcrum formed at its juncture with the walls of the oral chamber, and consequently carries forward the lower end and the parts attached thereto; that is, the whole mentum and the maxillæ. The posterior end of the maxilla is brought forward by the muscle *mx*[1] (fig. 4, lower portion of longitudinal section of head, showing muscle; and fig. 5), and this muscle is opposed by the muscles *mx*[2] and *mx*[3]. The lateral movements of the maxilla are produced by the action of a muscle found in its base (*mx*[4], fig. 5), which is inserted into the end of a dark chitinous strap (*j*, figs. 4, 5, & 6). This strap is hinged at one end to the side of the inner oral chamber at *h* (figs. 5 & 6). The contraction of *mx*[4] results therefore in drawing aside the whole organ, the elasticity of the hinge being sufficient to restore it again. The blade of the maxilla is extended by the muscle *mx*[5] and flexed by *mx*[6] (fig. 5).

The general appearance of the tongue is that of a slightly tapering brush-like organ densely covered with long hairs, which, when extended, is longer than the palpi. Within this, however, is a hyaline rod, which, arising from the central part of the end of the mentum (*l*, fig. 15, also fig. 8, longitudinal section of mentum, with tongue extended; fig. 9, the same, with tongue contracted; and fig. 10, section of tongue, A, taken near the root B, taken about halfway down). This rod terminates in a bifurcation upon a small ladle-shaped organ at the extremity of the tongue (*l*, A and D, fig. 11). The outer wall of the tongue is attached to it directly only at the anterior end. In section it will be seen that the side of the rod turned towards the bee is channelled by a groove which runs through its entire length. The outer wall of the tongue is not tubular, but is open along the back; the edges of this slit are united to each side of the rod by means of very thin expansions of membrane (*m*, fig. 10), one side of which is covered by hairs; the hairs at the anterior end are very short and are seated on irregular papillæ (fig. 18), whilst those at the posterior end arise from regular pointed papillæ and are somewhat longer (fig. 16, from above, fig. 17, from the side). The existence of this membrane may be easily demonstrated if the entire head of a recently killed bee with the tongue extended be placed in an ordinary live-box and be subjected to pressure. The rod, which is naturally curved, being pressed in the middle and being supported at both ends, is forced out of its place, and brings with it the membrane in question. Professor A. J. Cook, of Michigan, appears to think that the bee when feeding brings the rod to the outside and so increases the internal dimensions of the tongue by adding that of the second chamber formed by the membrane; and this opinion is shared by Mr. J. Spalding (Amer. Nat. Feb. 1881, p. 113), both authors giving illustrations in explanation. After many observations of bees when feeding, some made with the microscope, I cannot agree with this view; certainly it is not their invariable way of feeding, and, in fact, I have never seen any bee feed in this way.

The hairs covering the surface of the tongue are long and finely pointed, with flattened bases, and are arranged in regular whorls (fig. 15). The hairs near the base of the tongue are much shorter and broader, and are sometimes split into two or three points. Interspersed among these hairs are a number of bristles which occur on every fifth whorl. These bristles are similar in character with those found on the edge of the maxillæ, on the end joints of the palpi, and on the extremity of the tubular portion of the tongue itself. They all follow one type, viz. that of a bristle arising from the summit of a papilla. I am inclined to consider that they are touch-organs, and nothing more. It must be borne in mind that, covered with a hard skin, as all insects are, their nerves can hardly be susceptible to external influences to any great extent. These soft parts in their harness supply this deficiency. Then, it may be urged, why not consider those on the tongue as organs of taste? The answer is, that on two occasions, when desirous of making bees feed on coloured honey (one bee being under chloroform, and the other torpid through cold), no motion was produced in the tongue when honey was brought in contact with it. I do not presume to say the bee did not taste it, but it made no outward and visible sign that it did. Immediately, however, I moved the honey and touched the antennæ of these same bees with the same honey, the usual movements of the tongue were produced, although there was then no honey touching the tongue. I cannot therefore suppose that these bristles in the region of and on the tongue are taste-organs.

On the outer surface of the base of the tongue is a smooth groove (*n*, figs. 8 & 21, base of tongue, from above); this is only found in the workers. When bees feed one another, the tongue of the bee that is taking the food is applied to this groove on the tongue of that which is supplying it. The importance of it being free from hair is clear when it is remembered that an extension and contraction of the tongue is, except in one condition, the invariable mode in which the bee obtains its food; it would obviously be impossible for the tongue, thickly covered with hairs as it is, to pass over another surface as thickly covered, more especially when the hairs are in each case directly opposed to one another.

The posterior end of this feeding-groove is hinged to a lever (*o*, figs. 0, 8, & 9), the shape and position of which can best be understood from a reference to the figure. From the centre of the lower part of this lever arise two chitinous processes—one dark, curving forward, and uniting with the paraglossæ (*p*, fig. 8); the other hyaline, which, passing upwards, forms one side of the lower part of the salivary valve (*g*, fig. 8). To the lower end of the lever is affixed the muscle T; the contraction of this muscle will act upon the lower chitinous process running to the salivary valve, and serve to close it. The salivary valve just referred to is semicircular in transverse section (*t*, fig. 23); and, when viewed from above, is irregularly oblong (*t*, fig. 22). A pair of muscles (*s*¹, figs. 8 & 9) act upon it from below, and two other pairs (*s*² and *s*³, figs. 6, 8, & 9). At the posterior end it receives the salivary duct (*r*, figs. 3, 6, 8, & 9). This duct arises in the thorax, and, after there collecting the saliva, receives the products of the glands, found on each side of the head, and then passes into the mentum.

The tongue and paraglossæ, but not the palpi, are partially withdrawn into the mentum, in the manner shown in fig. 9, by the action of a pair of muscles (*r.t.* figs. 2, 3, 4, 6, 7, 8, & 9); they arise from the upper and hinder part of the head, and are inserted at the upper part of the paraglossæ.

In that part of the mentum surrounding the salivary valve is the chamber in which the syrup or nectar comes in contact with the saliva, and from which it passes upwards to the pharynx. This chamber is almost obliterated when the tongue is retracted and drawn within the mentum; while, on the other hand, on the protrusion of the tongue its capacity is considerably increased. This can be more readily understood by reference to the diagrams figs. 25 and 26, the asterisk (*) being the chamber.

Before considering the action of the tongue, a reference must be made to the ladle-shaped organ found at the tip of the tongue (fig. 12, from above, fig. 13, end on, and fig. 14, side view). Mr. Hyatt describes and figures it as a hollow cone or funnel which serves as a sucking-disk (Amer. Q. Mic. Journal, 1879, vol. i. p. 287). Others have spoken of and regarded it as a button. Upon the concave surface of this ladle-shaped organ are a number of curious hairs, shown at fig. 15; they are branched and divided in the manner shown, with the hairs turned inwards.

The true nature and function of the tongue has been the subject of discussion from very early times. Mr. Chambers, in the 'Journal of the Cincinnati Society of Natural History' (April 1878), summarizes the various views entertained at different times. It will be necessary briefly to refer to some of these theories. Kirby and Spence (Introd. vol. ii. p. 177) say the tongue, "though so long and sometimes so inflated, is not a tube through which honey passes, nor a pump acting by suction, but a real tongue, which laps or licks the honey and passes it down on its upper surface, as we do, to the mouth." Huxley follows this, and says, "Functionally this organ is a tongue, and enables the bee to lap up the honey on which it feeds." Newport goes more into detail, and says:—"It is not tubular, but solid ... the manner in which the honey is obtained when the organ is plunged into it at the bottom of a flower is by lapping, or a constant succession of short and quick extensions and contractions of the organ, which occasions the fluid to be accumulated upon it and ascend along its upper surface until it reaches the orifice of the tube formed by the approximation of the maxillæ above and the labial palpi and this part of the ligula below... At each contraction a part of the extended ligula is drawn within the orifice of the tube, and the honey with which it is covered ascends into the cavity of the mouth, assisted in its removal from the surface of the ligula by the little bunch of hairs with which the elongated second joint of each labial palpus is furnished." I have quoted this at length, as it is substantially the same as that given by Hermann Müller in 'Nature,' vol. viii. p. 189.

If a bee be put to a large drop of honey, it will be found to open slightly the whole of the organs of the tongue, and with a scarcely perceptible motion suck in honey, no doubt by means of, or largely assisted by, the muscular pharynx (s, figs. 3 & 4). Flowers, however, do not ordinarily contain nectar in such abundance nor in such convenient positions. The nectaries are described as usually only a small spot, which, without becoming more prominent, produces the nectar; but frequently they are in the form of a glandular protuberance, or project in the form of cushions, or, again, as shallow excavations (Sachs' 'Text-book,' 2nd ed. 1882, pp. 494–500).

In order to obtain the conditions more nearly approaching those in nature therefore, the honey should be presented smeared thinly on a bit of glass. If this be done, the bees will clear off every trace of honey, and leave the glass as clean as it was before the honey was smeared on it. This is done by the bee applying the lower and outer portion of the tongue to the surface of the glass, in the manner shown in diagram, figs. 25 & 26. The long joints of the labial palpi just touch the glass, the shorter joints being bent outwards at right angles. The tongue is then extended and retracted with great regularity and some speed, and to me it appears that the extension is a somewhat slower movement than the retraction. When the tongue is in this position the "ladle" will be turned with its concave side downwards, and that surface of the tongue which is split will be upwards. The pressure on the surface of the glass will move the rod to the opposite side of the tubular portion of the tongue in that part of it which is being pressed against the glass. This will cause the two membranes (m) to form a trough, which will of course be opened on its upper surface; and, although I have not actually observed the fact, it seems impossible to suppose that the honey does not pass into this trough. As the tongue is being retracted, the rod which was pressed against the inner side of the tongue will pass over to the front side, and so considerably enlarge the trough made by the membranes in the upper portion of the tongue, and the edges of the slit in the outer wall being closely united by interlocking hairs, the result will be the creation of a vacuum which will draw up the honey from the lower portion of the tongue. The tongue is then again extended; but now the salivary chamber is enlarging as the tongue is protruded, and the honey is so carried up still higher and into the mouth, whence it is once more drawn up by the muscular pharynx.

This, however, will not account for the bee being able to remove such minute traces of honey as it undoubtedly can. The hairs of the tongue will sweep backward the honey, that is to say, will drive it away from the mouth, towards the end of the tongue itself, and the ladle-shaped organ will then serve, as the tongue is being withdrawn, to collect and drive into the tongue the honey thus collected. When within the tongue, the capillarity of the narrow groove, assisted by the action of the salivary chamber, will afford a means, which the larger opening would not afford, of the smallest particle of honey being sucked up.

Professor Cook, in a paper reported in the Amer. Bee Journal, Nov. 1870, gives the following account of some experiments which support this view. He says:—"I have placed honey in fine tubes and behind fine wire gauze, so that bees could just reach it with the funnel [the ladle-shaped organ] at the end of the rod. So long as they could reach it with the funnel, so long would it disappear. I have in such cases seen the red axis when the bee was sipping coloured syrup. Subsequent examination by dissection revealed the red liquid still in the tube of the rod."

Bees always apply the forward and lower side of the tongue to the honey, even when it is put into a position in which almost any other way would appear more convenient.

The statement which has found its way into so many books that bees obtain the honey by lapping*, appears to me to be without foundation. The length and direction of the hairs, i. e. all pointing away from the bee, is sufficient to condemn it.

The next theory,—that propounded by Hermann Müller,—is as follows:—"The terminal whorls of hairs are filled with honey by adhesion; this honey is withdrawn into the sheath of the tongue [formed by the meeting of the maxillæ and the palpi], and is driven towards the œsophagus by a double cause: first by the pressure of the erect whorls of hairs, and secondly by suction." He elsewhere says the whorls of hairs are erected rhythmically, and that the suction here referred to is due to the action of the stomach. I cannot, however, accept this explanation, for (1) there does not appear to me to be any reason for supposing the hairs of the tongue are capable of being voluntarily erected; (2) the tapering shape of the tongue and the direction and length

* " Functionally this organ is a tongue and enables the bee to lap up the honey on which it feeds" (Huxley's ' Manual of Invertebrata ' p. 428). See also John Hunter, in Enc. Brit. 1875, " Bees ; " Shuckard, ' British Bees,' 1866, p. 57 et seq.

of the hair seem opposed to the idea that its withdrawal in the tubular surroundings would drive the honey towards the head; (3) the dense covering of hair seems to make such a mode of action impossible; (4) it does not account for the organs inside the tongue nor for the ladle-shaped appendage before referred to.

Shuckard, in his ' British Bees ' (p. 37), although he holds to the lapping theory, says that if a bee be observed whilst sipping any sweet liquid, the anterior portion of the tongue will be sometimes seen more swollen than when [? not] in action, and alterations will be observed in it of varying expansions. At another place he says the bee is also seen to curve the tongue about, causing from time to time the superior surface to become concave, to give, as it were, to the liquid with which it is loaded a downward inclination towards the head. The extremity is frequently above the surface of the liquid, and again the tongue can swell and contract; " these swellings and constrictions are observed to succeed each other."

These observations seem to me to support the theory I have here ventured to propound, namely, that the honey is drawn into the mouth through the inside of the tongue by means of a complicated pumping action of the tongue itself and its closely contiguous parts, and not in any sense by lapping.

DESCRIPTION OF THE PLATES.

PLATE XVIII.

Fig. 1. Longitudinal section through head of Bee, without muscles. *a*, Chitinous pillar supporting the front of the head; *b*, second pillar, from the side of which arises the thin chitinous wall *c*; *d*, cardo; *f*, base of maxilla.

2. Transverse section through same. *a, b,* and *d* as before; $hx\,m$ and $hx\,m^2$, muscles inserted into the head of cardo; *rt*, retractor of tongue.

3. Longitudinal section through head, with muscles. *h*, Thin wall of the upper side of mouth-cavity; *r*, salivary duct; *rt* as in fig. 2; *s*, pharynx; *g*, mentum; *e*, lora.

4. Longitudinal section through anterior end of head, with muscles. *a*, Portion of chitinous pillar as in fig. 1; *h, s,* and *rt* as in fig. 3; *j*, chitinous strap divaricating the maxillæ; *f*, base of maxilla; mx^1, mx^2, and mx^3 respectively, muscles of the maxilla.

5. Enlarged figure of the base of maxilla and adjacent parts. *d*, Cardo; *e*, lora; *f*, basal joint; *g*, mentum; *h* as in fig. 3; *j* as in fig. 4; mx^1, mx^2, mx^3, ends of muscles mx^1, mx^2, and mx^3 of fig. 4; mx^4, muscle lying behind *j*, which draws the maxilla outwards; mx^5, extensor of blade of maxilla, mx^6; mx^7.

6. Tongue of Queen Bee and adjacent parts, from above. *d*, Section through cardo; *e, f, g, j,* as before; *h*, section through thin wall of mouth-cavity, as in figs. 3 and 4; *o*, lever at root of tongue from above; *r*, salivary gland; *rt*, retractor of tongue; s^2, muscles inserted into sides of the outer wall of salivary valve; s^3, muscles inserted into the centre of same.

ANATOMY OF TONGUE OF HONEY BEE

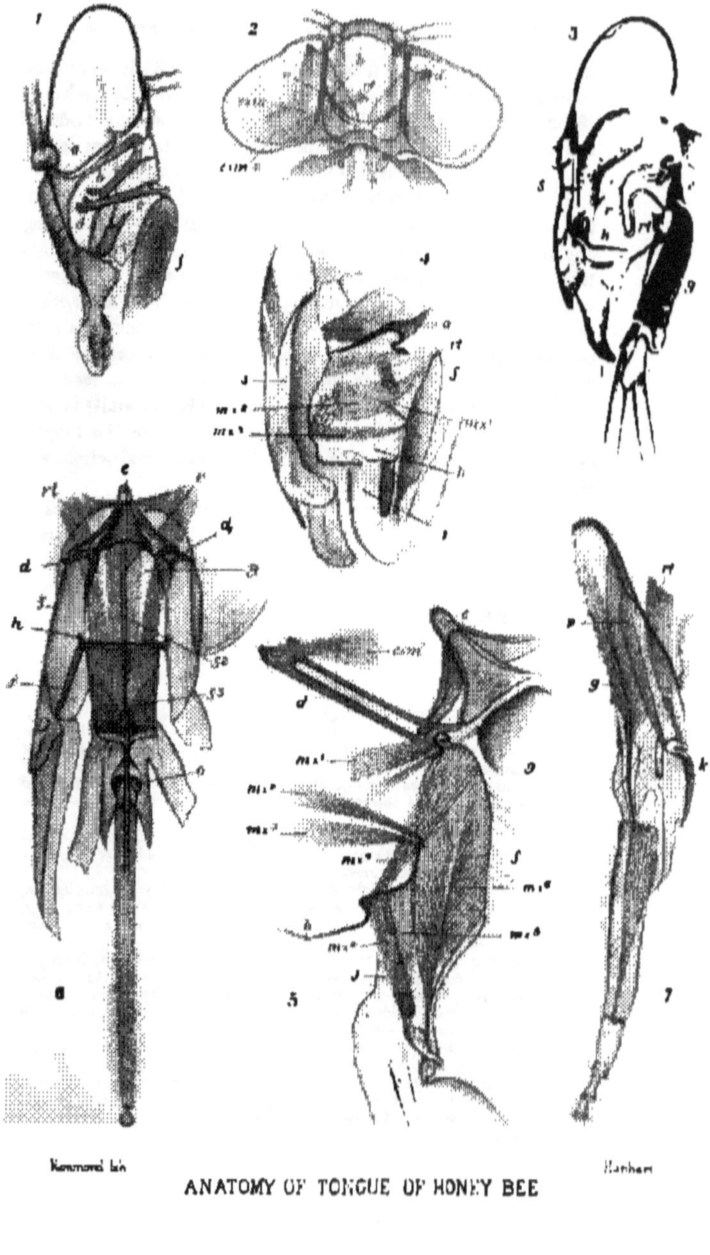

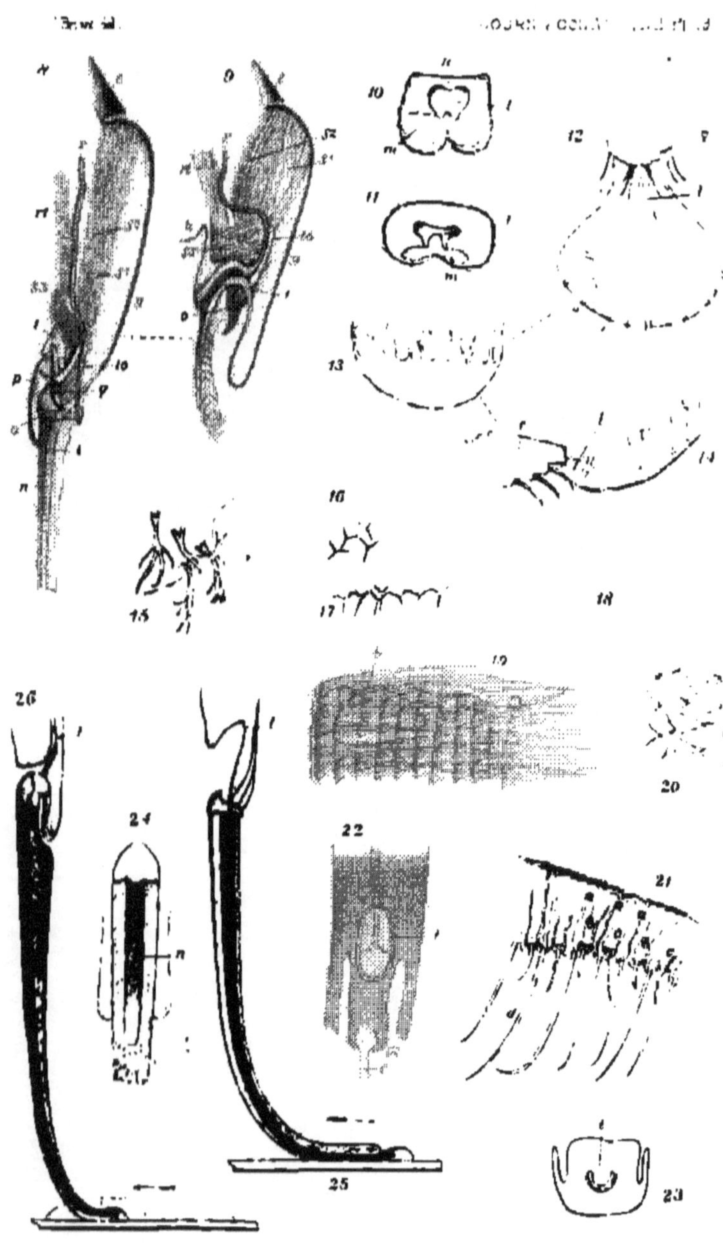

Fig. 7. Palpus, with portion of mentum, *g*, attached. *h*, Wall of mouth-cavity, as before; *k*, forward side of paraglossum; *p*, muscle inserted into paraglossum, and withdrawing same; *rt.* as before.

PLATE XIX.

8. Section through base of tongue and mentum, extended. *g*, Mentum; *e*, lora; *l*, hyaline rod of tongue; *n*, feeding groove; *t*, salivary valve; *o*, lever of tongue, as in fig. 6, side view; *p*, paraglossum; *g*, ridge from posterior side of salivary valve, united with lever *o*; *s'*, muscle acting on posterior side of valve; *s²* and *s³* as before; *to.* muscle inserted into foot of lever *o*, and throwing same forward.
9. The same, retracted.
Fig. 10. Transverse section through tongue near base. *l*, Hyaline rod; *m*, membranous bag; *n*, feeding groove.
11. The same, towards the end.
12. Ladle-like organ at end of tongue, sometimes called the "button." *l*, Hyaline rod of tongue, showing bifurcation.
13. The same, end view.
14. The same, side view.
15. Branched hairs on same.
16. Hairs on the inside of membranous bag, *m*, of figs. 10 and 11, from above, showing ridges of papillæ upon which they stand.
17. Side view of same.
18. Side view of same near the anterior end, showing irregularly shaped papillæ.
19. Hairs on surface of tongue with expanded bases. *b*, Sensory bristles scattered through same.
20. The same, from base of tongue.
21. Portion of blade of maxillæ. *aa*, Plications; *bb*, sensory bristles, the longer ones on shorter pillars; *cc*, the same, the shorter ones on longer pillars; *d*, longer hairs of same.
22. Anterior end of mentum (without muscles), showing salivary valve; *l*, Base of hyaline rod springing from chitinous tongue.
23. Transverse section of same.
24. Posterior end of tongue, showing feeding groove, *n*.
25 & 26. Diagrammatic view of tongue when feeding. *t*, valve. Fig. 25 is the position of tongue and internal parts as it arrives at the termination of the extension motion. Fig. 26, The same, at the termination of the retraction motion.

On a new Genus of Recent Fungida, Family Funginæ, Ed. & H., allied to the genus *Micrabacia*, Ed. & H. By Prof. P. MARTIN DUNCAN, F.R.S., Vice-Pres. Linnean Society.

[Read 5th June, 1884.]

(PLATE XX.)

Genus DIAFUNGIA, genus nov.

Corallum discoid, free, without trace of adhesion, not quite circular in outline, much broader than high. Base with a primary triangular piece extending beyond the centre, slightly projecting downwards, the rest of the coral grouping from its sides and apex, so that there is an appearance of former fracture and subsequent mending. Calice unsymmetrical from the prolongation of the larger septa of the primary piece beyond the

LINCOLNSHIRE PSEUDOSCORPIONS:
WITH AN ACCOUNT OF THE ASSOCIATION OF SUCH ANIMALS WITH OTHER ARTHROPODS.

H. WALLIS KEW, F.Z.S.,
London: formerly of Louth, Lincolnshire.

AT the time of the publication of the Rev. O. Pickard-Cambridge's memoir 'On the British Species of False-Scorpions,' in 1892, about 46 kinds were known in Europe, of which 20 had occurred in Britain, and no less than 14 in the single county of Dorset.[*] Several species are stated to be common and widely distributed, but they are seldom seen unless specially looked for, and thus it happens that for Lincolnshire, where no one has particularly attended to these creatures, we are as yet able to record four species only. Personally, while collecting in the county for several years, I found but one species, the *Chelifer latreillii* Leach; and during these later years, in what Londoners are pleased to call the home-counties, I have encountered but one other, the *Obisium muscorum* Leach, which occurred among dead leaves in Epping Forest.

The Lincolnshire species, though as yet only four, represent as many genera: *Chthonius, Chelifer, Chernes,* and *Chiridium*; and they leave unrepresented, of British genera, two only, *Roncus* and *Obisium.* They have been very obligingly identified, from *all* the Lincolnshire localities under-noted, by Mr. Cambridge, whose kindness I desire to acknowledge with much gratitude. In preparing the second part of the paper, I have had the good fortune to enjoy the co-operation of Mr. G. K. Gude, who in this as in other tasks has helped me with the literature. My thanks are due, moreover, to Mr. Beaulah, of Raventhorpe; Dr. George, of Kirton-in-Lindsey; Mr. J. E. Mason, of Lincoln; Mr. Carter, Mr. Goulding, and Mr. Larder, of Louth, who have contributed local notes and specimens; and also to Mr. F. M. Campbell, of Machynlleth; Dr. W. Hess, of Mulhouse (Alsace); Dr. F. v. Wagner, of Giessen; the Rev. A. Thornley, of South Leverton; and Lt.-Col. H. J. O. Walker, of Budleigh Salterton, who have favoured me with replies to inquiries and with references.

---

[*] O. P.-Cambridge, 'On the British Species of False-Scorpions,' Proceedings of the Dorset Natural History and Antiquarian Field Club, XIII. (1892), pp. 199-231.

I.

The four species identified from Lincolnshire are :—

Chthonius rayi L. Koch.   Sent to Mr. Cambridge several years ago by Mr. Beaulah from Broughton, near Brigg.   It occurs somewhat frequently under stones in Dr. George's garden at Kirton-in-Lindsey; and has recently been found by Mr. Carter under wood on the coast sand-hills at Trusthorpe, and under flints in a chalk-pit at North Ormsby.   Mr. Carter remarks on the creature's activity, and on its habit, when disturbed, of running quickly backwards.

Chelifer latreillii Leach.   Found by the writer, in 1886, under bark of dead-wood in a fence, near the sea, at Mablethorpe; and reported—as *Chelifer degeerii* C. Koch, a synonym by which the species was then known—in 'The Naturalist,' 1886, p. 339.   One had eggs attached to the under-side of the abdomen.   Subsequently others were found by me in the same spot; and some were brought thence to London by Mr. Gude. One or two of these were carrying eggs, which soon hatched, the parents becoming surrounded by numerous young.   The animal was again observed during the meeting of Lincolnshire Naturalists at Mablethorpe in 1893.[*]   Mr. Goulding found a specimen last year under an old boot on the Mablethorpe sand-hills; and Mr. Carter has sent me it from Trusthorpe, where he found it in some plenty under wood on the sand-hills. Mr. Cambridge mentions having received it from Mr. J. E. Mason, then of Alford,[†] by whom I am told that the specimens came from the coast sand-hills at Chapel St. Leonards, where the creature is not uncommon.

Chernes nodosus Schrank.   Among slides of Pseudo-scorpions mounted in Canada-balsam, which Dr. George has permitted me to submit to Mr. Cambridge, is one containing four individuals of this species from the neighbourhood of Kirton-in-Lindsey.   Mr. Larder has recently obtained a speci-men from the leg of a fly caught on the wing at Louth.

Chiridium museorum Leach.   Mr. Cambridge mentions having received this very little species—the Book-scorpion— from Mr. Beaulah, near Brigg, and from Dr. George, of Kirton-in-Lindsey.[‡]   I understand that Mr. Beaulah's specimens were. from Raventhorpe.   Dr. George found it, in July 1877, in great

----

[*] W. F. Baker, Naturalist, 1893. p. 261.
[†] O. P.-Cambridge, l.c.
[‡] O. P.-Cambridge, l.c.

numbers in a deserted sparrow's nest in ivy on the groom's cottage adjoining his garden at Kirton-in-Lindsey.

II.

It was in September last that I received from Louth, through the kindness of Mr. Larder, the above noted specimen of *Chernes nodosus*, together with the fly to which it was attached. His brother saw the fly on the wing in a warehouse in Mercer Row, observed that it was carrying an unusual object through the air, caught it, and found the object to be a Pseudoscorpion, clinging by closure of the pincers of one of the great pedipalps to one of the legs of the fly. On the following day another fly similarly encumbered was observed on the wing in the same warehouse. The questions involved in these observations are of considerable interest; but the subject is by no means new, and it has already been referred to in 'The Naturalist' itself, Mr. Cambridge having noted, in the volume for 1884-5, two cases of the attachment to flies of this same *Chernes nodosus*. One specimen was received from Mr. Meade, of Bradford; and the other from Mr. Roebuck with a note that it had been taken at Bradford by Mr. W. West attached to the leg of a house-fly.[*]

Poda, one hundred and forty years ago, made a reference to the subject, noting of a Pseudoscorpion supposed by him to be the Linnean *Acarus cancroides*: Repertus in pedibus *muscæ*, quos chelis suis firmissime apprehendit;[†] and in 1787 George Adams recorded the finding by Mr. Marsham of one of these 'lobster insects' 'firmly fixed by its claws to the thighs of a large fly, which he caught on a flower in Essex the first week in August, and from which he could not disengage it without great difficulty, and tearing off the fly's leg.'[‡] Hermann, in 1804, figured his *Chelifer parasita*, noting that it was found adhering to a fly.[||] The next available item appeared in 1831 in Loudon's 'Magazine of Natural History':

A LOBSTER-LIKE INSECT ATTACKING THE LEG OF A HOUSE-FLY. -As I was yesterday reading in the parlour, my attention was accidentally attracted to a common house-fly, which was chafing its fore-legs in a very unusual way. On closer examination, I found, to my surprise, that a small insect was firmly attached to one of its legs, which the fly was ineffectually endeavouring to dislodge. On applying a magnifying glass, my surprise was greatly increased by finding that the insect which had seized the fly's

---

[*] O. P.-Cambridge, Naturalist, 1884-5, p. 103.

[†] N. Poda, 'Insecta Musei Græcensis,' 1761, p. 122.

[‡] G. Adams, 'Essays on the Microscope,' 1787, p. 386.

[||] J. F. Hermann, 'Mémoire aptérologique,' 1804, p. 117.

leg had claws precisely resembling those of a lobster, with one of which it had grasped the unfortunate fly ; its body was flat, like a bug (Cimex), and resembled that insect in colour but was smaller. I unfortunately lost sight of the fly in an unsuccessful attempt to capture it. . . . O., London, July 19. 1830.*

The animal, as Professor Henslow suggested at the time, was certainly a Pseudoscorpion.† Subsequently the same correspondent recorded two other similar observations ;‡ and W. B. B. W. in the same magazine stated that he had often taken ' *Chelifer cancroides* ' and other Chelifers attached to the legs of the house-fly (*Musca domestica*) and two other Diptera.‖ A further observation was communicated, in 1835, by Mr. G. Moore to ' The Entomological Magazine ' :

Last summer I watched the manœuvres of a *Musca Domestica* that had one of these crab-like dependents [*Chelifer cancroides*] attached to its *femur*. It was in the window of a cold and damp out-office. The fly appeared but little annoyed, and continued to travel tardily about the glass, while its hanger-on busily occupied its free claw in seizing such minute objects as came in its way,—at least such appeared to be its business. On attempting to catch the fly, off it' flew to another window with its wingless passenger. I followed closely and quickly, when lo! the little appendix relaxed its grasp, and dropped itself into a crevice in the frame, where I secured it.§

An anonymous editorial note adds that the ' *Chelifer cancroides* ' is abundant on planks and bricks placed on decayed vegetable matter, and that *Lonchæa vaginalis*, a little fly commbn in the same situations during June, is particularly infested by it, and also by *Acari*. The fly, apparently uninjured, is seen on windows, the note says, with the Chelifers attached to its trochanters.** Dr. H. Loew mentions having found, in August 1841, another little fly, *Ulidia demandata,* running about in numbers on dry stems on a waste place on the parade-ground at Ofen, and so pursued by ' *Chelifer corallinus* ' that it was difficult to find specimens free from the attachment of this Arachnid.†† Dr. Gerstaecker, of Berlin, in 1862, reported the

---

* O., Loudon's Magazine of Natural History, IV. (1831), p. 94.

† J. S. Henslow, ibid., p. 284.

‡ O., ibid., V. (1832), p. 754.

‖ W. B. B. W., ibid., VII. (1834), p. 162 ; and see also ' Beobachtungen englischer Naturforscher über die Afterskorpione,' Archiv für Naturgeschichte, Jahrg. I. (1835), Bd. 2, p. 186.

§ G. Moore, Entomological Magazine, II. (1835). p. 321.

** Ed., Entomological Magazine, II. (1835), p. 322. Edward Doubleday is understood to have edited this volume in place of Edward Newman, who was responsible for the others ; but the note may be by Francis Walker, or some other member of the old Entomological Club.

†† H. Loew, ' Dipterologische Beiträge,' 1845, p. 29.

finding on an old oak of a Hover-fly (*Brachypalpus laphriformis*)
and a species of *Anthomyia*, each with an unidentified Pseudoscorpion clinging to one of the hind-legs.* Mrs. Lane Clarke
wrote of '*Chelifer*' in 1858:

This parasite attacks flies. I have seen a common fly run wildly about
upon the window-pane, shaking itself violently, and apparently in great
distress. Upon catching it, I found a small scorpion-like creature fixed
upon one of its thighs, by a pair of tremendous claws,—hardly could it be
detached for examination, and then it ran quickly, like a crab, sideways.†

Mr. Stainton told the Entomological Society of London, in
September 1865, that he had that autumn noticed an unusual
number of Chelifers on the legs of house-flies;‡ and other cases
have been reported by Mr. Bailey,‖ Professor Leydig,§ Mr.
M'Intire,** Mr. Bisshopp,†† and by J. S.‡‡ The last observer
compares the Pseudoscorpion hanging to the leg of the fly to
a parachute attached to a balloon. He sent the creature to 'The
Entomologist,' and according to Mr. Newman's identification it
was '*Chelifer cancroides.*'‖‖ In a case recorded by Mr. Macrae,
in 1869, the fly was small and weakly and the Chelifer strong
and active:

I saw the fly on the window at lunch, and noticed something attached
to it, but missed taking it. Strange to tell, it dropped in my wine-glass
at dinner, so that I secured both.§§

Mr. Preudhomme de Borre has reported an observation made in
July 1872, in a house in Liége, in which a Pseudoscorpion
attached to the leg of *Musca domestica* is said to pertain to
Chelifer panzeri C. Koch = *Chernes cimicoides* Fabr. A second
observation was made a few days afterwards.¶ Mr. C. W.
Dale, in enumerating the Pseudoscorpions of Glanville's

* A. Gerstaecker, 'Bericht über die wissenschaftlichen Leistungen im
Gebiete der Entomologie,' 1859-1860, p. 347.

† L. L. Clarke, 'The Microscope,' 1858, p. 146.

‡ H. T. Stainton, Transactions of the Entomological Society of London
(3), II. (1864-6), p. cxii. ; and Entomologist's Monthly Magazine, II. (1865-6),
p. 120.

 G. Bailey, Hardwicke's Science-Gossip, 1865, p. 227.

§ F. Leydig, 'Skizze zu einer Fauna Tubingensis,' 1867, pp. 16-7.

** S. J. M'Intire, Hardwicke's Science-Gossip, 1869, p. 246.

†† E. F. Bisshopp, Entomologist, V. (1871), p. 428.

‡‡ J. S., ibid., VIII. (1875), p. 185.

 E. Newman, ibid., p. 186.

§§ G. Macrae, Hardwicke's Science-Gossip, 1869, p. 283.

¶ A. Preudhomme de Borre, Verhandlungen der k.-k. zoologisch-botanischen Gesellschaft in Wien, XXIII. (1873), p. 36.

Wootton, in 1878, has noted of *Obisium muscorum* that it is
'fond of catching hold of the legs of flies';* but this, I understand, is a mistake, the Chelifer referred to being *Chernes
nodosus.* Mr. de Courtois' de Langlade, who writes from Arles-
sur-Rhône, states that one of his sons who had been examining
a heap of flies caught in a trap had found very small Scorpions
on the legs of a number of them;† and Dr. Hess, more recently,
has reported the occurrence of a Pseudoscorpion referred to
Chelifer cancroides on one of the front legs of a house-fly at
Mulhouse (Alsace); he records in this connection an interesting
experiment to which we shall recur.‡ A number of cases
observed in England from time to time were reported by Mr.
Cambridge in 1892. The Pseudoscorpion in every case proved
to be *Chernes nodosus,* specimens of which, found attached to
legs of flies, were received by Mr. Cambridge from Mr. Dale,
Granville's Wootton; Mr. Campbell, Hoddesdon, Hertfordshire;
Mr. F. O. P.-Cambridge, Carlisle; Mr. Stoddart, Bristol; Mr.
Bignell, Stonehouse, Devon; and twice, as above noted, from
Bradford.‖ Mr. Campbell informs me that his specimen was caught
on the leg of a blow-fly, on a window, in October 1887. The distinguished arachnologist, Simon, states that observations of the
present kind have been made not only in Germany, Switzerland,
France [and other European countries], but also in Algeria, and
in America.§ Of the American observations, Professor Leidy
mentions having occasionally met with *Chelifer cancroides?*
attached to the house-fly;** and Mr. Banks has reported the
attachment of his *Chernes pallipes,* in Colorado, to a fly of the
family Dexiidae.†† According to Dr. Hagen, *Chernes sanborni*
attaches itself to the legs of flies in Massachusetts, and *Ch.
loewii* in Panama. Hagen mentions also that a single *Obisium*
had occurred to him in America on a daddy-long-legs (*Tipula*).‡‡
Professor Berg has reported a case observed in a house by

---

*C. W. Dale, History of Glanville's Wootton, 1878, p. 325.

† F. de Courtois de Langlade, La Nature, XI. (1883), 1ᵉʳ semestre p. 71;
and see also P. Mégnin, ibid., XIV. (1886), 2ᵉ semestre pp. 241-3.

‡ W. Hess, 'Über die Pseudoscorpioniden als Räuber,' Zoologischer
Anzeiger, XVII. (1894), pp. 119-21.

† O. P.-Cambridge, 1892, l.c.

§ E. Simon, 'Les Arachnidés de France,' VII. (1879), pp. 11-12, 33-34.

** J. Leidy, Proceedings of the Academy of Natural Sciences of Philadelphia, 1877, pp. 760-1.

†† N. Banks, Entomological News, VI. (1895), p. 115.

‡‡ H. Hagen, Zoologischer Anzeiger, II. (1879), pp. 399-400.

Mr. Backhausen while engaged on the Argentine-Chilian Boundary Commission ;* and we have, moreover, the following interesting note from Mr. F. Knab, of Chicopee, Massachusetts :

A few days ago my father captured a troublesome fly, and, as he held it, found to his surprise that three Pseudoscorpions had left it and were crawling rapidly over his hand. Upon this more flies were captured and three found infested with Pseudoscorpions. Of fifty flies captured the following day two carried Pseudoscorpions ; one had two attached to a single leg. In each case the Pseudoscorpion hung on by a single pincer.†

More than one Pseudoscorpion, as we see from the just-quoted note, may be carried by a single fly. This fact, though concealed by me until now, has long been known. Dr. F. Löw has reported the occurrence, on a window in September 1861, of the little *Clidia erythrophthalma,* to the hind legs of which, clinging symmetrically, were two specimens of *Chernes wideri* C. Koch.‡ Another fly, to one of the legs of which two Pseudoscorpions were attached, was exhibited by Hagen in 1867 to the Boston Society of Natural History ;‖ the Pseudoscorpions in this case pertained, I believe, to the *Chernes sanborni* already mentioned. One gathers, moreover, that some of the flies referred to by Mr. de Courtois de Langlade had two or three Pseudoscorpions upon them ; and Mr. Stainton in the communication to the Entomological Society of London already quoted mentioned having seen a fly with three of these Arachnids on the same leg. Dr. Loew states that some of the *Clidia demandata* observed by him were beset with three or more Pseudoscorpions ; and the writer of the editorial note in 'The Entomological Magazine' refers to the attachment of from one to four to the legs of *Lonchaea vaginalis.* The Rev. L. Jenyns (afterwards Blomefield) mentions having taken, from one small fly, four specimens of ' *Chelifer geoffroyi* ';§ a *Musca uomestica* produced to Dr. Lukis, of Guernsey, in August 1832, had four specimens of ' *Chelifer cancroides* ' affixed to one leg;*

---

* C. Berg, 'Pseudoscorpionidenkniffe,' ibid., XVI. (1893), pp. 446-8.

† F. Knab, Entomological News, VIII. (1897), p. 13.

‡ F. Löw, Verhandlungen der k.-k. zoologisch-botanischen Gesellschaft in Wien, XVI. (1866), p. 944. Another example of the clinging of a Pseudoscorpion to a small fly is mentioned by Löw, ibid., XVII. (1867), p. 746.

‖ Hagen, Proceedings of the Boston Society of Natural History, XI. (1867), pp. 323-4 : Record of American Entomology, 1868, pp. 48-52.

§ L. Jenyns, 'Observations in Natural History,' 1846, p. 295 : the *Chelifer geoffroyi* Leach is a *Chernes.* The author adds—I do not know on what authority—that these animals 'are often found on *Tipula.*'

* F. C. Lukis, Loudon's Magazine of Natural History, VII. (1834), p. 163.

and Dr. v. Wagner (1892) has published an interesting account of a Tipulid fly (*Ctenophora pectinicornis*)—one of the larger daddy-long-legs—whose extremities carried the same number of individuals of a *Chernes*, not identified specifically, but thought to be *Chernes hahnii* C. Koch = *Chernes cimicoides*.[*] The fly, which was caught in Mecklenburg, is represented, with two of the Pseudoscorpions, in the accompanying figure. Dr. Schiner, further, has reported the capture, in August 1870, of the little *Clidia demandata* with no less than five Pseudoscorpions hanging to its hind-legs. The fly was on a window, and it is noted that it walked and flew in a lively manner, and did not seem inconvenienced by its numerous guests. These, as in the last case, were thought to be *Chernes hahnii* = *Chernes cimicoides*.[†]

A **Daddy-long-legs** (*Ctenophora pectinicornis*) with **Pseudoscorpions** (*Chernes* sp.) on its legs: slightly enlarged. The supplementary figure shows one of the Pseudoscorpions more enlarged. Both after F. v. Wagner, Zoologischer Anzeiger, XV. (1892), p. 435. The manner of attachment here shown, namely, by both pincers, is unusual. The animals generally hang by one pincer only.

But our limit is not yet reached, for at the Entomological Society of London, in September 1866, Mr. Stevens exhibited a house-fly to which six Chelifers were attached, and he stated that he had observed another on which were no less than eight.[‡] Finally, if Hagen was not mistaken, even ten have been seen on a single insect.[‖]

---

[*] F. v. Wagner, Zoologischer Anzeiger, XV. (1892), pp. 434-6.

[†] J. R. Schiner, Verhandlungen der k.-k. zoologisch-botanischen Gesell-schaft in Wien, XXII. (1872), pp. 75-6.

[‡] S. Stevens, Transactions of the Entomological Society of London (3), V. (1865-7), p. xxvii.

[‖] H. Hagen, 1868, l.c. : ' Many cases are quoted by naturalists who have observed one or more. Chelifers, even ten, strongly attached with their hands to the legs of insects.'

The animals do not confine their attentions to Diptera. Certain kinds are found in widely-separated parts of the world in hives and nests of bees; and Mr. E. T. Wells, writing from Cape Colony, has informed us that the creatures, at one time numerous in his hives, were sometimes seen hanging to the legs of the bees.[*] Another case concerning Hymenoptera is that of Menge, who reports the finding of a fossil Pseudoscorpion in amber attached to the leg of a fossil ichneumon.[†] We have one note concerning Orthoptera, Dr. Joseph having more than once taken his *Chernes cavicola* in the Grotto of Corgnale, Austria, hanging to the long-legged cave Locustid *Rhaphidophora cavicola*.[‡] The creatures are found also on Coleoptera, but as the association is here of different character we may first mention that they cling also to certain Arachnida, namely, to Phalangiids — the long-legged false-spiders or harvest-men. A note to this effect, by the Rev. W. W. Spicer, is found in one of the early volumes of 'Hardwicke's Science-Gossip':

In the course of a walk lately through a shady lane near Bath, I came suddenly upon three or four harvest spiders (*Phalangium opilio*). As they scampered away I observed that one of them had a dark object on its right fore leg, which evidently formed no part of its normal structure. On securing my long-legged friend, and examining the object with a lens, I found, to my great surprise, that it was a specimen of *Chelifer cancroides*, which had fixed itself to the leg, and was holding on 'like grim death.' Indeed, so tightly was the little creature attached, that I had some difficulty in making it let go, in order to transfer it to a bottle.

[*] E. T. Wells, British Bee Journal, XXVII. (1899). p. 126. The occurrence of Pseudoscorpions in bee-hives in Europe has been reported in the same journal by Mr. Hamlyn-Harris. In Pará, one has been found in numbers in nests of a social bee, *Melipona mutata* (Dr. Göldi); and it appears that there are Myrmecophilous and Termitophilous kinds. The finding of Chelifers in ants' nests was long ago noted by Professor Haldeman; and one has been reported, also from North America, from the nest of *Aphænogaster fulva* (Theo. Pergande). A small kind has been found living with *Camponotus cognatus* (Cape Colony, Dr. Brauns), and another with *Atta discigera* (Joinville, J. P. Schmalz). As regards Termites, the creatures have been found with *Termes tubicola* in Orange River Colony (Dr. Brauns), and with *Termes natalensis* in Natal (Dr. Haviland). These facts are from Wasmann, 'Kritisches Verzeichniss der myrmekophilen und termitophilen Arthropoden,' 1894, p. 193, and Deutsche entomologische Zeitschrift, 1899, p. 411. I have learned nothing of the behaviour of the Chelifers towards the *Melipona*, the ants, and the Termites. It appears from the remarks of Mr. Hamlyn-Harris that hive-bees avoid the creatures, apparently on account of their singular deportment and the threatening movements of the pedipalps.

[†] A. Menge, 1855, quoted by Hagen, 1868, l.c.

[‡] G. Joseph, Berliner entomologische Zeitschrift, XXVI. (1882), p. 22.

The Chelifer was attached to the hard tibia.[*] Professor Leydig, in his Sketch-fauna of Tübingen, has recorded observations of the same kind: he states that he has more than once seen Pseudoscorpions on the *Phalangium opilio*.[†] In the case of Coleoptera, Pseudoscorpions do not, as far as is known at present, attach themselves to the legs. They occur on the dorsal surface of the hind-body, hidden away under the wings and elytra; and according to Hagen the species thus found pertain mainly to *Chernes*.[‡] Several observations made in North America relate to the large and common elater *Alaus oculatus*. Professor Leidy, in 1877, recorded the finding of six individuals of his *Chernes alius* beneath the elytra of this beetle at Easton.[||] A similar observation — *Alaus oculatus* with one Chelifer — had previously been reported from Ohio;[§] and Professor Haldeman, in 1848, had recorded the finding of nine near the extremity of the hind-body, under the wings and elytra, of this same beetle.[**] Numerous cases have been reported from South America. Dr. v. Jhering, writing from Rio Grande do Sul, says that he has often found Pseudoscorpions under the elytra of two species of the brilliantly-luminous Elaterids of the genus *Pyrophorus*; and he once found one, similarly situated, on the great palm-weevil (*Rhynchophorus palmarum*).[††] Professor Leydig, in dissecting a spirit specimen of the harlequin-beetle (*Acrocinus longimanus*) — a great South American Longicorn — found a solitary Chelifer in the usual position;[‡‡] and Hagen once received three specimens from Surinam with a note that they were found under the elytra of

---

[*] W. W. Spicer, 'Helps to Distribution,' Hardwicke's Science-Gossip, 1867, pp. 244-5.

[†] F. Leydig, op. cit.

[‡] H. Hagen, 1879, l.c.

J. Leidy, l.c.

[§] B. P. Mann, Proceedings of the Boston Society of Natural History, XI. (1868), pp. 325.

[**] S. S. Haldemann, Silliman's American Journal of Science and Arts (2), VI. (1848), p. 148.

[††] H. v. Jhering, 'Zum Commensalismus der Pseudoscorpione,' Zoologischer Anzeiger, XVI. (1893), pp. 346-7.

[‡‡] F. Leydig, op. cit.; Verhandlungen des naturhistorischen Vereines der preussischen Rheinlande u. Westfalens, XXXVIII. (1881), p. 180; and 'Zum Parasitismus der Pseudoscorpioniden,' Zoologischer Anzeiger, XVI. (1893), pp. 36-7.

the same species of beetle.* Dr. Balzan mentions the occurrence of *Chernes argentinus* Thorell on a night-flying Longicorn of the genus *Achryson.*† Other observations relate to Lamellicorns of the genus *Passalus.* Mr. C. O. Waterhouse records the discovery of two specimens of a '*Chelanops*' under the elytra of *Passalus punctiger* from Rio Janeiro ;‡ and in Australia, according to Hagen, an undescribed Pseudoscorpion has been found on *Passalus politus.*|| Finally, we have a note from North Celebes by Professor Hickson. In pulling off the elytra of a Longicorn, *Batocera celebiana*, he found fixed to the wings, a large number of little creatures, which turned out to be Chelifers or tailless Scorpions.§

As regards the kinds of Pseudoscorpions in which the habits above noted obtain, it must be remembered that with animals of the present kind names, in the hands of writers other than specialists, have not the value they usually possess in more familiar departments of zoology. *Chelifer cancroides*, for instance, derived from the Linnean *Acarus* or *Phalangium cancroides*, was long a stock name for Pseudoscorpions of almost any kind ;** and its use, more especially by earlier writers, rarely implies any attempt at specific discrimination. Next to the Linnean species, in point of date of bestowal, comes *Scorpio cimicoides* Fabr.—afterwards *Chelifer* or *Chernes cimicoides*--and this title also, it can hardly be doubted, has often been applied to species other than the one to which it is now attached. The German arachnologist L. Koch states his experience that the species found attached to flies is always *Chernes reussii* C. Koch = *Chernes nodosus.*†† Stecker, referring to this remark, states that *Chernes cimicoides*, not *Chernes*

---

* H. Hagen, 'Chelifer als Schmarotzer auf Insekten,' Stettiner entomologische Zeitung, XX. (1859), p. 202 ; 1867, l.c. ; 1868, l.c. ; 1879, l.c.

† L. Balzan, Annali del Museo Civico di Storia Naturale di Genova (2), IX. (1890), p. 416 ; and Annales de la Société entomologique de France, LX. (1891), p. 498.

‡ C. O. Waterhouse, Transactions of the Entomological Society of London, 1875, p. xii. ; and Entomologist's Monthly Magazine, XII. (1875-6), p. 20.

H. Hagen, 1879, l.c.

§ S. J. Hickson, 'Naturalist in North Celebes,' 1889, p. 101.

** M. C. Cooke, Journal of the Quekett Microscopical Club, I. (1868), p. 15.

|| L. Koch, 'Uebersichtliche Darstellung der europäischen Chernetiden (Pseudoscorpione),' 1873, p. 6.

1891 July 2.

nodosus, occurred to him under these conditions.[*]　But the experience of Simon in France is in agreement with that of Koch.　All the European Pseudoscorpions found on flies' legs by Simon and by his correspondent Mr. Ray, of Troyes, proved to be *Chernes nodosus*;[†] and Mr. Cambridge, in England, who does not mention the finding of any other species thus situated, states that all, or nearly all, of the individuals of *Chernes nodosus* communicated to him from different parts of the country were obtained from the legs of flies.[‡]　To this species, moreover, Simon is inclined to refer the *Acarus cancroides* L. of Poda, and the *Chelifer parasita* Hermann.　In America, also, the fly-infesting species appear to be chiefly *Chernes*, and we have noted in this connection *Chernes sanborni* Hagen, *Chernes pallipes* Banks, etc. 'Those found on legs of harvest-men have not been critically examined; but that discovered on an Orthopteron was, as we have seen, *Chernes cavicola* Joseph. . We have already quoted the opinion of Hagen that the Pseudoscorpions associating with beetles are mainly *Chernes*, and of those which have been named we have *Chernes alius* Leidy and *Chernes argentinus* Thorell.

The meaning of the phenomena now detailed has been much discussed; but it was admitted by Simon in 1879 that no satisfactory explanation had been given.　J. S., who sent a Pseudoscorpion and fly to 'The Entomologist' in 1875, asking the name of the animal, and the object of its aerial journey, would hardly be satisfied with Mr. Newman's reply:

The first question is easily answered; the second is a problem more difficult of solution.　The insect is Chelifer cancroides.　I once found it in vast numbers under the bark of a willow tree on the banks of the New River. . . . Still we have to deal with its strange propensity to settle itself on the legs of flies.　It is, of course, very natural to suppose that these flies, having a decided weakness for settling on the trunks of willows, and that these scorpion-like creatures, having a similar weakness for the toes of a fly, should fix themselves thereupon; still there is something that requires explanation.[‖]

According to one view the Pseudoscorpion is parasitic, and according to another it is predaceous.　But the creature, compared with the insects to which it is found attached, seems too large to be a parasite and too small to be an animal of prey— *Chernes nodosus* is 2·5 mm. or slightly over one line in length—

---

[*] A. Stecker, Deutsche entomologische Zeitschrift, XIX. (1875), p. 314.
[†] Simon, l.c.
[‡] Cambridge, 1885, l.c., 1892, l.c.
[‖] Newman, l.c.

and thus a third view has sprung up, namely, that the animal is
a passenger, using the insect as a means of conveyance from
place to place, from one feeding ground to another.   There is
still a further theory, that the Arachnid resorts to the insect to
seize parasitic *Acari.*   This idea possesses a certain fascination;
but it is not supported by evidence; and Mr. Dale has dismissed
it (in a letter with which he has favoured me) with the remark
that some flies laid hold of by Chelifers have no infesting mites.

An early expression of the view that the Arachnid is merely
a passenger is contained in the already quoted communication
by Mr. Moore :

> Does not the *Chelifer* experience inconvenience, in consequence of its
> construction, when it would be pursuing its prey? and does it not take
> advantage of the leg which the fly so readily offers that it may ride out on
> its hunting excursions, and, by the aid of the fly's legs and wings, get
> cheaply conveyed from place to place?

This was the view of Hagen,[*] and it has been supported by
Simon and Cambridge, as well as by other observers, among
whom are Dr. v. Wagner and Professor Moniez.[†]   It is
favoured by the fact that Diptera, with attached Pseudoscorpions,
are seen flying through the air, and Phalangiids hurrying over
the ground, the Pseudoscorpions the while appearing in a state
of inactivity, passively hanging generally by but one claw to
a limb of the conveyor.   Hagen has remarked that the creatures
cannot obtain nourishment from the hard limbs, and that, except
when associating with beetles, they are always found on the
limbs, not on the softer body.   Mr. Spicer, referring particularly to Phalangiids, has made the same remark.   Simon and
Cambridge have emphasized the statement that the creatures do
not appear to injure their hosts, Diptera, etc., continuing to fly
freely notwithstanding the presence of their comparatively
formidable guests.   This has been remarked upon by several
observers, and we have seen that a small fly with five *Chernes*
attached yet flew and walked in a lively manner.   Further, in
support of the present view, we have a direct observation by
Mr. Moore, who saw a Pseudoscorpion which had been carried
by a fly from one window to another, relax its grasp and drop
into a crevice.   One can imagine that the attachment may be
a more or less accidental circumstance.   The little creatures are

---

[*] Hagen, 1867, l.c. ; 1868, l.c.

[†] F. v. Wagner, l.c.; R. Moniez, ‘A propos des publications récentes
sur le faux parasitisme des Chernétides sur différents Arthropodes,’ Revue
biologique du Nord de la France, VI. (1894), pp. 47-54.

accustomed to use the great pedipalps for seizing objects of various kinds,* and for attack and defence. They are exceedingly pugnacious, and when annoyed they brandish the pedipalps and open and shut the pincers in a ferocious, even ludicrous, manner. They are apt, moreover, to assume a condition of blind rage, and at such times they will grasp with the pincers any small object which opposes them. Mr. M'Intire, offering a camel's hair pencil to an angry Chelifer, found that it readily seized the brush and allowed itself to be carried some distance. We can understand, I think, from these facts, that Pseudo-scorpions annoyed by flies walking over them or entering their retreats would naturally seize the insect's legs, and it is obvious that the insects, being several times the size of the Arachnids, would have no difficulty in flying away with them. It is clear, moreover, that the creatures may thus be carried to considerable distances, for, refusing to acknowledge themselves beaten—and perhaps imagining that they have caught the fly—they often keep the pincer tightly closed and hold on for a long time with extreme tenacity. Dr. Hess, who kept a fly and Pseudoscorpion in captivity, did not observe any material change in the Arachnid's position after fifty-six hours. The creatures may detach themselves voluntarily as above noted, and they have been known to do so when the fly is caught by a naturalist; but this rarely happens, the Pseudoscorpion usually retaining its hold even when the fly is considerably handled for observation. One of Dr. Löw's specimens retained its grasp even when subjected to partial stupefaction with ether; and the other, though it became detached, immediately resumed its position on awakening. When the *Ctenophora* above mentioned was killed in alcohol two of the four *Chernes* fell off, but the other two kept their positions, falling off only when removed from the spirit. Professor Moniez mentions that he preserves Pseudoscorpions and a fly, plunged alive into spirit, but still in position; and we have, further, the case of the Chelifer in amber still attached to the leg of an ichneumon. This means of dispersal—if a means of dispersal only—is a remarkable one; but it is not without its parallel in nature. Bivalve molluscs often close their shells on the toes of flying water-insects and birds as well as on those of frogs, toads, newts, etc.; and this is clearly an accidental

---

* Albin, 'Natural History of Spiders and other Curious Insects,' 1736, p. 56: 'It had two long things,' says the author, of a Chelifer, 'like the claws of a lobster, and would use them as a crab or lobster doth to pinch or lay hold of anything.'

circumstance, serving the purpose of dispersal.　The creatures, thus clinging by closure of the shell, are carried through the air and along the ground just as Pseudoscorpions are while clinging by a closed pincer to the legs of flies, harvest-men, etc.　Operculate snails, moreover, occasionally cling accidentally to legs of insects, by closure of the operculum.　And in this connection one may refer also to the clinging of certain biting-lice to winged parasitic bird-flies : a habit which doubtless secures dispersal.[*] Dr. Lukis, referring to the case in which a house-fly had four Pseudoscorpions on the same leg, has doubted whether the attachment can be accidental.　If this be the case, he says, ' I am at a loss to conceive how so many . . had attached themselves to one limb?　If the fly had accidentally placed the limb in a nest of these insects, it seems natural to believe that it would have had sufficient sensibility to withdraw it ere the whole family had time to attach themselves.'　In reply, however, one might bring forward cases, of which I have elsewhere given particulars, of a water-bug with three bivalves accidentally attached to its toes—of newts with four, toads with six, and crayfish with eight shells similarly attached.　It might be argued, perhaps, that the attachment, at first accidental, but proving valuable as a means of dispersal, has been encouraged by natural selection, and has thus the character of a separate instinct.　Professor Moniez, who appears to go a step further, has supposed the attachment of Pseudoscorpions to be intentional, the creatures being believed to seize the legs of insects for the express purpose of getting themselves transported.　He relates that each time he had wished to exhibit Pseudoscorpions to his pupils he had easily obtained specimens by the following

---

[*] At a meeting of the Entomological Society of London, in 1890, Dr. Sharp exhibited *Ornithomyia avicularia*, from Dartford, to which were adhering—apparently by their mandibles—several specimens of a mallophagous louse (1).　The *Ornithomyia* is a flying Dipteron that infests birds, and it is believed that Mallophaga are transferred by this means from one bird to another (2).　Lt.-Col. Walker (3), moreover, has recently reported the capture of a specimen of the same fly which was leaving a recently-shot blackbird, and to which, hanging on like a bulldog, was a biting-louse agreeing with Denny's figure of *Nirmus merulensis*. This was the second instance which had come to the observer's notice of a mallophagous insect attaching itself to *Ornithomyia* ; in both cases it adhered to the posterior part of the hind-body.　(1) D. Sharp, Transactions of the Entomological Society of London, 1890, p. xxx. ; (2) D. Sharp, 'Cambridge Natural History,' V. (1895), pp. 350-1 ; (3) H. J. O. Walker, ' Bird-louse Changing Hosts,' Science-Gossip (n.s.), VII. (1900), p. 191.

---

proceeding, which had been inspired by the observations of his predecessors and by the ascertaining of the fact that the creatures occurred in some plenty in a manure heap in the open air at Lille. It sufficed to catch flies, to cut off a wing, and to place them under a bell-glass on the manure-heap; generally, in these circumstances, after a very little time, one might find the Pseudoscorpions fixed by their pincers to the legs of the Diptera, and Moniez's conclusion was that they could not resist the desire to quit the place where they were whenever the opportunity for a ride presented itself to them. It is noted, however, that while *Chernes nodosus, Chelifer cancroides*, and *Roncus lubricus* occurred in the manure-heap in about equal numbers, this supposed desire for passive aerial locomotion obtained only in the *Chernes* and *Chelifer*, the *Roncus* never attaching itself to the flies. The attachment, whether accidental or intended, obviously serves for dispersal; but it is probable that it is not a means of dispersal only, the phenomena having, almost certainly, a further significance.

It was the opinion of several of the earlier writers that the fly-infesting Pseudoscorpions are parasitic. This was the view of Hermann, and of Leach,* and also in more recent years of Professor Leydig;† and notwithstanding the Pseudoscorpion's diminutiveness it is probable that those found attached to flies, etc., are attacking the relatively gigantic creatures for the purpose of obtaining food from them. Several recent observers look upon the Pseudoscorpions under these conditions as predaceous rather than parasitic; and justly so I think; but the distinction is not of great importance, for it merely turns upon the question whether the Arachnids obtain their nourishment during the life of the insect or only after its death. These animals are generally stated to feed on minute insects and mites, and their larvæ, and they are seen to seize such creatures—book-lice, spring-tails, etc.—with their pincers and convey them

---

* W. E. Leach, 'On the . . . Scorpionidea, with descriptions of the British species of Chelifer and Obisium,' Zoological Miscellany. III. (1817). pp. 48-53.

† Professor Leydig compares the Pseudoscorpions, somewhat inaptly, to Hydrachnids or water-mites during their youth, at which time they are parasitic on the legs and bodies of water-beetles and -bugs. Reference might be made also to the larvæ of Trombidiids or velvety land-mites which we commonly see, like little red beads, adhering to harvest-men. These are cases of true parasitism, the attachment of the larvæ (whose imagines are free) being essential to their existence; and at the same time, doubtless, highly useful as a means of dispersal.

thus to the mouth.   It is probable that the greater part of the
food of most Pseudoscorpions consists of small fry of this kind ;
but it is certain that some sorts, more especially *Chernes*, occasionally or habitually attack larger creatures.   Mr. Blomefield,
as long ago as 1846, appears to have had no doubt on this
point, for he remarks of *Chernes* that their habitat appears to be
under bark, 'whence they probably spring out on their unwary
prey [flies] basking near.' According to Stecker, indeed, *Chernes*
sponges on flies and earwigs, *Chelifer* on bugs, and *Chthonius*
on woodlice, etc.* Dr. George informs me that he once saw
a Pseudoscorpion at Kirton-in-Lindsey seize a fly, first with one
pincer, then with the other, then with the mouth, and carry it
about like a cat with a mouse.   This note was made in 1879,
and Dr. George has now no clear recollection concerning the
fly, which was probably somewhat small.   The observation is
of interest, however, suggesting as it does that it is mainly
a question of size whether the attacked insect will be at once
overcome or whether it will lift the little assailant from its feet.
It is difficult to understand why *Chernes*, etc., to which presumably small prey are generally accessible, should make bold
to attack large creatures.   The house-fly in this connection is
sufficiently gigantic, while such creatures as *Ctenophora pectinicornis* and *Phalangium opilio* are relatively enormous.   It may
be remarked, however, that while *Chthonius* possesses four eyes,
and *Chelifer, Roncus,* etc. two, *Chernes* is blind ; and it may be
that it is unable accurately to estimate the size of the animals
whose legs it seizes.   It is true that the encumbered creatures
usually appear uninjured ; but this, perhaps, is because the
Arachnids have not had an opportunity of pressing the attack ;
and it is improbable, I think, that the hosts generally escape
injury or even survive.   We have already quoted the case in
which the fly was weakly and the Chelifer strong and active, the
two ultimately falling into a wine-glass.   The fly from which
Mr. Blomefield took four *Chernes* was 'so fettered in its movements by the grasping hold of so many aggressors at once, as
hardly to be able to crawl' ; and Mr. Stainton, in 1865, remarked
that house-flies were powerless to get rid of Chelifers, and that
these Arachnids, according to his experience, did not quit the
flies until the latter died.   Dr. Lukis, moreover, has informed
us of having seen '*Chelifer cimicoides*' dragging by the legs

---

* A. Stecker, Sitzungsberichte der k. Akademie der Wissenschaften
(Wien), LXXII. (1873), p. 517.

the dead carcass of *Stomoxys calcitrans*—a Dipteron as large as
the house-fly and resembling it in build.* The often-repeated
statement that Pseudoscorpions are always noticed on the legs,
not on the bodies, of flies is in need of modification. Donovan,
in 1797, recorded the finding of a Pseudoscorpion 'fastened on
the body of the *Musca Vomitoria* . . . from which it could
not be extricated without killing and tearing the fly into pieces';†
and in 1826 the following paragraph appeared in the pages of
Kirby & Spence :

> Another insect, remarkable for its resemblance in some respects to the
> scorpion—called in this country the book-crab (*Chelifer cancroides*), from
> its being sometimes found in books· occasionally is parasitic upon flies,
> especially the common blue-bottle-fly (*Musca vomitoria*). They adhere to
> it very pertinaciously under the wings ; and if you attempt to disturb them,
> they run backwards, forwards, or sideways, with equal facility.‡

A recent American writer mentions having received a Pseudo-
scorpion found, apparently, under the wing of a house-fly ; ||
and one gathers also that some of the Pseudoscorpions mentioned by Mr. de Courtois de Langlade were on the thorax of
the flies to which he refers. It thus appears that Chelifers
occasionally manage to leave the legs and effect a lodgment on
the bodies of their transporters ; and it is quite likely, in these
cases, that they contrive to suck the juices of the living animal.
But, from a consideration of all the facts above quoted, particularly those of Mr. Stainton and Dr. Lukis, and from certain
other facts still to be given, it is probable, I think, that the
creatures more usually remain on the legs till the insects die.
Perhaps they thus remain because they are unable to proceed
further, or possibly their policy is, by persistently clinging to
the legs, to tire out the insect, cause its death, and then suck
the juices of the carcass.

It would be interesting to know the fate of encumbered flies
kept in captivity. Mr. Moore put a Chelifer in a pill-box with
a fly, the leg of which it soon seized ; but next morning he
found that the Chelifer not the fly had died. This, however, is
not surprising, for confinement in pill-boxes is quickly fatal to
animals of many kinds. The anonymous writer in 'The Entomological Magazine' confined *Lonchæa vaginalis* and Chelifers
in a bottle, and afterwards added other flies :

---

* F. C. Lukis, Loudon's Magazine of Natural History, IV. (1831), p. 284.

† E. Donovan, 'Natural History of British Insects,' VI. (1797), p. 84.

‡ Kirby & Spence, 'Introduction to Entomology,' IV. (1826), pp. 228-9.

|| F. M. Webster, Entomological News, VIII. (1897), p. 59.

The other day we put several of both into a bottle, and often, when the fly approached the *Chelifer*, the latter immediately extended one of its claws, and seized the fly by the end of the *tarsus*; with the other claw it grasped either the middle of the *tarsus*, or the costal nervure of the wing, and then loosened the hold of each of its claws alternately till it arrived at the *trochanter*, where it remained fixed. We added three other flies, belonging to the genera *Anthomyia*, *Sepsis*, and *Borborus*. The first, a much more active insect than the *Lonchæa*, was soon seized by a *Chelifer*. It used its utmost efforts to disengage its *tarsus* without success; however, the *Chelifer* soon relaxed its hold of its own accord. When we looked at the insects the following day, the *Lonchæa*, the *Anthomyia*, and the *Borborus* were alive, and only the first had a *Chelifer* attached to it; so, likewise, had the *Sepsis*, whose death was probably occasioned by confinement not by any wound.

It is regrettable that these observations were not continued; but it is improbable that the behaviour of Chelifers in a bottle would safely represent that of individuals in a state of nature. That the attachment is not merely passive is indicated by the conclusions of Dr. Hess. We have already mentioned that this naturalist watched a house-fly with a Chelifer on one of its legs. He caught the fly at noon on 30th August and put it in a large glass. The Arachnid hung by one pincer to the tibia of the left front leg, the other pincer being free and ready for the fray. Frequently the creature grasped the right front leg with the free pincer; but it was obliged to release it, for the fly spreading out its legs liberated the right one. The two animals were kept for 56 hours without their mutual relations having changed; it merely seemed that the Arachnid had moved a little higher on the leg. To prevent the fly succumbing the observer frequently gave it a drop of milk. It walked about freely, and when resting was usually engaged in attempting to detach the Chelifer, using for this purpose the free front leg which it rubbed against that to which its assailant was hanging. The observation was accidentally terminated on the evening of 1st September, when too much milk was given to the fly, the Chelifer being found drowned on the following morning. It is unfortunate that the observation thus remained incomplete—the leg did not appear to have been injured—but Dr. Hess tells us that in view of the proceedings of the Chelifer, and the obstinacy with which it maintained its position, no doubt remained in his mind that its intention was to attack and feed upon the fly. In all probability the creatures sometimes realise that their chances of causing the insect's death are hopeless; and we have seen that they occasionally detach themselves. That they may be successful, however, seems clear from the observations of Mr. Stainton and Dr. Lukis, and is proved, I think, by those of Mr. Backhausen now to be quoted. The observations referred to were made in South America, and were reported in 1893 by Professor Berg, who had every confidence in the observer. A fly with a Pseudoscorpion hanging by one pincer to one of its legs was placed under a glass; and after an hour it was observed that the leg to which the Arachnid was attached became stiff. Next morning, Mr. Backhausen found the fly dead and the Pseudoscorpion fat and bloated under some scraps of paper. He next placed ten Pseudoscorpions on a tray with earth and leaves, put them under the glass, left them for a few days without food, and then imprisoned a few small flies. As soon as the Pseudoscorpions perceived the presence of the insects they came out of hiding and began to snatch at them, attaching themselves to their legs, always with one pincer, but using the other in their endeavours to obtain an assured holding. Once fixed they continued to cling to the leg. The observer was somewhat hindered by want of appliances; but according to Professor Berg he established: (1) that the imprisoned leg soon became stiff [this was not the case in Dr. Hess' observation]; (2) that the flies died while the Pseudoscorpions remained on the legs; and (3) that after the flies' death the creatures travelled along the legs to the body, and finally drew the insects under the leaves to suck out their juices. Similar results were obtained with a horse-fly (*Tabanus*); but its death occurred less quickly, as was expected from its greater size. Mr. Reeker, who has also written on this subject, has supported the views derivable from the last-quoted notes. This he does, however, merely on the strength of observations, of little importance, on the behaviour of Pseudoscorpions shut up by him and by Dr. Westhoff with somewhat small flies and beetles. He mentions, among other things, that a gnat (*Culex pipiens*) given to a Chelifer was seized by the leg—the Arachnid would not let go, and next morning the gnat was dead.* Further observations on the lines suggested by those of Dr. Hess and Mr. Backhausen are certainly desirable. The animals should be placed in large cages, the natural conditions of existence being preserved as nearly as possible; and, as pointed out by Dr. Hess, it is important that the insects should be properly supplied with food in order that the contest may have a normal termination.

---

* H. Reeker, 'Zur Lebensweise der Afterskorpione,' Jahresbericht des Westfälischen Provinzial-Vereins für Wissenschaft u. Kunst, 1894, pp. 103-8.

Attempts have been made to extend the dispersal theory to Pseudoscorpions associating with beetles. This has been done by Hagen, Moniez, and other writers; and the view has received doubtful support even from Dr. v. Jhering, who was well acquainted with beetle-infesting Chelifers in South America. It is assumed, apparently, that the little Arachnids seek out beetles, manage to effect an entry, and hide themselves away under the wings and elytra for the express purpose of getting a ride. This, as it seems to me, is incredible. It is equally difficult, no doubt, to regard the creatures as predaceous, for they can hardly hope to kill the huge beetles to which they resort. Professor Haldeman, Professor Leydig, Professor Hickson, and other naturalists have supposed them to be parasites, and it is highly probable that they have this character—unless, as might possibly be shown on further observation, they go to the beetles to hunt for infesting mites. Hagen dismisses the idea of parasitism in view of the character of the mouth-parts: ‘It is true,’ he says, ‘that *Chelifer* eats by sucking, but it is very doubtful whether it would choose for its food animals whose segments are very thick.’ The segments under the elytra of *Alaus oculatus* and of the great *Acrocinus longimanus*, he adds, ‘could never be perforated by the very small and soft maxillary apparatus of the *Chelifer*.’ But the writer would not attach much importance to this objection, for much smaller creatures manage to live parasitically on beetles, and we can well imagine that the Chelifers may find weak places in the armour. In the case of an Indian Pseudoscorpion (*Ectocerus helferi*) Stecker has called attention to the formidable character of the mouth-parts, and has supposed them to be suited for piercing the integuments of beetles. He was unacquainted with the habits of the creature, but in a museum-specimen he found a beetle’s foot in the mandibles.

SUMMARY.

Of the twenty British Pseudoscorpions, four only have yet been identified from Lincolnshire. They live under bark, stones, etc.; but one was discovered on a fly’s leg. The occurrence of the creatures on flies’ legs has been reported from various parts of this country; from Austria and Hungary, Germany, Switzerland, Belgium, France, etc.; from North Africa; and from North, South, and Central America. In Europe, the observations are generally made in late summer and autumn, and the Pseudoscorpion is commonly *Chernes nodosus*—a Chelifer about a third of the length of the house-fly. The Chelifers hang to the

leg by closure of the pincer of one of the pedipalps; their
legs, body, and the remaining pedipalp and pincer being free.
House-flies are observed on the wing carrying the creatures
from place to place, or walking with them on windows, etc.
Other encumbered Diptera are seen in gardens, waste-places,
etc.; certain small kinds occurring on decaying vegetable matter
are specially liable to be attacked; and great Tipulids do not
escape. Many infested flies sometimes occur in the same house
or about the same rubbish-heap; and not infrequently more than
one Chelifer hangs to the same fly. Individuals have been seen
carrying two, three, four, five, six, and even eight or ten; and
one had four on a single leg. Some Chelifers live in bees'-,
ants'-, and termites'-nests; and in South Africa one has been
seen hanging to legs of hive-bees. One has been found fossil in
amber, in Europe, still on the leg of an ichneumon. In an
Austrian grotto, a *Chernes* occurs on a Locustid; while in
Germany and England others have been seen on legs of False-
Spiders (*Phalangium*). The creatures also occur under the
elyta of large beetles. They have thus been seen, singly or
in numbers, in North and South America, in Australia, and in
the Malay Archipelago. In all these associations it is probable
that the creatures pertain mainly to *Chernes*. Those found on
beetles are presumably parasitic. Those on legs of flies, etc.,
have been supposed to have the same character; but the meaning of the phenomena has long been doubtful. When annoyed
with a camel's-hair brush, a Chelifer will seize it, and allow
itself to be carried away; and, as they are pugnacious, and
accustomed to use the pedipalps for attack and defence, the
attachment may be accidental. The attached creatures may
be carried to considerable distances, for they often hold on
tenaciously for a long time. In captivity one maintained its
position for fifty-six hours; and they will not always let go
when stupefied with ether or plunged into alcohol. We have
here, certainly, a means of dispersal—for which an accidental
circumstance might possibly have been converted into a special
instinct. Moniez maintains that the creatures seize the legs
intentionally for the purpose of obtaining a ride; but, from
various facts, it seems probable that they have another purpose
—and that the usefulness of the habit for dispersal is largely
incidental. Most Pseudoscorpions feed on minute insects, which
they seize with the pincers. Very small flies, whose legs are
seized, are at once overcome. Larger ones lift the assailants
from their feet, and carry them away. It is odd that large

creatures should be seized; but *Chernes* is blind and may not always know their size. The Arachnid occasionally effects a lodgment on the body of the living insect, and perhaps sucks its juices; but this is not usual; and it is true that the insects generally appear uninjured. Sometimes, however, they are in an emaciated condition; and according to Stainton's experience Chelifers remain on the legs of house-flies until the latter die. Lukis saw a Chelifer dragging by the legs the carcass of a Dipteron as large as the house-fly. The naturalist who watched a Chelifer and fly for fifty-six hours was convinced that the Chelifer was an assailant; and Backhausen, who kept a number of Chelifers and flies in captivity, is said to have established that the Arachnids remained on the legs till the flies died, and then travelled to the body and sucked its juices. The subject will bear further investigation; but from the facts now in our possession it seems impossible to avoid the conclusion that Pseudoscorpions found on the legs of other Arthropods — often relatively gigantic—are attacking the creatures for food, and that notwithstanding their diminutiveness they are to be regarded, not as parasites, but as animals of prey.

NOTE on NEUROPTERA.

Dragonflies Observed in the Huddersfield District.—On the 28th May I visited Cawthorne, and observed *Agrion puella*, *A. cyathigerum*, and *Libellula quadrimaculata* flitting about in considerable numbers amongst the vegetation of the disused Barnsley Canal.—W. E. L. WATTAM, Newsome, Huddersfield, 11th June 1901.

NOTE on HEPATICS.

***Morckia hibernica* and *Petalophyllum Ralfsii* in Yorkshire.** On 4th May 1901 I came across the former hepatic (which I have already recorded in 'The Naturalist') with abundant capsules on Coatham Marshes, and in a new habitat. On washing out the gathering, I found several plants of the very rare *Petalophyllum Ralfsii* (Wils.) Gottsche mixed with it. This latter is small, and looks like an outspread fan, with ridges or lamellæ running outwards from the stalk. Mr. Pearson, who has seen it, says this is one of the most important discoveries among the Hepaticæ of recent years. Its previous habitats were Ireland, Cornwall, and Anglesey, so it will be seen it is a very important addition to the Hepatic Flora of Yorkshire.—WM. INGHAM, York, 24th June 1901.

NOTES and NEWS.

'The Girl's Realm' for June 1901 has been sent to us by the publishers, Messrs. Bousfield & Co. Ltd., 10, Norfolk Street, London, W.C., who are not only to be congratulated generally on the excellence of the periodical, but specially on an article by the well-known naturalist-photographer, Mr. R. Kearton, F.Z.S., on 'Birds in their Little Nests,' illustrated by more than a dozen of the admirable photographs taken by Mr. Cherry Kearton, the artist's brother.

NOTES on MOLLUSCA.

Unusually fine *Planorbis nautileus* at Colton, near Leeds.—In the early part of April I was taken by my neighbour, Mr. Smith, to a pond in School Lane, Colton, near Whitkirk. At one end of the pond *Callitriche* grew most luxuriantly, and searching amongst it I found *Planorbis nautileus* very plentiful and more finely grown than I have met with it before, some of them measuring nearly 4 .mm. in diameter. Amongst the grass growing round the margin of the pond a few small *Limnæa truncatula* occurred, but, strange to say, there was no trace of *Limnæa peregra*.—WM. NELSON, Crossgates, Leeds, 18th May 1901.

Molluscan Gatherings near Brigg, Linc. N.—Our vicar, the Rev. E. Adrian Woodruffe-Peacock, M.C.S., offered the school children a number of little prizes for the best gatherings of our local species of snails. The result was not satisfactory from the collector's point of view. Hundreds of specimens were gathered, but the species were limited; only a very few being interesting. *Helix aspersa*, *H. nemoralis*, with a beautiful *compressa* variety and two fair *conica*. *H. arbustorum* is plentiful here, and the varieties *fuscescens*, *cincta*, *flavescens*, and *albina* were taken. *H. cantiana* had also been taken. There was one *H. caperata*, and it was the variety *ornata*, never taken alive in the parish before. There was one *H. rufescens*, and it was the variety *alba*, which was also new. This was strange, as the type and *albo-cincta* are common enough, even in the school garden. The Ancholme river, which was partly run off, supplied *Dreissensia polymorpha* only. Our next gathering will be later in the summer, and it is to be hoped will be more productive.—WM. BOOTH, Howsham School, Lincoln, 13th June 1901.

Reversed *Limnæa peregra* in Leeds.—There is a saying that 'All things come to the man who waits,' and surely there must be some truth in the axiom, for after collecting the Limnæidæ continuously for quite forty years, during which time I must have walked many hundreds of miles, searching the ditches and ponds of our county, and must have passed many thousands of specimens of *Limnæa peregra* through my hands, it was not until the beginning of the present month that I succeeded in finding the reversed form of this species.

During the first week in May I searched a pond situated in North Leeds which I had hitherto altogether overlooked. After searching some time I obtained specimens of the following Limnæidæ:—*Planorbis albus*, moderately fine and common; *Planorbis carinatus*, very fine and common; *Planorbis corneus*, rather fine but very scarce; and *Limnæa stagnalis* var. *fragilis*, very common and appearing to be enjoying itself floating foot upwards on the surface of the water. *Limnæa peregra*, on the other hand, was crawling on the muddy bottom of the shallow side of the pond; they were very fine grown shells of the *ovata* form, and after scooping a sufficient supply out with my net I was just for starting home when, having made what I thought was my last dip, I was at once struck by the singular appearance of one of the specimens, and could scarcely believe my eyes. It was, however, undoubtedly a specimen of monst. *sinistrorsum*. I will not attempt to describe my feelings, which can be readily imagined by any field naturalist who has suddenly found a long-sought-for rarity. After safely boxing my prize, I need scarcely say that I restarted searching with renewed vigour and care, peering into the shallow parts of the pond which the *Limnæa peregra* frequented, and putting every specimen that came within my vision through a critical examination. After a couple of hours' searching I found a few more beauties of the reversed variety.

The only vegetation I noticed in the pond was a grass which grows a considerable length, half of which lies on the water, and one of the water starworts (*Callitriche*).—WM. NELSON, Crossgates, near Leeds, 18th May 1901.

INTRODUCTION

OR

EARLY HISTORY

OF

BEES AND HONEY,

BY

WILLIAM CARR,

NEWTON HEATH APIARY,

NEAR MANCHESTER.

SALFORD:

J. ROBERTS, PRINTER, 168, CHAPEL STREET.

1880.

INTRODUCTION OR EARLY HISTORY OF BEES AND HONEY.

By Mr. William Carr.

The natural history of the honey-bee has been the marvel of all ages from the time of Adam, the greatest naturalist the world ever produced, who well knew her history when he named the bee "Deborah," which in the Hebrew means "she that speaks;" and the bees' speech is both as sweet and as wise as that of her namesake Deborah, whose wondrous song of victory is written in the book of Judges. Adam knew that the bee was able to speak, and teach proud man, with all his boasted intellect, many a wise saying, if he was only willing to learn at her school, and so he gave her that name. This was 4004 years before Christ.

The history of bees is found written in hieroglyphics on the Pyramids of Egypt, and on ancient tombs, long before writing was discovered, and this proves that the natural history and management of bees occupied the attention of man at the earliest period of which we have any record. Surrounded by a boundless variety of living creatures, he would naturally be led to notice their habits and economy; and no part of the world of insects would be more likely to engage his attention than the honey-bee.

Honey would, in all probability, constitute one of his earliest luxuries; and as he advanced in civilisation he would, as a matter of course, avail himself of the industry of its collectors by bringing them as much as possible within his reach; and by this means he would take an important step towards an acquaintance with entomology. But the progress made by our earliest progenitors, in this or any other science, is involved in the obscurity and uncertainty necessarily appertaining to the infancy of society and the difficulty of writing its history in hieroglyphics.

The first indication of attention to the bees' natural history is contained in the Old Testament, where it is mentioned in connection with honey and wax in no less than twenty of the books. In Genesis xliii. 11, the patriarch Jacob, in giving directions to his sons on going down into Egypt a second time, tells them to "take the best fruits of the land" with them, literally that which was praised the most, or "the song of the land," and among others he names "a little honey."

The things enumerated, as we are informed, grew well during a drought; and as a famine now prevailed, would be more highly appreciated in Egypt. Besides, we are led to the belief that honey was an article of commerce previous to this time. (Genesis xxxvii. 25, and inferences drawn from Homer and Herodotus, about 600 B.C., at a later date.) The whole of the twenty books conclusively prove the care that was taken of the bees, and how highly their produce was appreciated; and in Solomon's Song iv. 11, Christ's love for the Church is beautifully expressed, "Thy lips, O my spouse, drop as the honeycomb: honey and milk *are* under thy tongue; and the smell of thy garments is like the smell of Lebanon."

Honey was the first and last food that Christ partook of whilst on earth; and may not this account in some measure for his sweet disposition as a man? For

Isaiah prophecies the birth of Christ in the 7th chapter, 14th and 15th verses :—
" Therefore the Lord himself shall give you a sign ; Behold, a virgin shall conceive, and bear a son, and shall call his name Immanuel. Butter and honey shall he eat, that he may know to refuse the evil and choose the good."

The Jews in all countries where they are scattered to the present day do not believe that this prophecy has yet been fulfilled (and in the expectation that their first child may be the Messiah or Immanuel), import honey from Assyria to give their child when it is born.

I said the last food Christ eat on earth was honey, and that was just after his resurrection and before his ascension, and this is recorded in the 24th chapter of St. Luke and the 41st and 42nd verses. Christ said, " Have ye here any meat ? And they gave him a piece of a broiled fish, and of an honeycomb. And he took it, and did eat before them."

I said the bee was able to speak, and teach proud man, with all his boasted intellect, many a wise saying, if he was only willing to learn at her school, and the wisest man the world ever saw, was willing to learn from the bee, what all his wisdom could not teach him, I allude of course to King Solomon, as the following story shows :—

When Solomon was reigning in his glory,
  Unto his throne the Queen of Sheba came
(So in the *Talmud* you may read the story),
  Drawn by the magic of the monarch's fame,
To see the splendours of his court ; and bring
Some fitting tribute to the mighty king.

Nor this alone ; much had her Highness heard
  What flowers of learning graced the royal speech ;
What gems of wisdom dropped with every word ;
  What wholesome lessons he was wont to teach,
In pleasing proverbs ; and she wished, in sooth,
To know if Rumour spoke the simple truth.

Besides, the queen had heard (which piqued her most),
  How through the deepest riddles he could spy ;
How all the curious arts that women boast
  Were quite transparent to his piercing eye,
And so the queen had come—a royal guest—
To put the sage's cunning to the test.

And straight she held before the monarch's view,
  In either hand, a radiant wreath of flowers ;
The one bedecked with every charming hue,
  Was newly culled from Nature's choicest bowers :
The other, no less fair in every part,
Was the product of divinest art.

" Which is the true, and which the false ? " she said,
  Great Solomon was silent. All-amazed,
Each wondering courtier shook his puzzled head,
  While at the garlands long the monarch gazed,
As one who sees a miracle, and fain,
For very rapture, ne'er would speak again.

" Which is the true ? " once more the woman asked,
  Pleased at the fond amazement of the king,
" So wise a head should not be hardly tasked,
  Most learned liege, with such a trivial thing ! "
But still the sage was silent ; it was plain
A deepening doubt perplexed the royal brain.

> While thus he ponders, presently he sees,
>   Hard by the casement — so the story goes —
> A little band of honey, bustling bees
>   Hunting for honey in a Sharon rose.
> The monarch smiled, and raised his royal head :
> " Open the window ! " that was all he said.
>
> The window opened at the king's command,
>   Within the room the eager insects flew,
> And sought the flowers in Sheba's dexterous hand.
>   And so the king and all the courtiers knew
> That wreath was nature's ; and the baffled queen
> Returned to tell the wonders she had seen.
>
> My story teaches (every tale should bear
>   A fitting moral) that the wise may find
> In trifles, light as atoms in the air,
>   Some useful lesson to enrich the mind ;
> Some truth designed, to profit or to please,
> As Israel's king learned wisdom from the bees !

The records of its first progression are, however, entirely lost, and no regular history of this science exists prior to the days of Aristotle (300 years before Christ), who, under the auspices and through the munificence of his pupil, Alexander the Great, was enabled to prosecute with the greatest advantage, for the time in which he lived, his experiments and inquiries into every department of natural history. Alexander felt so strong a desire to promote this object that he placed at the disposal of Aristotle a very large sum of money, and in his Asiatic expedition employed above a thousand persons in collecting and transmitting to him specimens from every part of the animal kingdom.

Aristotle is therefore to be regarded as having laid the first foundation of our knowledge of that kingdom. He must likewise have derived great advantages from the discoveries and observations of preceding writers, to whose works he would probably have easy access. No individual naturalist could, without such assistance, have produced so valuable and extensive a work on natural science as that which Aristotle has bequeathed to posterity. And (bough the opinions of himself and his contemporaries have been transmitted to us in an imperfect manner, and abound in errors, still he and his illustrious pupil, Theophrastus, who succeeded him in the Lyceum, may be regarded as the only philosophical naturalists of antiquity, whose labours and discoveries present us with any portion of satisfactory knowledge.

Prior to the time of Aristotle and Theophrastus, we read of the philosopher, Aristomachus, of Sali in Cilicia, and of Philiscus, the Thasian, having devoted many years of their lives to an investigation of the manners and habits of bees. The contemplations of the former are said to have been almost solely occupied by these insects for fifty-eight years, and the latter spent so great a portion of his time in the fields in pursuit of the same object as to have acquired the name of Agrius. Both of these great bee-masters left behind them, in writing, the results of their experiments and observations ; but the original works have been long buried in oblivion. However small the contribution of knowledge which we have derived from these ancient worthies, they must have greatly aided the progress of their favourite science. and are at all events evidences of the zeal with which apiculture was prosecuted in their day.

About three hundred years after the time at which Aristotle wrote, his observations on the honey-bee were embellished and invested with a species of divinity by the matchless pen of Virgil, in his fourth Georgic (35 years before Christ), and it excites feelings of regret that poetry, which for its beauty and elegance, is so universally admired, should be the vehicle of opinions that are founded in error. The following is Virgil's description of an Italian queen bee in his fourth Georgic (35 B.C.):—

> "Glowing with yellow scales and dazzling hue,
> His body marked with golden bands to view;
> If safe this king, one mind abides in all—
> If lost, in discord dire and feuds they fall;
> Destroy their work, waste all their gathered store,
> Dissolve all bonds, nor are a nation more.
>
> If he but live, ruling the glowing hive,
> All are content, the fertile race survive.
> Him they admire, with joyful hum surround,
> While labour thrives and honeyed sweets abound."

You here see the grave mistake Virgil makes in calling the queen a king.

Virgil says "That the bee is a ray of the Divinity;" Plutarch, "That it is a magazine of the virtues;" Quintilian, "That it is the chief of geometricians;" and De Montfort, "That the bee surpasses, in architecture, the skill of Archimedes."

The extensive notice we find of "mead" and "metheglin," in the days of the Druids, would lead us to believe that bees were domesticated by the Britons; but we have no authentic information on this point, and the honey used in their drinks may have been collected by wild bees. The Romans, when they came (A.D. 43) no doubt taught the Britons how to hive and domesticate the honey-bee.

Mead was the ideal nectar of the Scandinavian nations, which they expected to quaff in heaven out of the skulls of their enemies; and, as may reasonably be supposed, the liquor which they exalted thus highly in their *imaginary celestial banquets* was not forgotten at those which they *really* indulged in *upon earth*. Hence may be inferred the great attention which must have have been paid to the culture of the bee in those days, or there could not have been an adequate supply **of honey for the** production of mead, to satisfy the demand of such thirsty tribes.

The mythology of Scandinavia (the religion of our Gothic ancestors) was imparted by Sigge or Odin, a chieftain who migrated from Scythia with the whole of his tribe, and subdued, either by arms or arts, the northern parts of Europe. In the singular paradise which Odin sketched for his followers, the principal pleasure was to be derived from war and carnage; after the daily enjoyment of which, they were to sit down to a feast of boar's flesh and mead. The mead was to be handed to them in the skulls of their enemies, by virgins somewhat resembling the houri of the Mahometan paradise, and plentiful draughts were to be taken, until intoxication should crown their felicity.

Hence the poet Penrose thus commences his "Carousal of Odin":—

> "Fill the honey'd bev'rage high,
> Fill the skulls, 'tis Odin's cry!
> Heard ye not the powerful call,
> Thundering through the vaulted hall?
> Fill the mouth and spread the board,
> Vassals of the grisly lord!
> The feast begins, the skull goes round,
> Laughter shouts—the shouts resound!"

The mead made in South Wales in the present day is not so potent as that drunk when King Ethelwald restricted the monks of his monastery to a certain quantum to be drunk between twelve of the brethren at supper. Howel Dhu, who was King of Wales about A.D. 490, made a code of laws relating to bees, fixing the various prices of a hive at different seasons; and so highly was mead thought of some thousand years ago that the mead-maker ranked in the Prince of Wales' household next to the royal physician.

The Anglo-Saxons, of the earliest period, were probably more anxious to domesticate bees than horses. Their produce was an article of food, necessary to brewing mead and extensively used in medicine. In the sixth and seventh centuries, bees were altogether wild. They swarmed in the woods, and formed their honeycombs in hollow trees, and were at first classed by law with foxes and otters, as incapable of private ownership, because they were always on the move.

Anyone who found them had a right to the honey and wax, though, from several ecclesiastical regulations in the seventh and eighth century, we may infer that their capture was a dangerous amusement, and that their half-naked captors were often severely stung. A favourite mode of taking them was to cut down the tree in which they were, saw off the part containing them, and carry it home. But as the country progressed in wealth, bee-keeping became more profitable. By the laws of one of the Saxon kings it was ruled that every " ten hides of land shall furnish ten vessels of honey."

The clergy earnestly encouraged bee-keeping, teaching that the bees had been sent from heaven, because the Mass of God could not be celebrated without wax. The first step towards their domestication was the formation of imitations in bark (*rusca*) of the hollows of trees in which they were found. After a short time a wild swarm became the quasi property of the owner of the trees in which they had settled for three consecutive nights; but if he omitted to discover it within that time, the finder had a right to fourpence, and if it were not paid, to keep it himself. This shows the difference in value between the wild and domesticated swarms, as a rusca of bees was worth six times fourpence, viz, twenty-four pence.

About the middle of the tenth century slaves (whose duty it was exclusively to attend to bees, and were called bee-churls) were ordinarily attached to wealthy establishments, and from the position of slaves they soon became servile tenants, whom their lord provided with a stock of bees, for which they paid a fixed amount of produce for life, the swarms continuing the property of the lord.

We also find about this time the Anglo-Saxon word *bee-cist* (bee-chest) and the Latin *alvaria* (bee-hives) usually substituted for " rusca," from which it may be inferred that these rough constructions were superseded by regular hives. Not long afterwards, the clergy induced Edward the Confessor (A.D. 1050) to tithe the bee-hives, an evidence that they had become numerous and valuable, which is confirmed by *Domesday Book*, where they are repeatedly mentioned.

But bees in those days were never more than semi-domesticated, nor even altogether private property, for if they flew away, and the owner did not recapture them within a short time, they belonged to anyone who could.

About the commencement of the Christian era (50 A.D.), Columella, who was a very accurate observer, and exhibited considerable genius as a naturalist, made some curious and useful remarks upon bees in his treatise, *De Re Rusticâ*, translated in 1745; but Columella, like Virgil, appears to have acquiesced in and copied the errors of his predecessors; and he states that the idea of deriving emolument from the labours of the bees was first entertained in Greece, after the introduction of the colony which accompanied Cecrops from Egypt to Attica, by whom bees were established upon Mount Hymettus. And the Cecropian bees have survived all the revolutions which have changed the features and uprooted the population of Attica; though the defile of Thermopylæ has become a swampy plain, and the bed of the Cephisus is laid dry, this one feature of the country has remained unaltered, and there are now upwards of five thousand bee hives on Mount Hymettus; the honey is very celebrated, being principally collected from wild thyme (thymus serpyllum).

> " And still his honey'd store Hymettus yields,
> There the blithe bee her fragrant fortress builds,
> The free-born wanderer of thy mountain air."

Columella must have handled queen bees, for he was the first to state the fact that a queen cannot sting a human being, and he gives a description of two kinds of bees.

After him, the elder Pliny gave a sanction to the opinions which he found prevalent, and added to them others of his own. But Pliny, though a laborious compiler, occupied himself with too great a variety of pursuits to attain excellence in any. As a naturalist, however, he is happy in some of his descriptions. To him we are indebted for the transmission to us of all that was actually known, or supposed to be known, of natural history in his day. I say—supposed to be known; for many of the opinions and conjectures which he has put forth have been shown by modern investigators to be ill-founded.

The notions of the ancients respecting natural philosophy rested on no rational foundation; ideas of charms and of planetary influence directed their most important pursuits, and led to the formation of very absurd theories. When Pliny recommended that the dust in which a mule has rolled should be sprinkled on persons who are violently in love, as a sovereign remedy for amatory ardour, and gravely tells us that snakes are sometimes produced from the human medulla,— with many frivolous conceits of the like kind, we may safely pronounce that he or his contemporaries, or both, were very credulous, and that the science of experimental philosophy was scarcely cultivated among them.

Melissus, King of Crete, was the first who invented and taught the use of bee-hives. I have a list of eighty ancient authors upon bees.

After the compilation of Pliny's vast compendium, nearly fourteen hundred years rolled away without anything being done for entomology or for natural history in general. The Arabians, who alone preserved a glimmer of science during those dark ages that succeeded the fall of the Roman empire, cultivated natural history only as a branch of medicine, and from their writings little can be gleaned in furtherance of our present object.

On the revival of learning in the fifteenth century, and after the discovery of the art of printing, various editions were published of the works on natural history, written by the fathers of that science.

Thomas Hyll, in 1568, produced his first work on Bees, sixth edition in 1608. Sir Edward Wotton, Conrade Gesner, and others, produced conjointly a work on insects, the manuscripts of which came into the possession of Dr. Thomas Penny, an eminent physician and botanist in the reign of Queen Elizabeth (A.D. 1570). After devoting fifteen years to the improvement of the work, the Doctor died, and the unfinished manuscripts were purchased at a considerable price by Mouffet, a contemporary English physician of singular learning, who, with great labour and at great expense, arranged, enlarged, and completed the work. When nearly ready for the press, he also died; and the papers, after lying buried in dust and obscurity for several years, at last fell into the hands of Sir Theodore Mayerne (*Baron d'Aubonne*), a court physician in the time of Charles the First, who gave them to the world in 1634.

The arrangement of this work is defective; but for the period in which it was written, it is a very complete and respectable treatise on Entomology. It was highly recommended by Haller; and as a storehouse of ancient entomological lore it has not yet lost its utility. Its pages are embellished with nearly 500 wood-cuts. An English translation of it was published in 1658. Prince Frederic Cesi, President of the Roman Academy of Sciences, wrote a treatise upon bees; but the work has not been preserved, and we are unacquainted with its merits.

Bee-keeping never flourished in any age of the world as it did after the sixteenth century. In 1609, Rev. Charles Butler, D.D., (the father of English Apiarians) produced his first work on bees. I see in the interesting article written by Mr. Henderson (page 179 *British Bee Journal* for February, 1877,) he claims for Mr. Butler the discovery of the drones being males, worker bees and queens females; for Butler says, on page 54, "I conclude that the drones are males, and that the ruler and the honey bees are all females, and that the bees are not copulative; but conceive in a secret, unknown way by the drones; that queens produce queens only, and that the common bees are the mothers of common bees."

Now Aristotle (writing 1939 years before Mr. Butler's first work) says in book 1, chapter iii., page 10, "That it is the opinion of others that bees breed by copulation, and that the drones are males and the honey-bees females;" but he calls the ruler a king. It was left for that clever bee-master, the Rev. Samuel Purchas, to describe the ruler by her true definition, namely, "queen mother." In his work *A Theatre of Political Flying Insects*, published in 1657, and on page 86 he says, " Bees will swarm any time of the day, between eight in the morning and four in the afternoon, but the chief time of swarming is between eleven and one. Signs of after swarming are more manifest and certain, for about eight to twelve days after the first swarm is cast, the next princess will begin to tune in her treble voyce a mournful and begging note, as if she did pray her *queen mother* to give her leaf to begone, unto which voyce, if the queen vouchsafe to reply, tuning her bass to the young princess treble, as commonly she doth (though sometimes not entreated for a day or two), then she consents, and the third day after expect a swarm. The first day after the grant from the *queen mother*, how fair soever the weather may be, they will not go ; and not ordinarily on the next day, except it be very fair; but on the third day, though it be somewhat close and cloudy weather, they will swarm ; but when it has been very cold and windy I have known them stay five or six days after liberty granted."

Sir Christopher Wren, the great architect of St. Paul's Cathedral, invented a three storied octagon hive in 1654.

Goedart (whose work appeared in 1662) spent forty years of his life in attending to the proceedings of insects,—" daily conversing with insects," as he expresses it.

Swammerdam published his celebrated work, *A General History of Insects*, in 1669; a more enlarged edition, in two volumes, containing the history of bees, was afterwards published in 1737, under the auspices of Boerhaave, from the manuscripts of Swammerdam. It appears that Swammerdam stated "that from one female, the only one in the hive, all these kind of bees are produced," viz. : queens, workers, and drones. This is the first distinct statement of the fact of the reproduction of bees, so Swammerdam has the credit of being the discoverer of this important fact.

Dr. Gedde, in 1675, published an excellent work on Bees, *The English Apiary*, and obtained a patent from Charles II. for his invention of octagon hives of three stories; so Gedde was the inventor of the storifying system, and the now called Stewarton hives. (This is the only patent ever taken out in England for a bee-hive.) What a contrast this is to America, where they have one thousand and one patent bee-hives.

Moses Rusden, Bee-master to the King's most excellent Majesty, published his work, "A Further Discovery of Bees," in 1679. Rusden improved Gedde's hive, and put a frame in it for the bees to fasten their combs upon. This is the first account we have of a frame being put inside a bee-hive.

In 1712, Dr. Joseph Warder published his first edition of his work on bees, "The True Amazons, or The Monarchy of Bees." This work went to the ninth edition, published in 1765.

Maraldi, a mathematician of Nice, in 1712, published the first edition of his work on bees. He was the first to invent a glass hive, in which the indoor proceedings of the bees could be seen; and his description of the manners, genius, and labours of the bees, which was published in the Memoirs of the Royal Academy of Sciences in 1712, gave a wonderful stimulant to the study of bees. Maraldi was the first to measure the angles of a bee's cell. He was struck with the fact that the three lozenge-shaped plates, forming the base of a bee's cell, always had the same angles, so he took the trouble to minutely measure them, and found that in each lozenge the large angles measured 109° 28′, and the smaller 70° 32′, the two making 180°, the equivalent of two right angles. He also noted the fact that the apex of the three-sided cup was formed by the union of three of the greater angles, 109° 28′.

Some time afterwards M. Reaumur, thinking that this remarkable uniformity of angle might have some connection with the wonderful economy of space, which is observable in the bee-comb, hit upon a very ingenious plan. Without mentioning his reason for the question, or telling him of Maraldi's researches, he asked Koenig, the celebrated mathematician, to make the following calculation:—"Given a hexagonal vessel terminated by three lozenge-shaped plates; what are the angles which would give the greatest amount of space with the least amount of material?"

Koenig made the calculations, and, by employing what geometricians denominate the "Infinitesimal calculus," he found the large angles should be 109° 26′, and the smaller 70° 34′, or about two-sixtieths of a degree, less or more, than the actual angles made use of by the bees, and measured by Maraldi.

Mathematicians were naturally delighted with the result of the investigation; for it showed how beautifully practical science could be aided by theoretical knowledge, and the construction of the bee-cell became a famous problem in the economy of nature.

In comparison with the honey which the cell is intended to contain, the wax is a rare and costly substance, as the bees consume about one pound of honey to make one ounce of combs. The wax is secreted in very small quantities, and requiring much time for its production; it is, therefore, essential that the quantity of wax employed in making the combs should be as little, and that of the honey contained in it as great as possible.

For a long time these statements remained uncontroverted; any one with proper instruments could measure the angles for himself, and the calculations of a mathematician like Koenig would hardly be questioned. However, Maclaurin, the well-known Scotch mathematician, was not satisfied. The two results very nearly tallied with each other, but not quite; and he felt in a mathematical question precision was a necessity.

So Maclaurin tried the whole question himself, and found Maraldi's measurement correct, namely, 109°28' and 70°32'. He then set to work at the problem which was worked out by Kœnig, viz., "What ought to be the angles of a six-sided cell with a concave pyramidal base, formed of three similar and equal rhomboidal plates, so that the least possible matter should enter into its construction?" Maclaurin found the true theoretical angles were 109°28' and 70°32', precisely corresponding with the actual measurement of the bee-cell.

Another question now arose. How did this discrepancy occur? How could so excellent a mathematician as Kœnig make so grave a mistake? On investigation, it was found that no blame attached to Kœnig, but that the error lay in the book of logarithms which he used. Thus a mistake in a mathematical work was accidently discovered by measuring the angles of a bee-cell; a mistake sufficiently great to cause the loss of a noble ship and the lives of all its gallant seamen, whose captain happened to use a copy of the same logarithmic tables for calculating his longitude. All honour due to Maraldi, Reaumur, Kœnig, and Maclaurin.

> " How most exact is Nature's frame!
>   How wise the Eternal mind!
> His counsel's never change the scheme
>   Which his first thoughts designed."
>
> " On books deep poring, ye pale sons of toil,
>   Who waste in studious trance the midnight oil,
> Say, can ye emulate with all your rules,
>   Drawn from Grecian or from Gothic schools.
>
> This artless frame?   Instinct her simple guide,
>   A heaven-taught insect baffles all your pride.
> Not all yon marshal'd orbs, that ride so high,
>   Proclaim more loud a present Deity.
>
> Than the nice symmetry of these small cells,
>   Where on each angle genuine science dwells,
> And joys to mark, through wide creation's reign,
>   How close the lessening links of her continued chain."—*Evans.*

The French natural historian, M. Reaumur, stands prominent among the students of entomology, for the unsurpassed enthusiasm and accuracy with which he has investigated some of its most intricate parts. To him the genus Apis is under greater obligations perhaps than to any entomologist either of ancient or modern times. See his immortal work, in 6 vols. 4 to. 1732, 1744, *Mémoires pour servir à l' Histoire des Insectes.*"

About this period also flourished the great, the illustrious Linnæus, whose labours diffused light over every department of natural science, and have justly caused him to be regarded as one of its brightest ornaments. He has generally been considered as the founder of the artificial system of arrangement; but a very near approach to it was made by that brilliant constellation of naturalists whom I have enumerated as having flourished at the close of the seventeenth century, and who may probably be regarded as having paved the way, and prepared materials, for the formation of his more perfect system.

Afterwards appeared the works of the celebrated M. Bonnet, of Geneva, in 1745, the admiring correspondent of Reaumur, and the patron and friend of Huber. This great physiologist became addicted to the study of entomology before he was seventeen years of age, from reading *Spectacle de la Nature*; and his decisive experiments upon Aphides do him the highest credit. His works are universally admired for their candour and ingenuity, as well as for their manifest tendency to promote the happiness of man, by exciting in him the love of knowledge and virtue.

The Rev. John Thorley's excellent work on bees, "The Female Monarchy," appeared in 1744, and was succeeded by the Rev. Stephen White, who invented the collateral bee-hives in 1756.

The Society for the encouragement of Arts, Sciences, Manufactures, and Commerce, in England, offered four hundred pounds to encourage bee-keeping in 1765 (a very large sum in those days). A premium of five pounds was given to every person who had in his possession on February 1st, 1766, being his own property, any number of stocks of living bees, in hives or boxes, not less than thirty; and also a premium of five pounds to every person who shall take ten pounds of merchantable wax, from any number of stocks of living bees, in hives or boxes, who shall preserve their lives till the 1st of March, 1767; but in case there shall be more claimants than the sum of four hundred pounds, shall be distributed between the candidates, in proportion to the number of claimants.

This gave such a great impulse to bee-keeping that I have a list with the names of the authors of no less than forty-two works written on bees during the next six years, amongst whom was the celebrated Wildman, 1768, who performed numbers of wonderful feats with bees, that have never been equalled in any country up to the present time. For instance, when he appeared before King George III., standing upright on horseback, with a swarm of bees suspended in garlands from his chin, like a great beard, and after transferring them from his chin and breast to his hand, stretched out to full length, and then on firing a pistol the bees all swarmed in the air and went back to their hive, with numbers of other equally wonderful performances.

The following is a copy of his advertisement :—"June 20, 1772. Exhibition of bees on horseback! at the Jubilee Gardens, Islington, London, this and every evening until further notice (wet evenings excepted). The celebrated Mr. Wildman will exhibit several new and amazing experiments, never attempted by any other man in this or any other kingdom before. The rider standing upright, one foot on the saddle and one on the neck, with a mask of bees on his head and face. He also rides standing upright on the saddle with the bridle in his mouth, and, by firing a pistol, makes one part of the bees march over the table, and the other swarm in the air and return to their hive again, with other performances too tedious to insert. The doors open at 6; to begin at a quarter before seven. Admittance :—Box and gallery 2s.; the other seats, 1s."

These performances were considered at that time as feats of legerdemain or witchcraft, but the secret of Wildman's skilful manipulation with bees is well understood now; it consisted of a careful holding and disposal of the queen, together with confidence in the generally inoffensive disposition of bees. Dr. Evans thus speaks of Wildman's feats :—

> "Such was the spell which, round a Wildman's arm,
> Twined in dark wreaths the fascinated swarm ;
> Bright o'er his breast the glittering legions led,
> Or with a living garland bound his head,
> His dextrous hand, with firm yet harmless hold,
> Could seize the chief, known by her scales of gold ;
> From 'mid the wandering train, her filmy wing,
> Or o'er her folds the silken fetter fling."

We now come to the physiological discoveries of Schirach, 1761 ; Hunter, 1789 ; Huber, 1796 ; and others, men who have wonderfully advanced the science of entomology by a series of experiments most ably conducted, by the most patient investigation, and the most accurate and enlightened observation, and placed it upon the solid foundation of rational induction.

Several other writers also, both in systematic works and in periodical publications, have contributed to throw much light upon the economy and habits of the bee. Amongst whom was John Keys, who published his first work " The Practical Bee Master" in 1870. My father was a disciple of Keys, and adopted his system, and never killed his bees to take the honey. He was a very humane good man, and almost the first thing he taught us was

> " Take not that life, thou canst not give,
> For all things have an equal right to live."

I have now some bees in a wood hive that my father got made in 1806, on Keys' system, and there has been bees in it from nearly that time to the present, yet it is as sound and good as the day it was made. This shows the great durability of wood over straw hives.

The immortal Thomson thus describes the barbarous practice of murdering the bees with sulphur, to take the honey, in his own energetic language :—

> Ah, see where robb'd, and murder'd, in that pit
> Lies the still heaving hive ! at evening snatch'd
> Beneath the cloud of guilt-concealing night,
> And fixed o'er sulphur : while, not dreaming ill,
> The happy people in their waxen cells
> Sat tending public cares, and planning schemes
> Of temperance, for winter poor ; rejoiced
> To mark, full flowing round, their copious stores.
> Sudden the dark oppressive steam ascends ;
> And, us'd to milder scents, the tender race,
> By thousands, tumble from their honeyed domes,
> Convulsed, and agonising in the dust.
> And was it then for this you roam'd the spring,
> Intent from flower to flower ? For this you toil'd
> Ceaseless the burning summer-heats away ?
> For this in Autumn searched the blooming waste,
> Nor lost one sunny gleam ? For this sad fate !
> O man ! tyrannic lord ! how long, how long,
> Shall prostrate nature groan beneath your rage.
> Awaiting renovation ? When obliged,
> Must you destroy ? Of their ambrosial food
> Can you not borrow ? and in just return,
> Afford them shelter from the wintry winds ;
> Or, as the sharp your pinches, with their own
> Again regale them on some smiling day ?
> See where the many bottoms of their town
> Looks desolate, and wild ; with here and there
> A helpless number, who the ruin'd state
> Survive, lamenting, weak, cast out to death.

For Thomson's humane appeal he has been thus apostrophised by Dr. Evans.

> " And thou, sweet Thomson, trembling alive.
> To pity's call, hast mourn'd the slaughter'd hive,
> Cursing, with honest zeal, the coward hand
>   Which hid in night's dark veil the murd'rous brand.
> In steam sulphureous wrapt the peaceful dome,
>   And bore the yellow spoil triumphant home."

I am pleased to be able to tell you that bee-murder is now practised by only the most ignorant people, as we have been able to show them at the meetings of the

British Bee-keepers' Association, that by murdering their bees, was like putting their hands in their pockets and throwing their money on the highway, as the bees are wanted to work for them next year.

Keys was succeeded by a host of writers on bees, including Sydserf, 1792; Bonner, the clever Scotch aplarian, in 1795; the illustrious Huber, 1796, the king of bee masters, who (although he was perfectly blind) made more true discoveries about bees than all the writers before him or since. Huber invented the first bar-frame hive; but his frames formed the hive, and the frames opened with hinges, the same as the leaves of a book. He was succeeded by Kirby, 1801; Buffon, 1812; Huish, 1815; and Dunbar in 1820.

Dr. Edward Bevan published his first work on Bees in 1827. This was the most scientific and useful work on bees that had been published in England up to that date, nay, I may say up to the present time it has not been surpassed by any English writer. He was succeeded by Thomas Nutt, who brought the collateral system so prominently forward in his work "Humanity to Honey Bees," published in 1832; and he says, "Is it not inhumanity to force bees to deposit their treasures in a garret, two or three stories high, when a far more convenient store-room may be provided for them on the first floor?" Now this sort of reasoning sounded very true and nice, but the bees' instinct taught them to reject his collateral boxes on the ground floor, and to deposit their honey in the highest, and consequently the warmest, part of the hive, as heat will ascend; so Nutt's collateral system has long since gone out of use.

Our late friend Rev. W. C. Cotton published his first work on bees in 1838, "Short and Simple Letters to Cottagers," of which 24,000 were distributed; and his enlarged work, "My Bee Book," in 1842, before he took the bees out to New Zealand, which so benefited the colony, as before the introduction of the honey-bee they had yearly to import fresh white clover seed (*Trifolium repens*), but by the agency of the bees they are now able to export it. We should have little seed or fruit if it was not for the agency of bees in carrying the pollen from the male to the female blossoms. On April 8th, 1870, I visited the residence, at Highgate, of our noble and good President of the British Bee-Keepers' Association, the Baroness Burdett Coutts, whose name is almost a household word. When I went into the peach house the gardener said to me, "See what a quantity of peaches I have got set." I looked round and said, "You have, indeed; how do you account for it." "Well," he said, "I have always kept bees to fructify my fruit bloom, but last autumn I bought a stock of Ligurian or Italian Alp bees, and they being hardier than the common English bees, they began working earlier, and got into the peach house just as the trees were coming into bloom, and the result is I have nearly double the quantity of peaches set I ever had before." So you see it is not only honey that we get from the bees, but nearly everything else that we grow. Mr. Cotton published and printed a work on bees in New Zealand in 1848, "A Manual for New Zealand Bee-Keepers." The natives called the bee the "White man's fly." In 1872 Mr. Cotton published a most amusing work, entitled "Buzz-a-Buzz; or, the Bees Done freely into English," from the German of Wilhelm Busch.

Major W. A. Munn published his first work on bees in 1844, and took out a patent for his bar-frame hive in Paris in 1843. Munn was the first to put a bar-frame inside a hive; but it was left to the Rev. L. L. Langstroth, in America, Rev. John Dzierzon and Baron Von Berlepsch, in Germany, unknown to one another at the time, to simultaneously invent the modern bar-frame hive in 1852, which quite revolutionised bee-keeping, and brought it to such great perfection that it has now become of national importance in many countries. These hives have rendered bee-keeping a more scientific study, as with them we have the full control over the bees, and can investigate all their proceedings whenever we like.

The Rev. John Dzierzon, the poor Carlsmark curate, published his first work on bees in 1846, and announced the discovery of the true doctrine of parthenogenesis in the honey-bee, or production by the queen, without having any intercourse with the male or drone bee. This is contrary to almost a universal law in the animal and vegetable kingdom, that he raised such a swarm of opponents, in nearly all the naturalists in Europe, who scouted the very idea of such a production, and raised such a host of objections against such a theory being true, that Dzierzon himself began to doubt the correctness of what he had seen with his own eyes. A number of them set to work to prove the fallacy of such a statement, but every experiment that was properly conducted only confirmed the correctness of Dzierzon's theory, and Professor Theodor Von Siebold (one of the most distinguished German naturalists and physiologists) fully confirmed this doctrine, after a laborious dissecting and microscopical investigation, he discovered a set of voluntary muscles for imparting some of the male element which is stored up in the spermatheca, to every worker egg, during its passage through the common oviduct. He also discovered lively spermatozoids in the semen of the drones, as well as in the contents of an impregnated spermatheca, and detected the same spermatozoids in worker eggs, whilst they were entirely wanting in those eggs that would produce drones.

This long and acrimonious dispute was at last conclusively settled, and it has explained many of the mysteries of the hive, in which the great king of bee-masters, the illustrious Huber, after discussing the effects of retarded impregnation, exclaimed, "It is an abyss wherein I am lost." All other great bee-masters have been equally lost in this abyss, until Dzierzon discovered the doctrine of true parthenogenesis, and it is now a confirmed fact that the queen bee has the power at will to lay drone or unfructified eggs, or fertilized worker eggs, and I have conclusively proved these statements with my own experiments.

All honour is due to pastor Dzierzon for his laborious observations, for which and his numerous other discoveries the Emperor of Austria in 1873 decorated Dr. John Dzierzon (formerly the the poor Carlsmark curate) with the Cross of the Knightly Order of Francis Joseph, and may he long live to enjoy his advancement and honours.

Dzierzon was succeeded by Miner, 1849; Rev. L. L. Langstroth and M. Quinby. who both wrote very excellent works on bees in 1853; and the Baron Von Berlepsch, who published his first work on bees in 1860; a second edition in 1868, in the production of which he bestowed immense labour, and it is said he read seventeen thousand pages, of the best bee-books in the world, to make it the most perfect bee-book ever published. The bee journals in different countries have done a great work in advancing bee culture.

I think I have now given you a short account of bee-keeping from the earliest date of which we have any records to the present time, the compiling of which has taken a very great amount of labour, and in conclusion I can truly say the culture of bees is indeed an object highly deserving the attention of the agriculturist, as well as of the natural philosopher. Their study is an endless source of pleasure, and the more you know about them the more you will want to know.

To go and sit down near your bee-hives when your mind is troubled with the cares, crosses, and afflictions of this life. the bees' soothing, happy hum, contented, busy

16

life, constantly going in and out of the hive, imperceptibly draws your attention from yourself and your great sorrow, for a time at least, and many an hour have thus been passed in comparative happiness by the poor sufferer that would otherwise have been spent in agony in mourning over his affliction or bereavement.

I will now conclude with the tale that some of you have probably heard of the good bishop and the curate.

Some years ago the Bishop was holding his first visitation of the clergy of his diocese in a town in one of the midland counties. Amongst those assembled he soon discovered an old college acquaintance whom he had not seen for a number of years. On comparing notes with his friend, he found he was still a country curate, at a stipend of £100 a year, and that he had a wife and a large family to support.

The worthy curate invited the bishop to spend a day with him, before he left the neighbourhood, and not wishing to appear proud, he accepted the invitation.

On reaching his friend's house he was surprised at the degree of comfort there was about everything, all the family being so well dressed, and the dinner was worthy of the traditional customary fare of his order.

After the ladies had retired, he said to his friend (knowing that he was originally a poor man) he was afraid that he had gone to an unusual expense to entertain him, and that it would entail privation upon him afterwards. "Not at all," replied the curate, "I can well afford to entertain an old friend once in a while without inconvenience." "Then," rejoined the bishop, "I suppose you must have got a fortune with your good lady." "You are wrong again, my lord; I had not a shilling with my wife. But I am a large manufacturer as well as a clergyman, and employ many thousands of operatives, which brings me in an excellent living. If you will walk with me I will show you them at work."

The bishop went with him into the garden, and there saw a splendid apiary, with a large number of bee-hives, the source of the curate's prosperity.

The bishop never forgot the circumstance, and frequently when he heard some poor curate complain of his income, he would cut the matter short by exclaiming, "There, there, let's have no grumbling. Keep bees, like Mr.———. Keep bees, keep bees."

If you wish for a pleasant and profitable recreation, I say with the good bishop of old, keep bees, keep bees, keep bees.

Longman's Magazine - XVI, 1885.

The Habits and Intelligence of Bees.

THE little busy bee has been a great favourite with the
moralists and philosophers of this much-preached-at world.
She and her works have been used to point so many morals
to the intended disadvantage of the lord of creation, when his
teachers take him to task in their sermons from the book of
nature, that it is time some one undertook a serious examination
of the claims of the little creature to be always posing as an
example to the rest of the world. Not that it is to be expected
that she would become less a subject of wonder and admiration,
but rather because it would be interesting to be able to judge the
exact amount of credit and respect to which she is entitled as an
intelligent author of her own exemplary conduct.

There is no doubt at all events about the place of the bee in
the insect tribe. In common with her cousins the ants, wasps, &c.,
she belongs to the order of hymenoptera, ranking first in the
insect series not only in the higher development of the cerebral
ganglia, and general intelligence in habits and mode of living which
this implies, but also in general completeness of form and structure. When bees are spoken of, the representative of the family
most familiarly associated with the name is the ordinary honey-bee
(*Apis mellifica*) which has for countless generations lived, laboured,
and died an ignominious death in the straw skeps of our rustic
gardens. The common variety is often known as the German
bee, its original home having been the woods and mountains of
Central Europe. A successful rival of late for the notice of the
intelligent apiarist is the Ligurian bee (*Apis ligustica*) introduced
from Italy, where in course of time, thanks to enforced separation
from its relations north of the high ranges of mountains which hem
in its native land, it developed those slight differences in structure
and colour which now mark it as a separate variety. Both
varieties were unknown in North America, until they were
introduced from Europe; but they have thriven and multiplied
enormously in their new home, especially in the Western States,
where they are still known amongst the Indians as the white

man's fly.   The other bees known in this country are the humble
bees, of which there are several varieties; but, although very
interesting in their behaviour and habits, as will be seen further
on, these are but the bumpkins of the bee family, who are content
to spend their rude lives in arcadian dulness, living from hand to
mouth, with no capacity for the aspiring life and higher civilisation
of their more gifted relations.

I am not a bee-keeper in the proper sense of the word.   In
my opinion, that occupation, on a large scale at all events, should
in this country be left entirely to those possessed of an unwaver-
ing faith in our variable climate.   My bees are not required,
as the British workman sometimes holds himself to be, to toil
from early morning to night, that the fruit of so much labour
may one day be thanklessly appropriated for the benefit of a
greedy master.   If they choose, they need trouble themselves
little for the future; for, if they have finished an unsuccessful
season spent in rummaging the gardens of my neighbours
around Clapham Common, the sweet stores of the nearest
grocer are always liberally drawn upon for their benefit.   One
small colony is quite at home on a small stand in my room,
having access to the outside through a little tube passing underneath my window-sill.   The little creatures are, however, quite as
anxious to get into the room as they are to go outside, for they
probably think from experience that the world would be on the
whole a very fine place to live in, if the good things thereof were
within such easy reach as they usually find them when they are
admitted from this side.   Let me draw up the slide a little.
There they are; the little heads thrust expectantly forward,
squeezing each other in the endeavour to force a passage underneath.   One little amazon has pushed her way through; and, as I
want to introduce her to you, we will shut the door on the rest.

She is too much preoccupied rushing about in search of
expected sweets to make her bow to the British public at the
present moment.   Look at her as she travels inquiringly round;
is she not a well-bred, intelligent-looking little creature?   Anyone
can judge for himself, without finding it necessary to take a slice
of her little brain to Professor Luys, to look at through his
microscope.   Intelligent in every motion, clean cut, compact in
form, with no gaudy patches of colour in questionable taste, but
refined, yet businesslike in appearance,—there is a general look
about her which stamps her at once as belonging to the highest
type of the insect race.   We do not entertain a proper opinion of

the importance of the little creature. In our dull way we are inclined to estimate her place in the world by the amount of sugar-water she and her tribe can contribute in the year, reserving a shrewd suspicion in the background that if the whole species were to be extinguished to-morrow it might unaccountably happen in these days of Yankee enterprise that the supply of honey in the market would be in no way diminished. But we greatly underrate the importance of our little friend. If the British nation were to be suddenly blotted out of the world, the even tenor of nature's ways would be very little disturbed; and, whatever the political world might do, the natural world would soon go on as smoothly and indifferently as if nothing had happened. But if our little friend the bee were to suddenly cease to exist, who shall describe the desolation and confusion which would invade the harmony of nature?   How many shy flower-virgins, in plain and hillside, would droop and pine for her coming! How many noble long-pedigreed families in wood and valley, finding life insupportable, would give up the struggle for existence, and become extinct!   How would nature herself change her brightest hues and dress herself in sombre colours to mourn our little friend!

In these days of popular science it is hardly necessary to make more than passing reference to the part which the bee plays in nature. In the vegetable world it is a vital necessity that the fertilising pollen from the stamens of certain flowers should be carried to the pistils of other flowers, and the mission of the bee is to unconsciously carry the precious dust from blossom to blossom in her search after the tempting drop of nectar with which the shy flowerets reward the winged bearer of their love-messages. A wonderful and fascinating chapter in natural history is that which treats of the relations existing between flowers and insects. Flowers may be divided into two classes, those fertilised through the action of the wind, and those in which fertilisation is effected through the intervention of in-sects or a like agency. Darwin and others have shown what interesting stratagems flowers of the latter class resort to in order to secure the services of insects in this respect. Every little foible and weakness of the winged visitor is pandered to. What is commonly called a flower is indeed nothing more than a skilfully devised trap to attract the attention of insects, and then ensure their services towards fertilisation. Our little friend the bee is æsthetic in her tastes, and behold the varieties of flowers vie with each other to beguile her attention in the display of the most artistic blending of colours and beauty of design. She likes sweet scents, and the laboratory of nature is called upon to distil the choicest perfumes to humour her. But these are but an advertisement for the nectar which it is the principal object of the bee to obtain, and when she has alighted in search of it, it is only to find that the flowers have in many cases devised the most exquisite little mechanical arrangements whereby she is unconsciously compelled to effect the object towards the fulfilment of which they have indulged in such a lavish expenditure of beauty and sweetness. It is all effected in the simplest manner through the great law of natural selection, here seen in operation in its severe simplicity; for the flowers of those plants which present the greatest facilities for fertilisation get their seeds set, and so ensure the continuance of their species, while the unsuitable and unaccommodating kinds remain barren and are gradually weeded out. In a babel of tongues, and since first he found a voice, the poet has sung of the loves and sorrows of mankind, but nature still waits for him to interpret her heart; if he ever learns to do so, there will be a new song in his mouth, for he will have a wonderful theme.

But nothing is perfect in this world, and I may, perhaps, be permitted a moment's digression here to refer to an instance on record of a wicked attempt to frustrate the design in all this adaptation of means to an end. My attention was first directed to the subject on the occasion of a letter which appeared in *Nature* some years ago referring to the export to New Zealand of two nests of our ordinary English humble-bees, in the hope that their descendants would come to the rescue of the colonists, who found that the red clover introduced from Europe would not set its seed and propagate its species in their country in the absence of the kindly help of the little attendants for whom it provides its honey. The writer expressed the hope that the humble-bees exported were not of a variety which he had observed had fallen into bad habits, in that the individuals, instead of obtaining the honey from the red clover in the manner intended by nature, had learnt to take unlawful possession of it by snipping a hole through the base of the tube containing it, without, of course, effecting the fertilisation of the flower in the act. I have myself often since had my attention directed to this habit in these bees, and it appears to be well established that this propensity to subvert the purposes of nature is largely developed in humble-bees under certain circumstances, and not only in the case of the flowers of the red clover, but also those of the scarlet-runner and other plants. It appears, indeed, that our hive-bees also, if they are not actually guilty of the practice, do not scruple to take advantage of the easy access to the honey thus provided for them. Such practices, if they were to become the rule, would soon bring their own obvious punishment.

Like many of the disreputable shifts resorted to in trade, this habit is in all probability the result of fierce competition for the means of obtaining an honest livelihood—another example of the action and interaction of the various causes which silently produce change and progress in nature. The hive-bee, thanks to its habit of storing up food for winter use, as well as to the protection of man, is able to start work early in the year, and during the months of April, May, and June, it practically has the range of our fields and meadows all to itself. The colonies of humble-bees, however, store up no honey, and do not live through the winter, only a few of the young queens of last season surviving. In April and May the poor queen-mother has to seek out a retreat in which single-handed she proceeds to rear what only towards the beginning of July becomes a large family. Now when these issue forth to forage in the fields they find in many districts that, what with a host of competitors of their own kind—and the hive-bees, which are masters of the situation, having already turned the best part of the year to account —they can eke out but a very scanty subsistence, and so, like others in reduced circumstances, they take to the mostly illegal occupation of living by their wits. The humble-bee, no doubt, finds it saves time to obtain possession of the honey in the manner described, the stratagem in all probability being principally resorted to in order to forestall her rivals by obtaining first access to the honey stored in young flowers which have not yet opened of their own accord. This interfering with the purposes of nature is not to be commended perhaps, but the poor humble-bees, for all that, deserve, in my opinion, considerable credit for the ingenuity thus displayed in seeking to hold their own under difficult circumstances in this hard world. Anyone may convince himself of the keen competition which prevails amongst bees of all sorts towards the end of the season if he will take the trouble to observe our fields or hedgerows for a very short space at this time of year, or if he will count the number of times in an hour that a particular blossom is visited by a bee—or would be visited if it contained honey, as it is not necessary for a bee to alight on a flower to know that she must go away empty. Darwin has left it on record, after carefully watching certain flowers, that each one was visited by bees at least thirty times in a day, and it cannot be supposed that the little visitors in such circumstances find much to reward their industry. Sir J. Lubbock has also shown that they will often visit from twenty to twenty-five flowers in a minute. It is very interesting to note that on such occasions bees always keep to the same species of flower during each visit to the fields, a seemingly unimportant fact first recorded by Aristotle, which has acquired new significance since we have learned what is the true relation existing between the bees and the flowers they visit.

Is the bee entitled to the eulogies which have been lavished upon her for so long as a tribute to instincts which some naturalists have held to be little short of reason? Entomologists of the present day seem to incline to the opinion that she is not. Despite the habits and wonderful social economy of bees, their acts upon analysis do not appear to be the result of such a highly developed intelligence as has been supposed.

For many generations naturalists have been loud in their praises of the architecture of the honeycomb, and they went into ecstasies when the mathematicians conclusively proved—after much disputing amongst themselves—that the bee in the structure of her hexagonal cell had solved the recondite problem of constructing her waxen storehouses with the maximum of strength and capacity combined with the minimum expenditure of material. Yet, however difficult it may be to believe it, it is now quite certain that the bee evinces no very extraordinary intelligence in producing the exquisite workmanship displayed in the honeycomb, with all its interesting arrangements of planes and angles. The first instinct of the bee was undoubtedly to construct a circular cell, and at present the work is always commenced by excavating a circular pit in the layer of wax from which the work proceeds. A moment's reflection will show that if all the cells were circular they would not fit closely together, and this would entail a great waste of space, as well as a large expenditure of wax in constructing a separate wall for each cell. Now, as the work of construction proceeds, both these undesirable contingencies are avoided in making the cell hexagonal, by simply straightening out, as it were, and eating away to a single thickness the original circular wall at the six points where it comes into contact with the walls of the surrounding cells.

If it were desirable to go into detail, it would be easy to show how easily and naturally this is accomplished in the manner in which bees work, and that without it being necessary to assume any extraordinary intelligence on the part of the little architects, who are guided by a few simple instincts, after the exercise of which the shape of the cell becomes a mathematical necessity.

Nevertheless, the honeycomb of the hive-bee is a wonderful instance of perfection in nature, and it has a place of its own in the story of evolution. Between it and the rude agglomeration of cells of the humble-bee there is a wide distance, and every step in the progress upwards has, no doubt, been taken through the operation of the law of natural selection.

The cells formed in the nest of the humble-bee arise in this way. The queen-mother commences by laying her eggs in a mass in a lump of matter composed of pollen and honey kneaded together, to form the food of the young grubs. When these are hatched out they burrow in the substance, and eventually spin their cocoons, and it is these cocoons, rudely fastened together with wax, which form the greater part of the irregular collection of cells found in the nests of humble bees. When the young bees have emerged, the empty cocoons are used for the storage of honey, and it is only when storage room of this sort is not available, that the bees display their rude attempts at the art of cell-building in forming rough waxen cups to hold the surplus honey. These last are the only cells which the humble bee actually builds, and in their structure it is not possible to trace even the rudiments of the wax-economising art of the hive-bee.

In tracing the development of the highly finished work of the hive-bee from such a rude beginning as this, it is only necessary to remember how vitally important to bees is the art of economising wax. It has been shown that the secretion of one pound of that costly material necessitates the consumption by the bees of from fifteen to twenty pounds of honey. It is easy to see, therefore, what an immense advantage it must have been to those colonies which long ago devised expedients for saving this precious material, and so were able to store up for winter use the large amount of honey which would otherwise have been consumed in its production. The advantage soon told in competition with other colonies, and so the progress was continued until the limit has been reached; for at the present time, in the structure of the honeycomb, perfection has been attained, there being simply no room for further progress.

The question to what extent bees possess the power of communication with each other has engaged the attention of many observers. Sir J. Lubbock's experiments with bees and also with ants were very interesting as tending to throw some light on this subject. He has shown that the ants of a colony recognised each other even after a separation lasting fifteen months. The bees of one colony always recognise each other also, even after prolonged absence, and, although it has not yet been clearly established, there seems to be good reason to believe that they do so principally by the sense of smell, and not by a pass-word or signal, as has been supposed. There is no doubt that bees possess a very keen sense of smell, and they are perhaps guided by it in many ways which it is difficult for us to understand. They evince a very strong dislike to all bad odours, and show a general preference for those smells which are pleasing to us.

An amusing instance of the dislike of bees to bad smells came under my notice some years ago. At the time in question there was in my father's garden a plot of early potatoes, some distance in front of a spot where stood several hives. Early in the season the rooks commenced to help themselves to the potatoes, grubbing the young tubers out of the ground, and doing so much mischief that some had to be shot, and the dead body of one was impaled in the middle of the plot as a warning and example to the rest. Soon after this a most unaccountable fury took possession of the bees. No one dared to approach them, for they attacked and instantly put to flight every person or animal which ventured into the garden. This went on for some days, with most unpleasant results, and the bees were fast becoming a nuisance in the neighbourhood, when the mystery was accidentally explained. Someone happening to pass by the impaled rook in the evening discovered the cause and centre of all the mischief. Every exposed part of the poor bird's body, especially about the mouth and eyes, was literally bristling with the stings of hundreds of bees, which had sacrificed themselves in a vain and senseless revenge upon its offensive presence. As the little creatures always die from the injury caused by the loss of the sting, the destruction must have been considerable amongst the bees, who in this case fell victims to their own extreme sensitiveness of smell.

It is often assumed that bees possess the power of communicating to each other ideas of a complex nature ; for instance, it has been stated that if a bee finds a store of honey, she will return with the news to her companions, who soon accompany her to share in the find. This is undoubtedly true of ants, but in their case the explanation is obvious, and observation and experiment leave no doubt that ants are guided principally by the sense of smell in following up the traces of a companion to the source from whence she has brought the food. This explanation, however, cannot be accepted in the case of bees, for it is not to be supposed that they could follow the track of a companion through the air by scent. It has not, however, been proved beyond doubt that a bee will lead her companions to a store of food in this way, though the experiments of Sir John Lubbock and others point to the conclusion that bees can bring friends, though they have not the power of directing them, to treasures at a distance.

As we owe to the bees' taste in colours most of the artistic arrangement of tints in our bright-coloured flowers, Sir J. Lubbock's experiments on the colour-sense in bees have attracted considerable attention. His experiments show that blue is essentially the bees' favourite colour; after which come, in order of preference, white, yellow, red, green, and orange. That there are not so many blue flowers as might be expected is explained by the probability that all plants with blue flowers are descended from ancestors with green flowers, which, under the influence of what may be called bee-culture, have passed through stages of white, yellow, and generally red before becoming blue.

Although the vision of bees is very good in some respects, they show little intelligence in finding their way in certain circumstances. Sir J. Lubbock experimented with a bee which he put into a bell-glass, turning the closed end to the light, only to find that she generally buzzed about for a long time in a vain endeavour to get out at the closed end, while flies placed in the glass in the same way soon made their escape.

I have always found bees very stupid in this way. Last summer I placed a nest of humble-bees in a large glass vase, some fifteen inches in diameter, and nine in height. I kept the nest in my room, and, for several days after it was placed in position, the workers crowded towards the side next the light, making vain attempts all day long to get out, and this although the top was quite open, and the surface of the nest only a few inches below the rim of the vase. It was some time before I noticed any of the bees get out, other than by what could only have been accident, although I watched the nest for some hours daily. It could not be said that the change in position of their home had unduly confused the older bees, for those born while the nest was under observation showed the same want of intelligence, and up to the end of the season in the daytime a few bees were always at the side of the glass next the light, beating about in a vain endeavour to get out.

Bees do not seem to possess the feeling of affection or attachment; even the respect for their queen savours of the coldest utilitarianism, and when through either accident or circumstances she ceases to be of use to the colony for the one purpose for which she is maintained, she is abandoned or superseded apparently without the slightest compunction or regret by her so-called subjects. Bees never seem to help each other in difficulty or distress, as is often done by ants. If you hold a bee captive by the leg, the others either take no notice of her struggles or do not attempt in any way to assist her. If you go further, and crush her to death, they quietly crowd around, and, in the most callous fashion, show their utter indifference by helping themselves to the sweet juices expressed from the body of their unfortunate companion. Yet if bees are fed regularly they often exhibit a kind of selfish friendliness somewhat akin to that displayed by the cats of the neighbourhood towards the cat's-meat man on his round. During several attempts which I have made to keep alive during the winter the queens of colonies of humble bees, I have particularly noticed it in those bees.

I first tried keeping the bees in little wooden boxes, which I always opened at feeding time, allowing the occupants to walk about for a little before putting them back in their boxes. I was surprised to find after a little time how the bees expected to be fed when the boxes were opened, coming familiarly on to my hand in search of food, and making themselves quite at home. One royal princess I had who always made such intelligent attempts to escape on these occasions that I was obliged to discontinue the practice in her case, and I fed her instead through an air-hole in the lid of her box. I, however, continued to take out her box with the others, and after a short time I was much amused to find her generally thrusting her long flexible tongue through the hole in the lid as soon as she knew that feeding operations were going on, as if she would by this means remind me that I must not overlook her. This bee I used to believe had a brilliant future before her, and it was a matter of great regret to me when I was one day the unintentional agent of her destruction. In mild weather she used to be always on the watch for an opportunity to get out of her box, and one fine

December morning when I lifted the lid she took a short flight across the room. In searching for her, I accidentally crushed her on the carpet beneath my slipper, and so ended her brief career.

Sir J. Lubbock, after many experiments on the power of hearing in bees and ants, states that he never could satisfy himself that these insects heard any sounds which he could produce. In the case of bees it would be a great surprise to many to hear that they are absolutely incapable of hearing, and it must not be assumed that they are so because experiments have as yet yielded no satisfactory result. From time immemorial it has been the habit with rustic bee-keepers at the time of swarming to invoke the aid of noise to hasten the alighting of the bees. With some, it takes the form of drumming on a tin kettle, others beat candlesticks together, or even put their faith in the strains of a concertina or violin. Everyone has his own theory as to the object of this performance. One does it to overpower the hum of the swarm so that the individual bees may think they are left alone, and so make haste to alight. Another does it to keep the bees in the neighbourhood with the charms of the music; and a third hopes to drown the notes of the guides which may be ready to lead off the swarm to distant parts previously explored in search of an eligible spot to alight in. It is remarkable, however, that all agree in assuming that the bees hear and are acted upon by the noise produced.

Sir John Lubbock has recently tried a further series of interesting experiments to decide the question as to how far the power of hearing is developed in bees. To what extent music has power to charm the bee or guide her instincts may be judged from the result of an experiment of which he read an account at a meeting of the Linnean Society in November 1882.

Some honey was placed on a musical box on his lawn, and the box was kept going for a fortnight, during which time the bees regularly helped themselves to the honey. The box and honey were then removed out of sight into the house, and, although placed near an open window and only seven yards from the previous position, the bees failed to find the honey, although those brought to it in its new position afterwards found the way readily enough. He, however, declines to say that bees are incapable of hearing, and thinks it not impossible that insects may perceive higher notes than we can hear, and may even possess a sense or perhaps sensations of which we can form no idea; for although we have no special organs adapted to certain sensations, there is no reason why it should be the case with other animals, while the problematical organs possessed by some of the lower forms favour this suggestion. He is of opinion that the sounds which bees hear may be not the low loud sounds but the higher overtones at the verge of or beyond our range of hearing.

It is, however, remarkable that bees certainly do seem to hear on some occasions. The note with which the old queen threatens the royal brood as they come to maturity, and swarming time approaches, and so well known to apiarists under the name of ' piping,' can often be distinctly heard some distance from the hive, and is evidently intelligible to the young queens, for they respond in tones perfectly audible to the listener. Although bees will take no notice of a very loud noise even quite close to the hive, it is, however, remarkable that the slightest tap on the hive itself, or any of its attachments, or even a heavy tread some distance off, immediately disturbs them.

Despite the study and observation to which bees have been subjected, their habits and instincts are still a promising and most interesting subject of inquiry. The strange relation of the sexes has received more attention than perhaps any other subject connected with these little insects, both on account of the interest attaching to it, and also because of its bearing upon other questions. The subject is, however, still full of difficulty, and the more it is investigated the more the interest attaching to it seems to grow.

In a colony of bees there are the drones (males), the queen (female), and the workers (neuters). It has long been known that the neuters are merely imperfect females, and the bees possess the wonderful instinct which leads them, in the event of the loss of their queen, to take a young worker grub or egg, and, by special feeding and the enlargement of its cell, to rear from it a new queen. It has been proved that parthenogenesis always prevails in the production of the male bee, the egg which produces a drone being always unimpregnated even when laid by an impregnated queen. A virgin queen will also lay eggs abundantly, and it has been conclusively proved that these eggs will come to maturity, and that they will invariably produce drones. Now, the bees always build a certain quantity of what is called drone-comb, in which the cells are larger than ordinary, and it is in these cells, and in these only, that the queen lays the eggs which produce drones. A knowledge of this circumstance first led to the assumption that the sex of the young bee was determined simply by the size of its cell, but this theory was soon abandoned, as it is settled beyond doubt that the sex of the egg is determined at the very moment at which it is laid. The theorists were then driven back on an ingenious explanation as to the mechanical effect of the shape of the cell upon the queen in the act of depositing the egg. This view has, however, also been rendered untenable by the result of experiments which place it beyond question that the sex of the eggs is altogether independent of the shape or size of the cells in which they are laid; for, with no drone-comb, the queen will sometimes lay drone-eggs in worker cells, from which eggs drones will be produced, and she will also, if necessary, though with great reluctance, lay worker-eggs in drone-cells. It would thus appear that we must concede to the queen bee the surprising instinct or intelligence which enables her to lay at will a drone-egg or a worker-egg, for in the hive she often passes immediately from the worker to the drone cells or *vice versâ*, depositing an egg at the bottom of each which always produces a bee of the sex intended. This instinct is rendered more wonderful when it is remembered that the number of drones produced in a hive is always regulated by the wants of the colony. The questions suggested by the manner of the production of the worker-bee are also highly interesting. It has been mentioned that the bees, when they require a queen, will take a worker egg or grub and by special feeding rear from it an ordinary queen bee. It has generally been stated that the young queen is in such cases fed with richer food known as royal food, but it seems by no means unlikely that we shall soon learn that this is slightly incorrect, and that the queen grub is in such cases simply fed with as much food as it requires. This would mean that the queen state is that to which all the worker-grubs would develop in normal circumstances, and that the bees deliberately and for social reasons prevent this natural development by a *régime* of low diet. Mr. Cook, Professor of Entomology in the Michigan State Agricultural College, who has made a special study of bees, gives it as the result of his observations that the bees feed the worker-grubs sparingly, as if fearing an excessive development—a truly wonderful instinct which has enabled the bees to solve one of the most difficult of social problems. In the construction of the honeycomb the bees anticipated the mathematicians: have they not here again anticipated the philosophers?

Benjamin Kidd.

Bretts Colonists' Cyclopaedia.
1883

SCIENTIFIC BEE CULTURE.

[By I. HOPKINS, APIARIST, MATAMATA].

NOW that the modern system of bee culture has opened to the country settler another profitable branch of industry, a work of this kind would not be complete without the necessary information upon the subject to enable the beginner to start operations. Although it is impossible to give minute details where the space is limited, still sufficient will be found in the following pages to give the reader, in a general way, the knowledge requisite to make a beginning, and to put him or her on the right road to success.

There is no branch of rural economy more interesting or profitable, when carried on systematically, than the culture of bees. Previous to the introduction of the movable-comb hive, artificial comb-foundation, honey extractor, and other improved appliances, bee-keeping was but a precarious calling. The rude hives and implements then in use did not conduce to systematic work, nor did they allow the bee-keeper to acquire an intimate knowledge of the habits of the bee— only to be obtained by a thorough acquaintance with the internal arrangements of the bee-hive—so necessary to their successful management, and without which the bee-keeper is but working in the dark. Ten to fifteen pounds of honey to the hive was then thought to be a fair crop, and this was often spoilt by the fumes of the sulphur used in murdering the bees to obtain it; while at the present time, with the improved appliances and method of management, it is quite common to obtain an average yield of 100 lbs. to the hive through an extensive apiary, and in single instances as much as 800 lbs. have been obtained by the use of the extractor, without necessarily the destruction of a single bee. Moreover, the honey can be obtained as pure as when brought in from Nature's own repository—the flowers. As the outlay for a hive, or a few hives, and bees to start with is so very small, it is within the means of every settler to test the matter without fear of much loss, even though he did not succeed. To every settler and suburban resident I would, therefore, say: Keep bees, but only as many as you can properly manage; for they will not only be found profitable, but you will gain a large amount of interesting and useful knowledge.

Before proceeding with the main part of this paper it will be necessary to give the beginner a few hints, which will be found valuable. First—study well the habits of the bee, for in this knowledge lies the foundation of successful management. Second—visit, if possible, an apiary conducted on modern scientific principles. And lastly—use only those hives and appliances which are in use amongst the most advanced apiarists; don't go striking out on a new line, as some are very apt to do, until you have gained experience, as those who have for years made bee culture their study are the people most likely to have the best knowledge of the subject.

INMATES OF THE HIVE.—During the greater part of the honey season, the main portion of which may be said to extend in this country from the beginning of October to end of February, the inmates of the hive consist of three kinds of bees—the Queen, Workers, and Drones. THE QUEEN (Figure 1), of which there is only one in a hive, is the mother of the colony, she being the only bee capable of laying eggs which will produce Workers or Queens. The loss of the Queen, unless the bees have the wherewithal to raise another, means ultimately the loss of the whole colony—so that it will be understood how important a matter it is to see that there is a healthy prolific Queen at the head of each hive. Her sole occupation appears to be laying eggs, her capacity for which is amazing.

FIG. 1.—QUEEN.

In the ordinary way, she commences to lay sparingly about the beginning of August, and, as the mild weather sets in, increases gradually, until honey is being gathered in considerable quantities, when she lays to her full capacity, which in a young, healthy Queen, will be over 2,000 eggs per day. As the Queen is in her prime the second season, it is better—unless she has some superior qualities—that she be superseded by a young Queen after the third season. Her development is as follows :—A cell is built on the edge or surface of the comb, somewhat resembling an American peanut in size and shape, in which an egg is deposited differing in no way from the Worker egg. In three days the egg hatches into a larva or grub, when it is fed profusely with a jelly-like substance. For the next five days the grub grows very rapidly, and is then sealed or capped over; and in eight days more, or in sixteen from the laying of the egg, the Queen comes forth a perfect insect. The impregnation of the Queen takes place while she is on the wing, and is usually accomplished within four or five days of her hatching, when she takes her "wedding flight" to meet the Drones. She commences to lay a few days after, and does not leave the hive again unless accompanying a swarm. She lives for four or five years under ordinary circumstances. She is furnished with a sting, but only uses it against a rival Queen. She may be recognised by her body being longer and more tapering than the Drone or Worker; her wings are much shorter in proportion to the other bees; and her abdomen is of a dark colour on the upper part, and lighter underneath than any of her offspring.

FIG. 2.—WORKER.

THE WORKER bees form the bulk of the population of a hive. They are undeveloped females, whose ovaries are not sufficiently perfect to admit of their laying eggs except under peculiar circumstances. They are fitted by nature for carrying on the whole of the labour of the hive—such as building comb, secreting wax, gathering honey and pollen, carrying water, nursing the young larvæ, and ventilating and defending the hive.

On the number of Workers in each colony depends the profitableness or otherwise of the apiary. A strong colony will contain from 40,000 to 60,000 bees during the height of the honey season; and these are the kind of colonies we should strive to have; for no bees, no honey. Weak colonies are at all times unprofitable and a nuisance. The development of the Worker is much like that of the Queen, except that the egg is laid in an ordinary cell, and it takes 21 days,

Instead of 16, before the insect is matured. The Worker is furnished with a sting, which it will freely use in defence of self or home if not properly handled. Its length of life is short during the honey season, being only about 45 days; but after the season is over it lives for several months.

The DRONES are the male bees, and their only office appears to be to impregnate the young Queens. They are only to be found in the hive during the swarming season, after which they are killed off by the Workers. They are physically incapable of carrying on the ordinary work of the hive. As a few Drones in each hive are sufficient, the breeding of them should be limited either by cutting out all surplus Drone-comb, or, what is much more profitable, using all artificial Worker

FIG. 3.—DRONES. comb-foundation. The breeding of Drones commences shortly before the swarming season begins, and their appearance may be taken as a sign of its approach. The development of the Drone is the same as that of the Worker, but takes three days (24) longer to mature.

VARIETIES OF THE HONEY BEE.—There are several varieties of the honey bee, but the most important of those now cultivated are the Italian (Ligurian), Cyprian, and Holy Land bee. From my experience of the Italian and Holy Land bees I can fully corroborate all that has been said of their superior qualities as honey gatherers, and would advise their cultivation in place of the common bee.

IMPLEMENTS OF THE APIARY.—First in importance is the Movable-Comb Hive. No systematic work can be carried on in connection with bees where the combs are a fixture, i.e., built to the sides of the hive. Every comb should be movable, so that they may be taken out at any time, either for deprivation or to examine the bees. Combs to be movable should be built within frames (see figure 4), which are hung in the hive for this purpose. These and the hives should all be made of well-seasoned wood, and the hives well painted before being used. There are several kinds of hives in use, but the one I would strongly recommend

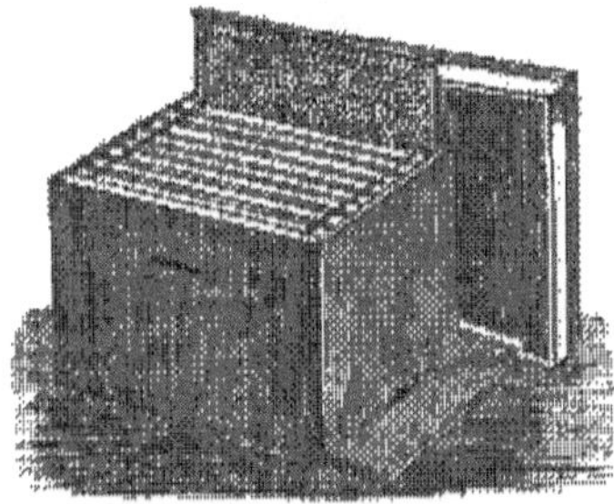

FIG. 4.—MOVABLE-COMB HIVE.

is the "Simplified Langstroth." After many years of experimenting with most of the principal hives I found this to be the best for all purposes. Its dimensions are: Body—length, 20¼ in.; breadth, 16 in.; depth, 10 in., outside measurement; and should be made of 1 in. timber planed on outside. Rabbets are cut on upper parts of ends, ⅜ in. down by ⅜ in. on, to form shoulders for the frames to hang on. The bottom board is made of 1 in. timber, 2 ft. long by 16 in. wide; two battens, 3 by 1 in., are nailed across the bottom to prevent twisting. The entrance is cut out of this (as in figure 4) ⅜ in. deep. The cover may be made either flat or sloping, as suits the maker's taste. The frames are ten in number and ⅜ in. wide; the length and depth are given in figure 5. They

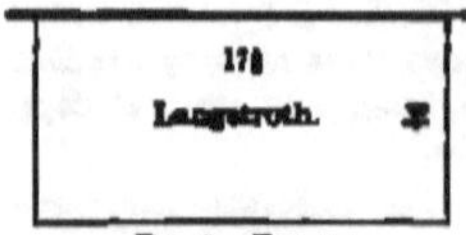

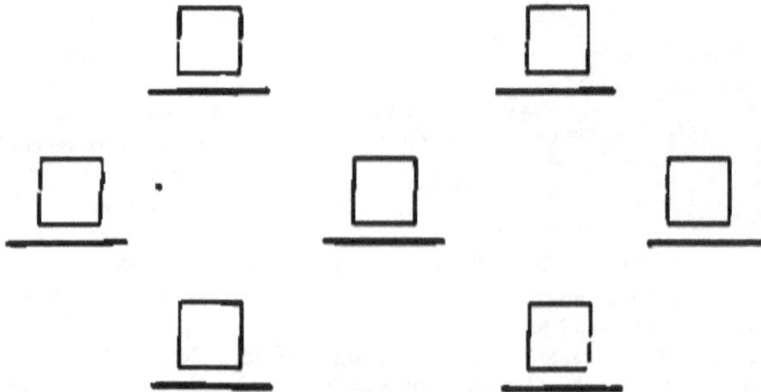

Fig. 6.—Frame.

should be made of ⅜ in. timber, except the bottom bar, which should be ¼ in., and left rough from the saw. Great care should be taken to have the different parts of the hive made to gauge, so that each may be interchangeable; and, above all things, do not use two kinds of hives, or trouble will be the result. The bodies of upper stories are made exactly like those of lower ones, and frames also when working for extracted honey.

BEE-VEIL.—All beginners should use a bee-veil, as it gives a sense of security against stings. It may be made of grenadine or any kind of gauze, and should slip over the hat, the lower part tucking in under the collar of the coat, as in figure 7.

THE APIARY.—There are very few places where bees may not be kept with profit; but in establishing a large apiary some previous knowledge of the district as to its honey-bearing plants is necessary. Near the bush, in a cultivated district, is one of the best positions for an extensive apiary. The hives should stand in a sheltered spot, near a shallow stream of water if possible, as bees require a deal of water during the breeding season. It is better that the spot be near the house, and away from stables or manure heaps, as bees dislike offensive smells. In preparing the stands for the hives, the bottom

Fig. 7.—Bee-Veil.

boards should be at least four inches off the ground, so that the air may circulate underneath and keep them dry. Four half bricks make a very good stand. In arranging the hives the plan given in figure 8 will be found the best. The entrances should be placed east or north-east if possible, and not less than six feet apart.

Fig. 8.—Hexagonal Apiary.

For shade, fruit-trees planted amongst the hives are both economical and the best shade that could be had; for the trees, being deciduous, would not prevent the sun warming up the hives, and drying the ground in winter. The workshop and honey house should be as near the apiary as convenient, and large enough to stack the spare hives and combs away in winter.

ARTIFICIAL COMB-FOUNDATION.—Next to the hive, nothing is so important in the apiary as comb-foundation. By its aid straight combs are insured, and built wherever required; it also saves the bees the greater part of their labour in secreting wax and building comb, thereby enabling them to gather more honey. I have a swarm of this season's that has built out fifty square feet and stored it with honey, and the season not yet ended (January, 1883). It is made by passing thin sheets of wax through a machine that imprints the bottom of the cells on each side. More broods can be raised and more honey stored in comb built on this foundation than in natural comb, as the cells are more perfect. It is invaluable to the apiarist, and there is nothing he can use with greater profit than comb-foundation.

FIG. 5.—HONEY EXTRACTOR.

HONEY EXTRACTOR.—This is an implement that no bee-keeper with a half-dozen hives can afford to be without. Combs built on foundation in frames can be emptied of their contents time after time, without injury, and be made to last for years. Honey taken by the extractor is as pure as when brought in from the flowers, and retains the respective flavour of each kind gathered from. The extractor (figure 6) works on the centrifugal principal; a wire basket inside a cylinder, into which the combs are put after being uncapped, is made to revolve rapidly; this motion throws the honey out of the cells into the cylinder, from which it is drawn off.

THE SMOKER.—No bee-keeper should be without a smoker. Smoke is the best bee-quieter known. It is not necessary to stupify them; a few puffs will cause them to rush to their honey, when they may be handled with little fear of getting stung. A roll of cotton rags, in the absence of a smoker, will answer the purpose, but is not so handy.

SWARMING.—From the middle of October to the middle or latter part of November constitutes the ordinary swarming season. The better condition the colonies are in the earlier will be the swarms. Swarming is the act of forming new colonies. As the warm weather of spring sets in, and honey is becoming plentiful, breeding goes on rapidly, and, as the hive is getting filled up, preparations are made to form a new colony by rearing young Queens. Although only one may be required to take the place of the old one, still the bees start several cells in case, I suppose, anything should go wrong with some of them. There are no indications of first swarms save the presence of Queen cells within the hive. The first swarm leaves the hive, if the weather permits, as soon as the first Queen cell is capped, or eight days before it hatches, so that a second swarm may be looked for about the ninth day after. If a second, or after-swarm, is not required, all Queen cells but one should be cut out soon after the first one

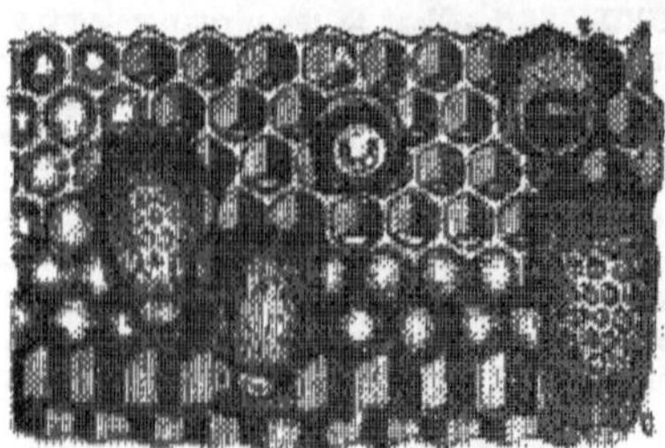

Description of Plate.—A, the ordinary Worker cell containing egg. B, Queen cell partly built, also containing egg. C, perfect Queen cell. D, cell built over Drone cell.

leaves. Figure 9, with explanation, will be a good guide to beginners in looking for Queen cells. Soon after the swarm leaves the hive it will settle on some tree or shrub near by, when it should be taken *at once*, by shaking them into any ordinary box and turning the box bottom up on a cloth spread for the purpose underneath. After a minute or so, raise one end of the box with a piece of wood or a stone, to allow any bees that are outside to go in, and shade the box from the sun. In the evening take the box and cloth to the hive they are to be located in, knock the bees out on to the cloth, and place the hive over them, taking care to have one end of the hive propped up to prevent the killing of any bees. After they are all up, place the hive on the bottom board and see the frames are all right, ⅜ in. apart. If working for surplus honey, the top box should be put on in four or five days, or as soon as the bees have three-parts filled the lower box, or they will make preparations for swarming again. When well at work in upper box, remove the frames as soon as filled and sealed and put others in their place.

ARTIFICIAL SWARMS may be made at any time when honey is abundant by taking the old Queen and three or four frames of bees and brood from a strong hive and putting them in another on a new stand. If there are any spare Queens on hand, one should be introduced to the old hive, or, if left to themselves, the bees will at once commence rearing another to take the place of the old one.

QUEEN REARING.— Every bee-keeper should rear his own Queens from his best stocks, and not allow the bees to breed them indiscriminately. A few should always be kept on hand for an emergency, as it may be the means of saving a colony. In raising Queens, select your best stocks, and, either by artificially swarming them, or taking frames of eggs from them and inserting them in other colonies, after taking out the Queens and all eggs and uncapped larvæ, a quantity of cells may be procured. These may be taken out about the fourth day after they are capped—leaving one, of course, in the hive—and inserted in combs, to be given to Queenless colonies or to nuclei to rear, and afterwards introduced wherever needed. A nucleus colony is made by taking one or two frames of bees and brood, *without the Queen*, and putting them into a small hive holding three frames; the other frame may contain an empty comb or sheet of foundation. By rearing Queens in this manner from an Italian stock the whole apiary may be Italianised in a short time.

INTRODUCING QUEENS.—This is done by making a small cage of wire cloth to confine the Queen you wish to introduce, and placing the caged Queen between two combs in the hive where you require her, after taking out the old Queen, or any Queen cells the bees may have built. The cage should be placed over some honey, so that the Queen may obtain food. In forty-eight hours release the Queen, and if the bees are unfriendly towards her, cage her again for twenty-four hours, and try once more. Usually she is accepted in from twenty-four to forty-eight hours, and there is no further trouble.

TRANSFERRING.—Bees and combs may be transferred from common boxes to movable comb hives any time during the honey season, but it is best done in early spring, before the hives are heavy with honey. Bee-keepers have different methods of transferring, but for beginners the driving process is the best. Have your smoker well alight, and a hammer and knife in readiness; also a small board, a cloth folded on the board, and the new hive. Blow a few puffs of smoke into the entrance of the box, and remove it a yard or two away, placing the new hive in its stead. Turn the box upside down, and place another box of about the same size on top to receive the bees as they are driven. Now take two small sticks, and lightly tap on the sides of the lower box for about fifteen minutes; by this time the Queen and most of the bees will be in the upper box, when it may be removed, and placed near the new hive.

The old box may now be taken to pieces, and the combs removed, one at a time, as required. Lay a frame on the folded cloth, and place the comb in it; if not large enough to fill the frame, fill up with pieces, as in figure 10. Now

fasten the comb in the frame with pieces of wire, bent at each end to clasp the top and bottom bars. These should be put on both sides, when it may be hung in the hive. Proceed in the same manner with the remaining combs, taking care only to put in *straight Worker* comb; that containing brood should be in the centre. After

FIG. 10.—PIECES OF COMB TRANSFERRED TO FRAME.

all is transferred, shake the bees on to a cloth, and place the hive over them as in hiving swarms. In two or three days the bees will have fastened the combs, when the wires can be removed.

ROBBING.—Bees, with their many good qualities, have one bad one—robbing. When honey is not to be had legitimately they will pilfer it or any saccharine matter if they have an opportunity. After the honey season is over, weak colonies have but a poor chance of existing, unless well looked after. If robbing is once fairly started it is sometimes a very difficult matter to stop it. Therefore, no honey should be left about where bees can get at it; and all entrances should be contracted. If a colony is strongly attacked by robbers it should be removed to a dark, cool place, and the hive closed up for forty-eight hours, taking care that it is well ventilated. When put back it must be watched.

DISEASES OF BEES.—Bees are only troubled with two diseases worth mentioning—dysentery and foul brood. Dysentery is usually caused by cold and dampness combined. It may be prevented by keeping the bees in warm; comfortable, well-ventilated hives. Foul brood is a disease to be dreaded. It is a fungoid growth that exists upon the larvæ, and when once introduced—unless in the hands of an experienced apiarist—is very likely to destroy the whole apiary. It may be known by its offensive smell, and the cappings of the brood cells being concave instead of convex, and having small pinholes in them. The only cure for a colony badly attacked is to destroy it and burn the hive. If detected in its first stages it may be cured by uncapping the cells, and spraying a solution of salicylic acid and borax over the infected combs. The recipe is 129 grains of salicylic, 129 grains soda borax, and 16 ounces of water.

ENEMIES OF BEES.—Bees, like other living creatures, have their enemies, the principal of which is the bee moth. Although I have experienced

FIG. 11.—BEE MOTH.

FIG. 12.—LARVÆ OF BEE MOTH.

very little trouble with it here, in some countries it is a great pest. The moth is often seen flying round the hives in the dusk of the evening. It deposits its eggs in or about the hives; these in a short time hatch into grey caterpillars, and it is in this form that they do the damage, by burrowing through the combs and destroying them. Italian bees are said to clear them out most effectually; but, I think, in this country they give but little trouble to the careful bee-keeper. If combs stored away in winter be attacked, put them in a close room or box, and fumigate them by burning some sulphur and keeping the place closed up for a day or two. This will destroy all the larvæ.

WINTERING BEES.—There is very little trouble in wintering bees successfully in this climate; all that is necessary is to have the hives properly made, and to prevent them becoming damp. Ventilation is one of the most important things to attend to, especially in winter, although a cold draught must not be allowed to penetrate the hive. If a one-inch hole be bored in each end of the cover, and covered with perforated zinc on the inside—to prevent insects getting in—and a stout porous mat be laid over the frames, it will allow of ample ventilation without a direct draught. In districts liable to heavy frosts the bees should be crowded on to as few combs as they can conveniently cover, and a division-board placed on each side of them, thus contracting the hive, and so leaving very little space for cold air. Division-boards are made to fit inside the hive from front to back, and should rest on the bottom board to prevent the bees getting outside of them. Cushions to lay on top of frames, under the cover, are capital things to keep the interior of the hive warm in winter. They should be made of scrim or some other substance, and filled with chaff. This will not stop the ventilation, but will absorb any moisture there may be in the hive, when it can be taken out and dried.

FEEDING.—Under the old system of bee-keeping the feeding of bees was looked upon almost in the light of a crime. Their owners considered they ought to " work for nothing and board themselves ;" and yet there is nothing that can be done in the apiary that will tend to make it more profitable when judiciously attended to. When taking honey, the bees ought never to be deprived that close as to be liable to leave them in a starving condition, should the honey season suddenly fail. In preparing the hives for winter, care should be taken to see that there is sufficient honey in them for winter stores : about five frames are ample for an ordinary colony. But if any require to be fed, it ought to be done before the cold weather sets in. Next to sealed honey, a syrup made of good sugar is best for feeding. To every pound of sugar add a half-pint of water ; place it on the fire, and keep it well stirred until it has boiled a few minutes ;

when cool it is ready for use. Great care should be exercised when feeding that it does not excite robbing. To avoid this each colony should have the feed placed within its hive. In early spring a little food given to a colony will stimulate it, and cause the Queen to lay a greater quantity of eggs, thereby getting the colony strong at an earlier date, and so be in a condition to take full advantage of the whole of the honey season.

BEE PASTURAGE.—One of the most important things to be kept in view by those who contemplate the culture of bees on a large scale is the necessity of being in the immediate neighbourhood of good bee pasturage. A good clover district within a short distance of a native forest (mixed) is, I consider, one of the best positions for an apiary. The greater variety of pasturage we can secure the better—more especially early and late varieties, i.e., anything coming in before and after clover. The following list comprises some of the best honey-producing plants and trees in North New Zealand, together with their time of flowering :—

Willows	...	...	September	...	3	weeks
Fruit Trees...	...	...	„	...	6	„
Ti-tree (native)	...	...	„	...	4	„
Kowhi	„	...	„	...	4	„
Tauro	„	...	„	...	16	„
Mahoi	„	...	„	...	8	„
White Clover	...	...	October	...	10	„
Hinau (native)	...	...	November	...	4	„
Rata	„	...	December	...	4	„
Flax	„	...	„	...	4	„
Red Clover	...	...	„	...	10	„
Cabbage Palm	...	...	January	...	4	„

To the above list may also be added the pohutukawa, kahikatea, puriri, matai, tawa, tariri, mirau, karaka, native fuschia, and nikau, which blossom between October and March.

PLANTING FOR BEES.—Cultivating for bees is now engaging the attention of the extensive bee-farmers of America. Large areas are now cultivated with honey-producing plants that blossom at a time when there is a dearth of honey from the main pasturage. They are also made to come in to fill up any gaps between the flowering of the principal plants that form the main pasturage, thus extending the honey harvest considerably.

Amongst the principal plants made use of for artificial pasturage are mellilot clover *(mellilotus alba)* and figwort *(scrofularia nodosa)*. These two plants I have grown myself, and from my experience of them I should say they are two of the best honey plants known. They yield a delicious honey, and remain a long time in blossom. Spider plant *(cleome pungens)* and buckwheat yield a great deal of honey, but are not so valuable in this respect as the two first-named. To sum up the matter, it will pay the bee-keeper well to cultivate such honey plants as will come into blossom at a time when there would otherwise be a scarcity of flowers.

MARKETING HONEY.—There is nothing that requires greater attention at the hands of the bee-keeper than the style of marketing honey. The time has now gone past when honey could be sent into market in any form, without regard to cleanliness or taste, and find a sale. The bee-keeper who is careless, and does not strive to send his produce in the best possible shape to market, will find himself left far behind his more careful neighbour, who, adopting the neatest style, will realise the highest price for his honey. Packages for extracted honey should hold not less than 2 lbs., while some may be made much larger for the local markets. Tin, of course, is the best material to use, although honey put up in glass finds a ready sale, but is more expensive. A handsome label should be put on each package, stating the name of the apiary and producer, and the source from whence the honey has been obtained. A show card should also be furnished the retailer, so that no opportunity may be lost in bringing the article before the public. For comb-honey, one and two pound section-boxes are best. These should be well filled, sealed, and stored at the time the best honey is being gathered. They should be packed in crates, to be left with the retailer until their contents are sold, when they may be returned. Crates holding twenty-four one-pound section boxes are a handy size for sending long distances. The sections should be packed tight within the crates to prevent the caps of the cells being broken, and so causing the honey to leak. The names of the apiary and producer should be painted on each crate in a neat manner.

CALENDAR, AND BEE-KEEPERS' AXIOMS—*From the "Illustrated N.Z. Bee Manual."*—The dates in this calendar are arranged for the latitude of Auckland, N.Z., where the willows and earliest flowering peaches blossom about the beginning of September. By carefully noting the time of flowering of the above trees, the calendar may be made suitable for any locality in this or the neighbouring colonies.

JANUARY.—Late swarms may be expected during this month. These are generally much smaller than those issuing earlier in the season, and when two or more come off the same day may be hived together, thus making one good colony. If increase is not required, swarming at this time especially should be kept down by the methods given elsewhere. Remove all surplus honey as soon as sealed. Comb-honey in sections should be packed away at once, and, if necessary, fumigated to kill the larvæ of the bee moth.

FEBRUARY.—This is usually a hot, dry month, with but little forage for bees, and on this account a sharp look-out should be kept that robbing is not started. Great care should be taken in opening hives that strange bees do not get in, as this is liable to start it. Contract entrances if robbers are about. Timber may now be stacked in a covered place to get thoroughly dry for next season's use.

MARCH.—Should rains come during this month a considerable amount of honey will be gathered from the autumn flowers coming into blossom. See that some is being stored in the lower hive for winter use, and if any is taken from the top story, keep a supply on hand to give them again if necessary.

APRIL.—If rains have not fallen there will still be a scarcity of forage, when all hives should be examined and top boxes removed. Any that are found to be short of stores should be fed, either by giving them surplus honey from other stocks, or thick syrup. Unite all weak or Queenless colonies, also Queen-rearing nuclei. Contract entrances, and beware of robbing. Stow away all spare combs in fumigating house for winter.

MAY.—If the instructions given last month have not been carried out, they should be forthwith. Before the cold weather sets in, contract the hives with division boards, and see that the combs within the chambers contain sufficient honey. Cover mat close down, and make all snug for winter.

JUNE.—If the foregoing instructions have been attended to, the bees will need little attention this month, beyond seeing that the hives are kept snug and warm. If, however, any colonies should require feeding during cold weather, give them candy.

JULY.—Now will be the time, during wet weather, to make up hives, section-boxes, etc., for the coming season, so that everything may be in readiness when required.

AUGUST.—All hives should be examined on fine days during this month, to see that they are well supplied with food. Colonies that have had but a scanty supply for winter use are now getting short, and should be fed. Breeding commences this month, when more food will be required by the bees, and if rapid increase should be desired, slow stimulative feeding will be necessary; but great care must be taken that the colony is kept nice and warm, or the brood will be liable to get chilled, in which case foul brood may be started, this being one of the principal causes of that dread disease. If the inside of the hives be nice and dry, and ventilated, there will be little fear of dysentery, which is prevalent among colonies kept under the old box-hive system, during this and the next months. The bottom boards should be cleaned occasionally, on fine days, during the winter, to destroy the eggs and larvæ of the bee moth. To do this, lift off the hive, and place it on a temporary board alongside while cleaning the bottom board. Fumigate spare combs, if necessary.

SEPTEMBER.—The population of healthy colonies now increases very fast, and those intended to raise cells for Queen-rearing should be ready for swarming toward the latter part of the month. Give plenty of room for breeding and storing by moving division boards. Unite weak colonies, for one strong hive now is worth more than three or four weak ones.

OCTOBER.—This *should* be the great swarming month. Prepare nuclei for Queen-raising. Supersede all impotent Queens by giving young and vigorous ones. Artificial swarming may now be proceeded with. Now is the time to Italianise the apiary. The early part of this month is the best time to transfer. Put on top storys with frames of comb or sections, and never allow them to get too full before "depriving." Enlarge entrances, and keep the hives clear of weeds and long grass.

NOVEMBER.—Keep down after-swarming. Remove all surplus boxes and frames as soon as filled and sealed, and put empty ones in their place. Keep a few spare Queens on hand in nucleus hives.

DECEMBER.—The instructions given last month will apply to this. See that the hives are well ventilated and the grass in the apiary cut close.

I commend to the notice of New Zealand bee-keepers the instructions given for the necessary work of each month, and would ask them to neglect nothing, but to do what is needful at the specified time: and if this advice is followed I feel assured they will never regret having kept bees.

BEE-KEEPERS AXIOMS.—The following axioms for bee-keepers, by Mr. Langstroth, are like Shakespeare's writings, not only for to-day, but for all time:—1st. Bees gorged with honey never volunteer an attack. 2nd. Bees

may always be made peaceable by inducing them to accept of liquid sweets.
3rd. Bees, when frightened by smoke or by drumming on their hives, fill themselves with honey, and lose all disposition to sting, unless they are hurt. 4th.
Bees dislike any *quick* movements about their hives, especially any motion
which *jars* their combs. 5th. Bees dislike the offensive odour of sweaty animals,
and will not endure impure air from human lungs. 6th. The bee-keeper will
ordinarily derive all his profits from stocks, strong and healthy, in early spring.
7th. In districts where forage is abundant only for a short period, the largest
yield of honey will be secured by a very moderate increase of stocks. 8th. A
moderate increase of colonies in any one season will, in the long run, prove the
easiest, safest, and cheapest mode of managing bees. 9th. Queenless colonies,
unless supplied with a Queen, will inevitably dwindle away, or be destroyed by
the bee moth, or by robber bees. 10th. The formation of new colonies should
ordinarily be confined to the season when bees are *accumulating* honey ; and if
this or any other operation must be performed when forage is scarce, the greatest
precaution should be used to prevent robbing.

The essence of all profitable bee-keeping is contained in Oettl's golden
rule—*keep your stocks strong.* If you cannot succeed in doing this, the more
money you invest in bees the heavier will be your losses; while, if your stocks
are strong, you will show that you are a *bee-master* as well as a bee-keeper, and
may safely calculate on generous returns from your industrious subjects.

MISCELLANEOUS PAPERS.

EXPERIMENTS relating to the MANAGEMENT of BEES, in a Letter from Mr. Geo. Hubbard of Bury St. Edmund's, to Mr. More.

[From the Ninth Volume of the Transactions of the Society for the Encouragement of Arts, Manufactures, and Commerce.]

" AS I am induced to become a candidate for the premium offered for stocks of bees, class 128, I beg leave to communicate to the society the following experiments; the result of which, I flatter myself, will afford some information towards the management of those useful insects. In my early acquaintance with these entertaining creatures, my endeavours to increase my stock were continually disappointed, particularly in the early months, by saving moderate stocks; which was a matter of surprise to me, as my strong stocks throve amazingly, whether I kept them for work or swarming.

" Now, to ascertain the matter with sufficient accuracy, I determined to sacrifice three hives every year, one strong and two moderate ones. Accordingly, on the first of February, I suffocated a strong hive, after Thorley's method; and when I took out the combs, it surprised me much to find an abundance of brood: the eggs and maggots were innumerable, and many were next to emerging from their cells.

" It was then obvious to me, that the queen had begun to lay her eggs in the early part of January; and this appeared the more extraordinary, as the month of January had been very cold, from severe frosts and snow; and it was evidently too sharp for a bee to stir abroad.

" This circumstance refutes the general received opinion, that the queen never begins breeding till the weather proves mild, and you see bees carrying to their hives, the little balls of farina on their legs: but to investigate the matter more fully, there appeared in the combs, vast quantities of farina; and what was very curious, some of it seemed covered with a kind of varnish substance, in order to exclude the air from it; besides on the top of the hive, there was a considerable quantity of water, apparently collected there from the same cause that it does on a window, where a room is hot, and the external air very cold. The foregoing consideration clears up a point that has puzzled many authors; I mean, the laying up such quantities of farina: White, and

some

some others, suppose it to be real food, mixed with honey, for the old bees.

"The second hive, which had not above three pounds of honey in it, I suffocated on the first of March; the queen of which stock had not produced a single egg: the third stock I examined the first of April, and there likewise found no eggs. In the second year, I repeated the same experiments with the strong and weak hives as before, and the result was the same in every respect.

"But the third hive I reserved till the 20th of April, by which time they begin to gather honey from the gooseberries: on examining this hive, I found some eggs produced. Let it be observed, that this hive I was under the necessity of feeding, to keep them alive.

"I cannot in this place forbear taking notice of the surprising foresight which these wonderful insects seem to be endowed with: in the weak hive, not a single egg is produced, till honey gathering commences; but in the strong hive, the increase of young bees is there carried on with surprising avidity at a time when they are generally supposed to be in a torpid state; and this increase is perfectly safe in a strong hive, for they are never observed to work in the early months, as weak hives do.

"From the above experiments, it is evident you gain almost four months between the two stocks: besides, early in May the strong stock is almost ready to swarm; whereas the weak hive, by its prodigious decrease, occasioned from their constant working, and no young ones being bred, generally dwindles to nothing. Once, on a hot day in April, I had five of these weak hives driven out by plunderers, with their

different queens: for the strong stocks never let the weak ones rest, when they find the latter are much reduced.

"Sometimes, if the months of March and April happen to be cold and wet, so as to prevent their going out, a little feeding may give them sufficient strength to defend themselves; but those stocks seldom turn to any account: hence the reason why keeping bees in colonies have always failed; I mean, in this country; for, if you imprudently reduce your bees, by taking too much honey from them, so as to prevent the queens breeding in the early months, they must miscarry in the following summer. I cannot help condemning two authors, that have written on this subject, viz. Messrs. White and Keys, particularly the former: their opinions have given a surprising check to the cultivation of bees; I mean, their idle notions respecting situation.

"A popular opinion prevails with us, that no village will support more than eight or ten stocks; consequently, the villages in our country do not contain above ten old stocks, one with another; whereas I am confident that twenty times the number might be kept. But let us examine what Mr. White has written on this business: he directs you to swarm your bees, and the same year to take part of their honey from them.

"Now it is well understood, that it requires a large swarm, aided with a fine season, to make them produce five and twenty or thirty pounds weight in October; which weight is absolutely necessary for their future welfare: he also affirms, that if you leave them eight or ten pounds of honey in August, it will very well support them through the winter. Further comments on such management

ment are needless, as the reason of his failure is too obvious to require the thought of a bad situation, to account for it.

"Keys seems to have copied his sentiments respecting situation; but from what I have advanced in regard to keeping such a number of flocks, it may be necessary to examine what the bees collect from. I will first mention the tare, that inexhaustible support to bees, from which they gather the whole summer; and it may not be improper here to note, that it is not from the flower, but a small leaf with a black spot on it, which in warm weather keeps continually oozing. But from careful inspection at the time of their gathering, this nectareous juice may be seen oozing from every joint of the stem. A hundred acres of tares are grown every year within the reach of my bees; yet it was always said to be a bad situation, and not able to support more than eight or ten stocks: besides, if the month of June proves hot, the collection from the oak, lime, and sycamore leaves, is astonishingly great; as well as from the profusion of flowers, which nature exhibits in succession throughout the whole summer.

"From these remarks and experiments it is evident, that success depends entirely on leaving your bees strong in October; for by this plan they naturally get into a habit of swarming early, and, by having the whole summer before them, always get rich. Whenever an unkindly season happens, to prevent this, it is an invariable practice with me, to give all my swarms sugar and water, or honey, sufficient to make each stock produce thirty or thirty-six pounds weight: besides, I am never disappointed of a swarm in May; and it is more frequent than otherwise, that these stocks will yield three

swarms each; the old stock likewise in general will be as rich as the prime swarm. On the other hand, if the stock is left moderate, though they may have honey enough to get them through the winter, yet some check may be given to the queen's breeding; of course it may be the middle of June, before they are ready for swarming; and if the weather turns out fine and hot, there is such a profusion of honey in the fields, and they are so intent after it, that no art can make them swarm; in that case, they will lie out the remainder of the summer, to the great loss of the owner. However, whenever this happens, I would advise all such stocks, after laying out a week, to be set on empty hives.

"I will now presume to offer a simple and easy mode of managing these admirable insects, the profits from which will far surpass that in common use. The owner must patiently wait till he has acquired twenty stocks, which may be soon accomplished by attending to the foregoing hints. In the month of April following, he must separate ten of the strongest hives for swarming; the other ten must be raised on large empty hives, the tops of which should be first taken off, and the joinings of the two hives secured with a little clay, which plan keeps the bees from swarming. In the month of September following, being the time I would recommend them to be burnt, each stock will seldom be found to have produced less than fifty pounds weight, provided it has been a kind season.

"The prime swarms from the other stocks, I would recommend to be put into three-peck hives, at least; for when they swarm so early, they are very likely to swarm again in a few weeks, which should always be prevented; and all the after-swarms

should

ſhould be united, two or three into one; for the great advantage ariſes from the large quantity of bees being kept together, ſince by that mode ten ſtocks will generally yield fifteen good ones. But the greateſt check to the cultivation of bees happens from inclement ſeaſons: I have experienced ſome ſummers, when it has rained, almoſt all the months of June and July, that not above one prime ſwarm in ten have been able to get a ſufficiency; this is really diſtreſſing; and on theſe occaſions, I have ſeen the ſtocks of villagers wholly ſwept off.

" This is another reaſon why double hives are ſo neceſſary; for, beſides the great profit ariſing from them in fine ſeaſons, it would prevent the decreaſe of ſtocks, which muſt unavoidably happen in bad ſeaſons. In the moſt unkindly ſummers, they are ſure to get enough to ſupport them through the winter: whenever it happens ſo, they ſhould ſtand till winter; and in a froſty day, the clay ſhould be removed, and a wire drawn between the hives, to ſeparate them; for by this time they will be all in the upper hive; and theſe ſtocks ſhould be reſerved for ſwarming the following ſummer.

" From a review of the above experiments, the reaſons are obvious, why people are ſo frequently diſappointed in the management of bees, eſpecially in the modern way; but, on the other hand, it ſhews what a ſurpriſing ſtate of cultivation they might be carried to; and ſuppoſing they could be brought to a ſtate of cultivation, that ten poor families in a village could keep twenty old ſtocks, beſides their own profit, it might become a national concern. Great pains have been taken, and

ſtill greater encouragement offered, for a plan to preſerve the lives of theſe uſeful and ſagacious inſects; which may be done by the intelligent; but cannot be expected from the cottager.

" My ſtock conſiſts of forty hives and boxes. The method I purſue in the management of bees is, to reſerve part of my ſtocks for working; for, by giving them room, they ſeldom ſwarm: and I always work them upwards; for, by that means, the queen is kept in the under hive, or box; and the honey ſo collected is of the pureſt quality.

" But is no eaſy thing to make them aſcend, to work through holes or bars ſo recommended by authors, as I have frequently known them ſwarm before ſo doing. My way is: if it is a hive, I take a piece out of the top, with a knife and chiſſel, ten inches diameter: thus, by laying a large ſurface of their comb bare, I am never diſappointed.

" But they will be induced to riſe ſooner, by placing a piece of empty comb, ſo as to reach from their own, to the top of the box or glaſs globe that is intended to be uſed: whenever it ſo happens, in wet ſummers, that each ſtock cannot get more than thirty pounds of honey, I always uſe Mr. Thorley's method, with the fungus; and I cannot help being ſupriſed that this ſimple method ſhould not be uſed, to ſave the lives of theſe uſeful inſects.

I am, Sir,

Your very humble ſervant,

Geor ge Hubbard."

Bury St. Edmunds,
October 29, 1790.

4. *Relation of a case of Poisoning caused by the Honey of the Lecheguana Wasp. By* M. Auguste de St. Hilaire.—" After having crossed the plains of the Rio de la Plata, I coasted the thinly-inhabited borders of the Uruguay, and arrived at the camp of Belem, on the locality of the town of the same name destroyed by Artigas. There I was told I should have to pass a desert destitute of habitations or roads, but that, in case of necessity, I could have recourse to two detachments of Portuguese soldiers posted on the banks of the river, and also that I could have a guide to the first detachment near the mouth of the Guaray. At the borders of this river I took another guide, who was to conduct me to the rivulet S. Anna, where I was told the second detachment was placed. Arrived at the rivulet, I and my men searched for

* Quarterly Journal, xvi. p. 388.

the detachment for two days; but our exertions being useless, I sent back the guide (he never having been farther), with one of the soldiers of my escort, to the river Guaray, directing the latter to return with another guide. In the mean time we waited on the borders of the rivulet, in a place inhabited only by a multitude of jaguars, immense troops of wild mares, stags, and ostriches, opposite the right bank of the Uruguay.

" For four days we were inconvenienced in this desert place, by heavy rains, and multitudes of annoying insects, with no other shelter than my cart. On the fifth day the weather became fine, and I went to botanize in the country about the river, accompanied by two of my men, all well armed against the attacks of jaguars. After some hours, hunger sent us back to the rivulet, and we ate of our usual food, the flour of the manhioc, and cow-beef, roast and boiled.

" During a short walk, the evening before, we perceived a wasps' nest suspended at about a foot from the earth, from one of the branches of a small tree. It was nearly oval, about the size of the head, of a gray colour, and of the paper-like consistence of European wasps' nests.

" After our breakfast, my two companions went to destroy this wasp's nest, and they took out the honey. We all three tasted of it. I ate most, but the quantity did not exceed two spoonfuls. The honey had a mild agreeable taste, and was quite free from the physic-like taste so often belonging to our bee-honey.

" After having eaten, I felt a pain in the stomach, not violent, but inconvenient. I lay down under my cart, and went to sleep; during which, those objects dearest to me were present to my imagination, and I awoke deeply affected. I rose, but felt such extreme weakness, that I could not take fifty steps. I returned to the cart, lay down on the grass, and felt my face bathed in tears. Blushing at my weakness, I laughed at myself, and notwithstanding my efforts, this laugh became lengthened and convulsive. Nevertheless, I had power to give some orders, and during the time my chasseur, one of the two Brazilians who had eaten with me, arrived.

" This man united, to rare intelligence, a light and fantastic character. Often, after long periods of amusing gaiety, he would, without any reason, fall into a dull melancholy state, continuing for weeks, and then he would find sources of irritation in the most innocent words and delicate attentions. His name was Jozé Mariano; he approached me, and said, with a gay but wild appearance, that for the last half hour he moved about the place without knowing where he was going. He sat down under the cart, making a place for me; I had much difficulty in reaching it, and feeling my extreme weakness, rested my head upon his shoulder.

" It was then that I experienced the most cruel agony, a thick cloud obscured my eyes, and I could perceive nothing more than traces of my men, and of the azure of the heavens traversed by a few light vapours. I did not feel much pain, but weakness of the extremest kind. Concentrated vinegar was placed near my mouth and nostrils, and rubbed on my face and temples; it reanimated me a little, and then I felt the pains of death. During this time, I preserved my memory perfectly, and remembered all that I had said, and that had been said; my recollections agreed perfectly with the recital of a young Frenchman who had accompanied me. A violent combat then passed in my mind, which continued, however, for but a few instants. I triumphed over my weakness, and resigned myself to death. That which affected me most was the fate of my Indian Botocudo, whom I had drawn from his forests, and who, I believed, would, after my death, be condemned to slavery. I conjured those around me to have pity on his inexperience, and to tell my friends that my last thoughts had been for that unfortunate young man. I felt an anxious wish to talk in my native language to the Frenchman who was earnest in his cares for me, but I was unable to find a single word in my memory which was not Portuguese, and I cannot express the shame and contradiction I felt at this want of recollection. I had at first endeavoured to take water and vinegar, but finding no relief, I requested warm water: each time that I swallowed it, I felt the cloud removed from my eyes for a few moments, and I began to drink it in very large quantities. I continually requested a vomit of my young Frenchman, but he could not find one. He searched in the cart, and I, being beneath it, could not see him. I nevertheless seemed to have him before my eyes, and reproached him for his slowness. This was the only error into which I fell.

" Whilst this was passing, the chasseur had risen without my perceiving it, but my ears were quickly struck with the dreadful cries he uttered. I was a little better at this moment, and none of his motions escaped me. He tore his clothes furiously, threw them far from him, took a gun, and discharged it. The piece was taken from him, and then he began to run about the place, calling the Virgin to his help, and crying out that all was on fire about him, that we two were abandoned, and that they were going to leave our portmanteaux and cart to be burnt. A Guarina man, (one of my suite) having endeavoured in vain to restrain him, was seized with fright, and fled.

" Until this time, I had had the attentions of the soldier who had joined us in eating the honey, but he was now very ill; he however soon vomited, and being of a robust temperament, he quickly recovered strength, though it required some time perfectly to re-establish him. I have understood since, that during the whole time he was extremely pale, his figure being frightful. On a sudden he said, " I shall go and tell what is passing at the Guard of Guaray." He mounted a horse, and galloped over the country, but the young Frenchman soon saw him fall; he rose, galloped a second time, fell again, and was found by my men profoundly asleep, some hours after, in the place where he fell.

" I then found myself almost dying, with no other than a man still furious, my Indian Botocudo, who was merely an infant, and the young Frenchman, who was almost distracted by these extraordinary events. All the morning we had perceived insurgent Spaniards on the other side of the river, and some even in the distance on the same side; they would probably have attacked us, had they known how small was our number. The dangers of my situation affected my spirits, and I felt myself worse.

" I had calculated the soldier would return with a new guide from Guaray on that day; I hoped to obtain help from them, and my imagination was divided between the desire of seeing them, and the fear of surrounding dangers. At one time I thought I saw their dogs, but I was mistaken, and returned to my former state. The dogs I had seen were some almost without master, in the deserts, which had been attracted by our food. The chasseur, Jozè Mariano, now came and sat by me; he was more calm, had fastened a cloth round his loins, but had not yet recovered his reason. " Master," said he, " long have I accompanied you, I have always been a faithful servant, I am on fire, do not refuse me a drop of water." Full of terror and compassion, I took his hand, and endeavoured to console him.

" The warm water, of which I had drunk a prodigious quantity, now produced the desired effect, and I vomited. I felt relieved, a numbness occurred in the fingers, but it was of short duration. I distinguished the cart, the pasturages, and the trees, and the cloud left my eyes, so that I could see all but the upper part of objects, or if it came on again, it was only for a few instants. The state of Jozè Mariano continued to cause me much alarm. I was also fearful I should not, myself, recover the entire use of my faculties. A second vomiting began to dissipate these fears, and procured me fresh ease. I saw objects more clearly, could talk French or Portuguese at will, my ideas became more clear, and I directed the young Frenchman where to find an emetic. I divided it into three parts, vomited abundantly, evacuating the food and honey I had taken in the morning, with torrents of water. Until I had taken the third portion of the emetic, I felt pleasure in long draughts of water; but after that time, I disliked it and took no more; the cloud disappeared, and after some cups of tea, I took a short walk, and, with the exception of strength, was almost in my natural state.

" Nearly at the same moment, reason returned suddenly to Jozè

Mariano, without his having vomited; he took fresh clothes, mounted a horse, and went in search of the soldier, with whom he shortly returned.

"It was about 10 o'clock in the morning when we had taken of the honey, and the sun was setting before we had recovered. The momentary absence of the Frenchman and the Indian Botocudo had prevented them from eating any of it. The soldier had offered some to the Guarina man, but he, knowing its deleterious quality, had refused to eat of it. The soldier laughed at him, and had not mentioned the circumstance to us.

"On the morrow I was still weak, the soldier complained of deafness, José Mariano had not recovered his strength, and said his body seemed covered with glue. As our guide had arrived the evening before, we parted, and continued our journey, glad to leave the place."

Having told his soldier that he should be glad of some wasps of the kind which had produced this honey, M. St. Hilaire was called, on the day following the memorable one, to look at a wasps' nest, exactly resembling that of the preceding day. It was recognised by the Guarini and the Indians the guide had brought with him, to be of the kind known in the country by the name of *Lecheguana.* Some of the animals, with fragments of their habitation, were secured, and have been deposited in the king's cabinet. The honey was red and liquid, like that of the preceding evening.

It appears, that notwithstanding the events of the preceding day, the Indian Botocudo, the Guarina man, and another, ate of this honey without the knowledge of M. St. Hilaire, but none of them suffered from it.

After-inquiry, in the more inhabited part of the country, elicited that two kinds of *Lecheguana* were known there, the one yielding honey white and innocuous, the other, such as is red; and this, though not always, yet often caused serious injury, occasioning a kind of drunkenness or delirium, which could be relieved only by vomiting, and which sometimes occasioned death.—*Mém. du Muséum,* xii. 293. (*1825*)

On the great advantage of giving premiums to farmers, manufacturers, and artists, with a proposal for the increase of apiaries in Ireland, by considering bees in the light of manufacturers; addressed to the Dublin society, by Sir James Caldwell, bart. F. R. S.

THE offer of pecuniary rewards to those who excel in any useful art or manufactory, has a much more powerful and extensive influence than appears at the first view: the benefit is much greater to him that obtains such a reward, than the mere acquisition of the sum to which it amounts; for it confers an honourable distinction upon him, to whom an increase of reputation is an increase of wealth. A reward of an hundred pounds offered to an artificer who shall excel in his profession, excites an emulation in proportion to the ultimate advantages it will produce to the winner, which is, probably, not only in the estimation of fancy, but of reason, more than twenty times the sum. The benefit that it produces to the public, is also in proportion to the benefit it confers on the individual: for the more powerfully it excites emulation, the more effectually it must produce improvement: it is at once both the cause and the reward of merit, in proportion, not to its intrinsic value, but its relative importance to the competitors: and in this view, the money appropriated to encourage ingenuity and diligence, is more improved than by any other application; for its value to the individual is increased, perhaps, as an hundred to one, by the manner and circumstances in which he acquires it; and with respect to the nation, the encouragement of arts and manufactures is an advantage infinitely greater than could arise, not only from employing the inconsiderable sums which are given in premiums another way, but from the whole produce of the mines of Mexico and Peru, if they could be transported into this kingdom, and wrought by the very hands that now ply the loom, or cultivate the ground.

Nor is the advantage of these rewards confined to the artificer, by whom they happen to be obtained: setting aside the national advantages arising from the general

general improvement which the competition necessarily produces, the competitor acquires some degree of eminence and honour, merely by entering the lists: if the scale hangs doubtful between several, the gain of all is nearly equal; for the mere pecuniary reward is but a very inconsiderable part of the whole; and even those whose performances do not hold the judges in suspense, will be drawn out of a state of obscurity, in which such abilities, as they possess, might be buried for ever; they will at least be known; they will have their partisans; they will be stimulated to new efforts to justify the partial opinions of their friends, who will naturally encourage them, in hopes that they will succeed.

The advantages that have already accrued from the Dublin society, an institution established upon these principles, and with these views, are so manifest and important, and the ability and integrity of the members are so well known, that the last session of parliament gave them the disposal of ten thousand pounds of the public money, and the present session has given eight thousand more.

As a new subject of public attention, and of this society, with respect to the rewards which they may hereafter offer, the encouragement of apiaries in this kingdom is now proposed to their consideration.

BEES have been often the theme of the poet, the legislator, and the philosopher; they have been considered as emblems both of public and private virtue, of subordination, diligence, and ingenuity; they have been exhibited in many characters, and have been the sub-

ject of many volumes; and the bee may very justly be now recommended to the Dublin society as a manufacturer, the maker of honey and of wax.

The excellence of a manufacture depends upon its being fabricated of cheap materials, so as to be valuable chiefly by the labour and skill of the artist, upon the facility with which it may be established, and the usefulness of the commodity to the public.

In all these particulars, the manufacture both of honey and of wax, must be allowed to excel. These articles are extracted by an instinct, wonderful indeed in its nature, but exercised with spontaneous facility, from a great variety of odoriferous plants, which, after this extract has been made, are as beautiful and as useful as before; the honey and wax are clear gain, like the corn picked up by poultry at a barn door: as this would be trodden under foot, and wasted, if not brought to our table, transmitted into the chicken that preserves it; so would the honey and wax, with all their salutary, pleasing, and useful qualities, perish in the flowers that produce them, if not extracted and fabricated by the bee. The little dwellings in which these manufacturers carry on their work, are constructed at the smallest expence, and the construction of them furnishes employment for the lame and the decrepit, those whom age and infirmity would otherwise leave to suffer, rather than to enjoy existence in total inactivity, weary to themselves, and a burden to others. The importance of these articles of trade deserves a more particular consideration.

That there is a consumption of
wax

wax in this kingdom, [Ireland], greater than its produce, is undeniable, because considerable quantities of it are imported; and that it is more for our advantage to produce than to import it, will scarce be denied: the encouragement of apiaries therefore with a view to the wax only, must be allowed to be a measure directly tending to the public benefit. It may, perhaps, be said, that the principal consumption of wax being in candles, one of the last refinements of a luxurious age, it would be more eligible to prevent than to provide for its gratification: but without shewing the folly of indiscriminately declaiming against luxury, or shewing, what would be easy to shew, that without the gratification, and even multiplication, of artificial wants, no nation, in the present constitution of things, could long support itself in a state of plenty and independence; it will be sufficient to observe, that no reason can be given why wax candles should not be substituted for tallow, by those who can afford it, which will not equally prove that tallow candles should not have been substituted for the lamps of rancid and fœtid oil used by our ancestors.

In a commercial view the great consumption of wax in candles, if we could produce a sufficient quantity at home, would be a national benefit; because it greatly increases our exports of tallow, from which a very considerable profit accrues.

It may also be observed here, that there is great probability of the government's increasing the consumption of wax in candles still farther, by directing wax candles to be burnt on board the navy. A proposal for this purpose has already been laid before the admiralty in England, in support of which it is alledged, that the burning tallow between decks, where candles of some sort must always be used, greatly increases the noxious and putrescent vapours which those close places render so fatal to lives, which it is of the utmost importance to preserve; that the great heat of those places causes the tallow to melt, so as to occasion great waste; that tallow candles become so soft as frequently to bend, and at length fall down, by which fires have often happened, and are perpetually liable to happen; and, in one word, that they are the cause of great filth, danger, and sickness These reasons, which will probably weigh with the state, did actually determine one of our admirals, several years ago, to burn wax on board his own ship, at his own expence, which he declared was attended with such advantages, that he would have continued it if the charge had been ten times as much as he found it; for, he said, the difference between wax and tallow for the year did not amount to more than ten pounds †.

Under these circumstances, the encouragement of apiaries becomes the more a national concern; for

* It must be remembered this is spoken of Ireland.

† This was told to a friend of Sir James Caldwell, by admiral Knowles, of himself, in the manner above related.

If we can not only supply our increased home consumption of wax, but export it, we shall turn the balance of commerce, in a very considerable article, in our favour, which is now against us, and must be more so, if, upon the increased consumption of wax, we must increase our imports in that article.

Besides the use of wax in candles, which is of all modern luxuries the most salutary and agreeable, it is an article absolutely necessary in many manufactures and trades, and in the public offices; it is also of great medicinal virtue.

As to honey, it is certainly a necessary of life, the want of which can be supplied only by sugar: in proportion as honey, a home produce, can be made cheap, sugar, a foreign commodity, will be less bought, and consequently less will be imported. Of honey we make mead, a most pleasing and salutary liquor: of honey is also made a kind of mum, called old ale, which in some families in Ireland is in great estimation. If honey is made cheap, it will greatly lessen the consumption of made wines, the principal ingredient of which is sugar; and the good effect will be, not only the substitution of a home for a foreign commodity, but of a wholesome for a pernicious liquor. But honey is still of more importance for medicinal than alimentary purposes: no physical writer, from Hippocrates to Huxham, has mentioned it without the highest encomium: it is penetrating and deterging, and is therefore good in obstructions of all kinds, especially those arising from viscid humours. It is also a

sovereign remedy in the torsures, a disease peculiar to this country, arising from its great moisture, which produces infarctions of the breast, with difficult perspiration, and other morbid symptoms. The inhabitants of Ireland in general have cold constitutions, the natural effect of their food and manner of life. This constitution renders them liable to phlegmatic disorders, for which honey is a most excellent remedy, and from which it is a certain preservative. Honey therefore should be brought within the reach of the poor; for the life and health of the poor are of infinitely more importance to the state, than the life and health of the rich.

The bee therefore seems to have a claim to the attention of the public in general, and in particular to the liberality of this society, with respect to both the commodities which he fabricates, honey and wax. This country is extremely well adapted, by circumstances and situation, both to his nature and trade, the climate being temperate, the spring early, the verdure perpetual, and the herbage abundant. This may appear, from honey and wax being mentioned, as articles of commerce and exportation, in all the old books of geography. The following proposal is therefore offered to the consideration of the society.

I. That one hundred pounds shall be allotted for the encouragement of apiaries, to be distributed on the third of October, 1765, in proportions, upon the conditions, and under the regulations following:

To the person having the greatest

est weight of honey and wax, above six hundred weight, including the hive and the bees, 30l.

To the person having the next greatest weight, above five hundred weight, 25l.

To the person having the next greatest quantity, above four hundred weight, 20l.

To the person having the next greatest quantity, above three hundred weight, 15l.

To the person having the next greatest quantity, above two hundred weight, 10l.

II. That the hives shall be weighed in the gross, the bees being alive, which is known by experience not in the least to prejudice them, by a proper person, in the presence of the minister or curate of the parish, or any justice of the peace in the neighbourhood, or any other person of a reputable character, known to a member of the society, and a person appointed by the proprietor of the bees [*].

III. That a certificate of such weight, and the number of hives, shall be signed by such minister, or curate, or justice of peace, or reputable person.

IV. That the person weighing the hives shall make an affidavit of their number and gross weight; that they are of the usual size and thickness: and that, to the best of his knowledge, no fraud has been practised to increase their weight [†].

V. That the proprietor of the bees shall also make an affidavit, that the number of old hives so weighed, attested, and certified, have been all his property six months before; and that all the new hives so weighed, attested, and certified, are swarms from the old hives; and that, to the best of his knowledge, none of those hives were above six Irish miles from his dwelling-house when weighed and certified, or for six months before.

VI. That such certificate and affidavits shall be produced by the claimants of the premiums, as the condition upon which alone they can receive it.

To this proposal the author can think of no objection, except the premiums that have already been given for honey. But as these premiums have been very small, and very much confined in the application, few persons in the kingdom, on that account, have increased their stock of bees; it is therefore hoped, that this present proposal does not stand precluded: the general utility of a premium for these articles being acknowledged, even by the very measure that has proved ineffectual for the purpose. The previous offer of premiums on these articles, there-

---

[*] The weighing of bees is by no means difficult: it is to be done after sun-set, in the following manner: A linen cloth is slipped between the hive and the stool, and knotted at the top of the hive, which is then lifted up by the knot, and put into the scale: after weighing, the hive is again put on the stool, and the cloth slipped from under it.

[†] Straw, rush, or bent hives, have been found, by long experience, to answer best; and no person shall be entitled to the premium that makes use of any other kind.

fore, rather supports than subverts the measure now proposed.

By this measure, it is hoped, bees will be greatly increased in a short time; for as the proprietors could not keep such numbers of bees without employing the poor, to the extent of six miles round them, to take care of them, which they would gladly do for a small gratuity, it is reasonable to suppose that, perceiving the advantages derived to the owners from the bees they look after, they would be induced to set up hives, and keep bees for themselves. From this single object, however inconsiderable, a habit of attention might be acquired by those who are now totally idle: hope of advantage might be awaked in the breasts of those whose industry is now depressed by despondency, and the advantages would be still more important and extensive than any that have been yet suggested, which are surely more than sufficient to justify an experiment which may be made at so small an expence as one hundred pounds.

It is to be observed, that this country, in many parts, abounds with heath and furze, which blossom in September, and are excellent pasturage for bees.

Description of a very curious and useful bee-hive invented by Mr. Thorsley, near the Mansion-house, London.

MR. Thorsley having found, from near sixty years experience, that bee-hives invented by him would be productive of much greater profit to the owners of bees, and also render that cruel and un-

generous practice of destroying these animals not only unnecessary but pernicious, presented a bee-hive of this construction to the London society for the encouragement of arts, &c. who readily purchased another of his hives filled with honey, &c. that they might be inspected by the curious, and brought into universal use. Nor did the society stop here: persuaded that the invention would prove of the greatest advantage to this country, they published a premium of two hundred pounds, in order to introduce either Mr. Thorsley's, or some other method of a similar kind, whereby much larger quantities of honey and wax might be procured, and, at the same time, the lives of these laborious and useful insects preserved.

The bottom part of this bee-hive is an octangular box, made of deal boards, about an inch in thickness, the cover of which is externally seventeen inches in diameter, but internally only $15\frac{1}{2}$, and its height 10 inches. In the middle of the cover of this octangular box is a hole, which may be opened or shut at pleasure, by means of a slider. In one of the pannels is a pane of glass, covered with a wooden door. The bee-hole at the bottom of the box is about $3\frac{1}{4}$ inches broad, and half an inch high. Two slips of deal, about half an inch square, cross each other in the centre of the box, and are fastened to the pannels by means of small screws. To these slips the bees fasten their combs.

In this octangular box the bees are hived, after swarming in the usual manner, and there suffered to continue till they have built their combs, and filled them with honey, which may be known by opening the door, and viewing their works through the glass pane, or by the weight of the hive. When the bee-master finds his laborious insects have filled their habitation, he is to place a common bee-hive of straw, made either flat at the top, or in the common form, on the octangular box, and draw out the slider, by which a communication will be opened between the box and the straw-hive; the consequence of which will be, that those laborious insects will fill this hive also with the product of their labours. When the bee-master finds the straw-hive is well filled, he may push in the slider, and take it away, placing another immediately in its room, and then drawing out the slider. These indefatigable creatures will then fill the new hive in the same manner. By proceeding in this method, Mr Thorsley assured the society, that he had taken three successive hives, filled with honey and wax, from one single hive, during the same summer; and that, after he had laid his insects under so large a contribution, the food still remaining in the octangular box was abundantly sufficient for their support during the winter. He added, that if this method was pursued in every part of the kingdom, instead of that cruel method of putting the creatures to death, he was persuaded, from long experience, that wax would be collected in such plenty, that candles made with it might be sold as cheap as those of tallow are at present.

Mr. Thorsley has also added an-other part to his bee-hive, which cannot fail of affording the highest entertainment to a curious and inquisitive mind. It consists of a glass-receiver 18 inches in height, 8 inches in diameter at the bottom, and in the greatest part 13. This receiver has a hole at the top, about an inch in diameter, through which a square piece of deal is extended to nearly the bottom of the vessel, having two cross bars, to which the bees fasten their combs. Into the other end of this square piece is screwed a piece of brass, which serves for a handle to the receiver, or glass hive. When the bees have filled their straw hive, (which must have a hole in the centre, covered with a piece of tin) Mr. Thorsley places the glass receiver upon the top of the straw hive, and draws out the piece of tin. The bees now, finding their habitation enlarged, pursue their labours with such alacrity, that they fill this glass hive likewise with their stores. And, as this receptacle is wholly transparent, the curious observer may entertain himself with viewing the whole progress of their works. One of the hives now deposited at the society's rooms in the Strand, is filled with the produce of the labours of those insects; and the glass hive is supposed to contain near thirty pounds of honey.

trance of a vaſt cavern, a body of real ſtone, of an irregular figure, but quite porous, which he had the curioſity to open. He was very much ſurpriſed to ſee the whole divided into oval cells of three lines in breadth, and four lines in length, placed all manner of ways about each other, but no where communicating, all of them lined with a very thin membrane, and what was more wonderful, each incloſing a maggot, or a fly perfectly like a bee. The maggots were very hard and very ſolid, and might paſs for petrified; but the flies were only dried up, and well preſerved as ancient mummies; and ſmall oval grains, which appeared to be eggs, were often found under them. There was at the bottom of many of the cells a thick juice, blackiſh, very hard, appearing red when expoſed to the light, very ſweet, making the ſaliva yellow, and inflammable as reſin. It was, in ſhort, real honey; but who ſhould ever think of finding honey in the boſom of a ſtone?

M. Lippi conceives that this was a natural hive, which at firſt had been formed in a looſe light, and ſandy earth, and afterwards was petrified by ſome particular accident. The animals that inhabited it were ſurpriſed by the petrification, and, as it were fixed in the ſtate they were then found. Their dried up mucoſity had formed the membrane that lined the cells. At the time when the hive was yet ſoft, the bees went out of it to ſeek their food, and make their honey in it.

Still ſeeking in the ſame place other particulars to clear up this fact, M. Lippi found, in ſeveral parts,

Account of a petrified beehive, diſcovered on the mountains of Siout in the Upper Egypt, by Mr. Lippi, licentiate in phyſic of the Army of Paris.

M. LIPPI found, on thoſe mountains, at the en-

parts, the beginnings of a like
hive. It was, as it were, the first
bed, formed of a number of little
cells, for the most part open, and
containing the animal in all its
different states, but dried up and
very hard as well as the hives. He
saw besides on one of the first beds,
a second composed of a heap of
little hillocks of about five lines in
height, and an inch diameter at
their base. They were grume-
lous, easily reducible into dust,
and nearly resemble the hills
thrown up by moles. M. Lippi
opened them by striking gently
against them, and found in every
one of them two or three oval cells,
filled with a yellow maggot, and
full of juice, which occupied them
entirely.

It is easy to conceive that on a
first bed once formed several others
are also formed, which constitute
the whole hive. But how are these
beds formed? Whence comes the
earth they are constructed of? Does
the animal carry it thither; and
how does he carry it, and in so
great a quantity? This is not yet
known; time alone can make us
acquainted with this branch of
knowledge.

A curious and interesting Account of a Substance, not before attended to, which the Bees collect and turn to honey. Extracted from a Memoire read before the Society of Sciences at Montpellier, by the Abbé Boussier de Sauvages, entitled, Observations sur l'Origine du Miel.

IT was formerly the opinion of naturalists, that the bees do not collect honey in the form we see it; the liquor they collect being digested in their stomachs, where both its nature and consistence are changed. But this opinion seems to be founded on erroneous principles: and it is now believed that the bees have no other share in the making of honey than simply collecting it; because the honey is, when properly diluted, subject to vinous fermentation, a property not found in any animal substance.

The flowers of many sorts of plants afford a quantity of honey, of saccharine juice, which the bees collect, and carry to their hives; but besides this liquor, the Abbé Boussier acquaints us, that he has seen two kinds of honey-dews, which the bees are equally fond of, both deriving their origin from vegetables, though in a different manner.

The first kind, the only one known to husbandmen, and which passes for a dew which falls on trees, is no other than a mild sweet juice, which, having circulated through the vessels of vegetables, is separated in proper reservoirs in the flowers, or on the leaves where it is properly called the honey-dew: sometimes it is deposited in the pith, as in the sugar-cane, at other times in the juice of summer fruits, when ripe. Such is the origin of the manna, which is collected on the ash and maple of Calabria and Briançon, where it flows in great plenty from the leaves and trunks of these trees, and thickens into the form in which it is usually seen.

" Chance (says the Abbé) afforded me an opportunity of seeing this juice and its primitive form on the leaves of the holm oak: these leaves were covered with thousands of small round globules, or drops, which, without touching one another, seemed to point out the pore from whence each of them had proceeded. My taste informed me, that they were as sweet as honey: the honey-dew on a neighbouring bramble, did not resemble the former, the drops having run together; owing either to the moisture of the air, which had diluted them, or to the heat, which had expanded them. The dew was become more viscous, and lay in large drops, covering the leaves; in this form it is usually seen.

" The oak had at this time two kinds of leaves: the old, which were strong and firm, and the new, which were tender, and newly come forth. The honey-dew was found only on the old leaves, though these were covered by the new ones, and by that means sheltered from any moisture that could fall from above. I observed the same on the old leaves of the bramble, while the new leaves were quite free from it. Another proof that this dew proceeds from the leaves, is, that other neighbouring trees, not furnished with a juice of this kind, had no moisture on them; and particularly the mulberry, which is a very particular circumstance, for this juice is a deadly poison to silkworms. If this juice fell in the form of a dew, mist, or fog, it would wet all the leaves without distinction, and every part of the leaves, under as well as upper. Heat may have some share in its production: for though the common heat promotes only the transpiration

piration of the more volatile and fluid juices, a sultry heat, especially if reflected by clouds, may so far dilate the vessel, as to produce a more viscous juice, such as the honey-dew.

"The second kind of honey-dew, which is the chief resource of bees after the spring flowers and dew by transpiration on leaves are past, owes its origin to a small insect called a vine-fretter: the excrement ejected with some force by this insect, makes a part of the most delicate honey known in nature.

"These vine-fretters rest during several months on the barks of particular trees, and extract their food by piercing that bark, without hurting or deforming the tree. These insects also cause the leaves of some trees to curl up, and produce galls upon others. They settle on branches that are a year old. The juice, at first perhaps hard and crabbed, becomes, in the bowels of this insect, equal in sweetness to the honey obtained from the flowers and leaves of vegetables; excepting that the flowers may communicate some of their essential oil to the honey, and this may give it a peculiar flavour, as happened to myself by planting a hedge of rosemary near my bees at Sauvages; the honey has tasted of it ever since, that shrub continuing long in flower.

"I have observed two species of vine-fretters which live unsheltered on the bark of young branches: they have a smooth skin, and those without wings seem to be the females, which compose the greater bulk of the swarm; or perhaps the young in their caterpillar state; before they are changed into flies; for each swarm has, in its train, two or three males with wings; these live on the labour of the females, at least I always saw them hopping carelessly on the backs of the females, without going to the bark to seek for food.

"Both species live in clusters, on different parts of the same tree, entirely covering the bark; and it is remarkable, that they there take a position which to us appears to be very uneasy: for they adhere to the branch with their head downwards, and their belly upwards.

"The lesser species is of the colour of the bark upon which it feeds, generally green. It is chiefly distinguished by two horns, or strait, immoveable, fleshy substances, which rise perpendicularly from the lower sides of the belly, one on each side. This is the species which live on the young branches of brambles and elder.

"The former of these species is double the size of the latter, and is that which I have now more particularly in view, because it is that from which the honey proceeds. These insects are blackish; and instead of the kind of horns which distinguish the other, have, in the same part of the skin, a small button, black and shining like jet.

"The buzzing of bees in a tuft of holm-oak, made me suspect that something very interesting brought so many of them thither. I knew that it was not the season for expecting honey-dew, nor was it the place where it is usually found, and was surprised to find the tuft of leaves and branches covered with drops which the bees collected with a humming noise. The form of the drops drew my attention, and led me to the following discovery. Instead of being round like drops which

which had fallen, each formed a small longish oval. I soon perceived from whence they proceeded. The leaves covered with these drops of honey were situated beneath a swarm of the larger black vine-fretters; and on observing these insects, I perceived them, from time to time, raise their bellies, at the extremity of which there then appeared a small drop of an amber colour, which they instantly ejected from them to the distance of some inches. I found by tasting some of these drops which I had catched on my hand, that it had the same flavour with what had before fallen on the leaves. I afterwards saw the smaller species of vine-fretters eject their drops in the same manner.

" This ejection is so far from being a matter of indifference to these insects themselves, that it seems to have been wisely instituted to procure cleanliness in each individual, as well as to preserve the whole swarm from destruction; for pressing as they do upon one another, they would otherwise soon be glued together, and rendered incapable of stirring.

" We may now with some probability account for the seeming odd situation in which they rest. Their belly is about twenty times larger than their head and breast. If the insect was placed in a contrary direction, it could not, without extreme difficulty, raise its heavy belly, so as to project it far enough outward to discharge the drop over its companions; whereas, when the head is lowest, much less effort is necessary to incline it forward; and even in this situation the insect seems by its flutterings to collect all its strength. When the winter's cold and rains come on, these vine-

fretters place themselves wherever they are least exposed; and as they then take but little nourishment, and but seldom emit their drop, they seem not to mind whether the head or tail be uppermost.

" The drops thus spurted out, fall upon the ground, if not intercepted by leaves or branches; and the spots they make on stones remain some time, unless washed off by rain. This is the only honey-dew that falls; and this never falls from a greater height than a branch where these insects can cluster.

" It is now easy to account for a phænomenon which formerly puzzled me greatly. Walking under a lime-tree in the king's garden at Paris, I felt my hand wetted with little drops, which I at first took for small rain. The tree indeed should have sheltered me from the rain, but I escaped it by going from under the tree. A seat placed near the tree shone with these drops. And being then unacquainted with any thing of this kind, except the honey-dew found on the leaves of some particular trees, I was at a loss to conceive how so glutinous a substance could fall from the leaves in such small drops; for I knew that rain could not overcome its natural attraction to the leaves, till it became pretty large drops; but I have since found that the lime-tree is very subject to these vine-fretters.

" Bees are not the only insects that feast on this honey, ants are equally fond of it. Led into this opinion, by what naturalists have said, I at first believed that the horns in the lesser species of these vine-fretters, had at their extremity a liquor which the ants went in search of. But I soon discovered

H " that

that what drew the ants after them, came from elsewhere, both in the larger and the lesser species, and that no liquor is discharged by the horns.

" There are two species of ants which search for these insects. The large black ants follow those which live on the oaks and chesnut: the lesser ants attend those on the elder. But as the ants are not like the bees provided with the means of sucking up fluids, they place themselves near the vine-fretters, in order to seize the drop the moment they see it appear upon the anus; and as the drop remains some time on the small vine-fretters before they can cast it off, the ants have leisure to catch it, and thereby prevent the bees from having any share: but the vine-fretters of the oak and chesnut being stronger, and perhaps more plentifully supplied with juice, dart the drop instantly, so that the larger ants get very little of it.

" The vine-fretters finding the greatest plenty of juice in trees about the middle of summer, afford also, at that time, the greatest quantity of honey; and this lessens as the season advances, so that in the autumn, the bees prefer it to the flowers then in season.

" Though these insects pierce the tree to the sap in a thousand places, yet the trees do not seem to suffer at all from them, nor do the leaves lose the least of their verdure. The husbandman therefore acts injudiciously when he destroys them."

Curious Experiments for preventing the waste of Honey, and preserving the lives of Bees during the winter. By a Gentleman near the banks of the Tweed. From the Repository for Select Papers on Agriculture, &c. Numb. II.

I Have tried several experiments for preserving the lives of bees, during the winter, and though, in general, with little success, yet I think I have reason to continue, and to advise others to follow what I practised last winter: the method is very simple, and not expensive; for it is no other than keeping the bees in a cold and dark place.

My reason for trying this experiment was, my having observed that a certain degree of cold brought upon the bees a stupor; and that the same degree of cold continued, kept them in the same state till they were brought into a warmer situation, which immediately restored their life and vigour [*].

With this view I kept two hives, shut up in a dark cold out-house, from the middle of September last, to the middle of April, without ever letting them see light; upon their being set out in the warmer air, they recovered immediately, and shewed an appearance of more strength, than the hives did which had been kept out in the usual way. This appearance of strength continued during the summer, and they multiplied faster than I had ever observed them to do before. They were rather later in swarming this year, than in some former summers, but this was the case with many hives in the neighbourhood; and even though this should always happen, yet I think other advantages will do more than over-balance it. Could I go into the country, early in the spring, to look after the bees myself, I would bring them into the open air some weeks sooner, carefully attend to the changes of the weather, and shut up the doors of the hives on a bad day; but this degree of care can scarcely be expected from servants and gardeners, who have many other things to attend to.

I intend to have four hives put up this season, in the coldest dark place I can find; and as an ice-house is the steadiest and greatest cold we have, one or two of my friends, who have ice-houses, have promised to put a hive upon the ice. By all accounts, the cold in Siberia does not kill the bees there, and in Russia, where the winters are extremely severe, bees produce much honey; so I think there is not any danger to be feared from any degree of cold we can expose the bees to.

If success continues to attend this experiment of keeping the bees asleep all the winter and spring, without consuming their honey, a great point will be gained: especially as Mr. Wildman has taught us to take the honey without killing the bees; for by what I have observed in this country, our bees are lost chiefly by being tempted to go out by a clear sun in the spring; though, perhaps, a frosty wind blows

* Mr. White says, in confirmation of Gedde's observation, that "bees "which stand on the north side of a building, whose height intercepts the "sun's beams all the winter, will waste less of their provisions, almost by "half, than others which stand in the sun; for seldom coming forth, they "eat little, and yet in the spring are as forward to work and swarm, as those "which had twice as much honey in the autumn before." See the Rev. Mr. White's Method of preserving Bees, third edition, price 1s.

and chills them, so as to prevent their being able to return to the hive; or an early warmth induces the queen to lay eggs, and a number of young bees are bred, which consume the little provision left, before the fields can afford any supply.

The following curious method of rearing Turkeys to advantage, is translated from a Swedish book, entitled Rural Oeconomy.

MANY of our housewives, says this ingenious author, have long despaired of success in rearing turkeys, and complained, that the profit rarely indemnifies them for their trouble and loss of time: whereas, continues he, little more is to be done, than to plunge the chick into a vessel of cold water, the very hour, if possible, but at least the very day it is hatched, forcing it to swallow one whole pepper-corn; after which let it be returned to its mother. From that time it will become hardy, and fear the cold no more than a hen's chick. But it must be remembered, that this useful species of fowls are also subject to one particular disorder while they are young, which often carries them off in a few days. When they begin to droop, examine carefully the feathers on their rump, and you will find two or three, whose quill part is filled with blood. Upon drawing these the chick recovers, and after that requires no other care, than what is commonly bestowed on poultry that range the court-yard.

The truth of these assertions is too well known to be denied; and as a convincing proof of the suc-

cess, it will be sufficient to mention, that three parishes in Sweden have, for many years used this method, and gained several hundred pounds by rearing and selling turkeys.

A very cheap and lasting Varnish, proper for pales and coarse wood-work.

TAKE any quantity of tar, and grind it with as much Spanish-brown as it will bear, without rendering it too thick to be used as a paint or varnish; and then lay it on the pales, or other wood-work, as soon as convenient, for it soon hardens by keeping.

This mixture must be laid on the wood by means of a large brush, or house-painter's tool; and the work should then be kept as free from dust and insects as possible, till the varnish be thoroughly dry. It will, provided the wood on which it is laid be smooth, have a very good gloss, and prove an excellent preservative of it against the weather, or moisture of any kind: on which account, as well as its being cheaper, it is far preferable to paint, not only for pales, but also for weather-boarding, and all other kinds of coarse wood-work, exposed to the weather. Where the glossy brown colour is not liked, the work may be made of a greyish brown, by mixing a small portion of white-lead and ivory-black with the Spanish-brown.

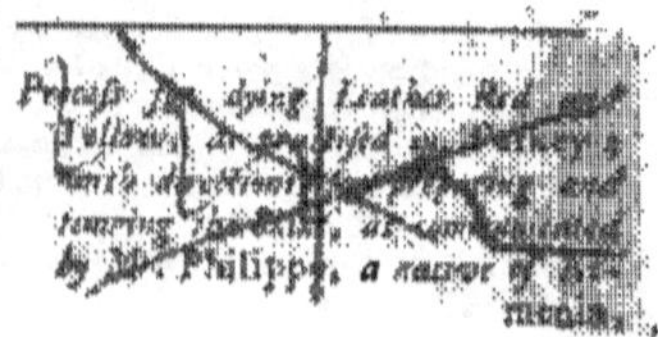

Kaſanka,
Mr. URBAN, May 1, O. S. 1785.

THE laſt place I wrote to you from was Schurafka, when I ſent you a drawing of the Slepetz (ſee p. 761); to the account of which I might have added, that Mr. Laxmann, in the year 1764, found an animal in the parts about Barnaul, in many reſpects very like it, to which he gave the name of The Rat-mole; it being a rat by the head, hinder feet, and teeth, but is a mole by the fore paws, by the ſmallneſs of its eyes, by its ſhort ears, and its manner of living. It is called, in the Ruſſian language, Zemlenui Medved, the earth-bear. But that animal has a tail, which the Slepetz has not. Notwithſtanding the bulk of his body, Mr. Laxmann ſays, there is no animal like him for burrowing in the earth. All the fields of Siberia, in the latitudes about Barnaul, are covered with the hillocks he throws up. They ſpoil all the roads and paths, by undermining them with their ſubterraneous paſſages. If we may judge of their numbers, ſays he, by the quantity of mole-hills, there muſt be many hundreds of thouſands of theſe rat-moles in Kolivan alone. But, notwithſtanding the prodigious detriment they do to the fields and highways, the boors leave them in perfect liberty, and you meet with many who have never given themſelves the trouble to ſee one.—I ſhall take up no more of your precious moments, Mr. Urban, about rats and mice. But as, by this time, I ſuppoſe you may be a little intereſted in what relates to me, allow me juſt to inform you, that I left Schurafka about the middle of laſt month, and, after paſſing through Bitſchok and Gorelofka, I arrived here at Kaſanka, which is about 130 verſts from Pavlofsk. I broke down, as uſual, on the way; but the travelling in a cabitka is attended with one very great advantage, which is, that, let what will happen to it, it is next to impoſſible but I am able to repair it the firſt tree I come to; eſpecially as I always ſling a couple of ſpare axletrees under it, and put a rope in the bottom, with a ſmall axe. I think, if you were once to travel in a cabitka, you would never uſe a poſt-chaiſe again.

Kaſanka is the firſt ſtanitza of the Koſacs of the Don, ſituated in an open plain, and has a ſtarſchina for commandant. Immediately on arriving, a

ſenſible difference is apparent in the country; not that the ſoil is not always the ſame, but becauſe every thing is wild and uncultivated, and, in ſhort, preſents nothing but a frightful deſert. Hitherto you ſee mankind turning the various advantages of nature to account. The inhabitants of the Greater and the Leſſer Ruſſias earn their bread by the ſweat of their face; but in this country of the Koſacs all is arid and bare; and this inhoſpitable, uncultivated deſert extends, without interruption, from Kaſanka to Tſcherkaſk. Excepting, therefore, the obſervations that natural objects demand, I can find but little, or rather nothing at all, to excite my attention.

To make amends for this, I will ſend you the manner of managing bees among the Baſchkirians, from my portfolio, which I ſhall be glad to empty a little, that I may adminiſter a needle and thread to it; for, by having been jolted ſo often under my head, and ſo often under my feet, I will venture to affirm no beggar's wallet in all London is half ſo ragged.

About four years ago I was at Bogorodſkoe, on the banks of the river Ufa, where I paid ſome attention to the manner in which the Ruſſians of thoſe parts, excited by the example of their neighbours the Baſchkirians, who are famous in this way, apply themſelves to the cultivation of bees, and were then applauding themſelves exceedingly on the rich ſtore of wax and honey they had got the preceding year. They excavate their hives in the trunks of different trees, giving the preference to ſuch as are of the hardeſt wood; and conſequently chuſe for this purpoſe the ſtrongeſt and the loftieſt trees of the foreſt. The hive is about five and twenty or thirty feet high from the ground, frequently even higher, if the length of the trunk allows it. They hollow them out length-ways, with ſmall narrow hatchets, and tools of a peculiar form, a ſort of chiſſels and gouges, with which they complete their work. The longitudinal aperture of this hive is ſtopped by a cover of two or more pieces, which are exactly fitted to it, and pierced with ſmall holes, to give ingreſs and egreſs to the bees.

No means can be deviſed more ingenious or more convenient for climbing the higheſt and the ſmootheſt trees than thoſe practiſed by this people, for the

conſtruction

conſtruction and ſituation of their hives. For this purpoſe they need nothing but a very ſharp axe, a leather ſtrap, or a common rope. The man places himſelf againſt the trunk of the tree, and paſſes the cord round his body and round the tree, juſt leaving it ſufficient play for caſting it higher and higher, by jerks, towards the elevation which he wants to attain, and there to place his body, bent as in a ſwing, his feet reſting againſt the tree, and preſerving the free uſe of his hands. This done, he takes his axe, and at about the height of his body makes the firſt notch or ſtep in the tree. Then he takes his rope, the two ends whereof he takes care to have tied very faſt, and throws it towards the top of the trunk. Placed thus in his rope by the middle of his body, and reſting his feet againſt the tree, he aſcends by two ſteps, and eaſily enables himſelf to put one of his feet in the notch: he now makes a new ſtep, and continues to mount in this manner till he has reached the intended height. The Baſchkirians perform all this with incredible ſpeed and agility. Being mounted to the place where he is to make the hive, he cuts more convenient ſteps, and, by the help of the rope, which his body keeps in diſtenſion, he performs his neceſſary work with the abovementioned tools, which are ſtuck in his girdle.

They carefully cut away all the boughs and protuberances beneath the hive, to render all acceſs as difficult as poſſible to the bears, which ſtill abound in vaſt numbers throughout the foreſts of the Ural, and, in ſpite of all imaginable precautions, do conſiderable damage to the hives. On this account they put in practice every kind of means, not only for defending themſelves from theſe voracious animals, but for their deſtruction too. The method moſt in uſe conſiſts in ſticking in the trunk of the tree old blades of knives, ſtanding upwards, ſcythes, and pieces of pointed iron, diſpoſed circularly round it, when the tree is ſtrait, or at the place of bending, when the trunk is crooked. The bear has commonly dexterity enough to avoid theſe points in climbing up the tree; but when he lets himſelf down, his poſterious foremoſt, he gets on theſe ſharp hooks, and gives himſelf ſuch deep wounds in the belly, that he uſually dies. It frequently happens that old bears take the precaution to bend down

theſe blades with their fore-paws, as they mount, and thereby render all this offenſive armour uſeleſs.

Another deſtructive apparatus is uſed with more ſucceſs, which bears ſome ſimilitude to the catapulta of the ancients, and is fixed in ſuch a manner that, at the very inſtant the bear prepares to climb the tree, he pulls a ſtring that lets go the machine, whoſe elaſticity ſtrikes a dart into the animal's breaſt.

Others ſuſpend, by long ropes to the fartheſt extremity of a branch of the tree, a platform, which they diſpoſe in ſuch a manner that they can bring it horizontally before the hive, and there tie it faſt to the trunk of the tree with a cord made of bark. The bear, who finds the ſeat very convenient for proceeding to the opening of the hive, begins by tearing the cord of bark which holds the platform to the trunk, and hinders him from executing his purpoſe. Upon this the platform immediately quits the tree, and ſwings in the air with the animal ſeated upon it. If, on the firſt ſhock, the bear is not tumbled out, he muſt now reſolve either to take a very dangerous leap, or to remain patiently in his ſuſpended ſeat. If he take the leap, either involuntarily, or by his own good will, he falls on ſharp points, placed all about the bottom of the tree; and if he reſolves to remain where he is, he ſurely dies by arrows or muſket balls. For explaining to you more ſenſibly this ingenious contrivance, I have annexed as good a drawing as I could make of it. (*See the plate annexed.*)

They go likewiſe, at the beginning of the night, to watch the bears from the top of ſome high tree, at a ſmall diſtance from the ſtocks theſe animals have begun to moleſt, or within the ſcent of ſome carrion. Laſtly, during the winter, they trace them by the ſmell, and after having rouſed them by their dogs, they kill them with their pikes. As this chace can only be carried on in pretty numerous parties, they agree upon certain times for that purpoſe.

The hives have ſtill another enemy in the black pie, or black wood pecker of Albinus, which the Baſchkirs keep off as much as poſſible by ſurrounding the aperture with all ſorts of thorns and brambles, and twigs of briar. In ſhort, the Tartars have the weakneſs to imagine that the very look of particular

perſons

The Baschkirian Bear Trap.

An Account of the MANNER of treating BEES in Portugal.

[From Murphy's Travels in Portugal.]

TO form a colony of bees, a spot of ground is chosen for the hives, exposed toward the south or south-east, well sheltered from the northern blasts, and surrounded with shrubs and flowers; of the latter, the best is rosemary. The richer the neighbouring grounds are, the better; for bees are said to range for food to the distance of a league from their homes. The situation being chosen, lanes must be cut through the shrubby thickets of five or six feet wide. The fences between the lanes should be about the same dimensions, and formed at intervals into small recesses, like bowers or niches, to receive the hives.

The figure of the hives used here in general are cylindrical; in height about twenty-seven inches by four-teen diameter. They are formed of the rind of the cork-tree, and covered with a pan of earthen-ware inverted, the edge of which projects over the hive like a cornice. The whole is fastened with pegs made of some hard and durable wood, and the joints stopped with peat. In the front of the cylinder, at the height of about eight inches, there is a small aperture where the bees enter. The inside is divided into three equal divisions, which are separated by cross sticks: here the bees form their combs or cells.

When the bees swarm, which is usually in the month of May or June, the hives are placed to receive them where they alight. If they descend on a tree, they are shaken off: the perſon who performs this operation muſt not be afraid of them, as they do not commonly ſting unleſs they are irritated; it will be ſafer, however, to cover the head with a wire maſk, and the hands with gloves.

Some bees are ſo wild, that they fly away in attempting to collect them, but they may be caught again in this manner: a ſheet is placed by night on the ground contiguous to the ſwarm, and when they alight, the hive is placed over them, with the entrance ſtopped, then the whole is covered with a ſheet, in which they are carried home. But they ſhould not be placed near the hive whence they had originally departed.

When the time arrives for taking out the honeycombs, which is generally in the month of June, when the flowers begin to decay, it ſhould be done in the heat of the day, as the greater part of the bees are then abroad, but not during a high wind, or at the commencement of a new or full moon. The hiver muſt have his face and hands defended, as abovementioned, and accompanied by a perſon holding a chafing-diſh, with a coal fire, covered with moiſt peat, to make the greater ſmoke: this ſmoke being infuſed among the bees from the top of the cylinder, they fly away, or remain intoxicated at the bottom, then the hive is taken to pieces, by drawing out the pins. The combs are cut out without deſtroying the bees, except two cells,

which are left around the hive; and leſt the bees ſhould feed on what remains, the inciſion is covered with pulverized clay; after this the hive is put together as before.

The combs ſhould not be taken out but when they are full of honey; it is rarely good the firſt year the bees aſſemble. In the months of March and Auguſt the wax is taken out, which is lodged in the firſt diviſion of the hive, after which the bees form other combs, and generate a young colony.

The hiver ſhould often viſit the ground, and repair any accidents that have happened. If ſnakes frequent the place, they ſhould not be killed, ſince they do not moleſt the bees, but deſtroy the toads and lizards, which are obnoxious to them.

When the hives are decayed, they are taken aſunder and fumigated; then the bees forſake their habitations, and take ſhelter in an adjoining hive, previouſly prepared for that purpoſe. This ſhould be performed in the ſpring, when the flowers begin to open and afford them ſuccour. The ſame method may be uſed in taking out the honey; but if repeatedly practiſed, it will extinguiſh the colony.

As the bees, in returning from their excurſions, are loaded and fatigued, there ſhould be nothing near the hives to obſtruct their deſcent, which is not in a perpendicular courſe, but in an oblique one.

'The Preparation of Coan Wine.

'Some boil three parts of must and one of sea water into a third of the quantity; but others mix with two measures of white wine one cotyla of salt, three cotylæ of sapa, one cotyla of must, one cotyla of flour of orobus, one hundred drams of melliot, sixteen drams of Celtic nard.'

As a fit liquor for women, a mixture of oil, wine, and pounded iris is recommended.

Will it be credited that 'the white poplar, being grafted or inoculated from the mulberry-tree, produces white mulberries?'

We cannot withhold from our readers the following prescription, with the translator's note:

'To make a Barren Tree bear Fruit.

'Having* girt and tucked up your clothes, and having taken an axe or a hatchet, approach the tree with resentment, wishing to cut it down: but when any body comes to you, and deprecates the cutting of it, as if responsible for a future crop, seem to be persuaded, and to spare the tree, and it will bear fruit well in future.'

A hollow stone, with a text of scripture inscribed on it, (Ps. i. 3.) is recommended to be hung on a tree to prevent the casting of its fruit.—We shall not specify other *charming* remedies against the maladies of the vegetable world: but, if the reader be not satisfied with those which we have adduced, he will find many more of the same nature by recurring to the production itself. That our medical gentlemen, however, may not be offended with us by total neglect, we shall furnish them with a recipe for the cure of a fever; which, we are confident, was never recommended by any of the College of Physicians: 'If you lay cucumbers of proportionable length near a sucking child, when he is feverish and asleep, he will be soon cured, for all the heat is attracted by the cucumbers.'

In the book concerning natural sympathy and antipathy, the subject of <u>Bees</u> is detailed, and a full account is given 'how bees may be produced from an ox, which is called Bongone.'

'* This opinion relating to the fructification of trees is of remote antiquity, which came from the east, and to which the parable of the fig tree seems to bear some analogy—*Luke*, xiii. 6. There is a passage in an Arabic writer, which shews that it was not unknown in the east. It relates to the fructification of the palm-tree, and runs thus: "The master, armed with an axe, approaching the tree with an attendant, says, I will cut down this tree, because it bears no fruit. Abstain, I pray, says the other; it will produce fruit this year. The master indeed without delay strikes it, but with the axe inverted: but the other preventing him, says, Spare it, I pray; I am responsible for it. Then the tree "becomes fruitful"—*Ibn Alvard.*'

It

It is impossible to resist transcribing this glaring evidence of antient folly, credulity, and cruelty:

' Let there be a building ten cubits high, and of the same number of cubits in breadth and of equal dimensions at all sides, and let there be one entrance, and four windows made in it, one window in each wall: then bring into this building a bullock, two years and a half old, fleshy, very fat: set to work a number of young men, and let them powerfully beat it, and by beating, let them kill it with their bludgeons, pervading the bones along with the flesh; but let them take care that they do not make the beast bloody (for the bee is not produced from blood), not falling on with so much violence with the first blows: and let all the apertures be stopped with clean and fine cloths dipped in pitch; as the eyes, and the mouth, and such as are formed by nature for necessary evacuation: then, having scattered a good quantity of thyme, and having laid the bullock on it, let them immediately go out of the house, and let them cover the door and the windows with strong clay, that there may be no entrance nor vent to the air, nor to the wind. The third week it is proper to open the building on all sides that the light and pure air may be admitted, except the side where a strong wind blows in; for if this be the case, it is proper to keep the windows shut on this side: but when the materials seem to be animated, having attracted a sufficient portion of air, it is again proper to secure the building with clay according to the former method: having then opened it on the eleventh day after this period, you will find it full of bees crowded in clusters on each other, and the horns, and the bones, and the hair, and nothing else of the bullock left. They say indeed that the kings are produced from the brain, but the other bees from the flesh. Kings are also produced from the spinal marrow. But those that are produced from the brain are superior to the others in size and beauty, and in strength. But the first change and transformation of the flesh into living creatures, and as it were a conception and birth, you will thus know; for when the building is opened, you will see things small and white in appearance, and like one another, and not perfect, nor yet such as may be properly called living animals, in great number about the bullock, all indeed motionless, but gradually increasing in size. You may then see the form of the wings with their divisions, and the bees assuming their proper colour, and seated around their king, and flying, but to a small distance, and with tremulous wings, on account of their want of practice, and the debility of their members.'

It is unnecessary, after these extracts, to discuss the merit of the translator; we can only lament that he has so unprofitably employed his time.

Removing Bees in France.

PASTURAGE OF BEES.

In the search of food, insects ramble far and wide. The vegetable kingdom presents to them a vast field for their banquets. Apart from the grasses and a few herbs and shrubs, the rest of the plants which cover the face of the earth, are to them either disgusting or absolutely poisonous. But from the gigantic banyan, which covers acres with its shade, to the tiny fungus, which the eye can scarcely perceive, there is a wide-spread provision of which insects may partake. It is probable that not a single plant exists, even of those kinds which to others are most offensive, that does not yield to some one or other of these creatures a delicious provision.

For them, indeed, a considerable portion of vegetable must have been provided. To mankind and the larger animals, for instance, the common nettle appears of little use, yet it yields food for at least thirty distinct species of insects. Nor is this all. The large herba-

ceous animals can subsist on no other part of plants than their leaves and seeds, either in a fresh or dried state, with sometimes the addition of the tender twigs or bark; but every part supplies proper food for different tribes of the insect race.

Some attack the roots; others the trunk and branches; a third class feed on the leaves; a fourth, with a more delicate appetite, prefer the flowers; and a fifth the fruit or seeds. Even a further selection takes place. Of those which feed on the roots, stems, and branches of vegetables, some grubs eat only the bark; others the albumen; others the resinous or other secretions; a fourth class the pith, and a fifth penetrates into the heart of the solid wood. Of those which prefer the leaves, some taste only the sap which fills their veins; others eat merely the pulpy substance; others only the lower surface of the leaf; while some devour its whole substance. Of the flower-feeders, some eat the petals; others, in their perfect state, choose the pollen, and a still larger class the honey secreted in the nectaries.

In the management of bees a great deal depends on supplying them with an abundant pasture. During a large part of the year a rich corn country is to them as a wilderness. They require, therefore, to be shifted from place to place, according to the circumstances of the season. Thus Celsus advised, that after the vernal pastures were consumed, they should be transported to places abounding with autumnal flowers; and hence in ancient times they were annually carried from **Achaia** to Attica, and from Euboea and the islands of the Cyclades to Scyrus. A similar course is pursued in France.

In Scotland the example is also followed. As soon as the bright flowers of summer are on the wane, the people of the lowlands despatch their hives in cart-loads to the blooming heather of the mountains, where the bees may enjoy an unfailing banquet of sweets. "It is indeed to be regretted," says a modern writer, "that our moorlands, in this respect, are so much more neglected than they ought to be. The very air of the highland hills is often redolent with the rich perfume, while here or there a solitary bee is seen or heard labouring with wearied wing among the inexhaustible stores of nature, and scarcely able to regain its lonely shielding in the distant vale." This is to be regretted, as the mountaineers are poor, and often want employment. It has been calculated that the pastures of Scotland could maintain as many bees as could produce 4,000,000 pints of honey, and 1,000,000 pounds of wax; and were these quantities tripled for England and Ireland, the produce of the British empire would be 12,000,000 pints of honey, and 3,000,000 pounds of wax annually.

But while we are thus neglectful, the people of Egypt, according to Maillet, imitate in some degree the industry and skill of their forefathers. One of their most admirable contrivances is, their sending their bees annually into distant countries, in order that they may procure sustenance at a time when they could not find any at home; and then afterwards bringing them back, like shepherds who should travel with their flocks, and make them feed as they go.

It was observed by the ancient inhabitants of Lower Egypt, that all plants blossomed, and the fruits of the earth

ripened, above six weeks earlier in [Lower] Egypt than with them. The mea[ns] used in consequence, to enable the[m] to reap advantage from the more [?] state of nature there, are still em[ployed] by their descendants.

About the end of October, al[l such] people of Lower Egypt as have hi[ves of] bees, embark them on the Nile, an[d con]vey them by that river into Upper [Egypt,] just at the time when the land ha[s been] sown and the flowers begin to bud. [The] hives thus sent are marked and num[bered] by their respective **owners**, and [placed] pyramidically in boats prepared f[or the] purpose. After remaining some d[ays at] the furthest station, and they are [sup]posed to have gathered all the wa[x and] honey they could find in the fields [within] the space of two or three leagues, [they] are conveyed in the same boats [some] three leagues lower down, and are [as] long as is necessary for them to [gather] the sweets of this spot also. Thu[s the] nearer they come to the place of [their] usual abode, they find their food f[ailing] in proportion. At length, about t[he be]ginning of February, after havin[g tra]velled through the whole length of [Egypt] gathering the rich produce of the [banks] of the Nile, they arrive at the [mouth] of that river, towards the ocean, w[hence] they set out, and from whence th[ey are] now returned to their several home[s. An] exact register is kept of every d[istrict] from whence the hives were desp[atched] in the beginning of the season, of [the] numbers, of the persons who sent [them,] and likewise of the mark or num[ber of] the boat to which they belonged.—*History of Insects.*

ART. IV.—*A Treatise on the Nature, Economy, and Practical Management of Bees; in which the various Systems of the British and Foreign Apiarians are examined, and the most approved Method laid down for effectually preserving the Lives of the Bees. Containing, also, an accurate Description, illustrated by Plates, of the Hives invented by Lombard, Ducouedic, Huber, Vicat, L'Abbé Della Rocca, and other foreign Apiarians; and of a newly invented Hive, for the purpose of depriving the Bees of their Honey with safety and expedition: forming the most complete Guide to the Study and Management of those valuable Insects.* By ROBERT HUISH, *Author of* "The Peruvians," *a Poem, &c. &c. Fellow of the Academy of Arts and Sciences of Gottingen: Honorary Member of the Imperial Apiarian Society of Vienna: and corresponding Member of the Agricultural Societies of Bavaria and Silesia.* 8vo. Pp. 404. Baldwin and Co. 1815.

WE sit down to the review of this work with a perfect acquiescence in the complaint and lamentation of the author,—

that a branch of rural economy, so important and profitable, as the
culture of bees, should be in such low esteem, or at least so little
attended to, in this country.   That the labours of these insects
are very profitable to the proprietors, who know how to manage
them, will be obvious to such as are not already aware of the
facts from their own experience, from the statements we shall
have occasion to make in the course of this article : few subjects, indeed, yield such large returns, in proportion to the
capital employed.   That it is also an object of national importance must certainly be admitted, if it should appear that
large sums of money are annually paid to foreigners for wax and
honey, which our own fields would furnish in great abundance,
were those winged ministers of man's necessities but cherished
as they deserve to be, and sent forth in sufficient numbers to
gather in the ample stores of treasure that lie scattered in gay
profusion over a fertile land, disregarded by the owner, and
totally lost to the community.   The harvest truly is great, but
the labourers are few; and most justly may it here be said,
while the present system of neglect is persisted in, that

> " Full many a flower is born to blush unseen,
>   And waste its sweetness on the desert air."

The national importance of bees will be seen in the strongest
light, when it is considered in how small a degree the capital
required for their maintenance, encroaches on the funds destined
for the support of any other species of industry ; and that, consequently, the greater part of the sum annually saved, by rendering
unnecessary the importation of wax and honey, would be so much
clear substantial addition to the wealth of the country, consti-
tuting a new fund for the maintenance of labour, and tending
still farther to promote the national prosperity.   What, then,
it may be asked, are the impediments to an extension of
aparian establishments, which are said to be so profitable to
the intelligent proprietor ? We may answer in brief,—bad management ;—a form of hive that necessitates the destruction of
the bees, whenever the produce of their labour is to be obtained ; and ignorance of the accidents which are to be guarded
against, and of the attentions which are necessary in particular
cases, to preserve the hives from desolation.   To ignorance
Mr. Huish adds superstition : in some parts of Great Britain,
he tells us, the people believe that a *purchased* hive never pros-
pers, and would not think of keeping one, unless it was *given*
to them : another species of superstition is, a fancy that the
bees ought not to be allowed to quit their hive on a Friday.
From the union of these causes there must necessarily result

much want of success; and they, who witness the ill fortune of their neighbours, are naturally deterred from engaging in a pursuit, which appears to *them* so full of trouble and vexation; with nothing more than a precarious chance of remuneration for their pains.

An improved system of management in this, as in every other branch of rural economy, must not be expected to become general on the sudden. A good example should be set by the gentry, who have opportunities of acquiring the requisite information; they should be communicative of their knowledge to those who wish to learn; and there can be little doubt that the peasantry will ultimately adopt what they see and feel to be a better method than their own. There is fortunately inherent in the very nature of man, a salutary dislike of innovation, which not only tends firmly to hold together the general frame of society, but continually preserves the mass of mankind from being deluded by the many futile, and not a few dangerous, schemes, which projectors of all kinds are ever calling upon the public to patronize. Yet it must at the same time be confessed, that the progress of improvement has been, and is, by this means retarded, though the evil is greatly counterbalanced by the good; for whilst error is beaten down by opposition, truth becomes established; it is mighty and will prevail. That system or doctrine, whether of husbandry, of philosophy, of religion, or of government, which has won its way to general acceptation, through a general conviction of its goodness, is set upon a firm foundation, it has stood the test, and can hardly be overturned but by a better.

The treatise of Mr. Huish is divided into thirty-two chapters, in which he appears to have omitted nothing that relates to the history or management of bees. He frequently engages in the discussion of questions, that have been the subjects of dispute to writers of this class in almost every age, and determines them with a tone of confidence, that could only proceed from " twenty years experience" of the nature and habits of these wonderful insects.

His zealous attachment, indeed, to this pursuit for so long a period, has enabled him to collect much useful information on the subject; some of which we shall take the liberty of communicating to our readers, in the extracts we are about to lay before them. The construction of a habitation for the reception of bees, is of primary importance, especially with a view to the spoliation of their combs, without destroying the colony; and the hive, described in the following passage, appears to be every way better adapted to that purpose, than the one which is commonly used in the country.

" My first object (says Mr. Huish) was to select those materials which I judged most suitable for the construction of a hive, and after repeated experiments on the various materials, I was convinced that there was none more proper than straw. This I know is deemed by Huber, but I must be allowed in this instance to differ from that celebrated apiarian. The shape of the hive was my next consideration. I had been so often defeated in my expectations in the deprivation of the common straw hive, and especially by the sticks with which they are necessarily furnished to prevent the combs from falling, that I was persuaded it was a shape fitted only for those persons who suffocate their bees, but to the deprivator it was the most inconvenient and unmanageable form that could be suggested. It was a flower-pot which first gave me the idea of the shape, and which appeared to possess peculiar advantages. It would, in the first place supersede the necessity of sticks; for the combs then acting like a wedge, being larger at the top than at the bottom, could not fall on the board. This was one great difficulty overcome; but then the impossibility of extracting the combs from the bottom of the hive presented itself; for upon the same principle that the combs acting as a wedge would prevent them falling down, so it would be impossible to extract them from the bottom, as they would be smaller there than at the top. One only method therefore presented itself of extracting the combs from the top, but this I knew could not be effected, were the combs all constructed on one basis, which is the case in the generality of hives. I therefore set my invention at work to devise a method by which each comb could have its separate foundation; but I was aware of the perverse and untractable temper of the insects under my management, and that from the very spirit of opposition, which, were I inclined to be severe, I might say arises from their being under the government of a female, they would not construct their combs in the particular manner consonant to my wishes. I had tried a hive on the principle of Huber, and I found that, notwithstanding the scientific and philosophical elucidation of Mr. John Hunter, that an edge forming a salient or even a returning angle, determined the foundation of the combs of the bees : they had nevertheless disregarded this principle, and had worked in the interstices between the frames. To give to each comb its own foundation was not a matter of any great difficulty; but in what manner the bees were to be prevented from working in the interstices, and at the same time to be forced to work on the foundation prescribed to them, cost me some little pains to determine. It suggested itself to me that a bee will never work on an unstable foundation ; and, therefore, that I should succeed in my design, if I could insert my net-work between the pieces of wood. Having obtained eight pieces of well seasoned wood, about three inches broad, and half-inch thick, I laid them equi-distant on the top of the hive, and having fastened them to the outer projecting band which serves as their basis, I covered them with net-work, over which I placed a circular board the whole size of the hive. Thus were the bees to attempt to fasten their combs in the interstices they would find the net-work, which being an infirm foundation, would oblige them to construct the combs on the single boards. I had, however, now given to my hive a flat top, which I knew was injurious to my bees, as it prevented the evaporation of the steam arising from their bodies. To obviate this, I made six holes in the circular board, which was placed upon the net, and which I closed with plates of tin, perforated with small holes. The whole I covered with a convex cover of straw, manufactured in the same manner as the hive; the interior form of which facilitates the flowing of the vapours down the sides of the hive; and the exterior form prevents any rain from lodging on it. This cover is well plastered down, to prevent the admission of any light into the hive. At any time or season, when I require some honey-comb, or at the end of the season, when I deprive my bees of their superfluous store, I open the top, and take the side-boards out, from which having cut the honey-comb, I replace them in the hive, and it facilitates the operation to have some vacant boards ready to supply the places of the full ones. This operation is very easily and speedily performed; it has the advantage of not disturbing the middle combs, and I have often deprived these hives of their honey without the loss of a single bee, excepting those few who were foolish enough to leave their sting in various parts of my dress. In the month of August, 1810, I obtained from one of these hives, eighteen pounds of beautiful honey-comb; by the end of September the void was again filled, and I extracted ten pounds more, leaving sufficient to supply them through the winter."

The principal advantages offered by the above hive are, the opportunity which it gives of easily inspecting the state of its interior,—the facility of extracting a portion of the combs, for the purpose of making room when the hive is crowded, and of taking a due share of the produce, and the means which it affords of preserving the lives of the bees, from year to year. But in order to be satisfied of the advantage of attempting to preserve their lives, we ought to see reason for believing that the natural duration of the life of a bee is extended beyond a year; this is a point which has hitherto been involved in considerable obscurity: though on many accounts it seems probable, and from the following observations almost certain, that a bee may live at least three or four years, if not prematurely destroyed. Mr. H. says,

" I can positively affirm, that the same queen has inhabited a hive for four years, and it is proved by the following circumstance;—in the spring of 1809 I had occasion to feed one of my hives, and in the evening when I took the plate from the hive, to my great mortification, I found the queen apparently dead, having been drowned in the liquid. I hastened with her to the house, and by the dint of as much attention as was ever bestowed by the most Philanthropic Member of the Humane Society, in recovering a drowned man, I succeeded in restoring my valuable patient to life. The act, however, which I committed, during the syncope of the queen, might be followed with great advantage in certain countries, for I *clipped the wings of royalty,* and then with a slight mutilation returned her to her longing subjects. This queen belonged to a strong second swarm of that year, and I clipped her wings for the purpose of ascertaining on the following year whether the old queen or a new one departed with the swarm. In the year 1810, after the swarm had departed from the hive, I drove the bees from it, and I found my mutilated queen still in the possession of her original kingdom. In the year 1813, I had occasion to unite a weak swarm to this hive, and in joining them I discovered my old mutilated friend again. This same hive was, however, from some particular cause, forsaken in the following year, and the fate of my quondam friend the queen remains to this day a secret to me. I however ascertained the fact, that a Queen Bee can live four years, and I draw the conclusion that a common Bee could live the same period, were it not exposed to particular dangers, exterior to the hive."

It is recommended that each hive should rest upon a separate stool, supported by a single pedestal; and in case of need, a chain and padlock may be so applied as to secure our property from the attacks of a dangerous two-legged depredator. To guard against the invasions of the numerous other enemies of the bees, a great degree of vigilance is required: every thing should be removed which can facilitate their approach to the hives; yet, in some parts of England, it is said, the hives are placed extremely low, and, as it were, to assist the mice, toads, and other enemies of the bees, a piece of board is placed gradually inclining from the opening down to the ground. We know not what the ladies will think of the author, on reading the ensuing passage, and a former one of the same nature; he certainly seems to entertain but an unfavourable opinion of the sex.

" In Sussex (he proceeds to tell us) this plan is generally adopted, and as I once passed through that country I stopped at several cottages where I saw the above plan adopted, and reasoned with the proprietors on the injury which must necessarily arise to their bees, by an adherence to such an injurious practice ; but to my great mortification, the hives generally belonged to, and were under the management of the female part of the family, who were so much devoted to the old method of managing bees, that they literally looked upon me as a person who knew nothing about the business, and my ignorance was greater in proportion as my advice departed from the long established customs of the country."

For the destruction of mice, the author keeps constantly round his apiary some traps of a very simple kind. A pea is soaked in water, and then strung upon a thread which is tied to a small stick at each end; these are fixed in the ground at the exact distance of the width of a brick, the brick is then placed on the thread, and the mouse coming to eat the pea, gnaws also the thread, and the support of the brick being then taken away, it falls and kills the mouse.

About the time of swarming, the young queen is said to make a particular noise, similar to *chip, chip,* which is distinctly heard two or three nights preceding the swarming. Respecting this circumstance we find it observed in a note, that

" 'The capability of the queen to utter any noise has been much doubted; on this subject the Abbe della Rocca relates a curious anecdote. A person, not very skilful in the management of bees, was appointed to deprive a hive of a part of its honey, and in the operation he wounded the queen. She immediately issued a most plaintive cry, and the bees attacked instantaneously all the spectators, and the animals in the vicinity. A horse of the Archbishop was by chance tied to a tree contiguous to the apiary, and it was attacked with so much fury, that it broke the reins, and took refuge in a country house; but the bees pursued it with so much acrimony, that it mounted the stairs of the first story, and burst into a room full of company, to whom he was, no doubt, an unwelcome visitor."

The author himself, on one occasion, saw a swarm alight upon the muzzle of an ass, which was tied to an adjoining post; "the patience of the animal could not brook the strangers, and it began to rub its muzzle on the ground. The indignation of the swarm was roused, and the animal was so stung that it died in three days. The swarm was consequently lost to the proprietor."

The value of a swarm is estimated by its weight; the best swarms are from five to six pounds: larger than these are not desirable, as they impoverish the parent hive too much. "Five thousand bees weigh about a pound; a good swarm consists therefore of about 20,000 bees." In this estimate it is not said whether the bees were weighed with their honey-bags full or empty, and, without some explanation of these circumstances, there seems to be a degree of inaccuracy in the following statement.

" The quantity of honey which a swarm carries along with it, for its sustenance, has been ascertained from the following curious circumstance:—in some countries, particularly to the south and south-east of Europe, it is customary to put a swarm into a bag, and this originates in the propensity of the bees to lodge themselves in the woods, in which it is the particular office of some persons to collect them. A person having once collected a swarm in a bag, he suspended it to a tree, whilst he went in search of some other swarms;—a most ardent sun killed the bees, but more than three pounds of honey were collected from them, leaving some behind. It may therefore be quoted, that about four pounds is the quantity of provisions which a swarm takes with it."

It has been much disputed, whether the bees fall into a state of torpor during the winter: our author concludes from some experiments, which he made in the severe winter of 1813, when he found the temperature of a hive to be twenty degrees above the freezing point, whilst that of the open air was twenty degrees below it; that two things are incontestably proved : first, that the bees, in a state of union, fear not the greatest colds of our climate; secondly, that they are not in a state of torpor during the frost, as has been asserted by some authors." P. 255.—Yet, with much apparent inconsistency, we find him, in p. 261, affirming that, " in the north the extreme cold preserves the bees in a state of inanimation, and prevents them from consuming their winter provender, which, on the return of spring, they find in great abundance, and thus escape the great evil of famine."

There exists also considerable unsteadiness in the directions given relative to the quantity of honey, to be left in the hive for winter store. At p. 260 he says, " at the conclusion of the season, it is the duty of every apiarian to weigh his hives, and he may with safety be allowed to deprive them of all their honey exceeding twenty pounds." In an old hive twenty-four pounds should be left, on account of the greater quantity of bee-bread which is found in it than in a new one. At p. 325, the apiarian is directed to take from his hives all above *thirty* pounds; and at p. 339, in speaking of the purchase of hives, it is said that, " if purchased in the autumn, the weight should not be less than thirty pounds ; one of twenty-five pounds may survive the winter, but is so very dependent on certain circumstances, and which in general happen nine times out of ten, that without the aid of food, the hive would perish before the ensuing spring." It is very possible, that in one place the weight of honey alone may be intended, and in the other, the weight of the whole hive; but, if so, there is certainly a want of precision in the language.

We shall now proceed to the author's statement of the profits attending an apiary, and leave our readers to judge for themselves. He informs us that nearly 80,000l. annually are spent by this country in the purchase of wax alone; and that

" In one ship, the Aurora, from Papinburg, was imported this year (1814) 41 casks of honey, weighing 68 cwt. 1 qr. 23 lbs. or 7667 lbs.; and in about a week afterwards, another vessel was entered at the Custom-house, London, bringing 8424 lbs., making, in two ships only, the enormous quantity of 16,088 lbs. of honey. The Zeelust, from Amsterdam, entered 19th May, 1814, brought over 4 hhds. and twelve casks of honey, weighing 50 cwt. 2 qrs. 14 lbs.

In the following passage, the price of a swarm is rated at the maximum; in the country it may be purchased for seven or ten shillings.

" I will state the profit of five years on a fair and equitable scale, making at the same time ample allowances for those losses, which even the most skilful apiarian cannot prevent. I will suppose a person to buy a swarm in 1812, for which he pays one guinea: there is little doubt of the bees making a sufficiency of honey to keep them until the ensuing spring; and after having diminished the entrance, and fastened the hive on the stool, the apiarian has no further trouble until the spring, when his bees begin to work. In the month of May or June his hive swarms, and in about ten days afterwards he obtains another swarm, which is called a cast. His apiary now consists of three hives, from one of which (the cast) it will be most prudent for him to take the honey; as from the smallness of the number of bees, and lateness of the season, it seldom makes honey sufficient for its support. I will suppose the cast to weigh fifteen pounds: these will bring him, if sold, twenty-two shillings. Thus in the first year the apiarian has received back the price of his original hive, and he has doubled his stock. The second year his two hives produce him four swarms. I would then advise him to sell his casts, which will bring him fifteen shillings each, and add his two swarms to his stock. He has now four good hives; and at the expiration of every year let the apiarian weigh his hives, and take from them all above thirty pounds, that quantity being sufficient for the support of the best peopled hive through the longest winter. I will suppose, on an average, that each hive could spare him ten pounds; the second year he has therefore received one pound ten shillings for two casts, and forty pounds of honey-comb, which at one shilling and six-pence per pound, (but which sells in the shops at three shillings and sixpence or four shillings) produce him three pounds. The third year his four hives produce him eight swarms. He follows the same plan as in the preceding years, and at the commencement of the fourth year, his apiary consists of eight stocks. At the beginning of the fifth year, his apiary has increased to sixteen stocks. I will now calculate the actual profit.

Dr.	£	s.	d.		Cr.	£	s.	d.
1812—To one swarm .	1	1	0		1813—By one cast - -	0	15	0
1813—To two new bee-hives - - .	0	4	0		By 10lbs of honey taken from the first swarm, at 1s. 6d. per lb. -	0	15	0
1814—To four new bee-hives - - .	0	8	0		1813—By two casts - -	1	10	0
1815—To eight new hives - - .	0	16	0		By 20 lbs. of honey-comb, taken from the two swarms -	1	10	0
1816—To sixteen new bee-hives - .	1	12	0		1815—By four casts -	3	0	0
1817—To, thirty-two new bee-hives	3	4	0		By 40lbs. of honey-comb taken from the four swarms -	3	0	0
To ten pounds of sugar for feeding the bees if necessary, at 8d. per lb. - - - .	0	6	8		1816—By eight casts -	6	0	0
To thirty-two stools for the hives, at 2s. each - - -	3	4	0		By 60lbs. of honey-comb taken from 8 swarms	6	0	0
To incidental expences - -	1	1	0		1817—By sixteen casts	12	0	0
					By 160lbs. of honey-comb taken from sixteen swarms -	12	0	0
						£46	10	0
					Deduct	11	16	8
	£11	16	8					

Actual profit in five years - £34 13 4
If the apiarian wishes to keep only ten hives, he can then sell twenty-two at £1 1 0 each - £23 2 0

£57 15 4

" Thus his profit at the expiration of five years, will be £57

15s. 4d.; and leaving him ten good stocks in his garden. I have not enumerated in this estimate, any probable profit which may be derived from virgin swarms, but I trust I have demonstrated the certain profit which can be obtained from a well-conducted apiary."

On many points of physiology Mr. Huish differs in opinion from Huber and several other writers of celebrity; but for the discussion of these topics, and for many important observations we must refer to the volume itself; which, though it be not composed with the elegance that will satisfy the fastidious reader, contains abundant materials for the gratification of a liberal curiosity, and will certainly repay the trouble of a careful perusal.

Critical Review—Jan: 1816 —

Sir,—It is my intention in this paper to point out the best and easiest method to those who are inclined to undertake the management of bees; and as my rules are derived from my own experience and practice, they may perhaps induce others to follow an example, from which both profit and much rational amusement may be derived. It will, in the first place, add much to the pleasure of those who are about to keep bees, if they make themselves acquainted with the character of those useful insects.

We should recollect that the minutest things in nature are appointed to some particular end and purpose; and that ' the Deity is as conspicuous in the structure of a fly's wing, as he is in the bright globe of the Sun itself.'

Of all the surprizing varieties of insects which have come under our notice, bees are most to be admired.

Independent of the profit derived from them, they serve as a pattern, by which man may in many instances govern his own conduct. Their cleanliness, their indefatigable industry, their courage and loyalty, are well known; and an instance of the latter quality deserves to be recorded, though it does little credit to the person who tried the experiment. A queen bee was taken from her hive, and by means of horse hairs fastened to a grass plot; she was followed by all her subjects; and as she could not quit the spot, the whole of them perished around her in the course of two or three days.

It would be carrying this article to too great a length, if I were to endeavour to excite your interest and compassion in favour of bees, by relating some of the many observations I have made on them. My chief object now is to endeavour to prove how little that person consults his own profit and interest who follows the old practice of suffocating these poor insects at that time of the year when, after all their labours, they have laid up a sufficient store to maintain themselves through the winter. A hive of bees should be considered like a sum of money in the funds. It will pay you good interest, and also increase your capital, by proper management; whereas, by destroying them, you lessen, if not annihilate your capital, and prevent the increase of that wealth you might otherwise have. The fact is, that a healthy hive of bees, in all tolerably good seasons, can afford to part with some of its hoard, and yet have sufficient to support themselves through the winter. To those who have little time or inclination to bestow on their bees, I would simply recommend the adoption of the following method of securing part of the honey of a hive. Take a common flower pot, the size to be in proportion to the strength of your hire; suppose one that would hold from eight to twelve pounds of honey: put a slender stick through the hole which is at the bottom of every flower pot, of a sufficient length to come rather below the edge of it; fasten the stick into the hole of the pot by means of a little clay; then with a sharp knife cut out two or three rounds of the straw at the top of your hive, so as to make a hole of three or four inches in diameter; place the mouth of the flower pot upon this hole, and keep it tight down by means of some more clay: a very small piece of white virgin wax fixed to the end of the stick will often induce the bees to begin to fill the pot with honey sooner than they would otherwise do. I would recommend the above operation to take place early in March; and in good seasons the pot will be found quite filled by the middle or end of June; when it may be taken off, and another put in its place; which in very good seasons will also be filled. Care however should always be taken that the bees have a sufficient stock of honey to last them through the winter and the early part of the spring; as many stocks are lost from a want of attention in this respect. A little honey or sugar is never thrown away upon bees at these seasons. Those who can afford to substitute glass instead of flower pots, will derive additional pleasure as well as profit from the change; as they will not only be enabled to see their bees at work, but honey made in glass is of a purer quality and sells for more money than that which is made in straw or earthern ware. The above mentioned plan is so simple and easy, that it may be adopted by any one who has a hive of bees.

To those, however, who may be inclined to have a colony of bees on a larger scale, I would recommend the use of Mr. Huish's hives. They may be purchased at a shop in High Holborn, and are admirably adapted not only to enable any one to remove a comb at pleasure, but to discover the whole internal state of the hive. His Treatise on Bees also is an excellent work, and will afford both instruction and amusement to any one who peruses it.

I think I could supply you hereafter with some interesting anecdotes of bees; and I trust that what has been already said may induce persons not to sacrifice the lives of these industrious insects for the sake of all their summer store; and will also implant a desire to cultivate them in a more extended manner than has hitherto been done in this country.   R. J.

ON BEES.

I AM anxious to rescue these industrious little insects from the unnecessary destruction which too frequently awaits them when their winter store has been collected. If one person should be persuaded to adopt the plan suggested in the last number, my time will not have been spent unprofitably: the following anecdotes of their surprizing instinct and sagacity, most of which are derived from personal observation, may excite a further interest in their favour:—

When Bees are attacked by wasps, or by Bees from other hives, they not only place an additional number of sentinels at the mouth of the hive, but will frequently contract the entrance, so that the approach to their treasures is more easily defended.

Mice are great enemies to Bees, and frequently get into the hive, where they sometimes lose their lives before they can make their escape. When the mouse is killed, it is not suffered to waste away by the common process of putrefaction, lest the health and safety of the whole hive should be endangered; to provide against this they embalm the body of the mouse in a case of propolis, and the remains thus gradually decay, without emitting any offensive odour.

When a snail with a shell gets into a hive, it costs the Bees much less trouble. As soon as it receives the first wound from a sting, the snail retires within its shell. In this case, the Bees, instead of pasting it all over with propolis, content themselves with glueing all round the margin of the shell; thus forming the shell into a tomb, and providing against all further mischief.

The walls of the cell are so extremely thin, that their mouths might be thought in danger of suffering by the frequent entering and issuing of the Bees, either to feed the young brood or to deposit the honey. To prevent this, they make a kind of rim round the margin of each cell, and this rim is three or four times thicker than the walls. This border round the top of the cell has another use; it effectually retains the honey, and thus the cell can be entirely filled with honey, even to taking a convex form, and then the pellicle of wax, with which it is covered for the winter's use, presses closely upon it, and prevents the admission of every humidity.

M. Huber asserts, that when Bees lose their queen, they will appropriate some of the common young brood to replace her. They begin by prolonging and enlarging the cells of those so selected; they supply them with food of a different kind, and with a greater quantity of it; and the brood reared in this manner, instead of changing to common Bees, become real queens.

Bees may frequently be observed in hot weather at the entrance and bottom of their hives, moving their wings with great rapidity. It is conjectured this is done for the purpose of promoting a circulation of air in the hive, which not only prevents the wax from melting, but also keeps the Bees cool in the upper part of the hive. The great quantity of air which these insects produce by this mode of ventilation, may be ascertained by any one who has a hive with an opening at the top.

In order to prove their economy of labour, a hive of Bees was brought from a distant place to a situation where food was to be had all the year round. The Bees soon relaxed from their usual industry, and discontinued to lay up their accustomed store of honey when they found that they could so readily procure it whenever they might have occasion for it.

Before Bees swarm, scouts are sent out, who fix upon a place for the queen to repair to: as soon as these scouts return to the hive, the whole swarm leave it and repair to the situation previously chosen for them. How this intelligence is conveyed is difficult to conjecture; but the fact is undoubted. (Vide Philosophical Transactions for 1807.)

The following anecdote is related by the Abbé della Rocca :—

‘ One day,’ he says, ‘ I was sitting on the top of a mountain, on which the wind raged with the greatest violence ; I saw a number of Bees which came to gather the honey; the wind blew with such violence, that as soon as the Bees presented themselves they were repulsed, and their resistance was useless ;—fatigued with this combat, many of them fell upon an expedient which I had read of, but had never before seen. Perceiving that they were too light to resist the wind, they collected some little stones ; and taking them up with their feet, they took their flight afresh, and finally succeeded in their design.’

I will conclude this paper with the words of a French author, who speaks of Bees in the following terms :—‘ In the vast creation of insects, there is not one whose history presents to us such a prodigious number of wonders as the Bee. How is it possible to refrain from transports of admiration in contemplating it ? This insect, so weak, so small in appearance, is seen working without relaxation in collecting the materials of its habitation ; forming them with so much art, and constructing those wonderful edifices, the architecture of which has been a subject of meditation for the most profound Geometricians.’　　　　　　　　　　　　　　　　　　　　　E. T.

A

COMPLEAT BODY

OF

HUSBANDRY.

CONTAINING

RULES for performing, in the moſt profitable
Manner, the whole Buſineſs of the Farmer and
Country Gentleman,

IN

Cultivating, Planting and *Stocking* of Land;

In judging of the ſeveral Kinds of *Seeds*, and of *Manures*; and
in the Management of *Arable* and *Paſture Grounds:*

TOGETHER WITH

The moſt approved Methods of Practice in the ſeveral
Branches of HUSBANDRY,

From ſowing the SEED, to getting in the CROP; and in Breeding
and Preſerving CATTLE, and Curing their DISEASES.

To which is annexed,

The whole Management of the ORCHARD, the
BREWHOUSE, and the DAIRY.

Compiled from the Original Papers of the late
THOMAS HALE, Eſq;

And enlarged by many new and uſeful Communications on
Practical Subjects,

From the Collections of Col. STEVENSON, Mr. RANDOLPH,
Mr. HAWKINS, Mr. STOREY, Mr. OSBORNE, the Reverend
Mr. TURNER, and others.

A WORK founded on Experience; and calculated for general Benefit;
conſiſting chiefly of Improvements made by modern Practitioners in
Farming; and containing many valuable and uſeful Diſcoveries, never
before publiſhed.

ILLUSTRATED WITH

A great Number of CUTS, containing Figures of the Inſtruments of
Huſbandry; of uſeful and poiſonous Plants, and various other Subjects
engraved from Original Drawings.

Publiſhed by his Majeſty's Royal Licence and Authority.

VOL. IV.

LONDON:

Printed for THO. OSBORNE, in Gray's-Inn;
THO. TRYE, near Gray's-Inn Gate, Holbourn; and
S. CROWDER on London-Bridge. MDCCLIX.

[illegible]

TO what we have published relating to bees, in the preceding volumes, and which we hope contains all that is
useful in the common practice: we have now something
to add from the correspondence of an ingenious clergyman
in Suſſex, who has beſtowed a great deal of his leiſure upon
the care of this uſeful inſect, and who, adding to the common advantages of obſervation and accuſtomed knowledge
under this head, a very perfect claſſical learning, has endeavoured to improve the common practice of England and
Holland, from that of the antient Italy; and has added to
Virgil, Varro, and Columella, as well as to the moderns,
a great deal from his own obſervation. I wiſh he had per-

S 3

mitted

mitted us to publish his several letters in his own words; but since that is not allowed, we shall be careful to preserve their meaning; and shall endeavour to render the instruction they convey plainer to the farmer, and in a shorter compass.

This gentleman's house is situated upon the edge of a vast heath: before it there is a large fertile space of ground, well enclosed and cultivated. Behind he is sheltered from the north by hills. Plantations, made a century ago, defend him from the east; and even the heath, to which he is open to the south west, is not without some shelter from stubbed oaks and brambles on the rising hillocks.

Among the other amusements of a retired life, the care of bees came early into this gentleman's thoughts; and he saw that his situation favoured them, because it was warm and well sheltered: but he found advantages in it, which exceeded expectation; and of which, at first, he could not guess the cause.

Virgil, from whom many of the other Romans copy their directions, advises the placing bees where they will be most quiet; and where the sun has power. This gentleman chose a situation, the warmest and most sheltered of any about his house, and where the servants had least occasion to come. He took into his own hands, the two or three pasture grounds which lay contiguous to his house, and keeping them principally for hay, few cattle were put into them.

The creatures therefore had rest and warmth; and he assisted them with all the comforts usually directed in books, or practised by those who keep bees. He observed, that they thrive better than those of his neighbours, and upon examining into the reason, he soon discovered that it was owing to their having larger room to rove: those bees, which belonged to a neighbour, whose house was near a publick road, and whose hives stood near his yard, he found scarce ever ventured farther than the garden, wherein the hives were placed: whereas, his went freely over all the fields, especially when they were laid up for hay; and what surprised him very much, they took the heath into their circuit, and seemed no where happier.

The success of his swarms, justified the doctrine of the antients on this head; and he soon found the means to encrease them yet more. It is a custom to rub the hives with baum, an herb very agreeable to the bees. This gentleman found they were much fonder of another herb, the

CE-

CEDRONILLA. The reader will find a full account of it in our body of gardening, with a figure, and its culture. It is a species of dracocyphalus; and the vulgar gardeners call it, from some resemblance in the smell to the balsam of Gilead, the balm of Gilead plant. The hives of the bees were rubbed often with this; and half a dozen flourishing plants of it were set round about the hives, and kept well watered. This had a great effect. The bees were always lively and chearful, and they soon became so numerous, as to form swarm after swarm, and require new habitations.

It often happens that late swarms are useless; but no such accident happened to this gentleman.

They found food in plenty, whatever were their numbers; and as they stood warm, they would venture out in search of it oftener than others would in suspicious weather.

The quantity of honey from these bees was greatly superior to the usual proportion, but there was a particularity in the colour: it had a pale reddish cast, but no other flavour than the honey of other people.

The proprietor of the hives had often wondered at the frequent visits his bees made to the heath, but he began now to suspect the cause.

He observed, that they were very fond of the flowers of the plant called HEATH, which grows in abundance on the grounds of the same name; and as the colour of that flower is red, he began to suspect this gave the tinge to the honey. The observations and enquiries he made in the succeeding seasons, gave him full proof of this. He found that all those who kept bees near the heath, had more or less of reddish tinge in their honey. In some who lay very near, but with a road between, the honey had little of that cast, because the bees would not venture among the cattle and the passengers; in others who had the passage free, it was more: and he found one farmer, whose little garden terminated at the heath, and whose house had its front upon the road, whose honey was so red, that none chose to buy it.

But with this there came also another discovery of more consequence, the redder the honey was, the greater was the quantity of it; and as this tinge does no real hurt to the honey, it is certainly of consequence that the quantity is so much encreased. The observation is certain, that bees will feed with great pleasure upon the flowers of heath; that

they

they get a great quantity of honey from them, and that the honey is as good as any other, the colour of it being somewhat particular. This should teach all who live on the borders of heaths, to keep abundance of bees: for they will be supported in such places with less expence and trouble than elsewhere, and they will produce a much larger profit.

The nearer a stand of bees is to a kitchen garden the better, not only for the health of the bees, but the flavour of the honey. The warmer parts of Europe abound with the fragrant and aromatick herbs wild; and it is for that reason the honey of those places is superior to that of England. The only chance we have of giving ours the same quality, is by planting such herbs near the hives. In a kitchen garden they are raised for the service of the table, and the bees will have their share of them. Thyme and favoury, hyffop, and sweet marjoram, all give this fine flavour to the honey; and the greater the abundance of them, the better it will be.

This gentleman observed, that the bees were very fond of borage; and he sowed a large femicircular bed of it at a small distance from the hives. This agrees with the direction we have given in a preceding chapter, for raising the plant vipers buglofs for the same purpose; for this is not very unlike borage in its nature. Indeed I have observed, that all the asperi foliate plants, properly fo called, such as buglofs, fage of Jerufalem, and the like, are very much fought after by bees; and many of the stellate kind, as the white lady's bedstraw, and such others.

CHAP. CXVI.
Of the use of the saffron plant for bees.

THE antients give us one direction which we have not followed, and which I am particularly furprized should escape this gentleman; it is the planting faffron near the places where bees are kept. I have observed the common garden crocus, which are true kinds of faffron, are always greatly frequented by the bees during their short times of flowering; and it is not a wonder, for we find their wine parts, which in all flowers are the peculiar organs that furnish the honey, are very rich and moift. The antients fay, the faffron gave not only a fine aromatick flavour to the honey of bees, which were kept near where it was planted,
but

but also heightened its natural yellowish hue to the colour of pure gold. Columella recommends the Corycian and Sicilian saffron for this purpose; but our farmer may be told, there is none equal to that of England.

The common saffron may be very easily propagated in gardens for this purpose; and its flower is as beautiful as any of the common crocus we plant for shew. But much more than this may be done for this purpose. We have brought the art of gardening to so much perfection now, that we can continue a shew of flowers, in the plants of the bulbous kind, much longer than their natural time. This is to be done by planting some parcels of roots later in the ground; and by this art, with the assistance nature gives of the variety of spring crocus and autumnal ones, we may have a blow of these flowers, for the service of the bees, nearly all the summer.

Beside the first mentioned use of giving, by this means, a peculiar colour and flavour to the common honey, this plantation will very well answer the purpose of those, whose honey suffers in colour, from their hiving in the neighbourhoods of heaths: the bees, by having a quantity of crocusses just before them, will be kept, in some measure, from the flowers of the heath; and the yellow from these plants will take off the redness which arises from the other.

A farther direction may be given on this head, which will be of great advantage. The farmer, who lives in a saffron country, should always keep bees; they will be particularly strong and healthy from the advantage they receive from this plant; they will swarm oftener and in larger number than others; and not only the quantity of honey will be great, but the quality excellent.

There is more difference in honey, occasioned by this article of the plants in the neighbourhood of the hives, than many think. The gentleman, to whom we are obliged for the remarks, whereon these additions to that article are founded, assures us, he can discover by the taste of the honey, what plants principally grow in the neighbourhood of the place where it was made. The farmer, who plants saffron, should always place a number of hives in that part of his garden which is nearest the saffron field, or from whence the bees can make their way the most easily to it. Or if others in his neighbourhood have saffron fields, tho' not himself, he should never fail to take the same advantage. It gives him a considerable benefit without any hurt

to the proprietor. The bees will give no disturbance to the
people employed to gather the saffron, for they only work
in the fields certain hours; and those creatures will not
come into it at that time, because they hate a disturbance;
they take their flights only when the gatherers have left the
field, and they enrich their combs without hurting the
saffron.

CHAP. CXVII.

Of other herbs which give a flavour to honey.

AMONG the flowers bees love most, come those of the
bean, but they are least useful to them. The quantity
of honey they obtain from these, appears, on nice examination, to be less than from many other flowers; and tho'
the bean flower itself be very sweet, it gives a kind of faint-
ness to the honey. Nothing but repeated and accurate
trials, by tasting the honey made at certain seasons, can
determine this point of the effect of various flowers upon
it; but those trials are worth making; and the effect is
easily known. This has been fairly tried by our corre-
spondents, and he has found, that the honey they collect
from these favourite blossoms, is pale, whitish, mealy and
sickly to the taste.

On the contrary, where there are turnips and cabbages
which stand for seed, the bees are fond of their flowers, and
though one would think these a very unpromising kind,
they encrease and improve the honey. There is no purer
honey than is collected from these flowers; its colour is a
pale yellow, and the taste is a perfect simple sweetness. The
first observation our correspondent made on this, was on the
honey of some bees which stood near a field of corn which
had been ill managed, and was over run with *charlock*, a
plant of the same class. He observed the bees were particularly fond of the flowers of this plant, and he had the curiosity to desire to taste the honey. This gave the first in-
timation of the effect of that plant, which more particular
observations afterwards confirmed.

Mathiolus, who has collected carefully from the antients
on this head, mentions, with wonder, the fondness bees
shew for the mustard plant: Virgil and Columella overlooked this among the favourites of the bee, but observation proves it to be true; and upon the principle just laid
down, there is nothing strange in it, for the mustard is of
　　　　　　　　　　　　　　　　　　　　　　　the

the same kind with charlock, turneps and cabbage, though different in the peculiar sharpness of the seed : the flowers are formed alike, and they are of the same class of plants.

Violets are a flower very agreeable to bees, for the time they last ; but let the farmer observe, that the common single violet, such as grows in hedges, is the proper kind ; for the double violets, usually planted in gardens for ornament, while they invite the bees by their smell, only tantalize them, for they contain no honey. There is a very peculiar sweetness in the honey collected in this early season, at a place where the violets, whether wild or planted, are abundant.

In all these accounts of the effect of various plants on honey, the reader is to expect only moderate changes, and these, according to the circumstances, greater or lesser in degree. The honey never shews the full effect of any flower, because the bees never feed from any one kind alone ; but from the garden plants in full flower, and which they are seen most attached to, some fair conclusion may be always made, that the honey of that time, though not collected entirely from these, yet is in great part owing to them.

There are also seasons when bees go less out than usual, or to a less distance. These shew the effect of certain plants more clearly, if there happen ten days or a fortnight of tempestuous weather, at a time when a parcel of seeding turneps are in flower in the same garden where the hive is, the bees will content themselves with what they can get from these, because it is disagreeable to them to go farther, and, in that case, the new made honey will, in a manner, be all made from that flower. These, and the like accidents, in the course of a life devoted to contemplation, have given opportunities of knowing the effect of particular flowers on the products of the bees, which have perhaps fallen in the way of few others.

Roses are a favourite flower of bees ; but it is only under certain circumstances they pay so much regard to them. It is not honey, but wax they collect from this flower ; and if they do not want wax, they slight it.

The red rose is the kind they most affect ; and the less double it is, the better they like it. The reason is plain from what we have explained before, relating to the nature of wax. The yellow buttons, on the threads of flowers, are the parts wherein it is originally formed by nature, and

from

from whence bees collect it.   Thefe are very numerous in
the rofe, therefore the bees love that flower; but the more
double the flower is, the lefs wax there can be in it, for
the leaves, which make this fulnefs, are formed out of the
threads and thefe yellow buttons ; fo that the fuller or
doubler the flower is, the fewer of thefe buttons there are,
and the lefs temptation the bees have to meddle with it.
When a rofe is perfectly double, there are none of thefe
threads or yellow buttons left in it ; and the bee no longer
regards it at all.   This difcovery, that the doublenefs of
flowers is formed in this manner, is new, but it is certain,
and in many inftances, particularly in the hollyhock and in
the double tulip, the button may be yet feen upon the new
leaves, fhewing their origin.   While thefe buttons remain
in any ftate in the flower, the bees will come to it for this
purpofe ; but they are fondeft of it in perfect finglenefs, which
is the ftate of nature, and in which the wax is found in
it in the greateft perfection.

The common broom is another plant, from whofe flowers the bees collect a great quantity of honey.   This is fuf-
fered, by a ftrange neglect, to over-run whole tracts of
hilly ground in fome parts of the kingdom ; and broom-
fields is a term by which the people exprefs fuch land.
Though they are very negligent who fuffer ground to be
thus over-run, the farmer fhould take the advantage of it
for his bees.   If he live near fuch a field, let him immediately fet up a ftand of hives in that part of his garden, from
whence they can get at the broomfield with leaft trouble ;
where the courfe is fhorteft, and the way liable to leaft dif-
turbance.   His bees will foon find the way to it, and he
will reap the benefit, in a great quantity of very fine honey,
and an extreamly thriving ftock.

In the year 1752, our correfpondent being on a journey
thro' a great part of Kent, examined, in his curious way,
the honey of feveral places where he had opportunities ;
and particularly that of two or three farmers, who had this
peculiar advantage for their bees, of a broomfield in the
neighbourhood.   He found the honey very good in all thefe
places ; but much of the nature of that collected from tur-
nep flowers that is pure and excellent, but with no peculiar
flavour.

In one farmer's houfe he found a honey thinner than the
reft, but not fubject to candy ; the colour a clear and fine
yellowifh, but the tafte highly aromatick.   Thofe who have
been

been accuſtomed to the taſte of the true foreign capillaire, will know what we mean by this; that ſyrup has it in perfection, and it is owing entirely to the honey, for the maiden hair, which is the only ingredient beſide, has no ſuch flavour. This taſte in the foreign honey, we know, is owing to the aromatick herbs, which are ſo abundant in thoſe countries: our correſpondent knew the broom flowers could not give it in this inſtance, and he examined the field to find ſome other cauſe. The ground was over-run with anthills; and there was in it an old gravel pit, long covered with weeds. All over theſe anthills, and upon the ſides of the old pit, there grew a vaſt quantity of wild thyme, the moſt fragrant of all the Engliſh aromaticks; from this the bees had collected enough to give fragrance to the abundance of pure honey they gathered from the flowers of the broom.

· This appeared to our correſpondent the very fineſt honey he had met with in England, and we may rely upon his judgment. Therefore, wherever there is an opportunity of a broom field with wild thyme, it will be worth while, even at ſome expence, to fix a ſtand of bees.

From the honey of theſe hives a CAPILLAIRE may be made of equal virtues, and equally pleaſant with that of Montpelier, and we may ſave the money, that goes out of the kingdom annually, for this frivolous article.

The only ingredient beſide is maiden hair; and our black maiden hair, which is common on old walls and under ſhady hedges in many parts of the kingdom, will anſwer the purpoſe of this very well.

Let the perſon, who ſhall attempt to make this ſyrup in England, get the right herb and uſe this fragrant honey, and he will not fail. He muſt not buy the plant at the herb ſhops, for they uſually ſell a common kind of fern in its place, which is nauſeous and has no virtue.

C H A P. CXVIII.

Of plants hurtful to bees.

ARISTOMACHUS, who ſpent ſeventy two years of his long life in obſerving the Œconomy of bees, does not ſeem to have underſtood them ſo well as the gentleman, to whom we owe theſe obſervations; nor has any one ſtudied them with ſo much regard to uſe. After examining by theſe moſt certain experiments, what thoſe plants

were

were which bees moſt loved, and what effect they took upon the honey; be beſtowed his attention upon thoſe kinds which were diſagreeable to them, and hurt them.

We have a weed called STINKING ORACH, ATRIPLEX OLIDA, an excellent medicine, but a very offenſive herb to bees. Unluckily it is common in farm yards and neglected gardens. Bees hate all ſtinks, and they ſeem in a particular manner to deteſt this.

Our correſpondent obſerved in a cow-keeper's garden near London, in 1748, a great quantity of this plant growing all about the beehives, and under the very ſtand. The man complained that his bees were always thin in the ſwarm, and produced little honey. He was adviſed to deſtroy all this weed, and digging up the ground, and throwing in ſome mould to plant baum and hyſſop, and winter ſavory In the place. He did ſo, and writing the gentleman, who gave him the advice, a letter of thanks, three years after, he ſaid his bees had throve excellently upon this change, and continued in the ſame ſtate ever ſince.

Elder ſhould never be planted near where there are bees. The flowers feed many inſects, but they are hurtful to theſe. There is a conſiderable quantity of wax to be collected from them; and ſometimes in diſtreſs, bees will ſeek it there, but their honey always get a ſickly flavour by it; and the bees themſelves become unhealthy.

The common ſingle narciſſus or daffadil, is another plant that does harm to bees. They get an ill-taſted honey from the bottom of this flower, but it does them nothing but harm: they grow faint and languid after it, and in places where this flower is very plentiful, the honey is greatly debaſed by it; becoming thick, and of a heavy and vapid flavour.

It is ſtrange, that experience here contradicts the doctrine of the antients, who, in general, have underſtood bees very well; they direct the narciſſus to be one of the plants cultivated near the hives: but there are many kinds of narciſſus; and it is not improbable they meant the white kind with the purple-circle, which we call the poetick daffodil. What effect this may have we don't pretend to ſay, having only obſerved the yellow kind.

Among ſhrubs, there is only one in our hedges which is yet known to be very hurtful: this is the DOGBERRY HASLE, called by the Latin writers, CORPUS FÆMINA. The flowers of this throw the bees into incurable diſorders. They

are

are tempted, on certain occasions, to use them freely, and great numbers perish.

In general, nature has very well taught this little creature what to seek and what to avoid; but the greatest danger to which it can be exposed, is that of being near a garden of foreign plants. Many of those, our curious people raise, are poisonous. I once saw a remarkable instance of a great number of bees being destroyed by a peculiar kind of apocynum, or dogs bane. This kills flies while they play about its flowers; and a gentleman having raised some of it not far from the place where his hives stood, the bees were fond of the flowers, and perished by their poison so suddenly, that multitudes of dead ones were found continually upon the ground, round about the plants.

There are many other herbs raised for curiosity, which are of the same poisonous nature, and bees are much more in danger from them, than from any which are the produce of our own country: whether the instinct, which directs them, be limited to the plants of our own growth, or howsoever it is, we find not only these small animals, but larger creatures also in much more danger from those herbs, which the art of man has introduced into the countries where they live, and feed them from all that are brought into their way by nature.

It is said, honey is sometimes rendered poisonous by the bees having fed on poisonous flowers, but we meet with no certain instance to confirm it; nor is the thing likely, since we find the bees themselves are affected by plants of this kind themselves, and would, after feeding on poisons, dye before they could discharge their honey into the cells of the comb. This seems one of the rash assertions of those men who place their imagination in the stead of observation; and repeat as facts, what their fancy has suggested; although it be what their mature reason would contradict.

It is an observation of Columella, that the elm is hurtful to bees. The flowers of this tree appear early in spring; and they are small and inconsiderable, they grow also on the tops of the trees, and therefore we scarce observe them, except when they are fallen off, in which state we find them scattered on the ground about the stems of the trees.

Our correspondent, who has been so curious on other heads in regard to the bee, did not omit his observations upon this: but whether the effect of climate, or whatever else, makes the difference between the bees of England

and

and thofe of Italy, it is evident, that here thefe flowers take no ill effect upon them. They afford a confiderable quantity of honey, at a time when thefe little creatures are in extream want of it; and therefore our bees feed greedily upon them; but without hurt, either to themfelves or their flock.

Two or three of the early flowering fhrubs are violently purgative, as the mezereon of our gardens, and the Laureola or fpurge laurel of our woods, of which we have given an account at the latter end of the third volume, treating of hurtful plants. The flowers of thefe fhrubs invite the bees which have had none for fo long a time; and they are killed by them in great numbers. To prevent this, our correfpondent has found an excellent medicine. He obferves, that the drug called Japan earth, is a remedy for the ill effects of thefe fpring flowers; and that its talte being fweet, the bees feed on it very readily when boiled up in water and mixed with honey. Columella names the fpring fpurge at the fame time as the elm; and attributes the diforders of the bees, at this feafon, to one as well as the other: probably it is this laureola he means, and that is a plant more likely to occafion the effect than the other. Whichever it be, or from whatever herb, this is a remedy. Certainly, where mezereon is common, the bees in fpring perifh by it, as if they were poifoned.

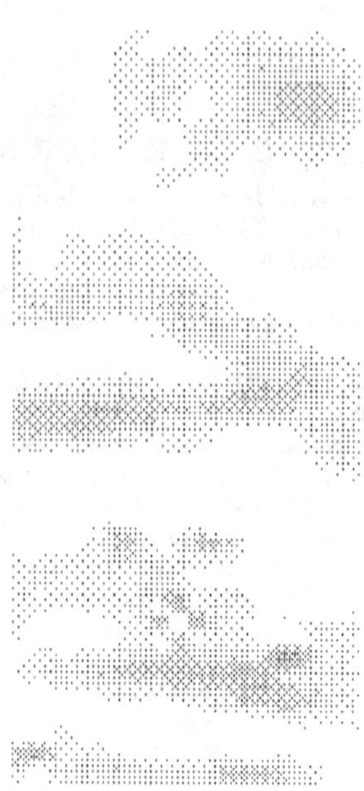

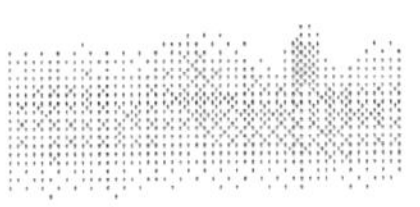

FRONTISPIECE.

RURAL RECREATIONS;

OR THE

GARDENER'S INSTRUCTOR;

EXHIBITING

In a clear and perspicuous Manner,

ALL THE OPERATIONS NECESSARY

IN THE

Kitchen, Flower, and Fruit Garden, &c. &c.

FOR EVERY MONTH IN THE YEAR:

WITH

A TREATISE

On the Management of Bees, &c.

To which is subjoined a complete Catalogue of

USEFUL & ORNAMENTAL TREES, SHRUBS & PLANTS.

With their Varieties, and Parts used,

FOR MEDICINAL AND CULINARY PURPOSES.

By a Society of Practical Gardeners.

LONDON;

Printed by E. Hodson, Cross-street, Hatton Garden;

FOR VERNOR AND HOOD IN THE POULTRY;

T. HURST, PATERNOSTER-ROW; AND R. BENT, COVENTRY-STREET, HAYMARKET.

1802.

ON THE MANAGEMENT OF BEES.

THE culture of Bees, as a branch of Rural Economy, has, until very lately, been considered only as an object of trifling concern; consequently improvements in the management of these useful insects have not been hitherto so much diffused, as the importance of the subject would seem to require. Few farmers in this island deem them an object worthy their notice, although they might certainly be rendered a source of considerable profit; besides, as most of the operations they require, are performed in the evening, or early in the morning, they could not interfere with more important business. While, however, we by no means wish that their culture should be wholly neglected by the Farmer, yet, for a variety of obvious reasons, we would still more particularly recommend them as deserving the attention of the Gardener. To the Country Gentleman, the admirable economy of these insects will afford a diversity of amusement, as well as prove a source of high gratification to the philosophic enquirer.

From these united considerations, the Editors would have deemed the present work defective, had not a few pages of it been dedicated to this interesting subject.

The Mellifica, or domestic Honey-Bee, is furnished with downy hairs; has a dusky-coloured breast, and brownish belly: the tibia of the hind legs are ciliated, and transversely streaked on the inside. Each foot terminates in two hooks, books, with their points opposite to each other, in the middle of which there is a little thin appendix which, when unfolded, enables the insect to fasten itself to glass or any other polished body. They likewise employ it to convey the small particles of crude wax which they collect from flowers into a cavity in their thigh. The *queen* and *drones* are not furnished with this cavity. The domestic Honey-Bee is likewise provided with a proboscis or trunk, which serves to extract the honey from flowers, and a mouth, situated on the fore part of the head, by means of which they feed on the farina of different plants. The belly is divided into six rings or joints, which, by slipping over each other, sometimes shorten the body. In the inside of the belly there is a small bladder or reservoir, in which the honey is collected, after having passed through the proboscis, and a narrow pipe which runs through the head and breast. This bladder, when full of honey, is about the size of a small pea. The sting, which is situated at the extremity of the belly, when examined by a microscope, is observed to be of a curious structure : It is composed of a horny sheath, including two bearded darts. The sheath terminates in a sharp point, through an opening, in which, at the time of stinging, the darts are obtruded : one of these is somewhat longer than the other; they penetrate alternately, taking hold of the flesh, till the whole sting is completely buried, and thence a venomous fluid is ejected through the sheath, from a little bag at the root of the sting.

When the bee is disturbed, the sting is left behind; otherwise the animal brings the hooks down close to the side of the dart, and thus withdraws the weapon, in which case, the wound is far less painful.

R 3

The

The *single female bee*, vulgarly styled the *Queen*, is easily distinguished from all the others. She is longer and larger, and her wings are much shorter than their's, in proportion to the size of her body; her hinder parts become regularly smaller, terminating in a sharp point, and her belly and legs are of a deep gold colour. She is armed with a shorter sting than the others, which she never employs but to oppose rival queens; she is rarely seen, and, if discovered by chance, instantly retires from observation. Her flight is unwieldy, and she seldom leaves the parent hive, except to settle a new colony; for although the bees become ever so numerous, or eager to swarm, it is impossible to establish them without the presence of the queen. On her depend the increase, prosperity, and permanency of a stock, for if, by any misfortune, the queen be killed, the bees quit the hive to associate with their neighbours, transferring their treasures along with themselves. It has been calculated, that in the course of a year, she usually lays forty thousand eggs, and frequently more; she has been observed to extrude forty immediately one after another, and her body, during this period, sometimes contains at once several thousand eggs, which she is compelled to drop, if a sufficient number of empty cells be not prepared for their reception.

The eggs are little white bodies, fixed, by the smallest end to the bottom of the cell. Those cells intended for the reception of the eggs which produce the *queen bee*, are constructed on the edges of the combs; when half finished, they resemble the cup of an inverted acorn, and are lengthened in proportion to the growth of the nymph. They hang in a perpendicular manner with the open end downwards; and when the egg has been deposited about three

days,

days, a maggot, in the form of a segment of a circle, appears at the bottom of the cell, surrounded with a white mucilaginous substance, which is continually supplied by the working bees, and serves it for nourishment. In the course of a week it becomes considerably increased in size, and ceases to take food; the cell is then covered up with a cap of wax, which in about twelve longer is burst open by the nymph, now metamorphosed into a *queen* bee: in cold weather this process is somewhat retarded. The *queen bee* is impregnated about August, by which means she is enabled to breed in the Spring.

The eggs, from which proceed the *drones,* and *working bees,* are hatched in the common cells, which likewise serve, when not thus occupied, for the reception of honey: those for the drones are usually the two middle combs of the hive, and are deeper than those for the working bees. They are usually hatched in twenty-one days.

The *drone,* or *male bee,* is larger than the *working bees;* of a clumsy shape, with large extremities, and the trunk or proboscis short and thin, the eyes large, and the body more hairy. In flying they make a much louder and harsher noise than the others, and having neither weapon of defence nor instrument to collect honey, they are sustained solely at the expence of the hive.

The dissection of the *drone* affords as evident a proof of its being the male, as that of the *queen* does of her being the female. Here there is not the smallest appearance of ovaries or eggs as in the *queen,* or any similarity to the structure of the working bee; but the whole abdomen is filled with transparent winding vessels, containing a white fluid, analogous to that in the males of other animals, which is destined to render the eggs of the female prolific: and this

R 4   whole

whole apparatus of vessels is evidently intended for the preparation and retention of this fluid, till the destined time of its being emitted. Soon after honey-gathering ceases they become destitute of this milky liquor, and are therefore discarded.

The *common* or *working bees*, are discovered, by the most accurate dissections, to belong to neither sex. They have no parts analogous to the ovaria of the queen, or that resemble the male organs of the drones. The young ones are readily distinguishable from those which are older, by their being of a light brown colour. They are not all of the same size; occasioned, probably, by the cells in which they are hatched being of different dimensions. This circumstance, however, although it may certainly explain the difference of their size, can never operate to effect a change in the sexual organs, as has been absurdly supposed by Schirach, and others. The *working bees* have the care of the hive: they collect the wax and honey, build the cells, feed the young, and defend the hive against all invaders. They are extremely quick at foreseeing an impending storm, and on such occasions make a precipitate retreat in great multitudes.

On the Apiary.

The aspect of an Apiary should be towards the south, or south-east, with a free opening in the front; and if possible situated in a lawn or valley, so as not to be much exposed to the influence of the wind: and in order still more to screen the hives from its violence, they ought to be so placed as to have trees, high hedges, &c. at their back or western side. The hives, however, should not be

so near to the trees as to be annoyed by their dripping; neither should dung-hills, weeds, long grass, &c. be suffered to
remain in their neighbourhood. The vicinity of rivers,
ponds, or large collections of water, is extremely ineligible
for an Apiary, as in such situations a great number of the
bees are frequently drowned. It is proper, however, particularly during a dry season, to place water near the hives,
in a shallow vessel, covered with duck-weed, to prevent the
little insects wetting their wings, or being drowned when
drinking; an accident which otherwise frequently happens.

The most approved arrangement, for an apiary, is that
of separate stands for each hive, constructed by driving four
strong stakes into the ground, at equal distances, corresponding to the dimensions of the hive floors to be placed
over them: their height from the ground should be about
16 or 17 inches.

These stands ought to be placed in regular rows, at about
the distance of three or four feet asunder, or from the wall
or fence behind them, and when the stocks become too numerous, it is better to divide them into different parcels, and
place these parcels at a distance from one another, to prevent quarrels; Eight or ten in one apiary is abundantly sufficient.

The best time for establishing an apiary is, generally
speaking, about the latter end of August, or the beginning
of the present month. The hive should be selected early
in the morning or towards the cool of the evening: they
are for the most part full, when the interstices between the
combs are crowded with bees, and the combs finished down
to the floor. When they appear white, or of a light yellow,
it indicates their being of the present year's produce, and
consequently fit for the purpose; but when, on the contrary

trary, they exhibit a very deep yellow, or brown colour, they are of the former year, and not well calculated to succeed; whilst those that appear blackish or dingy, being old, are altogether unfit to furnish a healthy or thriving apiary.

Should, however, the proper season for the purchase of hives be neglected, a *prime*, or *young swarm*, should be bought, at least, sufficiently large to fill half a bushel, and if that cannot be procured, two or three may be united, which will form a powerful stock.

In order to transfer the swarm, invert the hive into a pail, and lay two flat sticks across it, on which place the empty hive or box, and most probably the bees will enter it before the next day; should this, however, not be the case, beat round the lower hive with two small sticks till they ascend, which may be discovered by the buzzing noise in the upper hive.

In order to hive two swarms, strike the edge of the hives pretty smartly against the ground, on which a cloth has been previously spread, when the bees will tumble out in a mass, and then place over them an empty hive with one edge resting on a stick, covering the whole with a cloth.

Stocks should be removed either early in the morning, or in the evening, well tied up in a cloth, and suspended on a long pole carried on men's shoulders; and the first night after being brought home, it ought to be placed in the front of the bee-house, in order that the stragglers may find their way back to the hive.

The best material for hives is straw, which most effectually protects the bees from the extremes of heat and cold, although rushes, wicker-work plastered over, or sometimes sedges, are substituted in its place.

The

The plan recommended by those who have most experience, in the management of bees, is to have three hives
for each stock; which, by *storifying*, afford ample room to
the bees, and at the same time admit triplets to be sooner
taken off.

Their height ought to be nearly nine inches, and the
width of the area twelve, exclusive of the top. Three hives
require only one cover, which should be quite flat, and sufficiently wide to extend an inch beyond the edge of the hive.
The door must be left three inches long, and three eighths of
an inch in height, and besides the flat cover, all the three
hives must have wooden tops with seven openings cut transversely, each exactly half an inch wide. A long peg should
pass through the edge of the hive before and behind, to prevent the top from being displaced.

The opulent, to whom the appearance of straw hives will
perhaps seem inelegant, may have them concealed from the
view by a variety of contrivances, which will, at the same
time, add to the beauty of the apiary.

Although it is, we believe, pretty generally admitted, that
in point of real utility, *straw hives* are preferable to *bee-
boxes*, yet many choose the latter as being more ornamental;
as well as because by means of the windows constructed in
them, the operations carried on within may be observed.
With this view, glass hives have sometimes been employed,
but as little information can be gained from their use, and
as they are extremely disagreeable to the bees, they are now
generally laid aside.

Of all the methods hitherto divised, for the management
of bees, that of *storifying*, or placing one, two, or three
hives over each other, is supposed to yield the greatest profit,
and appears to be the most congenial to their habits and
style

style of working. In proof of which, a good *storifyer*
that has not swarmed, or has had the swarm returned, will
increase thirty pounds in seven days, when the season is
favourable: while, on the contrary, a single hived stock,
under exactly similar circumstances, that has been suffered to swarm, will not increase above five pounds in the
same time.

During Winter, stocks that are populous in the Summer,
frequently become greatly reduced. The re-plenishing the
hives therefore depends on the fecundity of the *queen*,
which provides those multitudes of young insects that constitute the swarms.

In consequence of this increase, the bees feel an impulse
to swarm, in defiance of every obstacle contrived to prevent
them. The swarm is not wholly composed of young bees,
but of old and young promiscuously.

The time of the year, in which they most generally swarm,
is from the middle of May to the end of June, according as
the season is more or less favourable. The earliest do not
always prove to be the best swarms, the weather being then
frequently so wet and cold as to greatly injure, and almost
deprive them of nourishment: whilst late swarms, on the
contrary, although not in danger of present famine, yet
have scarcely time to lay up a sufficient store for the winter.
About the swarming season, the door of the hive must be
enlarged to allow the bees more freedom to issue forth: It
should likewise remain in the same state for the convenience
of the young swarms during the first two or three weeks, as
they are then extremely busy in collecting stores, and it may
afterwards be gradually lessened.

After the first, or *prime* swarms have risen, the succeeding ones should be returned to the stock, which will otherwise

wise be so much impoverished, that little honey can be afterwards collected. Besides a sufficient number of bees will not remain to rear the young, which at this season are extremely abundant.

Stocks which have not swarmed from single hives, before the commencement of July, ought in general to be returned; but in this and similar cases, the propriety of particular measures must partly depend on local circumstances and situation, and must therefore be left to the skill and discretion of the apiator.

Those stocks which do not appear to increase, have for the most part a deficient number of *drones;* they should therefore be supplied with a dozen or two from another hive. To effect this purpose, take them singly with the finger and thumb, as they pass on the resting board, and put them into a phial till a sufficient number be obtained: then towards evening fasten the mouth of the phial to the door-way of the hive to be supplied with these *drones,* and they will have entered it before the morning.

To kill the *drones* in the Spring is a very injudicious practice; for as the *drones* are to *bees,* what males are to other creatures, we are thus cutting off the very means of their future increase. The only case in which it can ever be proper to destroy a few of them, is in Summer, when they are so numerous in a weak stock, as nearly to consume the honey as quickly as it is collected.

If the *working bees* do not as usual destroy the drones in August, a few may then be killed by the fingers; and by thrusting a small twig into the hive, the *working bees* will be induced, it is said, to complete the business: should this, however, not be the case, the cold weather will of itself, in a very short time effectually destroy them.

A great

A great number of *working bees* are bred before the queen
or *drones*, the last of which generally appears before May,
unless when the season has been uncommonly early; in
which case they are frequently observed among the most
populous stocks in April, and sometimes even in March.
Other hives, however, well often be so full of bees as to
cluster out, and even frequently swarm, without the smallest appearance of *drones*; although it is probable there must
be a few, which being weaker than the *working bees*, do
not shew themselves when the weather is unfavourable.

When the bees hang in clusters on the outside of the
hive, it is supposed by Mr. Wildman and others, to afford
a certain indication of their being ready to swarm. Some
later writers on this subject, however, consider this appearance as deceitful, and are rather inclined to explain it from
there being no *queen* ready to accompany them, as they frequently remain clustered in the same manner, during several weeks.

This clustering is very prejudicial, not only from the loss
of their labour, during the most productive part of the season, but from a habit of indolence which the bees acquire,
and which is not afterwards easily relinquished. It is besides attended with this farther inconvenience that as there
is no certain means of ascertaining when a *queen* will be
sufficiently restored to accompany them, constant watching is thus rendered absolutely necessary.

These disadvantages are admirably remedied by *storifying*:
but those who have not this convenience, may cut a door-
way in the back of an empty hive, and place it against that
of the stock, and fill up the vacancy left between the two
hives, with a piece of hay band, &c. taking care, at the
same time, to leave the passage of the two door-ways free,
and

and when the bees find additional room necessary, they will begin to find the empty hive.

Under such management, the bees will be constantly employed, which must be very profitable to the apiator, even should the stocks not swarm, although, in general, it is not prevented by *doubling*.

The profit to be derived from Bees depends, in a great measure, on the *swarms:* when these are lost, the increase of honey will be found trifling. The usual hours of *swarming* are from ten to two; but as this cannot be altogether relied on, constant watching from seven in the morning till four or five in the afternoon should not be neglected in fine weather, until the whole of the *prime* swarms have issued forth.

Old people or children may be employed for this purpose, at a very small expence, which will be fully compensated by the safety of the swarms, at the same time that it will prevent the anxiety and trouble of going backwards and forwards, which, after all is attended with a considerable degree of uncertainty.

Second swarms are seldom worth preserving single, but, by uniting two or three into one, a very good stock may be obtained.

On the rising of swarms, many bees just returning loaded from the fields are observed to join them, by which means they are sometimes enabled to construct combs immediately after settling, which they have been observed to do even on the branch of a tree when allowed to remain on it too long, without an attempt being made to hive them.

When the wind is brisk, a *swarm* generally flies in its direction, and will settle in that place, where they can be

best

best sheltered from its influence; without any seeming regard to their usual places of clustering.

A good *swarm* ought never to be less in bulk, when hived, than a *peck and a half*, though in some places a *peck* is esteemed a good swarm : less than this, however, can never be expected to prove productive. It is here, perhaps proper to remark, that a swarm appears much larger when it hangs on a bush, or the branch of a tree, than when clustered on the top of a hive.

The following table of the average number, measure, and weight of bees, is taken from the Bee Master's Farewell, a work of considerable merit on this subject :

		lb.	oz.	dr.
100	drones	0	1	0
290	workers	0	1	0
4640	——	1	0	0
915	——	0	3	2
1830	—— a pint	0	6	5
3060	—— a quart	0	12	10
29260	—— a peck	6	5	6

Winchester measure—averdupoise weight.

The preceding table is formed from the medium weight, &c. because two bees are rarely to be found of the same weight, on account of their various degrees of fulness, or to the difference of the load which they carry.

[*To be continued.*]

ON THE MANAGEMENT OF BEES.

(Continued from p. 232.)

On Hiving Swarms.

As bees frequently rise when least expected, Apiators ought always to have in readiness a sufficient number of empty hives, by which precaution they would almost always avoid the loss of their swarms. When these, however, are not at hand, the swarm may be put into a pail or basket, until the evening; then by inverting this vessel, and placing over it an empty hive, so as to rest on two flat sticks, the bees will thus be induced to ascend into it before the morning; but if not, their ascent may be facilitated by gently beating the sides of the vessel.

To prepare hives for the reception of swarms, the snags should be clipped off, and the inside rubbed very hard with a coarse cloth, to free them from loose straws, or other impurities, which would cost the bees considerable time and labour to gnaw away, which might be employed to greater advantage in constructing combs, &c. If boxes be used, any holes or crevices must be filled up with putty, or some other cement, to exclude the air, and prevent the entrance of vermin. If this be neglected, or improperly performed, the bees themselves make use of a resinous gum for this purpose, which is more tenacious than wax, and differs greatly from it. *Propolis* is the name by which it was

known

known among the ancients, and it is said to be found on the birch, the willow, and the poplar. It has an agreeable aromatic odour when heated, and by many is regarded as a most grateful perfume.

Two sticks, or *spleets*, placed in the form of a cross, near the bottom of the hive, are usually conceived to be necessary to support the combs; one from the front to the back, and the other from right to left. But in fact, common hives have very little occasion for any *spleets*, as may be observed by bees working in hollow trees, &c. and the two above mentioned are fully sufficient for any hive, even in the *storifying method*: those which are sometimes placed near the top, are extremely troublesome, and prevent the combs being readily removed. Some have recommended the employment of odoriferous herbs, such as bean-flowers, balm, &c. to rub the inside of the hives, on the principle that their fragrance may be grateful to the bees; but we apprehend that no other preparation or dressing is necessary, except smoothing the inside of the hive, as already mentioned: if *something* must be used, perhaps ale mixed with honey or sugar, and sprinkled in the top of the hive, will be found more alluring than any herbs whatever.

When a swarm flies too high in the air, they may be made to descend lower, and even induced to settle, by throwing amongst them handfuls of sand or dust: water is likewise sometimes employed for this purpose. It is usual at the same time to make a tinkling noise, which it is probable the bees mistake for that of thunder; as it is well known they return home from the fields with the greatest precipitation, when overtaken by a thunder-storm. The louder the noise, the sooner it is likely to succeed; in proof of which, the *watch rattle* used in London, has been frequently

quently found to answer the purpose, when the usual, and less noisy mode of beating on a kettle, or frying pan, has altogether failed. This noise should not, however, begin until a sufficient number of bees have arisen to form a good swarm, lest the *mother bee* be thereby terrified from issuing forth, in which case the bees will return to their hive, although they had previously settled. The noise should be made on the side opposite to that where we wish them to settle, and be discontinued the moment they are observed to cluster, as their buz will then be sufficient to attract those which remain on the wing.

Sometimes, after the swarm is hived, the *queen* is found on the ground, surrounded by a small cluster of bees; these should be placed near the door of the hive, otherwise the swarm will continue discontented and tumultuous. At other times, from having among them a couple of *queen bees*, they continue restless until one of them be sacrificed to the peace and tranquillity of the hive, which is usually done on the evening of the first day after the flight; or if it be delayed till the following morning, the youngest *queen* will endeavour, if possible, to effect her escape to the parent hive.

To prevent such disturbances, Mr. Wildman recommends seizing one of the *queens* alive, and imprisoning her with about 100 working bees, in a small box, with holes in it sufficient to admit air, but not so large as to permit the bees to escape. Here he feeds them with honey-comb for a few days, and thus has a *queen* in reserve, should she be required for another swarm.

Swarms should be hived as soon as possible after they have settled, lest any circumstance induce them again to take wing; or should another rising swarm attempt to join

the

the first, it must be covered with a thin cloth, and dust,
&c. thrown amongst the others, to induce them to settle
elsewhere.

Swarms will sometimes cluster in improper situations, in
which case, if they cannot be allured into an empty hive,
placed at a convenient distance, they may be dislodged by
blowing tobacco smoke forcibly amongst them from the
bowl of a pipe, previously covered with a piece of paper, in
which holes have been made.

The implements which it is necessary to have in readiness
for *hiving*, are an empty box or hive, a board, a table cloth,
two small wedges, and a long fork, or crooked stick: then
let the apiator invert the hive, and introduce it leisurely underneath the cluster, without disturbing the bees; afterwards let him give the bough two or three smart shakes with
his left hand, which will cause the greatest part of the cluster to fall into the hive, on which it should be immediately
removed, and placed with one edge on the board, previously
covered with the cloth, and the other on the wedges; draw
the cloth up over the hive, leaving the raised part open.
The bees may at first be expected to make a considerable
buz, but they will soon begin to ascend, and those on the
wing will gradually fly down and join their companions.
Let them remain in this situation until the evening, unless
they require to be shaded from too violent a sun, when
they may be removed to their destined stand.

' Whenever bees are clustered on a bush, hedge, &c. so
that a hive cannot be put under them, they must either be
shaken down upon a cloth spread on the ground, and afterwards have the hive placed over them; or it must be elevated above them, where they have settled, by means of forked
stakes, or cords; and by throwing a cloth over the whole,

X

the

the bees usually ascend in a few hours. Placing a handkerchief, or a hat, on a bush, will frequently allure a swarm, and prevent them clustering in an inconvenient situation; but when they have once settled, so that it is impossible either to shake them off into a cloth, or place under them an empty hive, a few bees may be gently taken up with a spoon, and turned out on the board, either within or near the door of a hive, the edge of which has been previously raised by a wedge: this should be repeated until the buz of those within the hive allure the others to enter it, which in general is not long; especially if the *queen* has been brought away among any of the spoonfuls.

When swarms settle on the extreme branches of very high trees, they must either be shaken off by means of a long crook, into a basket elevated for that purpose; or they may be disturbed, and induced again to take wing, by holding a pan of smoking substances beneath the tree, or employing similar contrivances. If lodged in a hollow tree, they may for the most part be displaced by beating about it's outside with a stone, or large hammer; having an empty hive over the hole at which they entered. If this method prove unsuccessful, recourse is usually had to *smoking* them out with burning rags, damp straw, &c. But when bees have settled in the roofs of houses, holes of walls, &c. where the sparks from fuming substances might be dangerous, water thrown over them, by means of a garden watering pot, is often found to effect the same purpose.

It is perhaps here proper to observe, that all operations connected with the culture of bees, should be performed in silence, otherwise the little animals will become alarmed, which will contribute not only to render the business troublesome, but in particular cases even dangerous.

In.

In fine warm weather all swarms begin to work as soon as
they are hived; but when the few first days turn out rainy
and unfavourable, it prevents them from prosecuting their
labour, and during a long continuance of such weather they
will inevitably die, unless relieved by early feeding.

On *Artificial Swarming.*

A variety of methods have been from time to time devised for the purpose of producing artificial swarms; but
none hitherto discovered have been calculated for general
use, or proved uniformly successful: But although wholly
inapplicable to general practice, the two following methods
may amuse the curious; and if unsuccessful, they will at
least not prove injurious to the stocks.

In the swarming season, by frequently looking into the
storied boxes, a *queen* may perhaps be discovered in one of
them; upon which let a divider be immediately pushed in
between the two boxes. Inspect these boxes, occasionally,
in the course of the day; and if the bees in both remain
quiet, introduce the other divider, and remove the duplet
to a station at some distance. But should the bees in either
of the boxes appear restless and discontented, it affords a
sufficient indication that no *queen* is amongst that portion
of them, and consequently the divider must be withdrawn,
unless an extra *queen* be at hand to introduce into the discontented swarm.

The second method, which is likewise recommended by
very experienced apiators, is, during the swarming season,
when the bees appear to be very numerous, to push a di-

X 2

vider

vider between a duplet in the morning, having previously
opened both doors; and if the bees quietly pursue their accustomed labours till the evening, the duplet may be removed as above directed.

The most certain mode, however, of acquiring an *artificial swarm*, is to unite into one hive, so many of the second or third swarms as to form one sufficiently populous.

On Wild Bees.

April or May is the most proper season to discover the
retreat of wild bees.   In the woods of America, bee-hunt-
ing affords a considerable source both of amusement and
profit; and it is not unusual, even in this country, to domesticate swarms of wild bees.   The directions given by
Mr. Wildman for discovering the abode of these useful insects, differ very little from the mode employed by the American hunter: it is proper, he observes, to watch early in
the morning, where there are plenty of flowers, to see whether many bees frequent those places; in which case we
may hope not only to find the stock numerous, but their
habitation not far distant.   As in dry weather, they frequently resort to springs, have some colouring materials
previously dissolved in water, into which dip a few twigs,
and sprinkle the bees as they alight, by which means you
may readily discover, after a little practice, whether they
return soon, or in great numbers.   A pocket compass will
greatly assist in determining their course, which, in their
return home, is always in a direct line for their habitation.
Should

Should this method not prove successful, take an entire joint off from a large reed with the knob at one end; bore a hole in the side, through which drop some honey into its internal cavity, and deposit it near the place to which the bees usually resort. After a few of them have been allured into this tube, by the odour of the honey, close the orifice by means of your thumb, and allow one of them to escape, which pursue as long as possible; then give a second its liberty, and if it flies in the same direction, continue the pursuit, by which means you will most probably be led to their habitation. Some rub empty hives with those aromatic herbs which are supposed to be agreeable to bees, or with honey, and then place them in their favourite haunts, by which means swarms are frequently induced to settle. When they are discovered in the hollow of a tree, they must be dislodged, in the same manner, as already directed respecting domestic swarms in a similar situation.

When this is done during the swarming season, such portions of the comb as are filled with honey, may be cut out, taking care to preserve those with the young brood, which, along with the empty ones, should be placed in the hive in the same manner, and at the same distance, as the bees themselves would have done.

A few individuals prefer employing aged people or children to watch the swarming of wild bees, in order that they may be hived in the usual manner; for whatever be the nature of their habitation, they cast out swarms, like the domestic bee. Having secured and carried off these, they return in Autumn, and take the honey produced by the labour of the stock during the preceding Summer.

On

On the Preservation of Bees.

It was a practice among the ancients to take away a part of the combs, without destroying the bees. To this purpose Columella gives a variety of judicious directions; as likewise Varro, and other ancient writers on this subject: the same method is now practised in Greece, and has been lately introduced into France by M. Prouteau and others. In our own country, Mr. Wildman has been particularly successful in saving the lives of these little insects; with this view he removes the hive into a darkened chamber, and by repeated quick strokes round its outside, induces the bees to ascend into an empty hive, which must be steadily supported on the edge of the full one; after which it is immediately removed to the stand whence the other was taken. He next examines the royal cells, and allows those which contain young *queens* to remain, as well as the combs with the brood of *working bees*, &c. and then proceeds to remove the *honey-combs* with a long broad pliable knife, such as is used by apothecaries. Having thus finished taking the wax and honey, and afterwards scraped the sides of the hive with a table spoon, to clear away what was left by the knife, he returns the bees into their old hive. It is hardly worth while, he observes, to rob a hive, before the latter end of June, nor is it safe to do it after the middle of July, lest rainy weather prevent the bees restoring the combs, of which they have been deprived, and laying up a stock of honey sufficient for the Winter. The attention and humanity of this ingenious apiator to the preservation

tion of the lives of his bees, cannot be sufficiently applaud-
ed, yet we must confess, that after the most accurate and
repeated experiments, it does not appear that the suffocation
of bees, reared in the common single hives, is in point of
profit prejudicial to the owners. The truth of this assertion
may easily be verified, particularly by those who cultivate
bees in boxes, with large windows, as they can readily perceive, that in December and January, very few bees remain
alive in the boxes, which were crowded in August. The
diminution is so great, that the fullest boxes are then reduced to about a quart by the death of the old bees; which
afford a sufficient proof that the only advantage obtained by
saving the bees, and uniting them to other stocks, is ultimately only the preservation of a quart; and as it is necessary the *queen* should be killed, they cannot add to the increase of the hive in Spring. Besides it remains to be considered, whether the multitude of bees united about August
will not gradually consume more honey before the Spring
gathering commences, than the quart left will compensate
by their labours, during the following season. Neither do
they contribute to the more early production of swarms, as
that entirely depends on the birth of the *queen-bee*, in which
they have no share : The truth of which is farther confirmed by experiments on such stocks, which will be found neither more forward, nor more productive than single ones
hived in the usual manner.

From what has been said, it must not be understood, that
we would wish to *perpetuate*, or *revive* the barbarous practice of suffocation, our only intention is to point out the
small profit to be derived from *saving bees* in the *single
hives*, and hence recommend storifying, which, equally
with

with the other, preserves the lives of these curious insects, whilst it affords to the apiator double or treble advantages.

Bees considered individually, live only about a year, pro-
gressively coming into birth, and as gradually decaying.
Hence, those produced in Autumn and Spring, or during
the intervening months, die about the same periods the succeeding year: but this is not perceived during the breeding
season, whilst the brood is rapidly increasing and counter-
balancing the chasms produced by the death of the old bees,
but is sufficiently evident from the thinness in the hives after this period. Hence, likewise, at the general time of
deprivation, the hives contain bees of all ages, from those
in embryo to those of extreme old age. Consequently, although individuals die daily, young ones rise to succeed
them; and by the storifying method the family may be per-
petuated, without the cruel necessity of putting the old and
young indiscriminately to death.

The method here recommended, can in no case be prejudicial, although the bees should even be thereby prevented from swarming (which is by no means the case) on the
contrary, it would rather be advantageous, since in that
case artificial swarming would not be necessary to perpetuate stocks.

[*To be continued.*]

T H E

ON THE MANAGEMENT OF BEES.

(Continued from p. 368.)

On Storification.

After what has been said of the advantages to be derived from this method of cultivating Bees, it may be thought necessary to give a few directions for the performance of Storification.

By storifying must be understood, the ranging hives over or under each other. In order to set on a *duplet*, loosen the cover of the stock, and slide a divider underneath it, keeping one hand on the cover. As soon as the divider is properly adjusted, remove the cover, and place an empty hive on the divider, which must be kept down with the hand until the divider is withdrawn.

When the duplet is to be under a stock, set a stool behind the stock and push the divider under it, then lift the hive and slider on the stool, and set an empty hive with its cover off on the stand whence the other was removed; immediately re-lift the stock and place it on the empty hive, pull out the slider with one hand, while the empty hive is kept steady with the other. Early in the morning, or towards the evening, is the proper time for conducting these or similar operations. A Triplet must be managed in the same manner.

It may be perhaps here not improper to add, that from a comparative estimate of stocks kept in single hives, and those placed according to the storifying method, it would appear, that by laying out 2l. 16s. for the extra apparatus of

the

the first year, a superior profit may be gained of 2l. 1s. 6d.
but in the succeeding years, it will amount to 4l. 17s. that
is nearly fifty per cent. per annum on the sum originally
expended, or an additional gain of 4l. 17s. a year, on *storifying twelve stocks*, than by a like number in *single hives*.

On taking up Hives of Honey.

When a stock has been prosperous and the triplet is filled
with honey, it may be taken off and another empty one
placed in its stead; in the most approved practice, the duplets are allowed to remain, and the triplets are separated as
often as they become full.

By looking through the windows of the boxes, we can
readily discover when they are full; but with regard to straw
hives it is different; in order to ascertain the state of the
combs in them, the apiator must strike round the body of
the hive, and if it feel hollow and a small buz only be heard,
these circumstances will afford a sufficient indication of its
being nearly empty, but on the contrary, if it feel solid,
give a dull sound on its being struck, and a great buz continue for a considerable time among the bees, he may safely
conclude that it is in a proper state to be *taken up*.

A triplet should only be *taken* during that season of the
year which is favourable for the production of honey, otherwise it ought not to be re-placed, but the stock itself must
be raised on an empty hive which is termed a *nadir*.

Place the triplet which was *taken* at a considerable distance
from the stock, and if, in a few hours, the bees become

A a 3   quiet,

quiet, it may safely be concluded to proceed from the presence of a queen or brood, in which case it must be again placed on the stock. When however, all the three hives appear to be crowded, some experienced Apiators have recommended, placing the door of the *taken* hive as near as possible to that of the stock, laying a slip of wood across, so as to form a bridge from the one to the other, and still to place an empty triplet on the stock. In this way, the brood continuing to be regarded as one family, will be reared, the cells filled with honey, and in about three or four weeks the hive may be removed.

Should the stock remain in confusion after *taking* the triplet, it affords sufficient evidence that the queen has been carried away, and in this case it must immediately be restored to its original position.

A *triplet* should never be separated in Autumn, unless the hive which is left be apparently full, and even then, except we can certainly determine in which hive the *queen* has taken up her abode; the most eligible practice will be to allow them to remain in their original situation.

The general time of *taking up stocks* must necessarily be various in different countries, according to the climate and temperature, but some time in August is the usual season in this island.

Bees in single hives ought to be taken when they begin to relax in their labour, which may readily be perceived by a diminution of their activity. At this period they feed on the hive honey, and the longer therefore they are afterwards permitted to stand, the less quantity of honey will be found in the hive. This reasoning is only applicable to stocks taken in the common way to be killed; for in the storifying method, as the life of the bees is always saved, no disadvantage whatever can arise from allowing them to stand.

At

At the usual time of *taking up* hives, there is for the most part much brood, the preservation of which is of far more importance than a greater number of bees indiscriminately taken from one stock and incorporated with another; yet regardless of this circumstance, they are frequently bruised along with the honey-combs, by which means the quality of the honey is considerably injured.

The brood combs should be handled with the greatest caution, and disposed in an empty hive, so as to touch each other as little as possible; for this purpose place slips of wood between them of a sufficient thickness to admit the extrusion of the young bees, and afford space for the ingress and egress of the older ones employed in rearing them, and in the evening replace them over the original stock, or some other which require to be augmented.

When storification is employed in the culture of bees, instead of the general deprivation of duplets in August, it has frequently been recommended to defer it until September, or even the beginning of October, by which time most of the brood will have left their cells, and as at this period it is probable no *queen* will be in the duplet, the bees, after a few hours will voluntarily desert it, without the necessity of *fuming*.

In general, stocks ought to be reduced to duplets before August; for which purpose the hives having the fewest combs should obviously be taken. Three or four light stocks may be incorporated together with advantage, and supplied with a sufficient quantity of honey; as weak stocks seldom survive the following Spring, or if they do, seldom compensate the trouble and expence of feeding them.

On the Pasture of Bees.

Bees do not fly to so great a distance in search of Pasture as some writers on this subject have supposed.—Their flight does not usually exceed half a mile, and even when a great number of favourite flowers on one continued spot of ground, joined to fine warm weather, allure them to extend their rambles, a mile or a mile and a half may be considered as their utmost range. In cold windy weather, although destitute of provisions, they will perish sooner than fly beyond that distance. Domestic bees do not feed indiscriminately on every species of flowers; several of the most splendid and odoriferous are wholly neglected by them, whilst they select others, the flowers of which are extremely small, and not possessing any very sensible qualities. Large heaths, sheltered with woods, are extremely productive of honey, as the thyme and other flowers with which they abound are not cut down by the scythe, and the heath itself remains very late in blossom. In Hertfordshire, and part of Hampshire, abounding with large heaths and woods, farmers have been known to keep from a hundred to an hundred and fifty stocks of bees.

Bees give a decided preference to those spots where a great quantity of their favourite flowers grow together. Fields of buck-wheat, or white clover, will be found thronged with these insects, whilst scattered plants, that afford more honey are neglected. When a variety of *bee-flowers* flourish in the same field, they will at first only collect from those which

which furnish the best honey : if, for example, several species of thyme be planted together, they prefer the lemon
thyme while its flowers continue.

A corn country may be considered as a barren desert to
bees, during the greatest part of the year ; neither do beans
nor orchard-trees afford a considerable quantity of honey.
Viper's Bugloss, or common viper-grass *(Echium Vulgare)*
which is a troublesome weed amongst corn, may be found
in great profusion in many places, particularly in chalky dry
soils, and even on old walls ; it is a biennial plant, and never fails to be productive of a considerable quantity of honey.   But the Borage *(Borago)* is eagerly sought for by
bees, and affords the greatest quantity of fine honey ; it is
an annual, and blossoms the whole year until destroyed by
frost ; in cold and showery weather the bees feed on it in
preference to every other plant, owing to its flowers being
pendulous.   The superiority of the Narbonne honey is supposed to arise from the bees feeding on Rosemary, which
grows wild in several parts of France ; yet Lavendar and
Balm, though equally aromatic, appear in our climate to
yield little or no honey.

The practice of other nations, who shift the abode of
their bees, is certainly well worthy of imitation.   From
Columella, we learn, that as few places are so happily situated as to afford the bees sufficient pasture both in the
Spring and Autumn, it was the advice of Celsus, that after
the vernal pastures are consumed, the bees should be transported to places abounding with autumnal flowers.   In
Greece, it was a common practice to convey their bees from
Achaia to Attica, and from Euboea to Scyrus ; in Sicily
likewise they were sent to Hybla from all other parts of the
island.

According

According to Pliny, the removal of bees was also practised in Italy in his time; and a much later writer, Alexander de Montfort, mentions the custom as still common a-
mong the Italians who live near the banks of the Po.

About the end of October, the inhabitants of Lower E-
gypt embark their hives on the Nile, and convey them to
Upper Egypt, so that they may arrive when the flowers begin to bud after the inundation. When they have remained some days at the most distant station, and are supposed
to have collected all the wax and honey they could find in
the fields within two or three leagues around; their conduc-
tors convey them in the same boats somewhat down the river, and again leave them to collect all the sweets of this
spot. In fine, about the beginning of February, after having travelled the whole length of Egypt, gathering all the rich
produce of the delightful banks of the Nile, they arrive at
the mouth of that river towards the ocean, whence they
set out.

In France, M. Proulant, who established a manufactory
for whitening wax near Petiviers, where the flowers become
scarce at an early period of the season, and indeed wholly
disappear after the corn is ripened, sends his bees into
Beance, or the Gatinois, in case it has rained in those parts.
This is a journey of about twenty miles; but if he conceives
that in neither of these places the bees can find sufficient
pasturage, he causes them to proceed to Sologne about the
beginning of August, knowing that thence they will meet
with a great many fields of buck-wheat, which will continue in flower until the end of September. Before trans-
porting them, his first care is to examine the hives, and
those combs which appear to be in danger of breaking, or
being separated by the jolting of the vehicle in which they
are

are conveyed, are fastened one to the other, and against the
sides of the hives, by means of small sticks, which must be
disposed differently, as occasion will point out. This being
done, every hive is set on a kind of packing cloth, the
threads of which are very wide. The sides of this cloth are
turned up and laid on the outside of each hive, in which
state they are tied together with a piece of small packthread,
wound several times round the hive. As many hives as a
cart, built for that purpose, will hold, are afterwards placed
in this vehicle. The hives are set two and two the whole
length of the cart, and over these are placed others, which
make as it were another story. Those stored with comb
should be inverted; whilst others that are less so may be
fixed in their usual position; taking care, however, to place
them so as not to exclude the air, which is essential to the
preservation of the bees, especially when they move about
very tumultuously, which is often the case during these
journies.

The horses which draw these *caravans* are led slowly along
the smoothest roads, and the owner embraces the first good
pasture to remove them from the cart. The hives are then
placed on the ground, and on taking away the cloth in which
they were tied up, the bees go forth in search of food.
When they are to be again removed, the hives are shut up
in the evening after the bees are all returned from the field,
and being placed in the cart they proceed on their journey.
When the *caravan* is arrived at the journey's end, the hives
are distributed in the gardens, or in fields adjacent to the
houses of different peasants, who, for a very small reward,
undertake to look after them. Thus it is, that in such spots
as do not abound in flowers at all seasons, means are found
to supply the bees with food during the whole year [*].

[*] Natural History of Bees, p. 428.

In

In our own island, this practice, were it generally a-
dopted, with a few modifications, would unquestionably
afford an ample recompense for the trouble; more particularly if, by such means, a sufficient quantity of wax could
be collected as to render it an object of utility in a commercial point of view.

Mr. Wildman, speaking on this subject, observes, that
in our vallies the plants bloom early, and are cut down more
early in the season. Rising grounds would in this case afford a better pasture; and if there is heath at a convenient
distance, the hives being carried hither, would considerably
lengthen out the season of collecting honey, for it continues
in bloom until late in August. The bees will themselves
go far in search of food*; but surely carrying them to the
spot whence they obtain their food, saves much of their time
and labour, and becomes a proportionable gain to the owner,
for by this means they collect the more honey in a given
time.

Mr. Wildman would prefer water-carriage, if equally
convenient: but where hives must necessarily be transported by land, they should either be carried by hand, or
suspended on a pole on men's shoulders. Each hive should
be rested, during the day, on a temporary stand, that the
bees may go forth in search of food, or that they may at
least have it in their power to go out; for a long restraint
would be extremely irksome to them. He reprobates the
practice of allowing the hives to remain in the boats, be-

* What distance this judicious writer may understand by the
word FAR, we are at a loss to determine; certain it is that several
experienced Apiators, as has been already observed, have limited
their range to a mile and a half; which if correct, affords an additional motive for the practice above recommended.

cause

cause many of them will be blown into the water and destroyed.

After recommending in the most earnest manner, the practice of occasionally removing bees in search of food, we should not omit to mention, that in this island many situations may be found capable of sustaining a great number of hives, which are either wholly neglected or but very thinly stocked. In fact it would be benevolent, as well as patriotic in land-holders and opulent farmers, were they to encourage a taste among their cottagers for the cultivation of these useful insects; unfortunately however, it is a melancholy truth, that in many counties the wages of cottagers are too low to enable them ever to purchase a *swarm,* especially when they have families; it would therefore be highly commendable in our British Noblemen and Gentry, were they to place a stock in the little garden of each cottager on their estates, or at least, bestow them as a reward for superior industry; thus, at a small expence, they might arouse a spirit of virtuous emulation, whilst at the same time, they afforded a healthful and profitable amusement to this useful and laborious class of men.

It is perhaps not unreasonable to suppose, that a small portion of ground might, in some situations, be profitably cultivated with the most productive bee flowers, it would at least be preferable to allowing large patches of land (which is the case on a variety of farms) to remain covered only with sour grass, rushes, furzes, &c. To answer the same intention, marshy wet soils, might be planted with sallows, osiers, lime-trees, or any other shrubs which are known to be productive of honey dew.

The *honey-dew,* which would appear to be an exudation from the leaves and stems of a few species of plants or trees, such

such as the maple, sycamore, lime, hazel, black-berry, &c. usually appears from ten to eleven o'clock in the morning, and continues about four or five hours. It is sometimes observed as early as seven, when the preceding day and night have been sultry, or when the rays of the sun are seen reflected through a cloud. The season of its appearance is in June or July, although it varies according to the heat or coldness of the weather, and in some unfavourable years it does not appear at all.

More honey is said to be collected in one week from such dews, than can be done in several from flowers. It must, therefore, be sufficiently obvious, that training up those species of trees on which it is produced in the greatest abundance, must be extremely advantageous in the vicinity of an apiary.

On Feeding Stocks.

Various methods have been proposed, and a great many different materials recommended, for affording nourishment to bees throughout the Winter.

During this season these insects are generally in such a torpid state as to require little food ; but as the weather is very changeable, and a warm sunny day revives and tempts them to go abroad, food then becomes absolutely essential.

Another circumstance which renders it likewise proper, is when a succession of bad weather follows immediately on their swarming; for then, being wholly destitute of provisions,

sions, and unable to fly out in search of them, they are in considerable danger of being starved.

The following observations on this subject may be found in the *Maison Rustique*:

Replenish the weak hives in September, with such a portion of combs full of honey, taken from other hives, as shall be judged a sufficient supply. For this purpose invert the weak hive, the operator defending himself with the smoke of rags; and after cutting out the empty combs secure the full ones in their place, by running pieces of wood across in such a manner, that they may not fall down when the hive is returned to its former position. The bees will soon fasten them more firmly.

If this method be thought too troublesome, a plate filled with liquid honey, unmixed with water, may be placed under the hive, with straws laid across, and over these a paper pierced full of holes, through which the bees will suck the honey without danger of being smothered.

Other writers recommend honeyed or sugared ale for this purpose, in the proportions of a pound of soft brown sugar to half a pint of mild ale. This is dissolved over a slow fire, until it attains the consistence of syrup, and is afterwards administered to the bees by means of *troughs*, made of the joints of elder, or angelica, slit down the middle, the pith and bark taken away and reduced to such a depth as easily to pass the door of the hives. Their length should be from six to eight inches, flattened a little on the under side, and the end closed with putty or other cement. These troughs, by passing a considerable way into the hive, enable the bees to come down and feed, without incurring any danger from the cold, which they would suffer by feeding at the door, .

and

and they are made so narrow that the bees cannot fall in and
suffocate themselves amongst the syrup.

When stocks appear to require feeding, one of these
troughs, which will contain about half an ounce, should be
pushed into each hive, filled with honeyed ale in the evening, and if the combs obstruct its entrance, pass a long slender knife to open it a free passage. This should be repeated
every morning and evening, by removing the empty trough
and substituting a full one in its stead. Feeding in this
manner will appear more troublesome than giving a sufficient quantity at once; but it is attended with this advantage, that the bees cannot overload themselves, which they
are but too apt to do when in their power, and which is not
only wasteful, but tends to produce diseases in the hive.
When this method is adopted, we would recommend, as a
substitute for the honeyed ale, brown sugar, or honey boiled
with a little water, to the consistence of thick syrup, which
would afford an equally nourishing, although a less stimulant food.

[*To be continued.*]

THE

ON THE MANAGEMENT OF BEES.

(Continued from p. 336.)

In vain will the apiator provide his bees with plenty of pasturage, and food, if he be not sedulous to guard them from the numerous enemies that either disturb, or endeavor to depredate on them. Among the first, we may rank snails, slugs, and a variety of other insects, which frequently creep into the hives, and occasion much confusion, particularly in wet weather, by preventing the labour of the bees, and soiling the hive with their excrements. They neither consume the honey, nor wax, and often find their way out of the hive; sometimes, however, they lie against the door way and prevent the ingress and egress of the bees; when discovered, in this situation, they may be taken out by means of a sharp-pointed wire in the form of a hook. Ants frequently construct their nests on the covering of hives, without however giving much molestation to the bees; yet neither these, nor spiders webs should be allowed to remain in the vicinity of an apiary.

Among the last, some endeavour to kill the bees, and live on the honey, whilst others only consume the wax. *Swallows, Sparrows,* &c. destroy a great number of these insects, especially in Spring, to feed their young. They are frequently observed watching at the door of the hive, in order to seize the bees as they issue forth; and a number of them are likewise caught by the *Wood-peckers,* when

collecting

collecting farina from sallows and other shrubs. It is almost impossible to form an effectual barrier against the depredations of birds; some place traps for them, baited with dead bees, in the neighbourhood of the apiary; whilst others advise the employment of children to rob and destroy their nests, in the Spring, with a view to prevent their future increase. Besides the immorality of this last mentioned practice; it can scarcely be expected to afford a sufficient remedy, unless it should become nearly universal.

Poultry, as well as *Lizards*, are very prejudicial to bees, by catching a prodigious number of them, as they proceed in or out of the hive. To guard against the cunning of these last mentioned animals, Columella advises to have two or three openings in the hive at a small distance from each other.

The entrance of *Field-mice* into the hive should be guarded against with particular care, especially on the approach of cold weather; indeed they seldom attempt to commit their depredations until this season, at which time the bees begin to decline in vigour. At first, they destroy the lower portions of the combs, but in proportion as the bees become more torpid, they ascend into the upper part of the hive; even here the evil does not terminate, since frequently, on the return of Summer, the bees are so much disgusted by the devastations, which have been made by these animals, as altogether to desert the hive. On the approach of Winter, the door-ways should be so much lessened, as not to admit these animals, and when the hives are thatched, they should frequently be examined to see whether any of the mice nestle in this covering, otherwise, in a short time, they will eat themselves a passage into the hive. Traps

D d 2

ought

ought to be placed in the neighbourhood of the apiary, in order to catch these mice; and a cat is frequently bred in the garden, and employed for the same purpose.

The *Wax-moth* is a much more formidable enemy to bees, than many individuals are willing to acknowledge : we have known several stocks wholly destroyed by this reptile, in an almost imperceptible manner. The female lays her eggs round the skirts of the hive, if she be prevented by the vigilance of the bees from depositing them in the inside; weaving a close strong web to defend the young. Mr. Wildman, speaking of this caterpillar, says, " It is tender in its frame, unarmed and defenceless ; and yet can subsist itself in the midst, and at the cost, of the most numerous hive. A few of these little caterpillars will destroy and break to pieces the combs of a hive, build up new edifices for lodging themselves in it, and finally force the bees to quit the place. This insect is of the species of the *False-moth*, and is extremely nimble. It is enough for it to get into a hive unawares. It runs so very swiftly, that it passes unperceived, and slides into some narrow place between the combs, perhaps inaccessible to bees, there to lay its eggs in security. This done it makes its escape as well as it can. From each of these eggs there proceeds a caterpillar, which escapes certain death merely by its extreme smallness, and the quickness with which it spins and enwraps itself in a covering sufficient to secure it from all harm. This covering or tube, is glued to the wax which the caterpillar feeds on, and the insect lengthens the tube as it eats the wax, till at last it shuts itself up in order to be turned to a chrysalis. Several caterpillars, and consequently several moths, must proceed from the eggs which the males and females engender. Probably the bees
destroy

destroy great numbers of the moths; however, if a single female has an opportunity to lay her eggs, she is so exceedingly prolific, that this second brood may quite overspread the hive. If one of the impregnated females escapes out of the hive by means of her great nimbleness, she seeks out another in which she spreads the same source of mischief. Old straw hives, or decayed rotten floors afford a lurking place for these and other small reptiles: hence the propriety of frequently shifting the hives, and cleaning, or renewing the floors before Winter. This was a practice common among the Romans; Columella, speaking on this subject, observes that, " The hives should be first cured by opening them in the Spring, in order that all the filth collected in them during Winter may be removed. Spiders which spoil the combs, and these small worms, or rather caterpillars, from which the moths proceed, must be killed. When the hives have been thus cleaned, the bees will apply themselves to work with greater diligence and resolution. From the Summer solstice to the Autumnal equinox, the hives should be opened, cleaned, and smoaked every tenth day, and then washed and cooled with cold spring water; and what impurities cannot be washed away, should be brushed off with the pinion of a strong wing. Particular care must be taken to sweep out every caterpillar that can be seen, and to destroy all the moths. For this purpose, a vessel with a narrow neck increasing gradually to a wide mouth, with a light in the neck, should be placed under the hive in the evening. The moths gathering around the light, are in that narrow space, scorched and killed."

Wasps are, perhaps, of all others, the most destructive enemies to bees, from their number and superior strength.

D d 3

They

They begin to be very formidable in July and August, except when the season has been extremely rainy, in which case, few of them are observed until September: soon after which, the *workers* die, but the female wasps survive the Winter, and begin to breed about April. A warm Spring, which has been preceded by a mild Winter, is so favorable to the increase of these insects, that the most unremitting attention is necessary, to guard the stocks from their depredations.

The *Wasp* is a very bold and daring insect, and will at any time readily encounter a very disproportionate number of bees; but on the approach of cold weather, when the bees become torpid, if no precautions have been adopted to prevent their entrance into the hive, they never desist, until they have robbed it of every particle of honey. At this season, therefore, when wasps are observed lurking about the hives, the door-ways should be contracted to half an inch, and the bees roused to defend themselves, and assail their enemies, by thrusting twigs, &c. within the door of the hive.

In the Spring, the female wasps may be found in considerable numbers, wherever there are any old decayed timber, with the filaments of which they compose their nests*; and likewise on the blossoms of gooseberries, and

rasp-

* M. de Reaumur, observing a *female wasp* at work on the frame of his window, which was open, immediately conceived that she was detaching from it materials for building. He caught her, and found she was loaded with pretty nearly such a quantity of materials as they usually carry to their nests; but they were not yet formed into a ball, or so much moistened, as when she cements them to her work. He examined this heap of filaments, which appeared very different from what it might have been expected the

insect

raspberries, in which situation they may easily be destroyed. The importance of destroying these females, before
they have deposited their ova, must be evident to every
person conversant in the management of bees, and who
has witnessed the havock which is produced by them,
among the stocks of these useful insects; more particularly
when we reflect that, according to M. de Reaumur, and
other naturalists, each female wasp gives birth, in the Summer, to nearly thirty thousand young. For this purpose,
phials half filled with ale or cyder in which honey has been
dissolved, may be suspended on the trees or shrubs when
in blossom; or placed in any other situation to which these
insects are known to resort. They will enter the phial, and
not being able again to ascend, their future increase will in
this way be greatly diminished. The nests of those which
remain, ought to be carefully sought after, and likewise
destroyed. That species of wasp termed the hornet, generally suspends its nest on the roofs of houses, &c. On a
rainy day, therefore, carefully approach the nest by means
of a ladder, and having a large mouthed bag, with running
strings, extend it so as to take in the whole nest; immediately draw the strings, so that the nest and hornets be at
once included. In this way, we are nearly certain of securing the females, as they do not readily quit the nest,

insect would have detached from the wood by nibbling; they were
each, at least, a line in length, and some of them much longer,
forming a sort of threads, similar to those of paper; and to obtain
which, she evinces a considerable degree of sagacity. She does
not merely cut the wood, which would only produce a kind of
saw-dust, but before cutting it, she presses the fibres between her
talons, raises them up, and by that means separates them one from
another.

and

and should a few males escape, they will soon perish, for on the females alone depends the duration of the state.

The wasps which construct their nests in the ground, should likewise be attacked in the evening, or morning of a rainy day, when none of them will be found abroad; a kind of squib made of damp gunpowder, may be introduced as far as possible into the opening by which they enter, and being covered with straw, which is kindled, the flame will be communicated to the gunpowder, the smoke of which, entering the nest, will instantly suffocate the insects. The nest should then be dug up, and thrown into water, so as to prevent the possibility of their recovering.

Bees are themselves the enemies of bees. In the Spring or Autumn, when no honey can be collected from plants, they frequently fight and plunder the well-stored hives of their neighbours. Dr. Warder supposes they are sometimes reduced to this necessity, by their own hives having been robbed, at a period of the season when it was impossible to repair the loss by any industry in the fields. Perhaps the best mode of preventing these destructive battles is, to give a regular and plentiful supply of food to the bees throughout the Winter.

A small red *louse*, about the size of a pin-head, is frequently found sticking to the breast of the bees. These vermin are not generally thought to be prejudicial, yet certainly, when abounding in a hive, they must greatly incommode the bees.

M. de Reaumur declares, that little is to be expected from a hive, in which the greatest number of bees have lice on them.

Madam Vicat relates, that observing one day a number of her bees endeavouring in vain to free themselves from
these

these troublesome enemies, she strewed over them a little Morocco tobacco, on which the lice instantly dropped off dead. In order to be satisfied that tobacco did not injure the bees, she confined a few which were infested with these vermin, under a glass, placed on paper strewed with tobacco. The lice died almost immediately, but at the end of three hours, the bees appeared vigorous and well.— Bathing the bees did not effectually rid them of these insects.

On separating the Honey and Wax.

After being taken up, the combs should be either immediately removed out of the hives, or they may be placed in a warm room, as the honey will more readily run out when in a fluid state: after reversing the hive, cut through the ends of the *spleets*, then with a broad thin knife cut likewise through the edges of all the combs, close to the hive, and afterwards place it in a clean shallow dish, having previously removed the straw cover. In this situation, the body of the hive may be easily forced up, by which means the combs will remain in their natural order: let them be then disengaged one by one from the frame of the bars, by cutting a notch out of each, where it is fastened to the spleet.

In the *common hives*, the combs cannot be removed whole, but by means of an iron implement in the form of the letter L. the shaft, exclusive of the handle, should reach the whole depth of the hive; the short foot must be sharp,

and

and made so as to cut with both edges; its length two inches, and its width half an inch. This instrument must be passed down between the combs to the top of the hive; afterwards, by turning it half round, and drawing it upwards, the combs are loosened from their fastening to the top of the hive. They may next be disengaged from the sides, &c. and managed as above directed.

Before placing the combs to drain, they should be carefully cleaned, and the crust with which the bees cover the honey, pared off with a sharp knife; the combs themselves should be divided horizontally through the middle, that the honey may flow freely out from both ends of the cells. In this state, they must be placed on sieves to afford a free passage to the honey, and allowed to remain whilst any continues to run out: what is obtained in this way, should be preserved by itself, as it is perfectly pure, and free from every kind of mixture. These combs may afterwards be broken by the hand along with others which were but partly filled, and left in the sieves, until the remainder of the honey run out. Some put the broken combs into a bag, and express the honey by means of a press; whilst others employ the assistance of fire. In both these cases, a considerable portion of wax will be found intermixed with the honey, which not only deteriorates its quality, but is extremely uneconomical, since the former bears the highest price in the market.

The honey brought to the London market is in general of a very coarse quality, principally from the very slovenly manner in which it is prepared. The method commonly employed is, to take the combs indiscriminately out of the hive by piece-meal, and mash them all together, dead bees, farina, brood, &c. which must necessarily impart to the
honey

honey a disagreeable, and frequently a very nauseous taste:
By this unskilful management, a very agreeable and salutary
article of diet has been rendered extremely disgusting and
inelegant.

The comparative taste, and fragrance of honey afford,
perhaps, the best criteria to judge of its excellence: that
collected in places abounding with aromatic plants, is
esteemed the finest; and that produced early in the season
is preferred to what is gathered towards its close. The
colour of the honey depends, in a great measure, on the
nature of the plants from which it is extracted. Hence,
honey collected from trees, is deeper coloured than from
flowers, and that from heath, is darker than any other
whatever. It ought never, from its acidulous or saline
quality, to be preserved in vessels glazed with lead; for
although its effects may not be immediately perceived in
persons of a strong and vigorous constitution, yet, when
its use is long continued, it cannot fail to prove, more particularly to the weak and delicate, highly injurious.

Honey may be clarified by putting it into a stone vessel,
and placing the vessel in water over a slow fire. When it
boils, part of the impurities will rise to the top, and must
be skimmed off. The heat however employed in this process,
destroys in a great measure, the fine flavour of the honey,
and will always be found unnecessary when the combs have
been properly managed from the beginning.

On Preparing and Bleaching Wax.

In order to obtain the wax in a pure state, the combs, after being separated from the honey, must be put into a copper with a sufficient quantity of cold water, and stirred over a slow fire, until they boil. When the wax is thus melted, it may be poured into strong bags, which should be either put into a press, or have the wax forced through them, by their sides being pressed between two strong sticks, tied together at one end, like a flail. The skim must be taken off as it rises, and the wax afterwards poured into vessels somewhat narrower at the bottom than the top. These vessels, and the other implements used in this process, should be rinced with cold water, as it prevents the wax from adhering to them: and the vessels or moulds, should be placed in such a degree of heat, that it may cool slowly, otherwise the cakes will crack and fall to pieces.

Bees wax is originally of a yellow colour, which it loses on exposure to the external air; but this effect only occurs at or near the surface. Hence the art of bleaching wax must consist in enlarging its surface. This may be done, either by passing the melted wax through a number of holes in the bottom of a vessel, into another filled with water; or by slowly pouring it upon a wooden cylinder, which is turned round in a vessel filled with water to such a height, that half of the cylinder is immersed. In the first case it undergoes a division, similar to what is termed granulation in metallic bodies; and in the second, the wax

is

is formed into a number of thin flakes, which do not adhere
to each other, but may be taken off and exposed to the
action of the air.

The dephlogisticated, or aërated marine acid bleaches wax
very speedily; from which we may reasonably conclude,
that it owes its whiteness, and the greater consistency it
acquires, during that process, to an absorption of oxygen,
or the vital part of the atmosphere.

On making Hydromel, or Mead.

Simple hydromel is honey diluted in nearly an equal
weight of water; and when this liquor has been subjected
to the spirituous fermentation, it is termed vinous hydromel,
or mead.

Honey, in common with all saccharine substances, is
susceptible of fermentation, and particularly of the vinous
or spirituous fermentation; to induce which, it is only necessary to dilute it sufficiently with water, and leave the
liquor exposed to a proper degree of heat.

To make good mead, a quantity of the best flavoured
honey must be put into a boiler, with more than its weight
of water, a part of which should be evaporated by boiling,
until a fresh egg will swim on its surface without sinking
more than one half into the liquor. During this process,
the skim must be taken off as it rises, and the liquor poured
into barrels when it appears to be sufficiently boiled : after
which it should be exposed to as uniform a heat as possible,

from

from 77° to 95°, of Fahrenheit's thermometer, taking care
that the bung-hole be slightly covered, but not closed.—
The vinous fermentation will continue two or three months,
according to the degree of heat; and during this process,
the barrels must be occasionally filled up with some of the
liquor, set aside for this purpose. After the fermentation
has ceased, the barrels should be placed in a cellar, and
well closed: at the expiration of twelve months it will be
in a proper state to be bottled.

Some brewers of mead, recommend it to be drawn off
the lees when it has stood six months, and again returned
into the casks after they have been well drained out, but not
rinsed. A two-ounce phial, with a long neck, containing
about an ounce of water, and half an ounce of marble dust,
or chalk, is then suspended, by means of a string, within
the mouth of the cask, after which half an ounce measure of
diluted vitriolic acid is poured into it, and the cask instantly
closed. The string should be well secured, before the bung
is fixed, to prevent the phial sliding down below the surface of the liquor.

The fixed air, or carbonic acid gas generated from
these materials, which in the quantity mentioned above
will answer for a nine-gallon cask, is absorbed by the
mead, and tends not only to fine, and preserve it from
acidity; but likewise gives to it the sparkling quality of
champagne; taking off the disagreeable sweetness so common in this liquor; and in four, or six months it may be
bottled. Malt, and other fermented liquors, are found to
be equally improved by a similar use of the vitriolic acid.

Mead is sometimes flavoured by having a small quantity
of preserved rasp-berries, or currants infused in it, when

set

set to ferment; and the juice of ripe sloes, or elder-berries, will give an agreeable roughness, and communicate a fine claret colour to this liquor.

Description of the Plates.

A Straw-hive, *pl.* i. *fig.* 4.

A Wooden-top, *pl.* i. *fig.* 4.

A Bee-box with a frame of glass in one side *pl.* i. *fig.* 2.

A Bee-house six feet long, for the reception of three boxes, *pl.* i. *fig.* 3.

Bee glasses *e e e e* placed over a box *pl.* ii. *fig.* 1.

An Adapter, or board of the size of the top of the box, on which the glasses are placed, *pl.* ii. *fig.* 3.

A Tree with a swarm suspended from one of its branches, *pl.* ii. *fig.* 2.

A Comb, *pl.* ii. *fig.* 4. *a* the royal cells, *b* the same cells elongated, with the maggots, or nymphs, sealed up in them.

The Queen, or female bee, *pl.* ii. *fig.* 6.

The Drone, or male bee, *pl.* ii. *fig.* 5.

The Common, or working bee, *pl.* ii. *fig.* 7.

THE

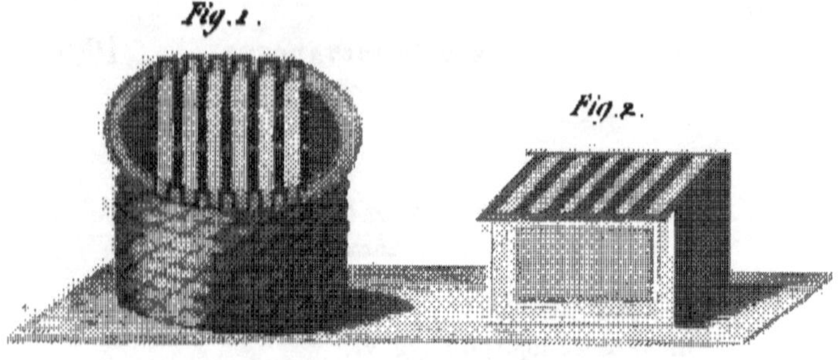

Fig. 1.

Fig. 2.

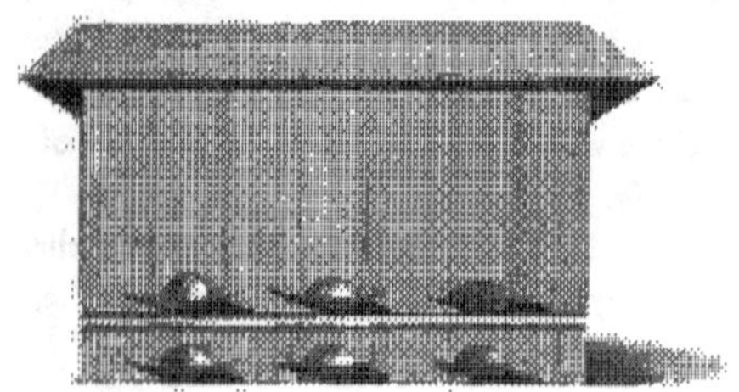

Fig. 3.

Fig. 4.

Publish'd Dec.r 1.st 1801. by Verner & Hood.

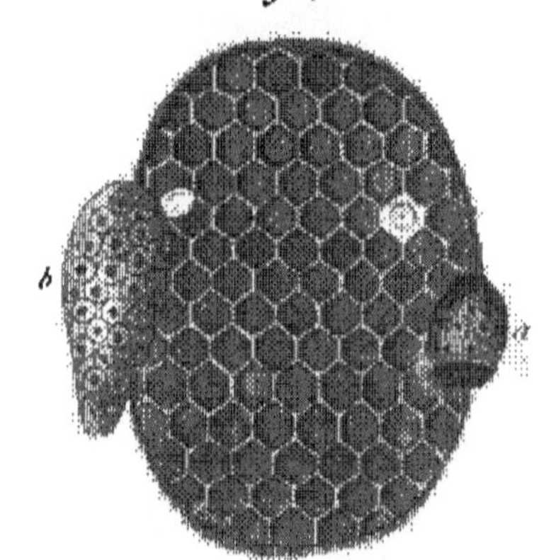

Publish'd Dec'r 1st 1801, by Vernor & Hood, Poultry.

Vol. XVI.   **MAY, 1888.**   **No. 5.**

THE BEE-KEEPERS' MAGAZINE.

50 CENTS PER YEAR.

Contents of this Number.

Subscription Rates

OF THE

BEE-KEEPERS' MAGAZINE

One Year . . . . 50 cts.
Six Months . . . . 30 "

Specimen Copy Free.

Postage to Foreign countries belonging to the Postal Union is 12 cents per year for each subscription. Others outside of the Union require to send 24 cents.

EXPIRATION.

Subscribers finding this paragraph marked with blue pencil will know that their time has expired. Another number will not be sent unless subscribers renew or drop us a postal saying they desire to continue, and will pay later. Bee-keepers are almost invariably honest, and we shall be glad to continue sending you the MAGAZINE if you will just let us know you desire it. Watch the date on your wrapper near your name.

Make Money Orders

Payable at RED HOOK, N. Y.

No stamps taken unless impossible to send money otherwise. Send one-cent stamps if possible.

For the Bee-Keepers' Magazine.

Legislation for Bee-Keepers Not Feasible.

The December number of the MAGAZINE was received with great pleasure, as usual, and read with interest, until I came to the report of the N. A. B. K. Society, the topic : "Legislation for Bee-keepers." I was astonished to find that any man would present such an idea or ideas as were introduced in that discussion. I have to say at once, monopoly, in the truest sense. I will have to ask the editor and readers of the MAGAZINE to bear with me, if I am pointed, in this article.

What better can any person want (unless they want all) than we had, and continue to have in the bee business? There never was a time in the history of bee-keeping that honey could not be sold at some price. This cry for legislation for bee-keepers is very common it seems, with bee-keepers. Suppose, for an instant, we should legislate that none but specialists should keep bees, how many bee-keepers would there be in the United States? and what would be the result therefrom. 1st. Very few bee-keepers. 2nd. And but very little honey. When Doctors, Lawyers and Preachers alone will produce honey for the consuming nations, we will eat but very little honey. Let every person keep bees, who loves the business. We can produce honey at five cents per pound, and have a profit. We are now realizing what high prices are, a great demand and a limited supply. I would rather have plenty of honey to sell at ten cents per pound, than to have high prices and no honey to sell. What say you bee-keepers? The questions before the bee-keepers should be, *how can we produce more honey, better honey, how can we care for our bees better ?* These are the points desired, not how can we effect the solidest monopoly. Pres. Miller says in this discussion : "Bee-keeping is not like traffic so much as is like farming, stock growing, etc. * * * What resemblance has one business to the other?

rather be a benefit. Hence bees do not trespass as do stock. Again he says : "How about farming? * * All farmers do not own land, but are farmers all the same." I will close, but do not conclude.   S. H. LINTON.

Burrows, Ind., 12—17, 1887.

[We think the question of legislation has been sufficiently discussed for the present. It is like the boy's perpetual motion machine, a very wonderful and beautiful machine, *only it wouldn't work.* Now that is just this legislation, in a nutshell. The idea, the theory, is all right, and we are very much inclined to feel that as Dr. Miller has fashioned it it wouldn't be a bad thing ; in fact a wonderfully beautiful thing, *only it wouldn't work.*

Mr. Linton is altogether mistaken we believe, in supposing the term "professional," as used by Dr. Miller, as applied to so-called professional men, like Doctors, Lawyers, etc. The term "professional" as used, referred to those making *bee-keeping a profession.* — ED.]

Would He Know Water?

A Melbourne correspondent of the Dundas *Advertiser* narrates what he consider an interesting proof of the provident and far-seeing instinct of bees : "Turning from men to insects, a singular circumstance is reported from a hot, dry valley in New South Wales. Last year the drouth there was of long duration, and the denizens of the apiaries suffered much from it. This year the bees have made provision against a similar emergency. They have filled a large number of external cells in every hive with pure water instead of honey. It is thought that instinct leads them to anticipate a hot summer.—*Western Rural.*

[We wonder how true this is ? Perhaps this correspondent hadn't seen water in so long a time he would not

Honey.

The forthcoming report of the Dairy Commissioner of New Jersey will contain notes on the quality of strained honey as usually sold in bottles and jars. Forty-two samples of bottled honey were analyzed and it was ascertained that out of thirty-one samples put up by packing houses only six were pure.

The samples purchased in small towns and villages, representing strained honey put up by farmers, were all pure.

Below is a table of the samples analyzed and the result of the analysis:

STRAINED HONEY.

Office No.	Where Purchased.	Name and Label.	Result of Analysis.
57	Paterson	Wm. Thompson, Wayne Co., N. Y., "choice comb honey"	Adulterated
58	"	McCool & Childrain Bros., N. Y. City; "white comb honey"	Adulterated
59	"	Same as 58	Adulterated
55	Hoboken	Klett, Philadelphia; no label	Adulterated
60	"	Wm. Collins, Worcester, N. Y., "choice comb honey"	Adulterated
61	Jersey City	J. V. Sharp Canning Co., Williamstown, N. J., "clover honey"	Pure
62	"	Wardell & Watson, Brooklyn, N. Y., "white clover honey from the apiaries of Central New York; warranted pure"	Adulterated
75	Newark	J. T. Durham, "superior quality of clover honey"	Adulterated
77	"	Thurber, Whyland & Co., N. Y., "pure California white sage"	Pure
78	Hoboken	E. A. Walker, Greenpoint, L. I., "superior XXX honey, warranted pure"	Adulterated
79	Jersey City	Wm. Collins, Worcester, N. Y., "choice honey"	Adulterated
80	Hoboken	E. A. Walker & Bro., 135 Oakland St., Brooklyn, N. Y., "choice honey"	Adulterated
81	Newark	Charles Israel & Bro., N. Y., "choice California honey"	Adulterated
82	"	C. G. Leslie & Son, Pittsfield, Mass., "choice extra clover honey"	Adulterated
83	"	"No Name," said to be Klett	Adulterated
84	Hoboken	Geo. D. Powell, "choice extra and Northern"	Adulterated
85	Newark	Wm. Thompson, Wayne Co., N. Y., "choice golden rod honey"	Adulterated
86	Hoboken	E. F. Watson, Brooklyn, N. Y., "pure California honey from growers of San Diego, there is none better"	Adulterated
87	Paterson	McCool & Hildreth, New York, "choice extra honey"	Adulterated
88	"	Code, Elick & Co., San Francisco, "extra choice Los Angeles"	Pure
89	"	Frank Chapman, New York, "white clover honey"	Adulterated
90	"	F. G. Strohmeyer & Co., New York, "pure orange blossom honey; is absolutely pure, no glucose"	Adulterated
91	"	Wm. Thompson, Wayne Co., N. Y., "choice golden rod"	Adulterated
92	"	Andrew Jackson, Deposit, N. Y., "pure honey"	Pure
1416	Burlington	K. J. Durham	Pure
1417	"	Sleeper, Wells & Aldrich	Adulterated
1418	"	Arthur Todd, Philadelphia	Pure
1424	"	Arthur Todd, Philadelphia	Pure
1425	"	Western honey	Adulterated
1427	Bordentown	R. K. Allen, farm honey	Pure
1429	"	Wm. Collins, Worcester, N. Y.	Adulterated
1431	"	Shipps & Sons, farm honey	Pure
1432	"	S. Garwood, farm honey	Pure
1434	Trenton	Wm. E. Johnson, Moorestown, N. J.	Pure
1435	"	S. P. Robinson, farm honey	Pure
1436	"	S. Holcomb, farm honey	Pure
1437	"	F. K. French, Dentonville	Pure
1438	Camden	Brown & Bros., State honey	Pure
1439	"	Arthur Todd, Philadelphia	Pure
1440	"	Wm. Collins, Worcester, N. Y.	Adulterated
1441	"	Gifford & Biller, State honey	Pure
1442	"	Philadelphia Pickling Co., "virgin honey"	Adulterated

For the Bee-Keepers' Magazine.

Introduction of Queens.

J. E. POND.

Years ago I was led to believe that it was a difficult task to introduce a strange queen to a queenless colony, and being fearful of results unless I followed the old road I pursued the plan of taking from five to eight days to do and stood the loss consequent thereon. At last concluding that a better method could be devised, I experimented in that direction, and now am able to introduce queens with no loss of time to egg production, and absolute safety. Thinking my method may be of interest to some of your readers I give it in brief. I am positive that it will prove a success, if the instructions are strictly followed as I have made use of it for several years with not a single case of loss.

On the afternoon of a fine day when the bees are flying freely, I remove the undesirable queen, at the same time removing every trace of a queen cell. In the evening of the same day, after the bees have all returned and quietness prevails in the hive, I allow the new queen to run in at the entrance. No further precaution is used save that to allow the hive to be and remain quiet for five or six days after the introduction. If desired I can give the theory on which I base the method, but this *modus operandi*, I deem sufficient for this article. I trust the method will be tested by other bee-keepers, and full reports made thereon.

No. Attleboro, Mass, April 10, '88.

[In the last edition of the British Bee-Keepers' Guide Book, Mr. Cowan says on page 131: "Mr. Simmins recom-what similar to yours, friend Pond, though yours is more simple. —ED]

For the Bee-Keepers' Magazine.

An Easy Way to Find Any Queen.

I have had one year's experience at bee-keeping, commenced in the Spring of 1887 with one swarm, and had a varied experience, and very, very much solid pleasure, (no honey) transferred, increased by division, and had one swarm come out, and now have, or had last fall, five swarms in chaff hives, one black and four Italians, but my great feat, if I can call it such, was in Italianizing a swarm of black bees. I followed the directions as laid down in the books at my command and all told me to upon the hive and examine each frame carefully for the queen, if not found close the hive and wait twenty minutes and look again. This I did again and again, every time with the same result, till I almost came to the conclusion that it was a queenless swarm, and looked at my beautiful yellow queen in her cage at a loss what to do with her. I thought of the following plan, and it worked well. I opened the hive again, gave them plenty smoke, jarred the hive, and gave time for every bee to fill with honey then took each frame out and brushed every bee into the box, set the frame back and put a trap made of perforated zinc at the entrance of the hive, placed a newspaper on the ground in front of the hive, and brushed all the bees out of the box on the paper, and let them run in through the trap into the hive, and as the queen could not get through the openings in the zinc, was found and caught. As soon as I had her safe, I put the cage containing the

Scientific Department.

IRREGULAR-CELL FOUNDATION.

The Important Discovery of J. W. Carlsson.

Editor Bee-Keepers' Magazine :

Last summer one of the former students of my apiarian school, by name J. W. Carlsson, wished to compel the queen not to enter the honey-room or supers of any kind, and that without *any sort of excluder.* He (as we all) had observed and known the fact, that eggs were never deposited in cells of *irregular shape.* He made a proper press for making foundation of such description ; then he placed these foundations at first in the honey room, then in supers, and lastly *in the middle of the broodnest*—always the same results, the cells were always filled with honey —never a single egg was deposited in those cells. You will easily find the value of this discovery ! A cottager of this country, living at the 60° m. lat., a bee-keeper of the old school, 1883 in the month of November, was bereft by thieves of one of his skeps, and to be sure the heaviest. The winter was coming on and as usually it was very cold—sometimes for days and nights the thermometer going down to 25° to 35° C., with plenty of snow later on in December. In March his daughter was going to the pasture ground, collecting sprigs of shrubs for fuel, when accidentally she tread upon this very skep, imbedded and covered with snow two or three feet deep. She brought it to her father, who cleaned the snow off the skep ; it had lain upon the ground *bottom up* and without the bottomboard and consequently was full of snow. When cleaned he found the combs taken away and the honey too, but still there were some small pieces of combs left in the top and upon these a lump of bees, which when disturbed and removed to a warm place, were awakened and soon very lively. The bees, of no use to him, were killed (while beginning to be too lively) without having tried to find the queen ; but probably she was amongst them ; if *not,* probably the bees would not have

badly arranged home. That for the "McFadden" and W. F. Clarke's hibernation theory.

For a copy of the *Luxembergdan Bee Journal* a gentleman, by name Carl Schröter, railway secretary, gives to the bee-keeping fraternity his way, since some years, to cure colonies diseased with foul brood. His system is to purify the air in the hive and kill the bacilli. Any one knows that in the open air carbolic acid very quickly evaporates. It will kill the bacilli but at the same time the bees cannot endure the smell, but will soon rush out of the hive ; they can not breath. Then he returned to a chemist who advised him to mix well the carbolic acid with tar of wood in equal parts, then it will evaperate slowly, the gasses being in some way bound. The bees tolerate this smell very well, never discontinuing their workings. The result of its use is : The bacillis are killed and the rotten substance in the cells will soon be dried up ; the bees then being able to clean the cells. Generally a single potion, or dose, is sufficient, but it is safe after three months to give the hive a new dose. Next spring you will closely observe such a hive and if necessary once more treat it in the same way. It will destroy the bee lice too. *Probatum est.* How to administer it : Take off all the combs, the very bad ones to be melted down, the other closely washed in a mixture of carbolic acid and water, and then either stored up until the bees want them again or put back at once. Then take two very thin boards—those of cigar boxes will do—cut them 10 cmtr. to 10 cmtr.* and to all the four edges of the one board nail on four pieces of lath 1½ cmtr. high to 1 cmtr. thick. Now place upon it a felt, quite covering it, this felt previously to have been moistened thoroughly in the above mixture of carbolic acid and tar of wood. Nail the other board on the first one, but before that you ought to place some pieces of boards or leather 3 mm. thick between the boards, the object being to prevent the evaporation of the carbolic acid. Place this little "case" exactly below the frames of the hive; shut it up except the entrance, of course, and the work is done.

Yours very truly,
H. STALLMAN.

Sweden Gottenberg, March 9th, '88

THE BACON BEETLE ATTACKS COMB.

Mr. John Aspinwall:

DEAR SIR:—The beetle which you send me for name, the larvæ of which apparently attacked some empty comb and riddled the wax, late last fall, is *Dermestes lardarius*, commonly known as the "bacon beetle" or the "larder beetle." It is one of the many pests that Europe has contributed to us for our annoyance and injury. Through commerce it has been distributed over many parts of the world.

The family of *Dermestidæ* of which it is a member, is of bad reputation, as it embraces several exceedingly destructive pests of the household, warehouses, etc., among which a notable example is the carpet-beetle, *Anthremes scrophulariæ*, which within the past few years has spread so extensively over the United States, carrying terror to the hearts of many provident housewives.

Another specie of the family is the leather beetle, *Dermestes vulpinus* Fabr., which, a number of years ago, committed such ravages upon the furs of the Hudson's Bay Company in its storehouse in London, that a reward of £20,000 ($100,000) was offered for the discovery of some effectual means for destroying it and arresting the ravages. Recently it has made its appearance as a destroyer of manufactured boots and shoes in wholesale houses in St. Louis, Mo., and elsewhere. Its operations, life history, and remedies for its attack have been written of by Prof. C. V. Riley, in the report of the U. S. Commissioner of Agriculture for the year 1885, pp. 258–264. In the illustrations of the insect on Plate vi, fig. 2, of the report, the figure of the larvæ

infesting bacon which had been hanging in garrets in heavy paper and in muslin meat sacks. It also feeds on other dried meats, as ham and smoked beef, and it occurs in the horns and hoofs of dead animals. Sometimes it becomes a museum pest, where it is attracted by the skins of the mounted animals, and it does not disdain, at times, to prey upon and rapidly destroy insect collections. Of course, it is only the larvæ that commits the injury, the beetle being harmless except as it is the parent depositing the eggs for the continuance of the species.

I have no knowledge of this insect ever attacking honey-comb, nor do I find any reference to such a habit in any publication at hand. Prof. Cook has not included it in his list of enemies of the bee, given in his excellent Manual of the Apiary. If the suspicion entertained of the larvæ feeding upon comb, shall be verified, it will be an interesting fact, as indicating a strange extension in its food habits.

A few words descriptive of the beetle and its larvæ may aid the readers of your journal in recognizing the insect should they meet with it in or about their hives. The beetle is of an oblong-oval form, black except the basal (front) half which is covered with a band of buff-colored or yellowish-brown hairs which is irregular or toothed behind, and bears a few small black spots on each wing-cover, of which the three across the middle are the most constant. On the body beneath and on the legs are some thinly scattered shining yellowish hairs. The legs are short, and the head bent downward so as hardly to be seen from above. Its length is from one-fourth to one-third of an inch with a diameter little exceeding one-tenth of an inch. The larvæ is about half an inch long when full-grown by one-fifth as broad, gradually tapering behind ending in a truncate cone, having a fleshy lobe at its tip which serves as a terminal proleg. The body is dark-brown above, whitish pair of short curved horney spines or hooks. The legs are short and scaly.

Since writing the above, the wax-eating of this insect is confirmed in a brief article contained in the *American Entomologist* for June, 1870, vol. ii, p. 246, which I had overlooked. The editor, Prof. C. V. Riley, in reply to a correspondent from Wisconsin who had sent samples of the larvæ to him for identification, after giving its name, states : " We never knew them to occur before in bee hives; but as they feed on feathers, horn, hoof, and other such (to us) indigestible substances, it is not surprising that they also relish wax. Those you sent fed ravenously upon it ; and after changing their coats several times, became beetles."

I am very glad that you communicated to me your observation of the occurrence of *D. lardarius* in honeycomb, since so far as I know, it is only the second time that it has been observed. It is an interesting addition to our knowledge of the insect, for we are now authorized to conclude that the first reported instance was not, as may have been thought, simply an abnormal manifestation of appetite, but that a larva taste for wax exists which will be gratified whenever the opportunity offers. Can it be that in some cases the operations of this larvæ have been mistaken for those of the beemoth, *Galleria cereana ?* Is there any resemblance in their manner of working ? Please favor us with a statement of the conditions under which the larvæ of the former were found by you in the comb, last year.

Very truly yours,
J. A. LINTER.

Albany, March 29, 1883.

Permit me to add another postscript.

In reply to an inquiry made of Professor Cook of any knowledge that he might have of the occurrence of *D. lardarius* in bee hives, he has replied that in the last edition of his Manual (mine is the second edition of 1878) he has stated that it often feeds on the dead bees and pollen in comb and so mutilates the fabric.

I also requested of Dr. Hagen, of at Cambridge, Mass., to inform me if he could find in their large library of European entomological literature, any record of *D. lardarius* feeding on wax or infesting hives in Europe, or if he had knowledge of such occurrence elsewhere. He has returned answer that in an extended search through a large number of works both in their library and in the public library of Boston, he has met with no record of the kind. Mrs. Hagen recalls the fact that yellow wax is sometimes injured in Europe by insects.

As Prof. Cook's statement is apparently at variance with that quoted from Mr. Walsh, the desirability of further observations in the matter is clearly seen. Will bee keepers please lend their aid.

POISONOUS HONEY.

Notes on Trebizonde Honey.

J. C. TRESH, D.SC., F. I. C.

Some time ago Mr. Holmes placed in my hands two samples of honey, which he had received from Mr. A. Biliotti, H. M. Consul at Trebizonde. This honey is reputed to be poisonous, and as the poisonous principle *is* by many writers ascribed to the ericaceous plants which abound around Trebizonde, Mr. Holmes desired me to ascertain, if possible, whether the honey contained " andromedotoxin," a poison isolated by Prof. Prugge from the Andromeda japonica, and which he has since shown to be present in other poisonous Ericaceæ. The results of my labors have not been altogether satisfactory, but the subject is one of such interest that perhaps no other apology is necessary for presenting them, together with an account of Dr. Stockman's physiological experiments with the poisonous principle.

Mr. Keith E. Abbot, writing from Trebizonde under date Dec. 10th, 1883 (*Lond. and Edin. Philosoph. Mag.,* vol. v., p. 313) gives an account of the poisonous properties of the honey, but does not mention anything peculiar about its taste or smell. He adds that the poison is supposed to be derived abundantly near, and when in blossom exhales a most luxuriant odor.

Hamilton ("Travels in Asia Minor," 155, 1842) says that all the poisonous honey has a bitter taste. He describes both the purple rhododendron and the Azalea pontica as abounding along the southern coast of the Black Sea, and prefers to believe that the poison is taken by the bees from the odorous azalea rather than from the odorless rohdodendron.

Still more recently Mr. A. Biliotti, H. M. Consul at Trebizonde, in his report for 1879 (c 2331, p. 1023), says that "bees are reared on a somewhat large scale in the province of Trebizonde, but the honey produced on the coast is unfit for food." He also adds: "It is presumed that the poisonous principle contained in the honey is gathered by the bees from the flowers of the Datura stramonium, which grows in abundance on the coasts. Beehives, therefore, are only remunerative for their wax." In a more recent letter to Mr. Holmes, which accompanied the honey, he says that the tins were obtained from different parts of the district, and that he is informed that cattle happening to feed on Azalea pontica are taken with giddiness, as also are people who sleep with large bunches of that flower in their rooms.

These statements, reports, etc., would lead one to infer that more than one kind of honey possessing poisonous properties is found in Asia Minor, and since Pliny, Dioscorides and others say that the bees which produce the poisonous honey, in some seasons produce good honey, it seems probable that the proportion of the toxic agent or agents varies from year to year, according to the character of the season. This appears to be confirmed by the fact that whilst one of the honeys received from Trebizonde undoubtedly contained a poisonous principle, it is probable that the other contained little or none.

It may be interesting to note here that poisonous honey has also been found in North America, and that in a district where the kalmia grows luxuri-

party of adventurers in New Jersey tried bee rearing in order to obtain honey. The bees throve splendidly and produced honey in abundance, but it proved to be of poisonous character, causing intoxication, dimness of sight, vertigo, etc., and in some cases vomiting, paralysis and death. Barton thinks the poison is derived from the kalmia, but also mentions andromeda, rhododendron, azalea and datura as possible sources.

The Trebizonde honey which I have examined was contained in a hermetically sealed, cylindrical tins, holding about 7 lbs. each.

Tin No. 1—The honey in this tin was quite granular, fawn colored, and with the usual agreeable characteristic oder. The flavor was at first like that of ordinary honey, but when the sweetness had passed off a certain degree of acridity could be detected even with small quantities.

[Dr. Thresh here gives a detailed account of his treatment of this honey and the extracts obtained by the use of chloroform and ether. No. 1 is extract soluble in the former and No. 2 in the latter. We omit this analysis, as it is purely chemical, and give the physiological experiments as being of more interest to bee-keepers.—ED. B. K. M.]

Not wishing to waste the very small amount of material at my disposal by trying unnecessary experiments. I decided to suspend the further chemical investigation until I had ascertained in which extractive the poisonous principle, if any, was contained. The remainder of the aqueous solution was therefore evaporated to a low bulk and labelled "No. 3. Extract, insoluble in ether and chloroform," and sent together with the extracts No. 1 and No. 2 to Dr. Stockman at Edinburgh for physiological examination. In these investigations the whole of the material was unfortunately used, so that a further chemical examination is impossible without acting upon a fresh supply of honey.

frogs and rabbits with the extracts sent to him, and furnished a report from which I can only quote briefly, since the details are more suitable for a physiological than a pharmaceutical society. He found that none of them affected the pupil of the eye, but that No. 2, when applied directly to the eye caused almost immediately a violent attack of conjunctivitis. Administered subcutaneously Nos. 1 and 2 were inert, or if they contained any toxic substance it was in too small a quantity to produce any apparent effects. Extract No. 3, on the other hand, proved to be exceedingly active, and therefore contained the substance of which we were in search.

A quarter of a grain of extract No. 3 dissolved in water and injected under the skin of a frog caused it rapidly to become paralyzed, the animal lying in whatever position it was placed, the only sign of life one hour after administration being a very sluggish action of the corneal reflex. Respiration had entirely ceased, but the circulation went on vigorously until the evening of the third day, when it died. Two grains were similarly injected under the skin of a rabbit. Shortly after, its gait became unsteady, and this effect increased until the animal appeared to have lost all control of its movements, and staggered about like a drunken man. One hour after, it lying down, unable to rise and respiration had fallen from 104 to 46 per minute. Two hours later it had nearly recovered, the only symptom of poisoning being slight unsteadiness of gait, which shortly afterwards passed off. A dose of 4 grains killed a much larger rabbit in a very short time. From these and other experiments Stockman concludes that " the toxic substance contained in Trebizonde honey is evidently a narcotic poison, acting very markedly on the respiratory center, by paralysis of which death is caused." On comparing its action on frogs with the action of andromedotoxin, as described by Plugge (*Archived Pharmacie*, [3], xxi., p. 16) there are certain points of agreement and disagreement. Both produce grad-

tion is arrested, whilst the heart remains little or not at all affected ; on the other hand, the vomiting movements, and the very marked fibriliary twitchings of the muscles observed by Plugge were absent.

The account given by Eykman of the effects on rabbits of asebotoxin (*Pharm. Journ.*, [3], xiii., 366) agrees with the results obtained from the honey extract in so far as gradually deepening paralysis occurred, with death from failure of respiration. As Dr. Stockman could not obtain, at the time of writing Eykman's original paper, a closer comparison was impossible.

Although our labors have not resulted in the isolation of the poisonous principle or principles, yet they enable us to speak with some degree of probability as to the nature and source of the poison. The reputedly poisonous plants growing near Trebizonde, and to which the toxic properties of the honey have been supposed by different writers to be due, are Azalea pontica, species of Rhododendron and Andromeda, Nerium oleander and Datura stramonium.

Since no trace of alkaloid could be detected in the honey, and the poisonous extract did not dilate the pupil there is little doubt the poison is not derived from the Datura stramonium.

Had the toxic agent been allied to the poison of the oleander we should have expected it to act as a cardiac poison, whereas it has little or no effect upon the heart. The little ascertained with regard to its chemical properties does not point to any relationship with neriin, oleandrin, neriantin or neriodorin ; it is very improbable, therefrom, that the poison is derived from the oleander.

The azalea, rhododendron and andromeda all belong to the same natural order, Ericaceæ and the researches of Plugge, Eykman and de Zaayer point to andromedotoxin or substances closely allied thereto as being the toxic principle in all poisonous Ericaceæ. There is now little doubt that the asebotoxin of Eykman and the andromedotoxin of Plugge are identical, and as shown the poison of Trebizonde honey so strikingly resembles that of the above mentioned principles as to leave little doubt as to their close relationship if not identity. Both are glucosides, soluble in water, not precipitated therefrom by normal lead acetate, but thrown down by the basic acetate, sparingly soluble in ether, and giving a distinctive color reaction with hydrochloric acid.

It is exceedingly probable, therefore, that the poison is derived from some Ericaceous plant, and as the azalea appears to be the most fragrant and abundant, so it is most likely to be its true source.

In conclusion, I must express my thanks to Dr. Stockman for his valuable assistance in undertaking the physiological experiments, and to Mr. Holmes, our Curator, for placing the honey at my disposal, and for his many interesting suggestions.

[There is no doubt that andromedotoxin is the poisonous property of The Kill Calf (*Andromeda Mariana*) honey of Long Island spoken of on page 49 of vol. xv. of MAGAZINE.—ED.]

Editor Bee-Keepers' Magazine :

Bees are all in good condition ; every one came through O. K. This now makes the fifteenth winter my system has taken our bees through without loss, on the summer stand. Am fully convinced that wintering is no hard matter if properly done. Fifteen times in succession should test it, in a place like ours especially. We are 2300 feet above sea level, and our bees are often confined to their hives from the 20th of November until the middle of March without a cleansing flight. Some years

Beginners Department

Motto—" Courage and Perseverance."

After purchasing your bees, as advised in last number, you should know something about their habits, before you can manage them with intelligence. The four products resulting from the labor of the worker bees are :

1. HONEY,
2. WAX,
3. POLLEN,
4. PROPOLIS.

They are here arranged in the order of their importance.

The first, third, and fourth are gathered from nature's vegetable sources by the worker bees. The second comes from the bees themselves, being what one might term their *fat.* It is produced in thin scales, between the rings of the under side of the abdomen, and is removed and molded by the bees into the honey comb so familiar to us all.

HONEY is a secretion of the flowers which the bees sip up with their tongue and hold in a *honey sac* situated in that part of the body which supports the wings and legs. This is not their own digesting stomach which is situated in the ringed portion of their body, but is simply a reservoir that by contraction forces the honey out through the tongue, when the bees desire to store the honey in the cells.

POLLEN is also derived from the flowers and is their fertilizing element. Bees gather it to use in feeding their young. It is often called *bee bread,* which by the way is not a bad name at all. Bees cannot raise their young without its presence in the hive. They do not take the pollen into the honey sac when gathering it, but place it on their hind legs, where nature has provided attempts to handle the frames of the hives, as bees not only stop cracks leading *outward*, but any cracks they find, and thus frame ends and rabbets, (the part on which the frame ends rest) become covered with it.

The *workers* then are the all important personages of the hive, and the *queen* and *drones* but instruments in the production of these little laborers. Long before any flowers secreting honey appear, plants such as the pussy willow and tag or swamp alder furnish the pollen necessary for the raising of young bees. Space will not permit us to go into the detail of brood rearing.

Brood is used to designate the bees while in the whole range of growth from the hatching of the egg to the coming forth of the perfect insect.

Egg is the first stage of the brood.

Worm or Larva is the second stage. Up to and including this stage the brood have not been capped, as from the hatching of the egg the bees have fed the larvæ constantly.

Pupa, sometimes incorrectly called *Imago*, is the third and last stage. When the worm is ready to be transformed, the cell is capped over and in this sealed chamber takes place that wonderful metamorphosis which astonishes and confounds the unbeliever.

For further information on these points see any of the standard works on bee culture.

Robbing.—Bees are not angelic creatures though we extol their virtues often. Could bees read, we should distribute printed copies of the eighth commandment about the hives. But we must not be too harsh on our pets. It is their only weakness, and could we say the same of humanity in general, we would not require so many penitentiaries. When a colony becomes weak so that there are not bees enough to cover two or three frames, then its stronger neighbors will pitch in and have a grand feast. They will bully those weaker brethren, invade their home and steal all their honey.

The weak stock, being without food, soon die. A little timely work, on the part of the apiarist, will prevent this

the entrance to this hive, when it is placed on its stand, so only one or two bees can pass in or out at a time, the weak brothers, or perhaps we had better say half sisters, will be able to guard their domain by seizing an intruder and dispatching him at their leisure.

Should robbing be well under way, and the weak colony thoroughly demoralized, a good method is to throw a handful of wet hay or grass over the entrance. The robbers in trying to struggle through this, become so wet that they give up their robbing and go home in disgust. Another method is to move the weak colony to some distant part of the apiary and shut it up for a day or two by placing wire gauze over the entrance, or else if you find that one colony is doing all the robbing, exchange the places of the two *i. e.* put the weak colony on the strong colonies' stand, and *visa versa*. A little flour sprinkled on the backs of the robbing bees as they emerge from the weak hive, will enable you to tell where they come from. The early fruit bloom is a great help in brood rearing, as it supplies a small but constant flow of honey. It is advisable to keep track of the bloom of the flowers, and the amount of honey coming in. This record will be invaluable in future years.

An eastern or southern slope is the best for an apiary, though it is not essential to success. A good way is to face the hives (turn the entrances) to east and south alternately. This enables the bees to mark their position better. In bees, the "bump of locality" is highly developed, and this must always be borne in mind when moving a colony a short distance, and upon this "bump" depends the success of the experiment of interchanging colonies when robbing. The robbers returning home find matters changed around and instead of a strong colony they find one weak with bees, hence they forget about robbing and go to protecting themselves.

The novice should never attempt to more than double his colonies if he

THE MYSTERIES OF VISION.

THE human eye presents itself to our common observation as consisting of two parts—the pupil, and the ball of the eye. The pupil receives the images of the objects we behold, which then pass through the eyeball; and many persons think that this is all that is requisite to produce perfect sight. If any of you entertain such an idea, you will be surprised when I tell you that the eye does not see at all. The eye has no more innate power of sight than a telescope or a looking-glass. It is an optical instrument for transmitting the rays of light, like the telescope; and it has reflecting powers like the looking-glass: but in itself it can do no more than either of the two instruments. It cannot accomplish sight; and we can, indeed, get all the impressions of vision, such as size, situation, and colour, without the eye being at all employed. This is constantly happening to us in our dreams; and whenever we have been more than ordinarily excited by pleasure, or depressed by grief, we are almost certain to experience these effects. Have you never dreamed that you have seen faces, figures, and sights? You have no doubt beheld in your sleep all these combined together, and had them so vividly pourtrayed as to retain the most distinct remembrance of passing scenes when you have awoke. But when a person is under the influence of an opiate, these impressions assume such distinct vividness, and exquisite beauty, as perfectly to entrance the mind at the time. No doubt is felt of the reality of the spectacle: its gorgeous colouring is of so bright a hue, as altogether to outvie the sombre scenery of our terrestrial globe. Take another instance—playing blindfold at chess: the board, with sixty-four squares, must be present to the mind; the pieces must all assume their proper shapes; their different moves must be distinctly recognised;—so that, in fact, the three great properties of vision—namely, colour, situation, and size—must be accurately impressed.

Allowing that there have been the most flagrant instances of imposture and collusion in mesmerism, yet still enough is verified to prove that internal impressions are made without the intervention of the organs whereby those impressions are generally produced. In some keenly-scrutinized instances, every act of the mesmeriser has been repeated by his automaton patient. Now, if a person imitate every movement I make with hand or foot, or head or lip, you would conclude that he sees me; at least, if he does not see, he does that which vision represents. In all these instances, the eye can have nothing to do with sight, for it is closed to all external objects. The eyelid is closely pressed upon the visual organ; so closely, indeed, that no image can enter its pupil—no light can pass through its ball. What, then, is the conclusion to which we are led? Clearly this—that if the sense of sight can be produced without the eye (that is, with the eye shut), the eye does not possess within itself the faculty of vision; and, consequently, if we would know the phenomena of vision, we must not rest satisfied with a simple inspection of the organ of sight.

Let us then consider the eye more closely with its accompanying machinery. The light of a candle which we see, enters the pupil of the eye, and passes through the various humours of its globe; it strikes against the retina—a thin delicate membrane at the back of the eye—and there the candle is reflected just as a face is reflected in a looking-glass. Now, embedded in this retina, are the pulpy ends of the optical nerves; and these nerves carry forward the impression of sight to the brain. This is confirmed by the fact that if these optical nerves are injured, vision at once becomes impaired, if not extinct. We trace vision into the eye, through the eye, and then along the optical nerves. These nerves end in a part of the brain which is called the seat of sensation, and into that particular part of it which bears the name of the optic ganglion; and that this optic ganglion receives the impression of the object which enters the eyeball, is made evident from the fact that if this ganglion receives any injury, however perfect every other part of the visual apparatus may be, the eye becomes quite dim.

I have now traced vision through the lengthened series of means which are designed for carrying it into execution. The eye receives the figure of the object, the retina reflects it, the optic nerve carries it onwards, it enters the brain, and at last it fixes itself in the optic ganglion. But then, can this optic ganglion produce the phenomena of sight? Why, it is only matter: be it composed of what it may, it is opaque matter, and there dwells in it no more favourable properties for seeing than you can find in either the skin of your hand, or your ear, or your foot. How, then, after all, can we explain vision? It is an unfathomable mystery. The naturalist knows nothing about it; to the philosopher it is an equal enigma; nor can the anatomist disclose the hidden secret.

From these observations, you will perhaps be led to this conclusion—that vision, though in its ultimate causation a direct exercise of creative power, is yet, so far as the mechanical apparatus of sight is concerned, more influenced by the optic ganglion and the optic nerves than by the eye itself. Let us, then, consider these two parts of the animal frame as the seat of vision. In what I have hitherto said respecting the theory of vision, I have had before me only the higher orders of animal existence; and I have alluded to the eye as found in what we may consider its most perfect shape. But we must not suppose that the eye is always so. In the insect tribes, in the worms and grubs, we shall discover a great variety of configuration, attended with a higher and lower degree of sight. In fact, vision is like an ascending series, beginning at so low a point that it is actually impossible to say where is its first existence. In some of the smallest animalcules there is a certain degree of sensibility to the rays of light—some choosing the light, and expanding to its influence, and others shrinking from it, as from an injurious agent. But in these microscopic creatures it is impossible, on account of their minuteness, to detect the presence of the optic ganglion or of the optic nerve. When, however, we come to creatures of a larger bulk, both these may be detected. Supposing, then, that the optic ganglion is the source of light, and the optic nerve has the power of being affected by the light, what would be the consequences if this optic nerve ended in the outer coatings of the skin—that skin being pellucid, and therefore offering no resistance to the light? In such a case, we should expect that the little creature would experience

of the optic nerve being merely like a little point inside the skin, it came through it, enlarging itself into a little globule, like the head of a pin, but smaller, we have then a somewhat greater degree of perfection in the visual apparatus; and we might then expect a somewhat nearer approach to sight. And this is the case in the common slug. It not only knows light from darkness, but has some idea of substance; for, from experiments that were made with the slug, it was repeatedly observed to avoid a small object presented to it—thus affording evidence of its possessing this sense, at least to such an extent as would enable it to find out its way, and to avoid what was injurious to its life. Next, suppose that instead of there being one pair of optic nerves, they branched out into many separate parts, each part, as before, ending in a distinct globule; then, there being so many more points for receiving the light, there would exist a proportionate extension in the degree of vision. In the leech, the optic nerve ends in ten such distinct points; in the caterpillar there are eight; in the centipede there are twenty-eight: and as there is a variety in the number of these rudimental organs of sight, so also is there no less variety in the perfection of the organs themselves. But still thus far we have met with nothing which can fairly bear the name of an eye; they appear to be little more than spots—in some like black grains of sand, in some red, and in some white. In others, these granules are of a somewhat larger size; and some experimentalists have imagined that they have detected some appearance of the germ of an eye, as in the slug and the leech. But it is unnecessary to dwell longer upon these creatures, which sink so low in the order of creation, and respecting which nothing can be affirmed with any degree of certainty, although numerous experiments have been made. I did not, however, think it well to pass them over, because they help to fix the ideas upon our minds of the theory of vision, leading us to trace them up to the optic ganglion, from thence to the optic nerve; making us to understand how a degree of sight could be imparted, when the visual organ was in its most imperfect and rudimental there is a pair of optic nerves; in others, four pair; in others, six; and in others, eight—each one ending in a complete visual apparatus. And hence it follows, that in the species of insects now under consideration, some have two, some eight, some twelve, some sixteen eyes, which are variously distributed about the head. Take the garden spider as a type of this class: it has eight eyes on its forehead, which are planted in three tubicles, four on the central one, and two on each side of the lateral ones; and that the spider has very distinct vision, will be evident to any one who has watched its movements. When a fly or a gnat is caught in the meshes of its web, how swiftly it comes down from its concealment, and pounces upon its prey! If the entangled captive is strong, and is striving to burst away, how dexterously the spider fastens an additional knot round the struggling limb, and binds it with elastic glue! The spider knows at once whether it is a wing or a foot that most requires the hand, and instantaneously the web is woven and fixed. And then look at the spider when the capture is complete—how it removes its prey, repairs the broken web, and, when all is fitly finished, goes back to its concealment.

But again, there is another kind of eye prevailing among a very large department of the insect tribes—what is called the compound eye; and the best way of conceiving the idea of these compound eyes, is to suppose that instead of the eyes being separated and distributed over the forehead of the insect, they are united together in two clusters, in which case we have eight or ten eyes united together on each side of the head, each having its own separate nerve, as being a distinct cause of sight. But, in fact, instead of there being only eight or ten, they vary from fifty to twenty-five thousand; and these are joined together in a way not much unlike the flower of the daisy. To look at the daisy, it seems but a single flower; but if we divide it in two, we soon discover that it is made up of a vast number of little florets, each one of which is a distinct and perfect flower, fixing itself in the receptacle. And so with the compound eyes, they are distinct and yet united. In the bee and wasp you will have observed a large black—or in the dragon-fly a dark-brown—hemispherical body, situated in front around the antennæ. On either side of the head is a mass of these eyes, they are packed to-

gether as the cells of a honeycomb, which in point of shape they closely resemble, being a six-sided cone, while the surface of these cones is flattened into very minute lenses. The ant has fifty of these lenses, that is, twenty-five eyes on each side of its head; the fly, eight thousand in all; the dragon-fly, twelve thousand; the butterfly, seventeen thousand; and in the mordella (a species of beetle), upwards of twenty-five thousand have been counted. Fortunately, from the great attention which has been given to this department of natural history, we may assign a reason for this. The eye of the insect is immovable, the head being in many instances fixed into the trunk of the body; the consequence is, that the insect can only see in one direction—straightforward, and with a peculiar limited range. It is, then, to compensate the little creature for this defect, that a peculiar organization has been provided. By the vast multiplication in the number of their eyes, their defects are compensated—a separate eye being provided, as it were, for every point to be viewed, by which means, although the orb of the eye is stationary, it can look in every direction, and catch every object, and has as ample field of vision as other animals; for it is quite certain, from observation of the movement of insects, that their vision is by no means deficient. Take, for instance, the bee: in the construction of its cells, what can be more exquisite? The distance of its flight is often great, and yet it knows how to find its way home. See it also among flowers, it always seems to have an object, and the very business of the bee is a clear indication of the perfectness of its range of sight. I have before alluded to the spider, and spoken of the exactness of its sense of vision. The same may be said of the ant and beetle kind, which are so frequently crossing our path in our summer walks. I will only add, that this perfection of sight in the various insect tribes, is just what we should have looked for if we had only seen the large quantity of optic ganglion deposited in the cavities of their heads. This has led naturalists to the conclusion that almost all the actions of insects are guided by sensations received through their eyes. Whether, therefore, we consider the optic ganglion, the optic nerve, or the compound eye itself, we perceive a series of contrivances no less remarkable for their complete adaptation to the wants of the insects, than they are admirable for the wonderful structure of their shape. All here is well done. The insect is abundantly compensated for the want of motion in its visual organ; the defect is amply supplied; and a degree of vision is secured which equals, if not exceeds, the sight of many other creatures.

In the higher order of creation, where the eye assumes that general character with which we are familiar, it will be found that the degree of sight depends very much upon the size of the organ, and upon its lustre. In the mole, where the eye is small, the creature has but imperfect sight; and if ever it gets out of its burrow, it is lost, and there is no great difficulty in taking it alive. The eye of the weasel is not large, but shines very bright; and unless you come upon it suddenly (when it is in pursuit of its prey), so rapid are its movements, from the keenness of its sight, that you must be an expert marksman ever to hit it with your shot. Again, the eye of the cow and the sheep, though large, are without much lustre, and their sight is inferior to that of the dog and cat, in which creatures great brilliancy often exists. And if we go into a menagerie, the eyes of some of the creatures, as the lion, the tiger, and the hyena, seem almost to flash fire, which is an indication not only of ferocity in tearing their prey, but also of their power to see it. The camel, the elephant, and the giraffe, have by no means bright eyes, and their habits do not require that intensity of sight which is necessary to guide the beasts of prey in making their spring. In fact, throughout the whole of nature we shall detect no waste. The vision of each creature is adapted to its mode of subsistence. The eyes of some birds seem altogether adapted for a vast range of sight. I may mention the vulture as an instance. When a caravan is crossing a desert, however expansive may be the plain of land, if a camel drops, there is soon seen, first in the horizon, then on high

white-headed eagle:—"Elevated on the high dead limb of some gigantic tree, that commands a wide view of the neighbouring shore and ocean, he seems calmly to contemplate the motions of the feathered tribes that pursue their avocations below. High over all hovers one whose actions instantly arrest all his attention. By his wide curvature of wing, and sudden suspension in the air, he knows him to be the fish-hawk, settling over some devoted victim of the deep. His eye kindles at the sight, and balancing himself with half-open wing on the branch, he watches the result. Down, rapid as an arrow, from heaven descends the distant object of his attention, the roar of his wings reaching the ear, as it disappears in the deep, making the surges foam around. At this moment the eager looks of the eagle are all ardour; and, levelling his neck for the flight, he sees the fish-hawk once more emerge, struggling with his prey, and mounting in the air with screams of exultation. These are signals for the eagle, who, launching into the air, instantly gives chase, soon gains on the fish-hawk; each exerts his utmost skill to mount above the other, displaying in their rencontres the most elegant and sublime aerial evolutions. The unencumbered eagle rapidly advances, and is just on the point of reaching its opponent, when, with a sudden scream—probably of despair and honest execration—the latter drops his fish. The eagle, poising himself for a moment, as if to take a more certain aim, descends like a whirlwind, snatches the fish in his grasp ere it reaches the water, and bears his ill-gotten booty silently away." From this graphic description we may form some general idea of the piercing vision of the eagle, and its kindred species. The Bengal sparrow is also a bird endowed with great quickness of sight; for when it is tamed, if a ring be dropt down from a height, it will fly down with amazing celerity, catch the ring, and bring it to its master. This feat has been performed down a deep well, and the thrown ring seized before it reached the of trees, to us invisible, would to this little bird be as large as a shot or peppercorn; and an insect to us a quarter of an inch in size, would appear to it as large as a common mouse. If it were not for the microscopic power so largely bestowed upon so many orders of the feathered tribe, our trees would soon be leafless, and our fields become barren and desolate. In fact, all the swarms of insects, and the countless hosts of grubs, would devour the kindly fruits of the earth.

There is yet another kind of vision, which, as it forms an important part in the economy of nature, ought not to be passed over without some remark. I mean nocturnal vision, or the capacity of seeing in the twilight, or nearly in the dark. The goat, the owl, and the woodcock, are all of them most active at night; and if disturbed by day, and obliged to fly when the sun is shining, they seem lost, and keep near the ground, or by the side of a hedge. In the dark twilight, the bat and night-jar move with great swiftness, and do much havoc among the moths and flies; the owl is at this time no less active upon its wings, as it brings a mouse every twelve or fifteen minutes to its young. We must notice, also, that beasts of prey are possessed of nocturnal vision. Now, to enable these creatures to see in the dark, they have a very peculiar organization provided. The pupil of their eyes can contract itself to almost nothing, passing away or vanishing to an invisible point, from which contractile power they can admit into their eyeballs just as much or just as little light as they require.

Some creatures see both on land and water; some by day and night; and some are fitted for all these various kinds of vision. It is, however, generally remarked that when there is a great enlargement of visual power in one particular, this can only be obtained by a corresponding loss in another; and that every excellence is just as incompatible in the eye as in any other part of the animal frame. Now, I cannot pretend to affirm whether there may be, or whether there may not be, any exceptions to this rule among the irrational works of creation, but certainly it applies with perfect truth to mankind. The human eye, if compared singly with the eyes of many other creatures in nature, may be found to be inferior to them in some particular. It has not the same exactness in telescopic power as the eye of the eagle; nor the same minuteness in

the microscopic power as the tit: it has not the same facility of looking downward as the ruminating quadrupeds: nor the same degree of nocturnal vision as the owl: it has not the quicksightedness of the cormorant; nor the same power of seeing in the water as the fish. In each of these particulars it must be regarded as an inferior organ. But then, although the human eye does not possess the very highest degree of power in all these departments, yet it does possess—what the eye of no other animal possesses — a quantity or an amalgamation of them all. What is wanting to a man in precision of sight, is made up in diversity and extensiveness of range. We have quantity against quality; and when all the numerous faculties, all the various properties of the human eye, are taken into account, and considered in the aggregate, instead of complaining of the inferiority of our sight, we shall regard this sense as existing in a higher state of perfection in man, than can be found elsewhere in the universe. One important property of the human eye is its ability to distinguish colour, in a higher degree than is possessed by any other variety of vision. The painter gives the idea of bulk, of distance, of figure, of expression; and that in so close a resemblance to nature, that one effort of art may make us laugh; another, depress our minds almost to tears; one may actually make us feel warm; and another bring over us the sensation of cold.

The eye is the greatest vehicle of our pleasures; all our enjoyments in life are brought to us through its medium. By it we recognise beauty in shape, symmetry in form, elegance in motion, and taste in dress. Every varied expression in passion —whether love, anger, indifference, satiety, or disgust—can be plainly read by the interested parties. So also may we trace the virtues which are of heavenly growth —reverence, veneration, submission, devotion, filial affection, piety, and charity. It were difficult to describe all the changes we see: but there is a change sufficient to pourtray all the varied emotions of the mind. It is this sense which enables us to carry on the various occupations of life, and is the most prolific means of supplying man's wants. It is just in proportion to its importance that it is defended and kept safe from injury. The eye is sunk deep into a bony socket, the projections of which help to preserve it from external injury. It is also defended by the thick skin of the eyelids, which cover it as with a case. Besides this, it is embedded in a fat, soft, yielding, and slippery substance, which from its very nature enables the eye to recede and slip away from a blow, if perchance one should fall on it. It is still further protected by the eyelid, which not only acts as a defence from injury, but also answers the purpose of a sponge—wiping the eye when dust or insects fly into it, and thus keeping it clean and bright. In the performance of this part of its office, it is assisted by the lachrymal glands, from which, when the eye is in a healthy state, three or four ounces of tears—that is, from six to eight tablespoonfuls — are discharged in the course of the day and night. We are not aware of this briny fluid, excepting when a flow of tears is produced by pain, or any violent mental emotion, or by getting anything into the eye. But under ordinary circumstances the same operation is going on in the eye constantly—the fluid, however, being drawn off as fast as it is formed; for there is a little duct at the corner of the eye, down which the tear drops into the nose, where it is evaporated by the air we inhale.

But the wonders of the eye are without limit: I know not where to stop. Besides the eyelid acting as a sponge to keep the orb moist and clean, there are also little glands at the bottom of the eyelashes, generating a sort of ointment (said to be like the white of an egg), which mixes with the tears, and with them is constantly passing over the eyes. Perhaps, however, the most important office of all that the eyelids perform, is that of preserving the eye from too much light; they close, by an involuntary movement, if the rays of the sun fall too suddenly upon the face. In some of the orders of creation this appendage is not supplied. The fish has no eyelids; but then the element in which

it lives renders such a covering unnecessary, as the water softens the rays of light. Even here, however, it may be observed that where a fish burrows in the mud—as is the case with the eel—there is a filmy skin provided which cases the eyeball, and prevents any injury from happening to the organ. Insects, too, have no eyelids; but then their visual orbs are horny externally, bearing the appearance of polished metal or cut glass; and they brush their eyes, and so keep them clear and bright, with their feet or antennæ. The birds—some of them, at least—have a third eyelid, called the nictitating membrane, which is drawn across the eye like a shade; and it is by the aid of this that the naturalists imagine the eagle can look unshrinkingly at the sun in all his meridian splendour. Such, then, are some of the wonderful contrivances in nature—some of the modes by which the eye is defended, and kept in a state of healthy action.

I have thus endeavoured to give a few gleanings from the wide book of nature, out of the page of vision. Imperfect as the sketch may have been, I trust I have said enough to impress the minds of all with a deep sense of the power, the wisdom, and the goodness of God. Well, indeed, has it been remarked by some of the profoundest philosophers of old, that vision was a cure for Atheism; so very plainly does the eye set forth and reflect the attributes of Deity. Let us, then, endeavour not to abuse but to improve this valuable faculty of vision, remembering always how much wisdom the Divine Author of our existence has employed in its development. Let us exercise it profitably, making our eyes the willing instruments of our advancement in useful knowledge, in refined civilization, and in natural and revealed theology.

THE BLIND PHILOSOPHER OF GENEVA.

" Of all the race of animals, alone
The bees have common cities of their own;
And, common sons, beneath one law they live,
And with one common stock their traffic drive.
Each has a certain home, a sev'ral stall:
All is the state's, the state provides for all.
Mindful of coming cold, they share the pain,
And board for winter's use the summer's gain.
Some o'er the public magazines preside,
And some are sent new forage to provide.
Their toil is common; common is their sleep;
They shake their wings when morn begins to
  peep.
Bush through the city gates without delay,
Nor ends their work but with declining day.
Then having spent the last remains of light,
They give their bodies due repose at night;
When hollow murmurs of their ev'ning bells
Dismiss the sleepy swains, and toll them to
  their cells."

Of all the deprivations to which man is subject, there is not one which to a greater degree shuts him out from the sources of pleasure, and the means of usefulness, than the loss of sight. He may lose the perception of odours and taste, without any diminution of the higher order of enjoyments; he may also be deprived of hearing, and yet may still have access to the widest field of instruction and delight. But he who has lost the power of vision is debarred, by the most formidable obstacles, from the perusal of that "book of knowledge," written by the fair hand of nature herself, in which are to be found, not the pictures of things, drawn by other minds, but the originals themselves. And yet there have been men, who have struggled with and overcome the difficulties of this affliction to a degree which would be incredible if it did not rest on the most indubitable proofs. How many instances have there been of blind persons, who have pursued knowledge with ardour and success, and have accomplished undertakings which would have done them honour, even if they had possessed all the bodily senses in the highest degree of perfection! The truth of the above remarks will be strikingly illustrated in the following pages.

Francis Huber was born at Geneva, in July, 1750, of an honourable family, in which quickness of intellect and a lively imagination seemed hereditary. His father, John Huber, had the reputation of being one of the wisest men of his time, and in this light is often mentioned by Voltaire, who highly appreciated his original conversation; he was also an agreeable musician, and wrote verses which were praised even at Ferney. The predilections of the father were inherited by the son. In his early years he attended the public lectures of the college, and, under the guidance of good masters, acquired a taste for literature, which was matured by the conversation of his father, to whom he was also indebted for his love of natural history. He was initiated in the physical sciences, by attending the lectures of M. de Saussure, and by making experiments in the laboratory of a relative, who ruined himself in the search for the philosopher's stone. Endowed with great warmth of feeling, his precocity was very remarkable, and he commenced the study of natural objects at an age when others are only beginning to be conscious of their existence. He was shortly to suffer the most grievous of all privations, and, as if instinctively, he laid up a store of recollections and feelings for the remainder of his life.

About the age of fifteen, his general health and also his eyesight began to be impaired; his ardour in the pursuit of knowledge and amusement,—the passionate eagerness with which he followed his studies by day, and the reading of romances by night (sometimes by no stronger light than that of the moon), wore the causes, it is said, which threatened the ruin both of his sight and of his constitution. His father at that period took him to Paris, in order to consult Tronchin on his health, and Wenzel on the state of his eyes. Tronchin, with the view of removing a tendency to consumption, sent him to pass some time at Stein, a village in the environs of Paris, that he might be out of the reach of every species of agitation: there he lived the life of a mere peasant, followed the plough, and occupied himself wholly in agricultural pursuits. This plan was completely successful so far as regarded his general health, which was ever afterwards unshaken, while he acquired a taste for the country, and a tender recollection of its pleasures which never forsook him. The oculist Wenzel considered his sight, however, as incurable; he thought it unsafe to risk the operation for cataract, which was then not so well understood as it is now, and announced to Huber the probability of his shortly becoming completely blind.

His eyes, however, in spite of their weakness, had, before his departure and after his return, encountered those of Marie-Aimée Lullin, the daughter of one of the Syndics of the republic. They had met each other frequently at the dancing-master's; an affection, such as is felt at the age of seventeen, sprang up between them, and became part of their existence, and neither of them believed it possible that their fates could be disunited. The speedy approach, however, of Huber's blindness determined M. Lullin to refuse his consent to their union, but as the misfortune of him whom she had chosen as her future partner became more certain, Marie regarded herself as bound never to forsake him. "But," said she, "now that he requires a guide to be every moment with him, nothing shall prevent me from being united to him." Her early attachment was rivetted by time, and afterwards became a species of generous heroism; and she resolved to wait till she had attained her majority (then fixed at twenty-five years), in order to be united to Huber. To all the temptations, and even to all the persecutions, by which her father endeavoured to shake her resolution, she remained impregnable; and the moment she attained her majority she presented herself at the altar, with the spouse whom she had chosen when he was happy and attractive, and to cheer whose melancholy fate she was now resolved to devote her life.

Being united to the object of her disinterested affection, their mutual good conduct soon obtained pardon for their disobedience. The constancy of Madame Huber was, in all respects, worthy of the juvenile energy which she had displayed; and during the forty years' continuance of their union, she never ceased to bestow the tenderest care on her blind husband; she was his reader and his secretary, made observations for him, and spared him every embarrassment that his situation was likely to produce. This excellent woman soon discovered a thousand means of alleviating her husband's unfortunate calamity. During the war she formed whole armies with pins of various sizes, and thus enabled him to distinguish the position of the different corps; she likewise stuck the pins in a map, which gave him a correct idea of the movement of the troops; and she formed plans, in relief, of the places they occupied. In a word, she had but one occupation—that of making the life of her husband happy,

and to such a point did this amiable woman carry her attentions, that M. Huber asserted that he should be miserable were he to cease to be blind. "I should not know," said he, "to what extent a person in my situation could be beloved; besides, to me, my wife is always young, fresh, and pretty, and that is no light matter." This affectionate instance of conjugal attachment has been mentioned by celebrated writers: Voltaire frequently alludes to it in his correspondence, and the episode of the Belmont family in Delphine, is a true picture, although somewhat veiled, of that of Huber and his wife.

We have seen blind men excel as poets; some have distinguished themselves as philosophers, and others as arithmeticians; but it was reserved for Huber to become illustrious in a science requiring the examination of objects so minute that the most clear-sighted observers find a difficulty in distinguishing them. The perusal of the works of Reaumur and Bonnet, and the conversations of the latter, directed his curiosity to the study of bees; his constant residence in the country inspired him, first, with the desire of verifying some facts, and afterwards of supplying some deficiencies in the history of these insects. But, for this kind of observation, it was not only necessary that he should have an instrument such as the labours of the optician might supply, but also an intelligent assistant whom he could instruct in the use of it. At this time he had a servant in his family, named Francis Burnens, equally remarkable for his sagacity and for his attachment to his master. Huber drilled him in the art of observing, directed him in his inquiries by questions dexterously proposed, and by means of his own youthful recollections, and the confirmatory testimony of his wife and friends, he corrected the reports of his assistant, and in this way succeeded in acquiring a clear and accurate idea of the most minute facts. "I am much more certain," he said to a friend one day, laughing, "of what I relate than you are yourself, for you publish only what you have seen with your own eyes, whereas I take a medium among the testimony of many." This, indeed, is very plausible reasoning, but will induce no one to quarrel with his eyes.

Huber discovered that the mysterious and remarkably prolific nuptials of the queen bee, the single mother of all her tribe, are celebrated, not in the hive, but in the open air, at an elevation sufficiently great to escape ordinary eyes, but not to elude the researches of a blind man, aided by a peasant; and he described in detail the consequences of the early or late celebration of this aërial hymen. He confirmed, by repeated observation, the discovery of Schirach, at that time disputed, that bees can at their pleasure transform, by an appropriate kind of food, the eggs of working bees to queens, or, to speak more correctly, neuters to females; he showed also how some working bees can lay productive eggs. He described with great care the combats of the queen bees with each other, the massacre of the drones, and all the singular circumstances that take place in the hive, when a foreign queen is substituted for the indigenous one. He showed the influence produced by the size of the cells on the growth of the insects reared in them, and how the larvæ of the bees spin the silk of their cells. Huber proved to demonstration that the queen is oviparous; he studied the origin of swarms, and was the first who gave an accurate history of the flying colonies. He pointed out the use of their antennæ in enabling the bees to distinguish each other; and, finally, from the knowledge he had acquired of their policy, he drew up good rules for their economical superintendence. For the greater part of these delicate observations on hitherto unnoticed facts, he was indebted to his invention, under various forms, of glass hives; one description of which he termed *ruches en livre*, or *en feuillettes*, book or sheet hives, and the other *ruches plates*, flat hives, which allowed the labours of the community to be witnessed in their minutest details.

These discoveries were greatly facilitated by Burnens, who, in his zeal for the discovery of truth, would brave, without shrinking, the wrath of an entire hive, in order to discover the most insignificant fact, and was even seen to seize an enormous wasp, in spite of the grievous stings of a whole nest of hornets. From this, we may judge of the enthusiasm with which his master (and I use the term here, not in the sense of employer but instructor) inspired all his agents in the pursuit of truth. The publication of his labours took place in 1792, in the form of letters to Charles Bonnet, and under the title of *Nouvelles Observations sur les Abeilles*. Naturalists were much struck, not only with the novelty of the facts detailed in this work, but with their rigorous accuracy, and the extraordinary difficulties which the author had combated so successfully.

The activity of his researches suffered no interruption, either from this first success, which might have satisfied his personal vanity, or from the embarrassing changes occasioned by the revolution and his separation from his faithful Burnens. Another assistant was necessary to him, and this office his wife performed for some time. His son Peter, who afterwards acquired considerable celebrity by his history of ants and other insects, next commenced his apprenticeship as observer to his father; and it was principally by his assistance that Huber made new and laborious researches into the history of bees.

The origin of wax was then a disputed point among naturalists, some affirming, but without sufficient proof, that it was formed with the honey; Huber, who had successfully cleared up the origin of the propolis, confirmed this opinion by numerous observations, and, in particular, showed, with the assistance of Burnens, how the wax escapes in the shape of flakes between the rings of the abdomen. He devoted himself to laborious researches on the formation of the bee-hive, and followed step by step its wonderful construction, which seems to resolve, by its perfection, the most delicate problems of geometry; he also pointed out the part which each class of bees take in forming the hive, and followed their labour from the rudiments of the first cell until the completion of the honeycomb. Huber first made known the ravages of the *sphinx atropos* in the hives which it enters. He even attempted to clear up the history of the senses in bees, and in particular to ascertain the locality of the sense of smell, the existence of which is proved by the whole history of insects, but the seat of which their structure has not yet enabled us to fix with certainty. He also undertook curious researches on the respiration of bees, and proved, by numerous experiments, that they absorb oxygen like other animals. The question, however, arose, how could the purity of the air be maintained in a hive plastered with mastic, and closed in all its parts, except at the narrow orifice which serves as the entrance? This problem required all the sagacity of our observer, and he finally arrived at the conclusion that the bees, by a particular motion of their wings, agitate the air in such a manner as to produce its renovation; after having assured himself of this by direct observations, he further proved it by means of the experiment of an artificial ventilation. These experiments on respiration required some analysis of the air in bee-hives, and this brought Huber into correspondence with Senebier, who was then occupied with similar researches on vegetables. Among the means that Huber had at first devised for discovering the nature of the air in bee-hives, was that of producing the germination of various kinds of seeds, in accordance with the notion that they never germinate in an atmosphere that has not its due quantity of oxygen. This experiment, although inadequate to the end proposed, suggested to the two friends the idea of occupying themselves with inquiries on germination; and the most curious part of this association is the fact, that very frequently it was Senebier who suggested the experiments, and Huber, deprived of sight, who executed them. Their labours have been published in their joint names, under the title of *Mémoires sur l'Influence de l'Air dans la Germination des Graines.*

The style of Huber is in general clear and elegant, and while not destitute of the precision required in didactic compositions, it is blended with that charm which a poetical imagination is capable of diffusing over all objects. That, however, by which it is particularly distinguished, is what would be least expected, the description of facts in so graphic a manner, that in the perusal we seem ourselves to see the objects which the author, alas! had not seen. In considering this singular quality of the style of a blind person, I have accounted for it by the efforts it must have cost him to connect the accounts of his assistants in order to form a complete idea.

His taste for the fine arts being deprived of the power of expatiating on form, was led to sounds. He loved poetry, but music had the greatest charms for him: his taste for it might be called innate, and he was greatly indebted to it throughout his whole life as a source of delightful recreation; his voice also was agreeable, and he had been initiated from his earliest youth in the beauties of Italian music.

The wish to keep up acquaintance with absent friends, without recourse to a secretary, suggested to him the idea of having a printing press for his own use;

it was made for him by his servant, Claude Lechet, whom he had inspired with a taste for mechanics in the same way that he had formerly instructed Burnens in natural history. A series of numbered cases contained small printing types, executed in bold relief, which he arranged in his hand. On the lines thus composed he placed a sheet of paper blacked with a particular kind of ink, and above that a sheet of white paper; with a press, set in motion by his foot, he succeeded in printing a letter, which he folded and sealed himself, greatly delighted with the idea of that independence of others which he hoped to acquire by this means. The difficulty, however, of putting the press into action made him soon abandon the use of it; but the letters and the algebraic characters of burnt earth, which his son, ever zealous and ingenious in his service, had made for him, were a source of occupation and amusement for upwards of fifteen years. He enjoyed also the pleasure of walking in the fields, and was even able to do this alone; by means of strings in his hand, and small knots made at intervals, he always knew where he was, and would direct himself accordingly. The activity of his mind made it necessary that he should have such occupations, or he might have been amongst the most miserable of mankind; his friends around him also had no other wish than to please and assist him, and it therefore ceases to be a wonder how he preserved that happy disposition which is so often destroyed by collision with mankind.

The conversation of Huber was generally of an amiable and pleasant cast; his wit was gay and lively; and to few departments of knowledge was he a stranger. He delighted in elevating his thoughts to the contemplation of the most lofty and important subjects, and he could also descend to the most playful and familiar. He was not learned, in the usual acceptance of the term, but, like a skilful diver, he explored the depths of every question with extraordinary tact and sagacity. When the conversation turned on subjects in which he felt more than common interest, his fine countenance became peculiarly animated; the vivacity of his physiognomy, by some mysterious charm, seemed to give expression even to his eyes, so long condemned to darkness, and the tones of his voice then became more solemn and impressive. To extensive knowledge M. Huber also joined an extraordinary memory: he related in a most graceful style a great variety of interesting anecdotes, and nothing could be more affecting than to hear him sing the words of the scene between Œdipus and his daughter.

This extraordinary man passed the latter years of his life at Lausanne, under the care of his daughter Madame de Molin, and from time to time he resumed his early pursuits. The discovery of stingless bees in the neighbourhood of Tampico, by Captain Hall, excited his interest, and his joy was great when his friend, Professor Prevost, was able to send him first a few specimens, and afterwards a whole hive of these insects. This was the last attention he paid to that favourite pursuit, to which he had been indebted for his fame, and what was more, for his happiness. Naturalists, who have followed in his track, although enjoying the benefit of sight, have found nothing of importance to add to the observations of one who was deprived of vision.

Hubert preserved his faculties, and was both amiable and beloved to the last. At the age of eighty-one he thus wrote to one of his dearest friends:—"There are moments when it is impossible to keep one's arms folded, and it is then, in unbracing them a little, that we can repeat to those whom we love all the esteem, the affection, and the gratitude with which they inspire us;" further on, he added, "I can only say to you, that resignation and serenity are blessings that have not been denied to me." He wrote these lines on the 20th of December, and on the 22nd he was no more, having calmly breathed his last in the arms of his daughter.

NOT LOST.

It is not lost,—the beautiful!
  That lights our changeful skies,
Although to dim its glory here
  Dark earth-born mists arise;
The summer, heaven's celestial blue,
  The sunset's parting ray,
The gorgeous clouds with purple hue,
  These have not passed away.

It is not lost,—the beautiful!
  Sweet sounds we loved of yore
Shall greet our ears in brighter worlds,
  "Not lost, but gone before:"
Soft plaintive notes that seem'd to raise
  Dead feelings by their strain;
The music of our bygone days
  Shall all come back again.

It is not lost,—the beautiful!
  The little star-eyed flowers
That bloomed so brief a time on earth,
  We scarce could call them ours:

Another clime shall give to them
  The life that here they lack,
And we shall see each floral gem
  We treasured once—come back.

It is not lost,—the beautiful!
  The long-remembered look,
Where myriad rays of feeling play'd
  Like sunbeams on a brook:
It will return—that transient gleam,
  And we shall see once more
The light that only lit our dream,
  Far brighter than before.

It is not lost,—the beautiful!
  These little sunbeams flown,
Are garnered with the things that hide
  In regions yet unknown:
The time will come—and then his hand
  (Whose pow'r was ne'er in vain)
Shall loose the captive spirits' band,
  And call them back again.

The Edinburgh Review – October 1815.

Art. V. *Nouvelles Observations sur les Abeilles. Par François Huber. Seconde Edition, revue corrigée, & considerablement augmentée. 2 Vol. 8vo Paris 1814.*

It is some time since we gave an analysis of the first part of these researches of Mr. Huber on the Natural History of Bees.* After an interval of twenty years since the publication of that work, a second volume has now made its appearance, in conjunction with a second edition of the former. Many circumstances of a private nature had discouraged the author from ......

* Vol. XI. p. 319.

The first edition of Huber's work was published at Geneva in 1792. 1 Vol. 8vo, 368 pages; 2 Plates.

undertaking the labour of revising the manuscripts for the press: but he has been at length induced to confide the task to his son, whose taste for natural history appears to have rekindled the dormant ardour of the father. The successful exertions of Mr P. Huber in some of the higher departments of this science, have already been displayed in his *Treatise on the Economy of the Indigenous Species of Ants;* our Review of which will be found in Vol. XXI., p. 143.

The first volume of the work before us had been written in the form of letters; but the second assumes the more didactic shape of memoirs. We cannot help thinking, however, that there is still room for a more methodical arrangement of the facts which it contains: for we find that many particulars and remarks relating to the same subjects, are often interspersed among the different chapters, when a closer connexion would have given them additional value. In giving, therefore, an account of this highly interesting volume, we shall not confine ourselves to the succession of chapters, but follow an order more strictly physiological than the one adopted by the author. We shall first take a review of the facts relating to the functions of secretion, reproduction, respiration, and sensation of bees; and afterwards proceed to consider the complicated questions which relate to their instincts and acquired faculties. We shall also beg leave to refer to our former review for an account of the leading features in the natural history of this insect, as introductory to the subjects that are treated of in this volume.

The origin of wax, the material with which bees construct their combs, had never been perfectly understood, although both chemists and naturalists had made repeated attempts to ascertain its properties and history. It was generally supposed that this substance was in some way or other formed from the pollen, or fecundating dust of flowers; or, as some have termed it, the farina. The proceedings of the bees in collecting and carrying off this pollen to their hives, and in laying up large stores of it in magazines for future use, had been observed and detailed with the most scrupulous attention to accuracy by Reaumur, Maraldi, and other naturalists. It was evident from the great quantity they collect, that some important use was made of it: and none suggested itself more naturally than its being the raw material whence the wax was prepared. Reaumur had indeed noticed the great difference that existed between pollen and wax, but conceived that the former was taken into the stomach, and converted by digestion into wax, after which it was returned by the mouth in the form of a frothy liquid. Mr Arthur Dobbs, on the contrary, asserted that wax was the excrementitious remains of the pollen after its digestion and passage through the alimentary canal.* One of the members of the ' Société des Abeilles,' established at a village called Petit Bautzen in Upper Lusatia, appears to have been the original discoverer of the fact, that wax is given out under the horny scales of the abdomen. This curious circumstance, which was stated cursorily in a letter from Mr Wilhelmi to Mr Bonnet in 1768, without mentioning the name of the author of the discovery, was probably not deemed worthy of much attention, and seems to have been almost entirely lost sight of. It appears, however, that Mr Duchet, in his *Culture des Abeilles*, which is quoted by Wildman in 1778, gave it as his opinion, that wax is formed of honey: as a proof of which he observes, that ' he ' has seen a comb broken in a hive overset, which has been ' repaired during bad weather, when the bees could not go a- ' broad in search of other materials.' Wildman, in his Treatise on the Management of Bees, † expressly states his having seen pieces of wax, in shape resembling the scales of a fish, at the bottom of the hive, which he thinks must have been moulded in the body of the bee. Observations of a similar kind were afterwards made by Mr John Hunter, apparently without any knowledge of the conjectures of his predecessors ; and were published in the Philosophical Transactions for 1792. He there considers wax as an external *secretion* of oil, formed between the scales of the abdomen of the insect. ‡ Mr Huber does not appear to have known the observations either of Duchet or of Wildman on this subject, although made long prior to those of Mr Hunter ; for he does not allude to them, while he quotes the whole passage from the latter. In 1793, Mr Huber's observations had led him to the same results as to the nature of the laminæ under the abdominal scales : but he has prosecuted the inquiry relating to their origin much more successfully than any preceding writer. He has found that these laminæ are contained in distinct receptacles on each side of the middle process of the scales : he has examined, with great care, the form and structure of these secreting cavities, which are met with only in the working bees ; and which had escaped the scrutinizing eyes of Swammerdam. Their general shape is an irregular pentagon ; and the plates of wax being moulded in them, preserve accordingly this form. On piercing the membrane with which they are lined on the side next to the abdomen, a transparent fluid

---

* Philosophical Transactions, XLVI. 536.
† P. 44.; 3d Edition.   ‡ Vol. LXXXII. p. 115.

was thrown out in a jet, which congealed on cooling, and in this
state resembled wax, and was again melted on the application of
heat.   A number of comparative experiments were made with
the substance contained in the pouches, and the wax of fresh-
made combs: a great similarity between these two substances
was thus made out: the latter, however, appeared to be somewhat more compound, having probably received some additional ingredient, while employed as the material for building.   The
secreting function of the membrane on the inner surface of these
cavities was farther evinced by a more minute examination of its
structure, which exhibited a number of folds, forming a hexagonal network, very analogous to the inner coat of the second
stomach of ruminating quadrupeds.   A very elaborate anatomical description of these organs is given in a letter at the end of
this volume.

Although it was thus ascertained that wax is a secreted animal substance, it still remained to determine what were the circumstances that give occasion to this secretion; and especially
whether it was the product of any particular kind of food.   The
opinion of Reaumur, that it was formed from pollen elaborated
in the stomach, and thrown up again into the mouth, was dis-
countenanced by the observation, that when fresh swarms take
up their abode in empty hives, they do not collect pollen, and
yet they construct combs; while, on the other hand, the bees of
old hives, where all the combs are completed, are seen to bring
home large quantities of pollen.   In order to determine this
point with greater precision, many experiments were instituted
by the author.   A fresh swarm was confined, with a sufficient
allowance of honey and water, in an empty hive.   In this situation, although they could have no access to pollen, yet at the
end of five days, they had constructed five combs of the purest
wax.   When these combs were withdrawn, and the bees replaced in the hive, they renewed their toil with unabated industry,
and had soon replaced the combs by others.   These last were
again taken from them; but the patient and indefatigable insects
still persevered in their labours, and began them afresh, although
five times in succession their works were no sooner completed
than carried off; and although, during the whole of this time,
they were fed only on honey and water.   On the other hand,
bees that were in a similar state of confinement, and were supplied only with fruit and with pollen, had, in the course of eight
days, produced no wax whatever, and of course had formed no
combs.   In order to prove that it was the saccharine principle
alone, and not any accidental admixture of particles of wax,
which might be contained in the honey that afforded the pabu-

lum for this secretion, the bees, still confined, were supplied with syrup made by dissolving Canary sugar in water; and comparative experiments were made in another hive where the bees were fed on honey. It was found that the former produced wax even sooner, and in larger quantity than the latter. It was further completely ascertained, that in the old hives the honey is warehoused, and that in the new hives it is consumed and converted into wax. The works always advance rapidly when the weather and the state of vegetation admit of a plentiful harvest of honey,—but are interrupted whenever rain, cold winds, a deficiency of flowers, or a very dry season, prevent the bees from collecting it.

Mr Huber has observed that there are two sets of bees in every hive: the one, who devour large quantities of honey, take upon themselves the office of furnishing wax, and of building the combs; the other, who collect the honey and immediately dispose of what they have collected to the former, retaining only a quantity sufficient for their own nourishment. Dissection showed that the stomach of the former class, which he calls the wax-making bees, is much more capacious than that of the latter, which he denominates the nursing-bees, as it appears to be their peculiar province to tend upon the eggs and larvæ. By putting a particular mark upon those belonging to one class, it was found that, in performing their several tasks, neither of them ever encroached on the province of the other: so remarkable is the extent to which the principle of the division of labour is carried among individuals of the same original formation: for it appears that the power of forming wax is common to both, from the circumstance that a small quantity is really found in the receptacles of the nursing-bees.

In the foregoing experiments, the bees had borne their confinement without betraying the least impatience; but, on another occasion, when they were shut up together with a brood of eggs and larvæ, and could have no access to pollen, though they were supplied abundantly with honey, they manifested strong symptoms of uneasiness and of rage, at being kept prisoners. Fearful of what might be the consequence of prolonging this state of tumult, the author allowed them to escape in the evenings, when it was too late in the day to collect provisions. The bees, therefore, returned home very soon after. This was repeated for five days successively; and, on examining the hive at the end of that time, it was found that the larvæ had perished, and that the jelly with which they had been surrounded on their introduction into the hive, had disappeared. The same bees were then supplied with a fresh brood, together with portions of a comb stored with pollen. Their behaviour was now very different: they eagerly seized upon the pollen, and immediately conveyed it to their young; order was reestablished in the colony; the larvæ went through their usual transformations; royal cells were completed and closed with wax; every thing went on prosperously, and the bees showed no desire to quit their habitation. Nothing seems more complete than the evidence furnished by these experiments as to the origin of wax, and the very different destination of pollen from that which had hitherto been assigned to it.

On the subject of the sex of working bees, which has given rise to so much speculation and controversy, a very curious anatomical discovery has been made, which must set this question for ever at rest. By adopting a peculiar method of dissection, Miss Jurine, the daughter of the distinguished naturalist of Geneva, has been enabled to bring into view the ovaria of the working-bee, which are perfectly analogous in their form, situation, and structure to those of the queen-bee, excepting that no ova could be distinguished in them. The occasional fecundity of a few of the working bees, a fact observed by Riem, is now in perfect conformity with the great discovery of Schirach: and every anomaly in the sexual theory of this insect, about which there has been so much dispute, is completely cleared away. Analogous facts have been ascertained with regard to the humble-bee and the wasp. The workers among the latter have been detected by Mr Perrot in the act of laying eggs; and these, like the eggs of bees in like circumstances, were universally found to produce males. The history of the ant tribe likewise affords parallel instances of the sexual functions being exercised by those individuals that are vulgarly denominated neuters.

As connected with the physiology of bees, we shall in the next place give an account of the author's researches with regard to their respiration, which is the subject of a very long chapter. Doubts have often arisen as to the absolute necessity of this function in many of the tribes of inferior insects, which are observed frequently to occupy situations that hardly admit of any renewal of air. Such, indeed, appears to be the condition of bees inhabiting a hive, of which the usual capacity is not above one or two cubic feet. In this confined space, are lodged frequently twenty or thirty thousand bees, in a state of high animal activity, and preserving a very elevated temperature. The only entrance into the hive is in the lower part, the situation, of all others, the least favourable to the escape of heated air; and even this passage is frequently much obstructed by crowds of bees, which are passing in and out during the heats of summer. Every other aperture is strictly closed up by the bees themrelves; and in addition, the hive is often covered over by the farmer with a coating of mortar. A lighted taper, enclosed in a glass-ball of similar dimensions, and with an opening on the side, of the same size as the door of the hive, goes out in a few minutes for want of a due circulation of air. How then, do bees, under similar circumstances, support life, if life require the uninterrupted continuance of respiration? The universal law, which the multiplied experiments of Spallanzani had so well established, appeared in this instance to be violated. Before attempting, however, to discover the cause of such a deviation, it was necessary to ascertain, with more precision, whether the anomaly was real, or apparent only. With this view, Mr Huber engaged in a series of experiments, which did away all doubt of the fact, that respiration was really carried on by bees. They fell into a state of asphyxia in the vacuum of an air-pump; and also, when confined in close vessels with a limited quantity of atmospheric air. In the latter case, the oxygen was found to be almost totally consumed. The admission of common air in both cases restored their animation, if the experiment had not been too long protracted; and the introduction of oxygenous gas was still more effectual in promoting their recovery. When confined in a given quantity of oxygenous gas, they were enabled to live for a period eight times longer than in common air. They perished speedily in carbonic acid, azotic, or hydrogenous gases. When previously rendered torpid, by surrounding with ice the vessel that contained them, they were totally unaffected by immersion during three hours in these same deleterious gases; and when removed and revived by the warmth of the hand, they appeared to have suffered no injury; which proves, that, in a torpid state, respiration, as well as the other vital functions, is completely suspended. Analogous experiments were tried on the eggs, the larvæ, and the nymphæ, with similar results; excepting that the effects of respiration were less considerable in these early periods of existence: thus, the larvæ consumed more oxygen than the eggs, and the nymphæ more than the larvæ; and the nymphæ were the most easily destroyed by a suspension of this process.

By immersing different portions of the body of a bee in water, Mr Huber next ascertained, that respiration was carried on by means of the stigmata opening on the corselet; and that it may be maintained perfectly well, if only one of these be left open. When wholly immersed in water, the play of these stigmata becomes evident by the appearance of bubbles of air, which for some time remain attached to their orifices, and which are alternately absorbed and repelled several times before they are quire sufficient size to enable them to rise to the surface. In this way, also, the author detected the existence of stigmata, which had escaped the observation of Swammerdam.

The next step was to analyze the air of the hive, and ascertain whether it was vitiated in the same manner as when bees were confined in close vessels. Mr Sennebier assisted the author in this examination; the air was found by the eudiometer to differ but slightly from atmospheric air in purity. Could it be supposed, then, that there existed in any part of the hive a power of giving out oxygen? Experiment showed, that neither wax nor pollen had any such property. It was evident, indeed, that if such were the case, the door of a hive might be closed without detriment to its inhabitants. This experiment was tried; and we shall give it without abridgment, as it was attended with a circumstance that led to the discovery of the whole mystery.

' Il ne s'agissoit que de renfermer exactement ces mouches dans une ruche dont les parois transparentes permettroient d'observer ce qui se passoit à l'intérieur; j'y consacrai l'essaim logé dans le récipient tubulé.

' L'activité et l'abondance regnoit dans cette peuplade; lorsqu'on en approchoit à dix pas on entendoit un bourdonnement très-fort. Nous choisîmes pour l'exécution de notre projet un jour de pluie, afin que toutes les abeilles fussent réunis dans leur habitation. L'expérience commença à trois heures, nous fermâmes la porte avec exactitude, et nous observâmes, non sans une sorte d'angoisse, les effets de cette clôture rigoureuse.

' Ce ne fut qu'au bout d'un quart d'heure que les abeilles commencèrent à manifester quelque malaise; jusque-là elles avoient paru ignorer leur emprisonnement; mais alors tous leurs travaux furent suspendus, et la ruche changea entièrement d'aspect. On entendit bientôt un bruit extraordinaire dans son intérieur; toutes les abeilles, celles qui couvroient la face des gâteaux, comme celles qui étoient réunies en grappes, quittant leurs occupations, frappèrent l'air de leurs ailes avec une agitation extraordinaire. Cette effervescence dura environ dix minutes. Le mouvement des ailes devint par degrés moins continu et moins rapide. A trois heures trente-sept minutes les ouvrières avoient entièrement perdu leurs forces: elles ne pouvoient plus se cramponner avec leurs jambes, et leur chute suivit de près cet état de langueur.

' Le nombre des abeilles défaillantes alloit en croissant, la table en étoit jonchée; des milliers d'ouvrières et de mâles tomboient au fond de la ruche; il n'en resta pas une seule sur les gâteaux, trois minutes plus tard toute la peuplade fut asphyxiée. La ruche se refroidit tout d'un coup, et du terme du vingt-huit degrés la température descendit au niveau de celle de l'air extérieur.

' Nous espérâmes rendre la vie et la chaleur aux abeilles asphysiées, en leur donnant un air plus pur : on ouvrit la porte de la ruche ainsi que le robinet fixé sur la tubuture du récipient. L'effet du courant qui s'établit alors ne fut pas équivoque ; en peu de minutes les abeilles furent en état de respirer ; les anneaux de leur abdomen reprirent leur jeu ; elles se mirent simultanément à battre des ailes, circonstance bien remarquable, et qui avoit déjà eu lieu, comme nous l'avons dit, au moment où la privation de l'air extérieur avoit commencé à se faire sentir dans la ruche. Bientôt les abeilles remontèrent sur leurs gâteaux, la température s'éleva au degré où ces Insectes savent l'entretenir habituellement, et à quatre heures l'ordre fut rétabli dans leur demeure. Cette expérience prouvoit indubitablement que les abeilles n'avoient dans leur ruche aucun moyen de suppléer à l'air qui venoit du dehors.'   p. 335—337.

It was proved by this experiment, that the air of the hive was renewed from without, since the bees had perished when it was closed. After many fruitless conjectures as to the mode in which this renewal took place, it occurred to the author, that the vibration of the wings observed in the experiment, and which was accompanied by a loud humming sound, might be instrumental in this change. The wings are agitated with a rapidity that renders them invisible, except at the extremities of the arcs of vibration, which are equal to a complete quadrant of a circle ; and the bees remain all the while firmly fixed by their feet to the table, so that the progressive motion of flying, which would take place were they at liberty, by the reaction of the air, is prevented : the whole force of the wings is therefore exerted on the air, which is thus impelled in a continued stream. This current is very sensible on approaching the hand to a bee, which is thus performing the part of a ventilator.

During fine weather in summer, a certain number of bees are always seen vibrating their wings before the door of the hive ; but if the interior of a glass hive be inspected, it will be seen that a still greater number are engaged in this duty on the floor of the hive. These bees have their heads turned towards the door, while those on the outside have their heads from the door ; so that both cooperate in producing a current of air in the same direction.

' On diroit que ces mouches se placent symétriquement pour s'éventer plus à l'aise ; elles forment alors des files qui aboutissent à l'entrée de la ruche, et sont quelquefois disposées comme autant de rayons divergens ; mais cet ordre n'est point régulier, il est dû probablement à la nécessité où les abeilles qui s'éventent sont de faire place à celles qui vont et viennent, et dont la course rapide les force à se ranger à la file pour n'être pas heurtées et culbutées à chaque instant.

' Quelquefois plus de vingt abeilles s'éventent au bas d'une ruche ;

dans d'autres momens leur nombre est plus circonscrit; chacune d'elles fait jouer ses ailes plus ou moins long-tems: nous en avons vu s'éventer pendant vingt-cinq minutes; dans cette intervalle elles ne se posoient point, mais elles sembloient quelquefois reprendre haleine en suspendant la vibration de leurs ailes pour un instant indivisible: aussitôt qu'elles cessent de s'éventer, d'autres les remplacent, ensorte qu'il n'y a jamais d'interruption dans le bourdonnement d'une ruche bien peuplée.' p. 942.

By means of light pieces of paper suspended from a thread, it was ascertained, as might have been expected, that a double current took place, of which the strength was proportioned to the number of inhabitants in the hive. This ventilating process, which is indicated by a humming sound within the hive, is continually going on, both in summer and winter; and indeed appears sometimes more active in the depth of winter, than when the external temperature is more moderate.

In order to ascertain whether the assigned cause was adequate to the production of the whole of the observed effect, an artificial ventilator, consisting of a small windmill of tin, with eighteen vanes, which could be made to turn round by machinery, was adapted to an aperture in the bottom of a glass cylinder, which was closed at both ends, after a lighted taper had been introduced. The taper continued to burn as well as in the open air, so long as the ventilator was kept in motion; and went out when this motion was not given to it.

The author next inquires into the immediate cause which prompts the insect to perform the actions above described. This he conceives to be the sensation of heat, and the presence of vitiated air.

' L'idée la plus simple qui s'offrit à nous fut que les abeilles ne s'éventoient qu'afin de se procurer une sensation de fraîcheur, et une expérience nous convinquit effectivement que ce motif pouvoit être l'une des causes immédiates de la ventilation.

' On ouvrit le volet d'une ruche vitrée, les rayons du soleil dardoient sur les gâteaux couvertes d'abeilles; bientôt celles qui ressentirent trop vivement l'influence de la chaleur commencèrent à bourdonner, tandis que celles qui se trouvoient encore à l'ombre demeurèrent tranquilles.

' Une observation qu'on peut faire tous les jours confirme le résultat de cette expérience: les abeilles qui composent ces grappes qu'on voit au-devant des ruches pendant l'été, incommodées par l'ardeur du soleil, s'éventent alors avec beaucoup d'énergie; mais si un corps quelconque porte son ombre sur une partie de la grappe, la ventilation cesse dans la région obscure, tandis qu'elle continue dans celle qui est éclairée et rechauffée par le soleil.' p. 357.

' On séparoit quelques abeilles de leur ruche en les attirant avec

du miel, puis on approchoit d'elles du coton trempé dans l'esprit de
vin pendant qu'elles mangeoient, il falloit le mettre près de leur tête,
pour qu'il les incommodât; mais alors l'effet n'en étoit pas douteux,
les abeilles s'écartoient en agitant leurs ailes, elles se rapprochoient
ensuite pour prendre leur nourriture.   Lorsqu'elles étoient bien éta-
blies on recommençoit l'expérience, elles s'écartoient de nouveau,
mais sans retirer tout à fait leur trompe ; elles se contentoient de
battre les ailes en mangeant.' p. 359.

It is a remarkable fact, that the drones, though they appear
to be affected by strong odours in an equal degree with the work-
ing-bees, have never recourse to the same expedient.   This mode
of ventilation, by the action of the wings, is a process peculiar
to the working bees ; and the drones, in this as in other instances, participate in none of the active labours of the hive ; and,
independently of the part they perform in impregnation, are
merely *fruges consumere nati.*

Two chapters are occupied with observations relative to the
senses.   M. Huber asserts, that we have no positive proof of
the existence of the sense of hearing in bees; although the common method practised by the country people, of preventing the
escape of a swarm by loud noises, is founded on a contrary sup-
position.   They undoubtedly possess great powers of vision with
regard to remote objects; for they distinguish the situation of
their own hive from considerable distances, and fly towards it in
a perfectly straight line, with the rapidity of an arrow.   But it
is in the accuracy of the sense of touch, more particularly, that
they excel other insects.   The antennæ are the principal organs of this sense ; and it is by the help of these instruments
that, while secluded from the light, they construct their combs,
replenish their magazines, feed and watch over the larvæ, ascertain the presence of the queen, and minister to all her wants.
Their taste is probably the least developed of their senses, the
bee appearing to have very little discrimination in the qualities
of its food or drink.   For the purpose of quenching thirst, they
frequently choose the most stagnant or putrid water, and neglect the purest dew drops.   Honey is the great object of attraction, wherever it may be found ; and it is sought for even
in the most acrid, fœtid, or poisonous flowers: It is known to
differ remarkably in different districts, or when collected at different times of the year ; and in many parts of America it occasionally partakes of the deleterious qualities of the plants from
which it was obtained.   Quantity, and not quality, appears always to be the motive of preference in their selection of the
flowers they visit.   They appear in this to be guided altogether
by the sense of smell, which must be very subtle, from the great

distances at which they can perceive the presence of saccharine substances. This was ascertained by several direct experiments, in which honey was concealed in boxes with small holes, not allowing of a sight of the contents, but admitting of the escape of a small portion of the odorous effluvia. When small valves of card were adjusted to these holes, the bees, after going round the boxes, and examining every part, discovered the contrivance, and readily found means to raise the valves, so as to get at the honey.

Another proof of intellect was afforded by some bees, which, during the autumn, had been supplied with a quantity of honey placed on an open window. The honey had been removed, and the shutters had continued closed during the whole of the ensuing winter: but in the spring, when the window was again opened, the bees were seen to return to the same spot where they had before been entertained, although no honey had since been put there. The lapse of several months, therefore, had not obliterated the memory of their former adventure. The author has endeavoured to ascertain the seat of smell, concerning which, as relating to insects in general, so much diversity of opinion has existed. A hair pencil dipped in oil of turpentine, to which bees have a strong aversion, was presented successively to different parts of the body of a bee that was occupied in sipping honey. Although brought in succession near every part of the abdomen, and trunk, including the stigmata, it did not occasion the least disturbance to the bee, until it came to the neighbourhood of the mouth, when the insect immediately quitted the honey, and set about ventilating itself violently, but in a short time renewed its meal. Oil of rosemary produced similar effects still more quickly. It is presumed from this experiment, that the organ of smell is situated somewhere either in the mouth or its appendages; and this is corroborated by repeating the experiments upon bees whose mouths had been plugged up with paste, which was allowed to dry before they were set at liberty. While the organ remained thus obstructed, the bees appeared to be totally insensible to all odours, even to those for which they usually evinced the most violent aversion: they even showed no repugnance in walking along the pencils impregnated with the poisonous fluids. Although much affected by the effluvia of turpentine and other essential oils, as also by the vapours of powerful chemical agents, such as the nitrous and muriatic acids, ammonia and alcohol, they are but little incommoded by the smell of musk, and appear to be perfectly indifferent to that of assafœtida, devouring honey that is mixed with it with as much avidity as usual. They manifest a strong

antipathy to camphor; but they are capable of overcoming their
dislike, by the stronger attraction of honey, which they will entirely drink up, though with some-deliberation, when its surface
has been sprinkled over with camphor.   In another experiment
it was ascertained that the vapour of alcohol was fatal to them
when they were subjected to its influence in a confined space:
although a large spider, under similar circumstances, did not
appear to suffer.

The odour of the poison which accompanies the sting of the
bee, produces a remarkable effect on these insects,—awakening
their choler, and exciting them to immediate acts of hostility.

' Nous mimes quelques abeilles dans un tube de verre fermé seulement à l'une de ses extrémités, nous les fîmes engourdir à demi
pour qu'elles ne pussent pas sortir par le bout qui étoit resté ouvert.
On les ranima ensuite par degrés, en les exposant au soleil.   On in-
troduisit après cela dans le tube un épi de blé, et l'on irrita les abeilles en les touchant avec ses barbes; toutes tirèrent leurs aiguillon et
des gouttes de venin parurent à l'extrémité de ces dards.

' Leur première signes de vie furent donc des démonstrations de
colère, et je ne doute pas qu'elles ne se fussent enferrées les unes les
autres, ou jettées sur l'observateur, si elles eussent été en liberté :
mais elles ne pouvoient ni se mouvoir, ni sortir malgré moi du tube
dans lequel je les avois placées.

' Je les pris une à une avec des pinces, et je les enfermai dans un
recipient pour qu'elles ne troublassent pas mon expérience.   Elles
avoient laissé dans le tube une odeur désagréable, et c'étoit celle du
venin qu'elles avoient dardé contre ses parois interieures.   Je pré-
sentai son extrémité ouverte à des abeilles qui étoient groupées au
devant de leur ruche.   Ces mouches s'agitèrent dès qu'elles senti-
rent l'odeur du venin; mais cette émotion ne fut pas celle de la
crainte ; elle nous prouvèrent leur colère de la même manière que
dans la premiere epreuve.

' Il y a donc des odeurs qui n'agissent pas seulement sur le phy-
sique de ces insectes, mais qui produisent jusqu'à un certain point
sur eux une impression morale.'   p. 987.

The author has next attempted to investigate the principles
of a variety of complicated actions exhibited by these insects,
which have hitherto been seldom made the subject of philosophical inquiry, but which are contemplated by the vulgar with
blind admiration, while the passive curiosity of the naturalist is
satisfied with referring them to the inscrutable agency of instinct.   How far, it may be asked, are bees influenced by the
mere impressions of their senses ? how far are they under the
direct guidance of appetite ?   What is the nature, and the degree of those internal faculties which wear so much the sem-
blance of reason, and which would seem to imply a knowledge

of various relations among external objects, an anticipation of future events, and a power of combining means for the accomplishment of particular purposes? What variations of conduct do they exhibit under diversities of external circumstances; to what extent are they capable of profiting from experience; and what is the origin of those social habits which so eminently distinguish them above all the other insect tribes; and which imply a mutual coöperation for objects of general utility, and a subdivision of labour conducing materially to the advancement of those objects? In this wide and difficult field of inquiry, Mr Huber has selected a few of the more striking features in the economy of bees, as particularly susceptible of illustration. When they have lost their queen, it is now well established that they select out of the young larvæ in the hive some individuals, which, by a particular process of nourishment and education, they convert into so many new queens. The *rationale* of this part of their conduct deserves especially to be examined. The utility, nay the absolute necessity, of their so doing, for the future prosperity and even existence of the colony, is sufficiently manifest: but what is the immediate principle or motive which leads them to take such a step? If it were the mere absence of the queen, they should set about the formation of royal cells immediately on their being sensible that they had lost her: but a considerable time elapses before they determine upon this proceeding. What happens on these occasions cannot be better conveyed than in the descriptive style of the author:

' Lorsqu'on enlève une reine à sa ruche natale, les abeilles n'en paroissent pas d'abord s'en apercevoir; les travaux de tout genre se soutiennent, l'ordre et la tranquillité ne sont point troublés: ce n'est qu'une heure après le départ de la reine que l'inquiétude commence à se manifester parmi les ouvrières; le soin des petits ne semble plus les occuper, elles vont et viennent avec vivacité; mais ces premiers symptômes d'agitation ne se font pas sentir à la fois dans toutes les parties de la ruche. Ce n'est d'abord que sur une seule portion d'un gâteau que l'on commence à les apercevoir; les abeilles agitées sortent bientôt du petit cercle qu'elles parcouroient, et lorsqu'elles rencontrent leurs compagnes elles croisent mutuellement leurs antennes, et les frappent légèrement. Les abeilles qui reçoivent l'impression de ces coups d'antennes s'agitent à leur tour et portent ailleurs le trouble et la confusion: le désordre s'accroît dans une progression rapide, il gagne la face opposée du rayon, et enfin toute la peuplade; on voit alors les ouvrières courir sur les gâteaux, s'entrechoquer, se précipiter vers la porte et sortir de leur ruche avec impétuosité; de là elles se répandent tout à l'entour, elles rentrent et sortent à plusieurs reprises, le bourdonnement est très-grand dans la ruche, il augmente avec l'agitation des abeilles: ce désordre dure

environ deux ou trois heures, rarement quatre ou cinq, mais jamais
d'avantage.

‘ Quelle impression peut causer et arrêter cette effervescence ;
pourquoi les abeilles reviennent-elles par degré à leur état naturel,
et reprennent-elles de l'intérêt pour tout ce qui sembloit leur être
devenu indifférent ? Pourquoi un mouvement spontané les ramène
t-il vers leurs petits qu'elles avoient abandonnés pendant quelques
heures ! Qu'est-ce qui leur inspire ensuite l'idée de visiter ces larves
de différens âges et de faire choix parmi elles des sujets qu'elles doivent élever à la dignité de reines ?

‘ Si on visite cette ruche vingt-quatre heures après le départ de
la mere commune, on verra que les abeilles ont travaillé à réparer
leur perte ; on distinguera aisément ceux de leurs élèves qu'elles ont
destiné à devenir reines ; cependant à cette époque la forme des cellules qu'ils occupent n'a point encore été altérée ; mais ces alvéoles
qui sont toujours au nombre de ceux du plus petit diametre se font
déjà remarquer par la quantité de bouillie qu'ils renferment : ils en
contiennent alors infiniment plus que les berceaux des larves ouvrières.   Il résulte de cette abondance de matière alimentaire que les
larves choisies par les abeilles pour remplacer un jour leur reine, au
lieu d'être logées au fond de l'alvéole dans lequel elles sont nées,
sont placées tout auprès de son orifice.

‘ C'est probablement pour les amener là que les abeilles accu-
mulent la bouillie ou pâtée dernière elles, et qu'elles leur font un lit
si élevé : ce qui prouve que ce tas de bouillie ne sert point à leur
nourriture ; car on le retrouve encore tout entier dans les cellules
quand le ver est descendu dans le prolongement pyramidal par lequel les ouvrières terminent leur logement.

‘ On peut donc connoître les larves destinées à donner des reines
par l'aspect des cellules qu'elles habitent avant même que celles-ci
ayent été elargées, et qu'elles ayent acquis une forme pyramidale.
D'après cet observation, il étoit facile de s'assurer au bout de vingt-
quatre heures si les abeilles avoient pris le parti de remplacer leur
reine. '   p. 396.

A difficulty that occurs on the very threshold of this inquiry,
is to explain the mode in which all the bees become apprized of
the absence of their queen.   Do they collect this knowledge by
the information of the sight, the smell, the touch, or of some
unknown sense ; and how is the news communicated from one
to another till it becomes general throughout the hive ?   In order to elucidate this subject, the following experiment was made.
A hive was divided into two separate compartments, by the
quick introduction of a lattice, of which the wires were too
close to admit of any bee passing through the interstices, but
allowed of a free circulation of air between the two divisions,
while the escape of the bees at the doors was prevented in a way
that did not impede the passage of air.   Great agitation prevail-

ed in that division of the hive which was deprived of its queen;
but in the course of two hours it subsided, and in a few days the
bees had commenced the construction of three royal cells. From
that moment these bees conducted themselves as the inhabitants of a separate colony, never associating with their former
companions; and having soon acquired a queen of their own,
were thus completely independent of their former queen. Neither the sight nor the smell could in this instance have led to the
knowledge that the queen, which was so near at hand, was unable to cross over to that part of the hive which had thus been
insulated. That the absolute contact of the queen was necessary to their being assured of her presence, was proved by an experiment, in which she was separated from the other bees by a
thin lattice, which admitted the antennæ of the bee to pass
through, though it was too close for the passage of the whole
head. Under these circumstances, no disturbance took place
in the hive; the labours were not interrupted; and a constant
intercourse was kept up with the queen through the medium of
the antennæ.

' Ce qu'il y eut de très-remarquable pendant la réclusion de cette
reine, c'est le moyen que les abeilles employèrent pour communiquer
avec elle : un nombre infini d'antennes passées au travers de la grille,
et jouant en tous sens ne permettoient pas de douter que les ouvrières
ne fussent occupées de leur mère commune ; celle-ci répondoit à leur
empressement de la manière la plus marquée, car elle étoit presque
toujours cramponnée contre la grille, croisant ses antennes avec celles
qui la cherchoient si evidemment ; les abeilles s'efforcerent de l'at-
tirer au milieu d'elles, leurs jambes passées au travers du grillage,
saisissoient celles de la reine, et les tenoient avec force ; on vit même
plusieurs fois leur trompe traverser les mailles du fil de fer et notre
captive nourrie par ses sujettes depuis l'interieur de la ruche. ' p.407.

The same experiment repeated with a double lattice, with an
interval too great to admit of the antennæ reaching to the space
beyond, was attended with all the perturbation which ensues on
the loss of a queen, and led immediately to the construction of
royal cells. The importance of the antennæ is further shown
by the consequences which result from their amputation. When
deprived of these organs, the bee appears to have lost all its former instinct ; it desists from its labours, remains at the bottom
of the hive, seems attracted only by the light, and takes the
first opportunity of quitting the hive, never more to return.
That the antennæ are the principal substitutes for the sense of
sight, appears from the use they make of them during the night,
when they guard the door of the hive from the entrance of
moths which are fluttering around. It is curious to observe with
what skill the moth avails itself of the imperfect vision of the

bee, when not assisted by strong day light; and what scrutinizing activity the bees exert in discovering the presence of so dangerous an enemy.   The vigilant sentinels parade in circles round their habitation, expanding their antennæ to the full extent, and moving them incessantly on either side.   Destruction awaits the luckless moth that comes within their reach.   Aware of the danger, the latter displays considerable dexterity in avoiding the slightest contact, and in surreptitiously gliding between the sentinels, who are stationed to intercept it.

The singular art displayed by bees in the construction of the combs, has often attracted the attention of philosophers, and has given rise to much speculation among mathematicians as well as naturalists.   A structure which appeared as a model of perfection, uniting the advantages of strength and economy of materials, and satisfying every condition of a refined geometrical problem, was contemplated with a degree of admiration that drew off the attention from the physical means employed in its execution; although it is evident, that without understanding these, all our reasonings on the principles from which so curious a species of architecture results, must be vague and hypothetical.   Buffon has advanced with much confidence a theory, which may account in a plausible and summary manner for some of the appearances; but nothing shows more clearly the insufficiency of the most brilliant imagination, even when united with extensive knowledge, towards explaining the hidden processes of nature, if unassisted by the careful observation of facts, than the very erroneous views entertained on these subjects, by this specious and eloquent writer.   No naturalist, indeed, prior to Huber, had ever been able to see the bee actually at work, and to follow up the several steps of the operation.   Reaumur, whose diligence was unrivalled, and whose sober judgment never ventured to form conclusions with regard to facts without the support of actual observation, acknowledged that he had not seen enough of the proceedings of these insects, while they were engaged in building their habitations, to satisfy himself of the justness of his own conjectures. Glass hives, of any ordinary construction, are insufficient for this purpose, because the bees never carry on their architectural labours without being surrounded by a throng of assistants, which suspend themselves from the top of the hive, and form a thick curtain before the workers, impenetrable to the eye of the observer.   It occurred to M. Huber, that this obstacle might be removed, if he could by any means deprive the auxiliary bees of the means of supporting themselves from the top, by obliging the bees to build upwards instead of downwards, which they always do when they find it possible. After many attempts, he succeeded, by a particular contrivance, in effecting this; and by looking at them from below, on which side the light was admitted through glass, he was enabled to continue his observations throughout the whole process. He has given us a copious detail of each step of their operations, with a minuteness that appears unnecessary, and a prolixity that renders it very fatiguing to the attention. It is, however, well illustrated by plates, which exhibit the successive forms assumed by the work in every stage of its progress. We shall endeavour to give such a general outline as may be intelligible, without reference to figures.

The combs of a bee-hive are built up in vertical plates, severally composed of a congeries of partitions, which enclose a number of small cells. The form of each cell is that of a hexagonal prism, opening by one of its bases at the surface of the plate, and separated from the cells which open on the other side of the plate by a partition, so disposed as to form a pyramidal cavity at the bottom of each cell. This pyramid consists of three rhomboidal planes, which form an apex by the meeting of three of the obtuse angles; while the other angles meet the several sides of the prism. The lateral partitions being common to the adjacent cells, no interstice is left between them. The same effect also results from the adjustment of the cells on each side of the plate; for in the partition which divides them, the apex of each pyramid of the one set of cells forms one of the angles at the base of the other set. The three planes which compose the terminal pyramid of each cell, respectively concur in the formation of the bottoms of three cells on the opposite side; and the axis of the former, if produced, would be the common line of junction between the three latter. The most perfect symmetry, therefore, on each side of the comb, and in every cell, must result from this structure.

The junction of the rhomboidal planes, composing the terminal pyramid, with the six lateral planes of the hexagonal prism, could not be effected unless a portion of each of the latter were cut off obliquely at the base; the effect of which truncation will be to produce, in each of the lateral planes, an acute angle on one side and an obtuse angle on the other, instead of the two right angles with which they would have been terminated in a regular prism. The most remarkable circumstance in the form of the honey-comb, is, that these angles are exactly equal, respectively, to the angles of the terminal rhombs. There must evidently be six solid angles formed where the six sides of the cell meet the pyramid by which it is closed at the bottom; and these angles are constituted in the following manner. Each acute angle at the base of the sides of the prism, is next to the acute angle of the adjoining side; and, in like manner, each obtuse angle is next to another obtuse angle; and these angles succeed one another in pairs alternately. Each pair of acute angles will join with the acute angles of two of the terminal rhombs, to constitute a solid angle, which will thus be formed of four acute angles. The pair of obtuse angles will join with the obtuse angle of one rhomb only, and the solid angle thus formed, will be bounded by three plane angles only, and all of them will be of equal magnitude. This latter solid angle, which is repeated at three of the angles of the base, is therefore exactly equal to the one at the apex of the pyramid; a condition which can obtain only when the ratio between the shorter and the longer diagonals of the rhomb, is the same as that between the side of a square and its diagonal. That the employment of rhombs of this particular shape requires a less expense of materials, than that of any other possible form, has been demonstrated by many mathematicians of the greatest eminence. The problem has been solved by Kœnig, Maclaurin, Cramer, Boscovich, L'Huillier, and Le Sage: Several remarks on the methods employed for this purpose, are contained in the work before us; and a demonstration of Cramer's, which is remarkable for its elegance, is given in the Appendix.

It does not appear to have been observed by former writers, that the first row of cells, or those nearest to the roof of the hive, from which the whole comb is suspended, have a form very different from any of the others. Their openings, instead of being hexagonal, are irregular pentagons, in consequence of two of the sides of the hexagon being cut off by the plane from which the comb arises. The partitions at the bottom of these cells deviate still more widely from their usual pyramidal form; for they are composed, on the one side of the comb, of two trapeziums, joined with one rhomb: and, on the other, of two rhombs only, without any third side. The work must therefore begin by the construction of these primary cells; and the design of them is sketched out by one or two bees, who appear to act as superintending architects; and who, by laying, as it were, the foundation stone of the future edifice, determine the relative situation of all its parts. For this purpose, then, the bee takes out, with its hinder feet, the plates of wax which are contained in the receptacles under the abdomen; and, by means of its fore feet, carries them to its mouth; where the wax is moistened and masticated, so as to give it that degree of softness and ductility which fit it for being worked. When thus prepared, it is applied to the roof of the hive; and other bees contributing fresh materials in quick succession, a sort of block of wax is raised, of a lenticular shape, thick at the top, and tapering towards the edges. Hitherto no trace of the angular forms which are to be given to it, can be discerned: this is effected by a series of operations, in the following manner. A single bee takes its station on one side of the block of wax, and scoops out a vertical channel of the breadth of an ordinary cell, along the middle of that surface; accumulating the materials thus dug out all round the margin. No sooner has the line been traced, than other bees arrive in succession, relieving one another, often to the number of twenty, before the cavity on that side is sufficiently cleared out. They next operate on the other side, where two bees take their station, one on each side of the middle line, the situation of which they are enabled to distinguish from its being slightly prominent in consequence of the force with which the depression has been made on the other side. Each of these bees are now employed in excavating the wax at its respective station, so that the foundations of two cells are laid, the line between them corresponding to the middle of the cell on the opposite side. By degrees, all these hollows are rendered deeper and broader; their line of junction becomes a straight ridge; their sides assume the form of planes; their curved margins are fashioned into straight lines, which meet in regular angles. When the pyramidal partition at the bottom of any cell is finished, the bees build up walls from its edges, so as to complete the prismatic part of the cell. The second, and all the succeeding rows of cells, are formed exactly by similar steps: a wall being first raised, and modelled into the shape of a pyramidal partition, from the edges of which the lateral plates of the cells are built. The projecting parts of one side of the partition being made to correspond with the depressions on the other, an equal thickness is preserved throughout. As the building of one set of cells advances, others are begun; so that several rows at once are receiving additions, and room is allowed for the employment of a great number of workers at the same time. The row first constructed is the groundwork of that which succeeds; and this, in its turn, determines the situation of the next; the form and disposition of the parts of every cell being ultimately dependent upon that of the original cell raised by the founder of the comb. While the work is still proceeding, the recently formed cells do not attain the same length as those begun at an earlier period; the comb has a semi-lenticular form, broad at the base and centre, and tapering below and towards the sides; but when there is no longer any space for its lateral extension, all the cells acquire an equal depth, and the two surfaces become planes, exactly parallel to each other. The author concludes, from all that he has observed, that the geometrical relations, which are conspicuous in their works, are more the necessary result of their mode of proceeding, than the principle by which their labour is guided.

The deviations from their usual methods of building, present many curious subjects of inquiry. Those rules of architecture, which, under ordinary circumstances, appear to be so rigidly prescribed, give way on various occasions where new ends are to be attained, or unusual obstacles are to be overcome. It is indeed highly interesting to watch these insects, impelled, as it might appear to a superficial observer, by some principle which determines them to a particular routine of conduct, occasionally emancipating themselves from these rigid laws, and assuming the prerogative of interpreting the intentions of their legislator. Many such anomalies will be recognized by an attentive scrutiny of the methods employed by bees in the construction of different parts of the comb, and will appear totally repugnant to the idea of their following some blind instinct. They will be found to change the direction of the combs, in order to avoid certain obstacles, such as a pane of glass, on which, from its smoothness, their feet can have no hold; and this change is always begun before the work has reached the glass. Portions of combs which have been broken off, and have fallen in different positions are joined to the entire comb by new cells, in which new modes of construction are resorted to, suited to the particular circumstances. Very different methods are employed in connecting the sides of the combs to the interior surfaces of the hives, according to the nature and the position of these surfaces. The compensations which are made in the size and disposition of the planes, which compose the terminal pyramid, in order to adapt them to these new forms, and to the varying capacities of the cells, are equally indicative of choice and selection, and are generally those best adapted to the end in view. The larger cells, in which the male larvæ are hatched, usually occupy the middle or lateral parts of the combs; and yet they are joined to the smaller cells without disturbing the general regularity of the construction. This is effected by the interposition of three or four series of what may be called cells of transition, of which the bottoms are composed of four, instead of three planes, viz. two rhombs and two hexagons. This transition of form is gradual; and it connects in the most regular manner the perfect pyramidal forms of larger and smaller dimensions, belonging to the larger and the smaller cells: The same gradation is also observed in passing from the rows of the former to those of the latter.

These deviations which Reaumur and Bonnet had cited as examples of irregularity and imperfection, appear, when accurately studied, to be in reality proofs of the most accurate geometric adjustment of particular structures, destined for different purposes. The principal circumstance which determines the last described modification in their architecture, is the sort of eggs which the queen-bee is preparing to bring forth: another cause of deviation may be pointed out in the abundance of provisions which they can lay in store, and for the reception of which they prepare larger and deeper cells, having their axes more inclined to the horizon. Thus do we see every apparent irregularity determined by some sufficient motive, and compensated in other parts by some corresponding change: and so great is the flexibility of the faculties of these insects, that the work can be always adapted to the intended object, whether that object relate to external circumstances, or to domestic policy, whether it concern the interests of individuals, or the welfare of the community at large. The real operation of instinctive, or rather of implanted principles, appears to be restricted to a smaller number of objects of the first necessity, than is commonly imagined; the execution of other points being left to the determination of circumstances, and being modified by a degree of sagacity, of which the operation resembles much more that of choice than of habit or involuntary mechanism. In the architecture of bees, Buffon could see nothing but a necessary result of the efforts of great numbers of insects simultaneously exerting equal degrees of pressure laterally against a mass of soft wax. As the uniform operation of the law of cohesion on the particles of a basaltic stratum disposes them in equal prismatic columns, so does he suppose that the equal pressure of a distending force, would convert a number of similar cylinders, compressed in a limited space, into regular hexagonal prisms. He finds examples of a tendency to assume the hexagonal form in the lines on the membranous wing of the bat; in the reticular folds of the second stomachs of ruminant animals; in the impressions on some flowers, capsules and seeds of vegetables, as well as in the configuration of crystals. But he does not condescend to show how such a principle might apply to the pyramidal forms of the terminal partitions, or to the curious mutual adaptation of the cells on opposite sides; nor does he stop to inquire whether all the cells are of the same dimensions, or how those of different sizes are adjusted to each other. Above all, he thinks it unnecessary to ascertain whether the actual practice of the bees, when building, is conformable to his hypothesis; and whether they all work at the same moment, each for himself alone, without relation to any general design, or reference to the objects of the community. Loose analogies from other departments of science are caught hold of in support of a crude but sweeping theory, calculated only to satisfy the hasty and superficial gazers on Nature's productions, but crumbling into dust as soon as we attempt its application to the real matters of fact. It is not by such attempts to scale the walls, that we can expect to gain the recesses of the labyrinth.

In the course of the preceding inquiries it was remarked, that the combs, when recently made, had a very different appearance to that which they assumed after a certain time. At first they are perfectly white, semitransparent, soft, but exceedingly fragile, and smooth, without being polished. In a few days they acquire more or less of a yellow tint; their edges become thicker and stronger, so that the comb will now yield considerably before it breaks; their surfaces have a gloss as if varnished over; and they bear a higher temperature before they melt. It was ascertained that these qualities are given to them by the addition of a kind of varnish, with which the whole surface, but more particularly the edges of each plane, are covered, and which is also employed in large quantities as a solder at the junction of the planes which compose the partitions. When chemically examined, this varnish was found to be of the same nature as the propolis with which the interior of the hive is lined. This substance appears to be a gum-resin, and it has long been conjectured to be of vegetable origin; but the particular plants from which the bees collected it, had never been exactly determined. M. Huber ascertained that the buds of the wild poplar can supply them with this material. The matter which imparts to the wax its yellow colour, differs essentially from propolis, being wholly insoluble in alcohol: its colour is destroyed by the light of the sun, and also by nitric acid. The source of this colouring material could not be discovered. The following account of their labours in distributing the propolis on the cells, contains many curious traits of ingenuity.

‘ Un tems serein, une température élevée engagèrent enfin les abeilles à la récolte; on les voyoit revenir de la campagne, chargées de cette gomme résine, qui ressemble à une gelée transparente; cette substance avoit alors la couleur et l'éclat du grenat: on la distinguoit aisément des pelottes farineuses que les autres abeilles apportoient en même-tems. Les ouvrières chargées de propolis se joignirent aux grappes qui pendoient du haut de la ruche, on les voyoit parcourir les couches extérieures du massif: quand elles étoient parvenues aux supports des gâteaux, elles s'y reposoient: leles s'arrêtoient quelques fois sur les parois verticales de leur domicile, en attendant que les autres ouvrières vinssent les débarrasser de leurs fardeaux. Nous en vimes effectivement deux ou trois s'ap procher de chacune d'elles, prendre avec leurs dents la propolis sur les jambes de leurs compagnes, et partir aussitôt avec ces provisions.   Le haut de la ruche offroit le spectacle le plus animé ; une foule d'abeilles s'y rendoient de toutes parts ; la récolte, la distribution et les divers emplois de la propolis étoient alors leur occupation dominante : les unes portoient entre leurs dents la matière dont elles avoient déchargé les pourvoyeuses et la déposoient sur les montans des chassis ou sur les supports des gâteaux ; les autres se hâtoient de l'étendre comme un vernis avant qu'elle fut durcie, ou bien elles en formoient des cordons proportionnés aux interstices des parois qu'elles vouloient mastiquer.   Rien de plus varié que leurs opérations ; mais ce que nous étions le plus intéressés à connoître, c'étoit l'art avec lequel elles appliquoient la propolis dans l'intérieur des alvéoles.   Nous fixames donc notre attention sur celles qui nous parurent disposées à s'en occuper, on les distinguoit aisément de la multitude des travailleuses, parcequ'elles avoient leurs têtes tournées vers la glace horizontale.   Lorsqu'elles en eurent atteint la superficie, elles y déposèrent la propolis qui brûloit entre leurs dents, et la placèrent à peu près au milieu de l'espace qui séparoit les gâteaux. Nous les vimes alors s'occuper à conduire cette substance gommo-résineuse au véritable lieu de sa destination ; profitant des points d'appuis qu'elle pouvoit leur fournir par sa viscosité, elles s'y suspendoient aussitôt à l'aide des crochets de leurs jambes postérieures, et sembloient se balancer au-dessous du plafond vitré ; l'effet de ce mouvement étoit de porter leurs corps en avant et de le ramener en arrière ; à chaque impulsion nous voyons le tas de propolis s'approcher des alvéoles, les abeilles se servoient de leurs pattes antérieures qui étoient restées libres, pour balayer ce qui avoit été détaché par leurs dents, et pour réunir ces fragmens répandus sur la surface du verre ; celui-ci reprit sa transparence lorsque toute la propolis fut amenée auprès de l'orifice des cellules.   Quelques abeilles entrèrent dans celles qui étoient vitrées ; c'étoit là que je les attendois, et que j'esperois les voir travailler tout à mon aise : celles-ci n'apportoient point de propolis, mais leurs dents appliquées contre la cire étoient employées à polir et à nettoyer les alvéoles, elles les faisoient agir dans les sillons angulaires formés par la rencontre de leurs pans, elles leur donnoient plus de profondeur, elles ratissoient les parties raboteuses de ces bords ; pendant ce travail les antennes sondoient le terrain ; ces organes placés au devant de leurs mâchoires leur indiquoient sans doute les molécules protubérantes qu'elles devoient enlever.

 ' Lorsqu'une de ces ouvrières eut assez limé la cire dans l'espace anguleux que ses dents parcouroient, elle sortit de la cellule en reculant, s'approcha du tas de propolis qui se trouvoit le plus à sa portée, y plongea ses dents et tira un fil de cette matière résineuse ; elle le rompit aussitôt en écartant sa tête brusquement, le prit avec les crochets de ses pattes antérieures, et rentra dans la cellule qu'elle venoit de préparer.   Elle n'hésita point à placer le filet entre les deux pièces qu'elle avoit applanies, et au fond de l'angle que celles-ci formoient ensemble; mais elle trouva, sans doute, ce cordon trop long pour l'espace qu'il devoit recouvrir, car elle en retrancha une partie; elle se servoit tour-a-tour de ses pattes antérieures pour l'ajuster et l'étendre entre deux pans, ou de ses dents, pour l'enchâsser dans le sillon anguleux qu'elle vouloit garnir de cette manière. Après ces différentes opérations, le cordon de propolis parut être encore trop large et trop massif au gré de cette abeille, elle se remit tout de suite à le ratisser avec les mêmes instrumens, et chaque coup tendoit à en enlever quelque parcelle : lorsque ce travail fut achevé nous admirâmes l'exactitude avec laquelle le cordon étoit ajusté entre les deux pans de l'alvéole. L'ouvrière ne s'en tint pas là, elle se retourna vers un autre partie de la cellule, fit agir ses mâchoires contre la cire sur les bords de deux autres trapèzes, et nous comprîmes qu'elle préparoit encore la place que devoit recouvrir un nouveau filet de propolis. Nous ne doutions pas qu'elle ne s'approvisionnât de cette gomme sur le tas qui lui en avoit fourni précédemment ; mais contre notre attente elle tira parti de la portion qu'elle avoit retranchée du premier filet, l'arrangea dans l'espace qui lui étoit destiné, et lui donna toute la solidité et le fini dont il étoit susceptible. D'autres abeilles achevèrent l'ouvrage que celle-ci venoit de commencer ; tous les pans des alvéoles furent bientôt encadrés par des filets de propolis, les abeilles en placèrent aussi sur leurs orifices ; nous ne pûmes saisir l'instant où elles étoient occupées à les vernir, mais il est facile de concevoir actuellement de quelle manière elles doivent s'y prendre.' p. 264.

The expedients which bees resort to for defending their hive against numerous enemies, furnish perhaps the most curious instances of ingenuity and contrivance of any part of their policy ; and are the more deserving of study, as they often admit of direct comparison with human artifices. The sphinx atropos, a very large species of moth, commits great devastation in the hive, whenever it can succeed in getting into the anterior   A hive that has been visited by this nocturnal depredator, is generally soon after deserted by its inhabitants; and on examination, is found to be entirely robbed of its honey, of which it had before contained an ample provision. It was some time before the cause of these frequent losses of bees was discovered; and when detected, it was found that the only effectual method of securing the hive from the attacks of this formidable moth, was to contract the door-way, so that the large body of the sphinx could not pass through, while sufficient room was left for the entrance and exit of the bees. It is very remarkable, that in some hives where the cultivator had not employed this expedient, the bees had, of their own accord, adopted a similar contrivance, and had built up, within the hive, and immediately behind the door, a thick wall, in which several holes

were left just sufficient for the passage of the working bees. In
different hives, considerable variety in the construction of these
lines of defence was observable; different plans of fortification
had been followed by these expert and sagacious engineers.
Sometimes a single wall was turned into arches at the top; at
others, several buttresses were placed in succession behind each
other, as if in imitation of the bastions of a citadel; doors were
constructed, which were masked by walls in front, and opened
in the face of another series of ramparts, and in situations which
did not answer to the original entrances. On other occasions,
a series of massive arches were built, so as to cross one another,
and thus leave a very narrow aperture: and the whole formed a
compact and solid structure. When the danger is less pressing,
when the population of the colony has much increased, and
the abundance of flowers abroad requires the constant passage
of the bees to and from the hive, all these fortifications are de-
molished, until fresh subject of alarm arises. Those raised in
1804 were destroyed in the ensuing spring. The sphinx did
not make its appearance either that year or the next; but in
the autumn of 1807, they returned in considerable numbers;
the bees immediately barricadoed their doors, and thus succeeded in saving themselves from the danger which threatened
them. In May 1808, they again dismantled the fortress, to
make way for the swarms that were sent off. If the farmer
should have already taken the precaution to straighten the entrance, the bees, finding that they have been anticipated in their
labours, do not employ any additional measures of security.

It is for those who deny the existence of any degree of reflection in insects, to explain these facts on some other principle.

The volume of which we have now given an account, must
recommend itself to all who pursue philosophical inquiries, by
the excellent specimens it contains of the methods of investigating the processes of nature in the animal world. The history
of discoveries on the subject of bees, about which so many volumes have been written, and to which the attention of the a-
griculturist as well as the naturalist has been directed from the
earliest times, is highly instructive, as disclosing the progress of
the human mind in the attainment of knowledge. In the works
of Aristotle, Pliny, Virgil and Columella among the antients,
and of Swammerdam, Maraldi, Reaumur, Hatlorf, Riem, Schirach, Debraw, Bonnet, Hunter and Huber among the moderns,
we may trace the rise and fall of various opinions, and the slow
confirmation of truths, which, now that they are established,
we wonder could ever have been disputed. We are in the situ-

ation of a spectator who looks down from a commanding eminence on the tangled paths which wind up the ascent, and for-
gets the labour and perplexity of the traveller who first explored
his way over the craggy steeps.   We are amused with the motley admixture of truth and error apparent in the works of the
older authors, and the indolent acquiescence with which those
errors have been copied and transmitted through succeeding
ages.   While we gather confidence in results which are founded
on legitimate induction, we are at the same time taught a salutary scepticism with regard to those theories which rest on less
direct evidence.   We learn what difficulties impede us in the
very outset of our inquiries ; how laborious and arduous is the
task of collecting accurate observations ; how liable we are to
delusion from the magic power of imagination, which persuades
us that we see what is not before us, which dresses up what we
expect or desire in the guise of reality, and which insensibly
lures us into partial or exaggerated statements.   A conjecture
thrown out at random has sometimes reached the threshold of
an important discovery, which has yet remained unexplored till
a long time afterwards, when inquiry has led to it by a very different path.   Truth often lies concealed near the very spot where
we had looked for her in vain ; her subtle essence eludes our
grasp in a thousand ways; and, even when fully in our view,
she appears in such unexpected shapes, and fantastic disguises,
that we fail to recognize the object of our search.

Edinburgh Review – Oct: 1815 –

[L]   [Price One Shill.

"That I may see my shadow as I pass."—*Shakspeare.*

INDUSTRY.

A MORAL SONG.

"Industry *must* prosper.   Glorious day for the Beehive!"—*Old Farce*.

How doth the little busy bee
  The sprawling hours knit closer,
By gath'ring honey constantly
  For every opening—grocer.

How skilfully she builds her cell—
  (It seems the *busy* bee,
Who rears the home and stores it well,
  Is, after all, a "she,"

With full maternal powers contrived
  To rear a buzzing brood,
But who, from childhood's dawn, deprived
  Of elbow-room and food,

And labour-doom'd, must aye forego
  A mother's joy and care—
The fate of luckless females who
  Go early out to "chair!")

I 've mused upon the busy bee,
  I 've watch'd her ways of late;
I 've mark'd the social theory
  That rules the apian state.

INDUSTRY.

Some twenty thousand working bees
   Each straw-built homestead hives;
They are the smallest kind one sees,
   And lead the shortest lives.

Their numbers vary with the clime,
   They swarm in summer's breath;
They 're apt, towards the winter time,
   To freeze (at work) to death.

Each tiny slave—a sage declares—
   Well fed and housed, had been
Possess'd of all the powers, the airs,
   And honours of a queen.

But hives are small, and flowers are few!
   Who wants save what he sees?
Ambition's wind is temper'd to
   These shorn and stunted bees.

In stifling nurseries consign'd—
   Half fed, untaught—to lurk,
These paupers think the fortune kind
   That sends them out to work;

To breathe the air, and feel the sun,
   And sniff the opening flowers,
Like merry masons laughing on
   An emperor's rising towers.

Their skins, perspiring, yield the wax
   The cloister'd town to build;
With "pollen" on their legs and backs,
   Their sacks with honey fill'd,

They buzz along—these working bees—
   To build and stock the hives:
They are the smallest kind one sees,
   And lead the shortest lives.

SHADOW AND SUBSTANCE.

There is another kind of bee,
    We christen him the drone;
A heavy-swelling insect he,
    To labour never known.

'Tis easy to distinguish him
    From the industrial fry;
His limbs are stout, his aspect grim,
    He hath a wondrous eye.

Ay, and a voice (the toiling bee,
    Who builds the city wall,
And stocks the common treasury,
    Hath ne'er a voice at all).

He ever heralds his approach
    By a tremendous din:
In building time he calls his coach;
    " The workpeople are in ! "

And travels till the month of May,
    When all is in repair;
The hive laid out, the season gay,
    The flowers and sunshine fair !

Then to his town-house comes he up,
    To sport him on the green,
To quaff the sparkling honey cup,
    And buzz about his queen !

THE QUEEN !   Ah ! who shall dare invade
    That sovereign bee's repose;
Discuss her tribute, gladly paid,
    From every conquer'd rose?

Who shall dispute her sacred right
    To house in roomy cell,
Where homage, plenty, space and light,
    And all the comforts dwell?

The matron of the teeming home,
  They pinch that she may thrive!
.Who would not make his mother's room
  The snuggest in the hive?)

For her the cheery workers toil,
  And hold the labour sport,
Of storing barrack rooms with spoil
  To feast her dronish court.

They hide her from the eyes of men,
  They die to guard their queen;
In her bright form they joy to ken
  The thing themselves had been—

The proved perfection of their race;
  The ripen'd charms and powers
Of each—were hives less scant of space,
  And earth more rich in flowers!

'Tis much that some score thousand bees
  Can yield one perfect queen.
Who would begrudge her wealth and ease,
  And happiness serene?

Who rob the toilers of their aim,
  The tie that binds them closer?
Ah! luckless rhyme (it *is* a shame)
  That brings me back to " grocer!"

The little state is organised,
  The constitution plann'd;
The town in narrow streets devised,
  And built, and stored, and mann'd.

Warm quarters every princelet house,
  By loyal builders skill'd;
The lordly drones at ease carouse;
  The treasuries are fill'd.

The worker to her cell retreats
  (No spacious home or sunny),
The queen within her parlour eats
  Abundant bread and honey.

Let winter come ; the task is done !
  Of peace sets in the reign ;
When, lo ! invasion's booming gun
  Is heard across the plain.

The grim resistless conqueror comes
  Encased in sting-proof mail,
The match is lit, the fortress hums ——
  But why prolong the tale ?

Fell, sulph'rous smoke the homestead chars,
  Dead bodies strew the ground ;
Spoilt honey sells, in earthen jars,
  At tenpence for the pound !

————

I weep : 'tis for the royal bee,
  That insect, hothouse-nursed,
The best of a community,
  So glorious in its worst ;

And also for her noble drones,
  That stalwart courtier train
Of jovial guards and stout dragoons
  Cut off for selfish gain ;

But mostly for the working bees,
  Who plann'd and stock'd the hives :
They are the smallest kind one sees,
  And lead the shortest lives !

No. 65
DECEMBER 1900

PRICE
ONE SHILLING

THE BADMINTON MAGAZINE

· MAGAZINE ·

OF SPORTS & PASTIMES

EDITED BY

ALFRED E. T. WATSON

APIS INDICA

BY A. P. BERESFORD

A GOOD many years have passed now since I went out to join my regiment in India. We were quartered at Jubbulpore, a town situated on the Nerbudda, in the Central Provinces. I was very fond of fishing and most anxious to make the acquaintance of the lordly 'Mahseer' about whom I had heard so much, but none of my brother-officers were fishermen; they preferred the more exciting sports of shooting and polo, and it was not till after some inquiry that I got hold of a native 'shikarry' named Abdul Rahman, who initiated me into the art of fishing. I abbreviated his name into 'Abram,' and together we had some very fair sport.

He used constantly to talk about a place some eight miles off, where he said the fishing was very good, but when I suggested going there he used to refer to some drawback, and my knowledge of the language was not sufficient to make out what the difficulty was. He branched off into some subject other than fishing, and seemed to talk about flies. My curiosity being aroused, I got one of my brother-subalterns to interpret for me, and found out that the place was the 'Marble Rocks' and the drawback was '*The Bees.*'

A spice of danger gives zest to an adventure, so I determined to go up there, have a day's fishing, and see these bees of whom all the world stood in awe.

The following Sunday we set out. I persuaded my interpreter, Percy by name, to come with me. We took our lunch and up-stream this takes some time to travel. 'Abram' spent the time in telling us tales of what the bees had done to those who, wittingly or unwittingly, had interfered with them. A party of natives had been fishing there, and one of them thoughtlessly lit a pipe. The smoke from it had infuriated the bees, and in a few minutes they were set upon. The men kept their heads, cut their boat adrift to float down with the stream, wrapped themselves in their blankets, and let the boat take its own course. They must have had a miraculous journey, as the river is by no means easy; but eventually, more dead than alive, and more than half frightened out of what life was left, they reached the town. The fate of another party was more tragic. Four soldiers who had rowed up the river, shooting as they went, found their way into the Marble Rocks; when there they fired at a passing pigeon. Instantly the bees were on them ; with mighty swarms round them they tried to save themselves by jumping into the river. But they found death instead of safety. Every time they showed their heads above water thousands of bees set upon them : they were drowned, and four disfigured corpses floated down the lordly ' Nerbudda,' a warning to all. Animals, too, had met with a similar fate ; deer, pigs, and even—so Abram assured us—the lordly tiger had paid the penalty of indiscretion. They had accidentally roused the bees, and when set upon had sought refuge in the water and had been drowned. Thus Abram droned on with his terrible tales till gradually we reached our destination. The country round Jubbulpore is flat, but as you ascend the river the banks get hilly, and at the Marble Rocks these hills close in and form a sort of rocky gorge through which the river rushes. The rocks vary from one to two hundred feet in height, and in some places almost touch overhead. As we forced our way up the gorge we noticed that the sides were full of deep cracks and fissures. In these fissures we could see great dark masses hanging. They were the bees.

I fished that day and had fair sport, but my heart was not in it, and my eyes kept wandering away from the water to where the bees were : I pictured to myself what they would be like when they were roused, and felt almost awe-struck to think that these small people were able to defy the powers of man and beast. After our day's sport was over we drifted back. On the way I kept thinking and thinking, gradually my thoughts took a definite shape: I would rush in where

in his den; I would attack the dreaded bees of the Marble Rocks.

This was my resolution, there remains to tell how I carried it out.

Now I had hived a swarm in the garden at home; I knew a little about bees and what they will do under given circumstances, and had therefore a fair idea of how to set about my job. I began by designing a suit of defensive armour. It was constructed by the local dirzee, or Indian tailor, and consisted of a sort of overall suit, which was tied round the neck with tape. I had a good bee veil made which I was going to tuck into the garment; the legs I stuffed into riding boots, and a pair of gauntlets and two pair of gloves were to protect my hands. Such was the armour, but before entering into the great encounter I thought it best to test it, so, knowing of a colony of bees in a place down the river, I set out alone to tackle it. The place was near the river, and I went down to it in a boat. Besides the armour I took with me a sulphur smoker (half measures are no good with the 'Apis Indica') and a pail to bring the honey away in. The bees were in a little temple about two hundred yards from the river. I went quite close to it and armed myself.

There was a large stone in front of the door on which the faithful used to put their offerings; it was covered with marigolds and little odds and ends of food, and pushing past this altar, I entered the temple. Opposite me I saw a figure of the elephant-headed 'Ganesh' which nearly filled up the low room.

The bees had started building from the roof, and the combs now reached down so low that they were fixed to the head of the benevolent god. The insects had begun to be attentive directly I entered, so I thought it was no good delaying matters, but made my attack at once.

After the first sulphur puff the enemy came at me in earnest, and the fun began. I could protect myself very well on one side, thanks to my sulphur-smoker, but I was attacked on four.

I will not describe a skirmish, with a battle to recount ahead of me; suffice it to say that I filled my bucket and got back to my boat. I did not escape scatheless, two stings in the hands showed me my gauntlets were not sufficient; a prod in the foot taught me that a determined bee can force his tape round my veil. On the other side I should say the casualties were heavy. I often wonder what happened to the next devotee who went to lay his offering on the shrine of 'Ganesh.' I expect he found the god angry.

Having thus got ten pounds of honey and some not very dearly bought experience, I decided that when the fatal day came the joints of my harness should be sewn, and hoped that this would make them bee-tight. I divulged my scheme to Abram, and, though he was very much frightened, faith in the 'Sahib' and promises of large 'backsheesh' turned the scale. Percy did not know or care anything about bees, but an appeal to him to back me up, a promise that there would be plenty of excitement, and an offer to do his turn of church settled the matter ; so two more suits of bee-armour were ordered and made.

The army was mobilised and equipped, the enemy was located, and his dispositions and probable tactics only too well known. We were ready to start.

Sunday is the day of leave in India, but two days were required for this campaign, so, getting leave for Saturday as well, we started early and made our way quietly up the river. Our army consisted of two boat loads ; it included ourselves, Abram, some boatmen, and a tailor. That night we reconnoitred the position and were to start operations the next day. I had a well thought out plan of campaign which will reveal itself as my story is told. We camped just below the Marble Rocks, and I went to bed that night with the feelings that Wellington must have had on the eve of Waterloo. I woke up at daybreak and marshalled my forces. We donned our armour and were sewn into it by the tailor, every joint and cranny was closed, and we put on our trousers over our riding boots, and bandages over them. Abram and I, armed with a bucket and two coils of rope, were to climb up to the back of the hills, so as to get above the bees, and Percy, with the two boats, ascended the rocks. He went to the edge of the river which was under the part we intended to attack, and made his boat fast ; all the natives then got into the second boat and returned to cantonments.

Abram and I climbed up till we thought we had got opposite the place, when I left him and crawled cautiously forward. As I got to the edge I could hear a sort of all-pervading hum have opened a hive are familiar, partly honey, partly wax, and partly bee.

I found that I had judged the distance pretty accurately, and that the place fixed on was only about a hundred yards further on. I returned to Abram and together we made our way out to the appointed spot. The cliff was sheer, in fact, if anything, overhanging. Leaning over I could see the dense masses of bees and comb about fifty feet below me, and another fifty feet below that I could see the boat and my faithful ally. There was a tree growing at the edge of the cliff ; round this I put the rope, gave one end to Abram, and went over.

When I first showed at the top the bees began to be attentive, and, as I was lowered, they began to buzz round me. I sank down until I was opposite the place where I meant to alight, and found that I should have to get a swing on to reach the ledge on which I wished to stand. Hanging down on to this ledge from above was about ten or fifteen feet of comb. I could just reach the rock with my hand, gave a vigorous push, swung out, then back again scrunch into the middle of the comb, and gained my feet with a scramble. Now when I was hanging opposite the ledge I was beset by as many bees as there seemed to be room in the air for, but all that had gone before was as child's play to what happened now. The whole air reeked with that curious acrid smell which is familiar to all who have been stung ; the noise of the water rushing below was drowned by the screaming hiss of the angry bees, well known to all who have been mobbed by them. I was completely blinded as they swarmed over my veil, blocking out the light. When I touched my body with my hand to make sure I had got one, it seemed to me, through my glove, as if I was covered by thick soft fur—all bees ! For a few moments I was completely stupefied. As Daniel felt when cast into the lion's den, as a man feels who has been treed by a furious man-eating tiger, as one feels who finds a shark has come to bathe with him, so I felt—except that with them death was an appreciable distance off, with me it was screaming and hissing within an inch of my face.

After a minute or two I realised that my armour was trustworthy and that I was safe. I gave two tugs to the rope as a signal to Abram, and he lowered the bucket to me. My vision was completely blocked by bees and I could see nothing, but I felt about for the comb, and, as well as I could, filled the bucket.

I did my best, but had no control over the circumstances under which I was working, and they were, to say the least of it, unfavourable.

I lowered the bucket down to Percy; my original scheme had been to haul the bucket up again as soon as he had emptied it into a jar we had brought, but I saw that if we could get off with a trophy we should have done very well and that any idea of making a big bag of honey was out of the question. A muffled shout came from below to let me know the bucket had arrived, and I in my turn shouted to Abram to lower me. He told me afterwards that he could see nothing of me and that all that was visible was a brown whirling mass round the place he had last made me out. I really don't know how I accomplished that descent. To be lowered a hundred feet under the most advantageous conditions is no child's-play : I suppose the good genius that presides over drunkards and adventurous subalterns had me in his charge. I swung out in the dark and felt myself being gradually lowered, bumping hither and thither as I went. At last, after what seemed an age to me, I felt an arm clutch me, and knew that I was at the bottom. I brushed away the bees from my veil, and there opposite me, through a driving mist of bees, I saw a cluster of bees in the shape of a man. It was my companion.

We shouted at each other to say that the sooner we could get off the better ; and we tried to shout to Abram but he could not hear. There was, indeed, a sound of rushing wings, and though they were not mighty, they made up for it by being innumerable and intensely earnest. We cut the rope and let ourselves drift.

There were so many bees attacking us when we started that it is hard to say that their numbers increased, but still as we drifted through their stronghold I think a few more countless thousands, roused by the smell which a stinging bee emits, and which seems to act as a battle cry to all his fellows, came and joined in. Again I think a special deity protected us. The river is not easy to navigate and we had a good many millions of other things to think about. At last, however, we reached the place where we put up the night before and made for shore. With a great deal of trouble we got the sulphur smoker alight and tried to clear ourselves of bees. After a bit we were joined by Abram. He was much as we were only less so, and he was thoroughly frightened to boot.

We worked away for some time, and what with the bees

that appeared to be following us up, we managed to keep the numbers about the same. We moved down another mile and again landed, and this time got rather the better of our enemies ; twice more we landed, on each occasion improving our position, and the fourth time, having come down five miles, we really collared them. The bees had left off following us, and the powerful fumes of my sulphur-smoker finished off those that remained. All praise be to the dirzee ; our dresses had held out, none of us were stung. We struggled out of them, and cleared up the boat, finally getting back to our quarters late for dinner. When we strained off the honey we found we had got just 15lb.

To obtain this three of us had held our lives in our hands for about six hours. I do not think that it can be considered as cheaply bought. We sent a message to the cantonment magistrate to tell him that we had been up the river, that something seemed to have annoyed the bees at the Marble Rocks, and that we thought that it would be dangerous for any one to go up there for a day or two.

This closed the incident as far as I was concerned, but the story went round the bazaar, and I do not think untold gold would persuade Abram, or any one to whom he has related his story, to try again. I went up to the place about a month afterwards. The bees were quite settled then and I shall never disturb them more. I still keep bees, and now whenever I get the smell of the stinging bee into my nostrils (they say that memory is more easily awakened by the sense of smell than by any other) my mind flies back to the day when the Indian bees came at me in their millions, and I picture to myself the mighty rushing river, the gloomy rocks over head, lit up where the sun breaks through the trees that crown them, and the masses of the 'little people' who hold their store against all the wide world.

THE HONEY BEE: THE NATURAL HISTORY, CULTURE, UTILITY, GEOGRAPHICAL DISTRIBUTION, AND COMMERCIAL VALUE.

By the Rev. T. SLEVAN, Poulton-le-Fylde, Lancashire.

[Addressed to the Members, at the Memorial Hall, Wednesday, February, 4th, 1891, at 7·30 p.m.]

THE great fire in London, by clearing away the nests of disease and death, thus making way for open streets, &c., did great good. So a fair and honest apology like mine may clear the ground and put me right with those who hear. To those present who may have given critical and scientific attention to this subject I have nothing to say. To those who stand on the border of this interesting wonderland in an inquiring spirit I have a little to say. I don't know much about bees. Well, the fact is, the man who knows most on this subject admits that he has but touched its border lines. What I have to say is not new, but true, and there is a sense in which what is true is new. My findings on this subject are the result of extensive reading, careful observation, and some practical experience. Like the bee, I have for years been gathering knowledge from every opening flower. And just as the bee gives a new character to the sweet nectar she gathers from every opening flower, so have I endeavoured to give to all I have heard and read the colour and strength of my own thought and experience. At the outset, let me say that I am greatly indebted to Mr. H. Carr. Newton Heath, Mr. W. B. Carr, of London, and specially to the two great kings of bee-keepers, Messrs. Cowan and Cheshire, and many another beside.

Poised one day on the crest of a North Sea wave, with the genial Secretary of the Manchester Geographical Society by my side, I made a rather rash promise. Whether I was too much excited by strong sea-breezes, or a too free use of toast and water, I can't tell, but I did promise that in return for a lecture on the Mediterranean delivered at Poulton I would come to Manchester and speak about bees. In anxiety ever since I feel sure that I have paid very dearly for my whistle. I would have retreated, but found the bridge burnt behind me. Like the man who rides a bicycle, I felt that I must either go on or go off. To go off and lick the dust would be unworthy of a north-countryman. So here I am to do my best, and leave the rest to critics. I have no serious intention of delivering a lecture, properly so called, but to talk familiarly so as to interest you in the honey bee, its history, culture, and utility; and, if possible, to so interest you that when you see a bee you may not feel it to be your duty to kill it, nor even to be afraid of it, but that when you sip the delicious honey, or burnish your chairs or light your room with wax, you may rejoice in its "sweetness and light."

Every man should have a hobby (not a fad). If he have not brains for a big one, then get a little one; but be careful that you do not ride it to death. Just take it out for a little trot now and then, just to secure a little healthy recreation as a relief from or preparation for the larger and more important duties of life. Not that I think the study and culture of the honey bee a little thing. The novice may so regard it, but as he intelligently advances he finds himself in the presence of the infinitely great. God and Nature are never so great and so grand as when we bend to examine what we in our ignorance call the infinitely little. Every jot and tittle of Hebrew writing is significant, so is every living organism, however small. The daisy has never been a little flower since Robert Burns apostrophised it. To the thoughtless and unobserving it is still but a daisy. You remember the words put into the mouth of Peter Bell by Wordsworth, that

> " A primrose by the river's brim
> A yellow primrose is to him,
> And it is nothing more."

To many people a beehive is only a skip or box of mysterious mischief, a point of danger, a thing to be dreaded. I want to make it more than that. Our old friend Adam had an early knowledge of the bee, to which he gave the name " Deborah," or one that speaketh. Speech is not always in words. Men speak with their eyes and by clever attitudes. In this case the tongue of the bee speaks in honeyed deeds, which are always more eloquent than honeyed words. In more than twenty books of the Bible we read of honey and wax. Old Jacob was a generous bee-master. Seeing his sons preparing to go down into Egypt he said, " Take the man (Joseph) of the best fruits of the land," and among other things a " little honey." In the Bible the highest style of living is connected with milk and honey. " With honey out of the rock will I satisfy you." The good time coming is described as a " land flowing with milk and honey." The only riddle in the Bible, and the oldest riddle in the world, is about honey, and in a queer hive, too. The most remarkable reference, however, is that the first and last food of Jesus Christ was honey. " Therefore the Lord himself shall give you a sign. A virgin shall bear a son, and his name shall be called Immanuel; butter and honey shall he eat, that he may know to refuse the evil and choose the good." To this day the Jews give honey to their new-born babes. After the Resurrection, " Have you here any meat? And they gave him a piece of boiled fish, and of an honeycomb, and he did eat before them."   The earliest records testify to man's appreciation of the wisdom and value of bees.   In Hindoo mythology, in representations of Persian worship, on coins of Athens and Ephesus, we find reference to the bee as a symbol of fecundity.   It is figured in the Egyptian hieroglyphics as denoting a people obedient to a king. Virgil says, "The honey bee is a ray of divinity." Plutarch says, "The honey bee is a magazine of virtue." Quintillian calls her "the chief of geometricians;" and Dr. Montford says that "the honey bee surpasses in architecture the skill of Archimedes."   The notice given to mead in the days of the Druids would lead us to believe that bees were domesticated by the Ancient Britons; but we have no authoritative information on this point, and the honey used in their drinks may have been collected by wild bees.   The Romans when they came (A.D. 43) no doubt taught the Britons how to hive and domesticate bees. Mead was the ideal nectar of the Scandinavian nations, which they expected to quaff in heaven out of the skulls of their enemies; and, as may reasonably be supposed, the liquor which they exalted thus highly in their imaginary celestial banquets was not forgotten, as those which they really indulged in upon earth.

> " Fill the honey'd bev'rage high,
> Fill the skulls, 'tis Odin's cry !
> Heard ye not the powerful call,
> Thundering through the vaulted hall !
> Fill the mead and spread the board,
> Vassals of the grisly lord !
> The feast begins, the skull goes round,
> Laughter shouts—the shouts resound."

The King of Wales, about the year A.D. 490, made a code of laws relating to bees, fixing various prices of a hive at different seasons; and so highly was mead thought of 1,000 years ago that the mead-maker in the household of the Prince of Wales ranked next to the royal physician.   The Anglo-Saxons of the earliest period were probably more anxious to domesticate bees than horses.   Their produce was an article of food necessary to brewing of mead, and extensively used in medicine.   In the sixth and seventh centuries bees were altogether wild (some think them wild yet).   They swarmed in woods and formed their honeycombs in hollow trees, and were at first classed by law with foxes and otters, as incapable of private ownership, because they were always on the move.   Anyone who found them had a right to the honey and wax, though from certain ecclesiastical regulations in the seventh and eighth centuries we may infer that their capture was a dangerous amusement, and that their half-naked captors had often a bad time of it.   A favourite mode of taking them was to cut off the branch of a tree in which they had lodged themselves, taking care, of course, when sawing off the branch to sit on that part of the branch nearest the tree, then taking home their treasure. As the country grew in wealth and intelligence bee-keeping became more profitable. By the law of one Saxon king it was ruled that " every ten hides of land shall furnish ten vessels of honey." The clergy encouraged bee culture, teaching that the bees had been sent from heaven, because the mass of God could not be celebrated without wax. It has been said that man alone is capable of living in all lands, and of migrating freely to any portion of the globe; that each species of animal, as well as vegetable, has an organisation fitting it to the climate of a certain portion of the earth's surface, and that when they are removed from their natural districts they cease to exist, or, if the change is not too violent, they vary their habits so as to adapt themselves to their new conditions. For instance, if a fine-woolled sheep be taken to the torrid zone the wool is changed to hair. The dog of the tropics is naked. The elephant and the camel do not, as a rule, live long in temperate zones. The arctic bear and the lion cannot exchange places. Therefore to man alone has been attributed the power of inhabiting all climates; for, whether in the polar regions, where now and then mercury freezes, or in India, where at times the thermometer marks almost semi-boiling heat, his body maintains an equable temperature, his blood having (under ordinary circumstances) in all those places its natural warmth of 98° Fahrenheit. Man is not alone in his proud pre-eminence in this respect, for the honey bee, in an organised colony, during the working season, has the power of maintaining an equal temperature in the hive of 70°, regardless of the heat or cold outside, and, during the winter, of living in any climate with less protection than man. More: however short the summer, wherever vegetation blooms, it can gather its own food. So the bee belongs to all nations, climates, and men. The honey bee is one of the most fortunate of insects, for, unlike most of its class, having a practical " bearing," and sometimes a painful " bearing," it has obtained more attention from naturalists than even its interesting economy would have attracted, and repays, in a tangible form, the care that man has bestowed upon it for his own pleasure and profit.

There is a charm in modern bee-keeping which never existed when the hive was a sealed book and the bee supposed to possess two points of interest only, and those at its extremities—its tongue and its sting—which had nothing particular between them, to use the words of a humorous writer, save " skin and squash." Here the naturalist and the trader find a common point of interest. The hive is the home of the honey bee. On this point I have but few remarks to make. While David dwelt in a house of cedar he failed to feel comfortable when the Ark of God dwelt within curtains. The bee is the friend of man. Our interests are bound up together. Let us be as careful for the bee's comfort as for our own. It is true that hives gather no honey, but in so far as they effect the objects we have in view they are the cause of much being gathered. Environment and home comfort go for much among men ; they are not less important among bees. Therefore, turning from the clay pipe of the Egyptian and the straw skip of the peasant, we direct our attention upon those modern inventions which have given to bee culture its high place among the industries and studies of this practical age. There is great difference between hives for bees and hives for the bee-keeper. Just step inside the hive, if you please ; the accommodation is not large, but the work and workers are full of interest. There are three kinds of bees in the hive at certain seasons and two at others—the queen, the drone, and the worker. The queen is the mother of the hive, and the only mother. The drone is her royal consort. The worker is the neuter on whom there comes the honour and dignity of labour. The queen bee lays an egg, and in 24 days it becomes a worker bee. The same egg that produced a worker would by different feeding and environment in 16 days produce a queen. She lays an unfertilised egg, and in 25 days there comes forth a drone. The great charm of the hive is the queen. She is supposed to be the centre of influence and authority. She differs widely from those around her. While not so bulky as the drone her body is longer, and as it is tapering she has a waspish appearance. Her wings are much shorter than those of other bees, her colour is brighter, and her movements slow and matronly. No colony can long exist without her. She is treated with the greatest possible affection. Her dutiful children attend her every want. They back out of her way like so many courtiers as she moves about. Her shy and retiring disposition is a manifest disadvantage to the bee-keeper. When the hive is opened she hides among her children, preferring to be heard, not seen. She is a wonderful creature, sometimes laying as many as 2,000 eggs per day. Her wings are short, rendering her incapable of long and continuous flight; in fact, she seldom leaves the hive more than twice—first, when she goes off on her wedding tour ; and, secondly, when she leaves the hive with a swarm in order to make room for a younger and more vigorous successor. Wonders multiply when you come to know more about this illustrious lady. A queen may be produced from a worker larva, when the larva is less than three days old. This is a great mystery. These royal scions simply receive a more abundant and sumptuous diet, and occupy a more comfortable home. Not only are the ovaries developed and filled with eggs, but the mouth organs, the wings, the legs, and the sting ; yes, and even the size, form, and habits are all wondrously changed. That the development of parts should be hastened, and the size increased, is not so surprising, because it is well known that the kind and quality of food helps or retards growth in other insects; but that food should so essentially modify the structure, is certainly a rare and unique circumstance, hardly to be found except here and in related animals. The queen has a sting, but so far as at present known she never uses it, except in combat with another royal lady. Nature has evidently taught her that a common foe is unworthy of her steel. So then, when you have the chance, you may handle a queen bee as freely and fondly as you would a baby.

I come now to the drone—the father of the hive and the best-abused member of the bee community. "Big, fat, and burly, and studious of his ease," he is an ill-used bee. He appears in May, and often stays until November. The drone is shorter than the queen, being less than three-fourths of an inch in length. He is more robust than either the queen or the workers. He makes his presence felt by his loud humming noise. Mark, the beehive is not the only place where those who make the most noise do the least work! But does he do less work? Less certainly, but he is by no means the proverbial idle fellow he is often described to be. Inside the hive he helps to hatch the young by increasing the temperature of the hive. Outside his cheery song and well-to-do appearance gives to the hive an air of respectability. The drone has no sting and no pollen pockets, and no proboscis suitable for honey gathering. No wonder, then, that he is ill-used, for how can a utilitarian age like this think well of a member who has neither power to get, nor keep, nor fight? We have the best German authority for saying that the drone is the product of an unimpregnated egg. Many curious reasons, more or less reasonable, are given for the wholesale destruction of drones. One, and the most likely, is this: A check in the fine summer weather indicates famine. In view of this the cautious, far-seeing bees stay all proceedings likely to increase the population of the hive, and to be an unremunerative strain on the food supply. After all the drone has a merry life, though a short one. When the queen goes off on her marriage flight he is to the fore. The drone who follows the farthest, thus proving both his strength and his affection, is chosen as the royal consort. Alas! poor fellow, he never again regains the hive. Dr. Evans thus describes a drone:—

> " Their short proboscis sips
> No luscious nectar from the wild thyme's lips;
> From the lime's leaf no amber drops they steal,
> Nor bear their grooveless thighs the foodful meal;
> On other's toil in pampered leisure thrive,
> The lazy fathers of the industrious hive."

In a hive we have a population of from 15,000 to 40,000—one queen, 600 drones, the rest workers, emphatically "the bees."

The workers are of two kinds—small ones called sculpturers, and larger ones called waxworkers and outdoor labourers. The age of bees is always a subject of interest. Those hatched in the autumn will (with care) survive the winter and start the work in spring. Those reared in the spring wear out in three months. In the busy season few live more than thirty days—they usually die of nervous exhaustion. Bees never live through a year. One great secret of success is to get a strong stock of young bees in the autumn ; in the spring, to stimulate the queen to egg-laying, so that by the time flowers bloom there may be an army of workers ready to take the field.

I now come to the product of the hive, but not being learned in chemistry I can only say a little. Honey is the main point. Beekeeping has been called the grace of agriculture. Still, it has a very prosaic side. However poetic and romantic, we still look for "divy" in the shape of honey and wax. What is honey? A Chinaman called it the juice of bees.* Honey is not gathered, but made. It is first nectar, or sweet water, found on or in flowers, and containing cane sugar. Received by the bee it is changed into grape sugar, then an entirely new character is given to it by the bee, which differentiates it from all sugars. The short season and the quantity won is the great marvel.

Pollen is the dust of flowers, and is gathered to be the food of young bees. It is most needed where there is least to get. So we advise our friends to make artificial crocuses, and fill them with peameal or fine oatmeal, and place them in the garden where the bees may find them.

Wax is an important product of the hive. It is a solid, unctuous substance—a fat-like material. It is secreted by the bees, and may be seen in scales under the abdomen.

Comb Building : The bees first gorge themselves with honey, then hang themselves in festoons in a cluster, and by a swinging motion get up great excitement, the temperature rising to a great height. Then the wax exudes from the body, the bees disengaged come to the cooler part of the hive, the fatty substance sets in layers on the abdomen ; they then proceed to the place for comb building, and are relieved of their load.

The Sting : I have intentionally and appropriately left this until the last. It is what the Americans call the business end of a bee. Many have a very wholesome but needless dread of bees because they sting. Never go near in windy weather. Why? Bees think that you cause the disturbance. Nor in gloomy damp weather. Why? The bees are discouraged and ill-tempered. Always move quietly, firmly, and decidedly. People can get accustomed to stings. Keep calm, and the ill-effects are almost *nil.*

---

* Aristotle believed that honey fell like dew from heaven, where it formed the food of the gods and of the industrious. Pliny calls it the juice of stars.

Lastly, its *Commercial Value:* The honey possibilities of this and other lands it is hardly possible to believe. In the United States we have 400,000 million of acres yielding 1lb. of honey per acre per year. In England alone, and without occupying a single bit of land useful for other purposes, it is said that one million fruit trees might be planted with marked advantage. Mark! the success or failure of such a planting depends more on bees than at first sight appears. The want of interest in bee culture renders fruit trees and clover crops less productive, and hundreds of tons of honey are annually wasted, for when honey is not gathered the flowers simply " waste their fragrance on the desert air." Scotland alone could maintain a sufficient number of bees to provide four million pounds of honey and one million pounds of wax each year. Our flowers will bear very favourable comparison with those of Russia and Hungary, and yet not a single mile from John o' Groats to Land's End is sufficiently stocked with bees. Why should the farmers of Lancashire complain of poverty when they allow all this land to waste? Let the nobleman with his miles of heather, the squire with his park and woods, the farmer with his bean and clover fields, and the cottager with his garden, all join together this rich harvest of good things. Bees are free roamers. They never trespass, for they have right of way everywhere, and are ever welcome. The German Government encourages bee culture in every way possible. Teachers paid by the State travel through the rural districts giving instruction on the best methods of bee culture. Schoolmasters before receiving their certificates must pass examination on this question. Bee clubs are common in the villages, money for prizes and expenses being freely and heartily given by the Government. Here, then, you have an illustration of the principle of the " three acres and a cow." The result of this fostering care is that Germans are the most skilled apiarians. With the German it is a science as well as a grace.

Let us all love bees. Mahomet made an éxception in favour of bees when he condemned all flies to be killed. This love of bees made Napoleon prefer as a national emblem of industry the bee instead of an idle lily. The Athenians ranked the honey bee among their national blessings; and so should we, did we understand it rightly and care for it wisely by adopting rational methods of culture. When you see the busy bees in your garden do not kill the friend of man, but think of Him who made both them and you—think of the part they play in the economy of Nature, as high priests at the marriage festivals of flowers; remember their industry, their love of home, their bravery in the defence of it, their strict and zealous attention to the business of their lives, and the joyous hum with which they set about their daily task; their division of labour, and how willingly each one performs his allotted task, whether it be that of courtier in attendance on the queen, or, as Shakspere has it—

> " The singing masons building roofs of gold ;
> The civil citizens kneading up the honey ;
> The poor mechanic porters crowding their heavy burdens
> at the narrow gates."

Is it not enough, think you, to excite the interest of the dullest minds when we consider that within so small a body should be contained apparatus for converting the " virtuous sweets " which it collects into one kind of nourishment for itself, another for the common brood, and a third for the royal lady of the happy home ? More. Glue for its carpentry, wax for its cells, poison for its enemies, and honey for its master ! Think ! This little busy bee has a tongue almost as long as its body, which it can contract or lengthen at pleasure ; and a sting so sharp, with a point 1,000 times finer than the finest needle you ever saw, and, more wonderful still, that that sting is a hollow tube ! All these wonders in a body less than half an inch in length, and only two grains in weight ! Well may our thoughts turn from Nature to Nature's God. Whether we contemplate the minute or the majestic in Nature we may exclaim—" Great and wondrous are thy works, Lord God Almighty ; just and true are thy ways, thou King of Saints. Who shall not fear thee, O Lord, and glorify thy name ? " " There is something better than honey, more to be desired than gold, yea, than much fine gold ; sweeter also than honey in the comb."

Brehm's Zoological Atlas, classified in 55 sheets, folio. About 900 illustrations. Ruddiman Johnston and Co., Limited.—This is a selection of some sheets of the *Thierleben* of Brehm. The classification has been revised and the English popular names supplied. The pictures are very beautiful, and to anyone wishing to interest children in Natural History are very valuable. They are correctly drawn, and the relation of the picture to the size of the creature is indicated. This is one of the books which make it a delight to teach and a pleasure to learn something of the creatures, both tame and wild, inhabiting our globe. The book is not expensive.

A New Geography on the Comparative Method. With maps and diagrams. Fourth edition. 1890, 504pp. Index.

The British Empire: Its Geography, Resources, Commerce, Land Ways, and Water Ways. By J. M. D. Meiklejohn, M.A. 336pp. and Index. Diagram maps marked in colours, the natural products, &c. 1891. Simpkin, Marshall and Co., London.

The comparative method is the only true method of teaching Geography, and Professor Meiklejohn, in these two volumes, gives us examples of the application of the method in a practical form. The diagram maps in the " British Empire " are very useful and valuable, and the books will be heartily welcomed. There are some things in the volumes which might be altered, but we are not concerned with little blemishes. We are concerned to welcome any attempt to make the study of Geography more interesting both to teachers and pupils, and these two books do that well. They are very well printed, and not too trying to the eyes.

B

The Honey Bee.

FROM a boy I have loved the bee with a love that even the mild impertinences of Dr. Watts could not quench. Scarce any sound in Nature is, to my ear, more soothing than the " murmuring of innumerable bees," heard in an hour of idleness beneath the fragrant limes. Scarce any sight is more pleasant than the reiterated pilferings of my choicest blossoms by these ever-welcome little pillagers. Nor has my love been a sordid one. I have never been a bee-keeper. I have never had occasion to rejoice over a good take, nor suffered anxiety from foul brood. Not that I despise the sweet product of the honey-bee's industry. But much as I have ever admired the products of innate power or industrious application in man or bee, articulate or inarticulate, I have always felt a keener admiration—an admiration touched with reverence—for the living and breathing producer. Thus my love for the bee is a purely personal one. Of me, the untiring worker can say, as of Lord Ronald, Lady Clare—

> " He loves me for my own true worth,
> And that is well."

It does not matter how you take a bee. She is full of interest all over. In the head are eyes simple and compound ; feelers with great delicacy of touch and smell, and a tongue—silent, indeed, which gallantry compels me to regard as a defect, but otherwise well-fitted for its special task—to sip the sweets of life ; in the mid-region of the body or thorax are four delicately veined and closely interlocking wings, and six legs adapted for progression on surfaces rough or smooth, and as full of additional contrivances as is a school-boy's pocket-knife ; in the abdomen are wax organs, and that " centre of painful interest," the sting. Nor are its habits less interesting than its structure.

Full of that concentrated unconscious wisdom which we call instinct, she displays also, at times, mental powers of a more plastic kind.

Some interesting experiments have recently been made by Mr. Romanes to test the homing faculty of bees. The house where he conducted his observations is situated several hundred yards from the coast, with flower-gardens on each side and lawns between the house and the sea. Bees, therefore, starting from the house, would find their nectar on either side of it, while the lawns in front would be rarely or never visited, being themselves barren of honey-sweets and leading only to the sea. Such being the geographical conditions, Mr. Romanes placed a hive in one of the front rooms on the basement of the house, and made suitable arrangements by which he could liberate a score or so of bees at a time and observe how many returned to the hive. He found that bees liberated at sea, on the sea-shore, or even on the lawns in front of the house, failed to find their way home; while bees liberated in the gardens, amid the flowers they were wont to frequent, returned to the hive within a few moments of their liberation. From such observations Mr. Romanes justly concludes that these bees were guided by local signs—by a special knowledge of the flower-gardens— and not by any general sense of direction, instinctive and innate.

Much has been written (and preached) upon the cell-building instinct of bees, concerning which a curious cell-myth has arisen. According to this myth, Maraldi is said to have sub-mitted the problem of cell-structure to Kœnig, the mathe-matician, whose solution differed from Maraldi's actual measure-ments by only the 30th part of a degree. Not contented with an accuracy already exceeding the possibilities of observation— even with instrumental appliances at that time undreamt of— Maraldi begged the mathematician to re-examine his calcu-lations. The obliging Kœnig did so; and was thus enabled to correct a printer's error in the mathematical table he had used. His results and those obtained by actual measurements were then, so runs the myth, in exact accord. Since when, the bee has stood upon a pinnacle of perfection fraught with danger. For human folk cannot permit perfection to go long un-challenged. No sooner is the eye of man described as an optical apparatus without flaw, than a Helmholtz comes forward to say that, were his instrument-maker to provide him with no better work, he would promptly return it for alteration and correction.

Recent measurements and observations have tended to dissipate the cell-myth, and to show, not only that the honey-comb is far from regular, but that such regularity as it has is due to merely mechanical conditions. Mr. Frank Cheshire tells us in his recent volume, that careful measurements of the finest pieces of comb, built with every advantage for securing regularity, show that, so far from every cell being geometrically accurate, it is difficult to find a hexagon presenting errors of less than three or four degrees in its angles. On the other hand, there is a growing tendency to accept a modification of Buffon's explanation of the origin of cell-structure. Buffon attributed the regularity of the cells to mutual pressure ; in illustration whereof he packed a closed vessel with dried peas, and filled up the interstices with water. The peas, which were thus caused to swell, assumed, under the pressure which resulted, the form of more or less accurate geometrical figures. Perhaps a still better illustration of this principle of mutual interaction is seen in soap-bubbles. If a little soapy water be placed in the bottom of a tumbler and air be blown into the water through a tube until the upper part of the glass is full of bubbles, the hexagonal form which these bubbles assume under mutual pressure, and the trilateral pyramids at their bases, will be readily seen. Not that these geometrical figures are the same as those which the wax assumes, but they illustrate the principle. For, at the temperature of the hive, the wax, pared thin by the smooth-edged jaws of the workers, has all the plasticity of a fluid membrane. The bee has indeed to avoid the danger of paring away too far, and thus making a hole through the wall. But even here she may be aided by mechanical conditions. If we take a thin piece of soap and pare away one face with the blade of a pocket-knife, we shall soon form a transparent patch where the soap is very thin. But if we continue to pare, we do not cut through the soap at this point ; but, for a time at least, we merely enlarge the area of the transparent patch. The thin film of soap yields at this point, and the stress of the blade falls on the thicker and less-yielding edges. Some such mechanical yielding of the wax may guide the bee in her work.

Do not suppose, kind reader, that I would hereby reduce the whole function of cell-making to a matter of mere blind mechanism. I have far too high an opinion of the bee to cast such a slur on her intelligence. And the size of the cells is in any case determined by no mere mechanical principles. Nor is the size invariable. For the worker-brood, cells one-fifth of an inch in diameter are constructed ; for the drones and for honey-storage, smaller cells one-fourth of an inch in diameter are made ; between contiguous groups of these cells, transitional cells of more or less irregular contour are interpolated ; while the royal cells for the future queen-mothers are irregularly rounded in form and constructed with lavish expenditure of costly wax.

For the wax of which these cells are made is a product of the vital activity of the bee. It is no mere extraneous substance which needs only to be collected for use ; it is a bit of individual organic home-manufacture. If you examine the under-surface of a cell-building worker, you will find beneath the abdomen four pairs of white plates projecting from as many pockets in the encasing rings of this part of the body. These are the wax-plates, made from the life-blood of the worker. Examine now with a lens one of the hinder legs. You will find that the stoutest joints are very square-shouldered at the hinge, and that the hinge is well over to one side ; so that the shoulders form a pair of jaws, which open when the limb is bent, and close when it is straightened. The upper jaw has a row of spines which bite on a plate on the lower jaw. With this apparatus, piercing it with these spines, the worker withdraws a wax-plate from its pocket, transfers it to the front legs, and thence to the mouth, where it is laboriously masticated with a salivary secretion. Unless it undergoes this process, it lacks the ductility requisite for cell-making.

Within the cells thus constructed of this costly material, the queen-mother lays silvery eggs, from which will be developed workers, drones, and queen-mothers, each in their appropriate cells. And how comes it that, from eggs apparently similar—for each egg is a glistening white oval embossed with delicately netted lines—there issue three different kinds of bee ? These three stand to each other in the relation of males (drones), fertile females (queen-mothers), and infertile females (workers). But how comes it that the males are all developed in one set of cells ; that the majority of eggs, those in the larger hexagonal cells, produce females that are infertile ; and that only the few, laid in royal cells, reach their full sexual development ? It is well known that most of the higher animals are developed from eggs in which a male and a female element have entered into fertile union. It is not so with drones. The queen-mother, after her short marriage flight, carries with her a special storage reservoir, that with which she can fertilize each egg as it is laid. From eggs so fertilized female bees, perfect or imperfect, are developed. But from eggs from which drones are to spring, the queen-mother withholds the fertilizing fluid. That drones are unfathered is one of the strange results of modern zoological investigation.

The difference between queen-mothers, with fully developed egg-producing organs, and workers, in which the egg-producing organs are present in an undeveloped condition, would seem to be determined by diet. The grubs which issue from the silvery eggs are fed by young workers, hence termed nurses, with the product of a special gland in the head. This secretion, which is only formed in early life (the older workers giving up nursing and taking to foraging), is termed royal-jelly, and resembles water-arrowroot. Of the three forms of bee-food, pollen, honey, and royal-jelly, this is the richest and the most concentrated. It seems to have a wonderfully stimulating effect on the reproductive organs. More is supplied to drones than to workers; most of all to the queen-mother, who throughout life is provided with this stimulating food by nurses who are ever ready to minister to her wants.

It is well known that the queen-bee can brook no rival, and that when there are several royal nymphs in a hive the first-born throws herself upon her unprotected sisters, still sleeping their strange chrysalis sleep, and pierces them with her sting. But what if the queen should die, and the hive be thus left motherless? The workers then proceed to the cells in which are worker eggs newly laid. They tear down the partition walls so as to throw three cells into one. Two of the embryonic inhabitants they sacrifice; but the third they feed right royally. And under the stimulating effects of a liberal supply of royal-jelly she becomes a queen-mother. Not only are her egg-producing organs thus stimulated into full development, but this change is accompanied by all those other differences which serve to distinguish the queen-mother from her infertile but, in most other respects, superior sister.

It is commonly supposed that the queen-mother is in every respect as superior as the humble worker-bee, as the worker is herself superior to the idle, ill-conditioned, good-for-nothing, reprobate drone. This is, however, a mistake. The brain of both queen-mother and drone is markedly inferior in relative size to that of the worker. In powers of flight, as judged by the relative areas of the wings, the queen-mother is inferior to the worker. For though the wing-area of the worker is somewhat less (by one-sixth) than that of her fertile sister, her body is relatively much smaller. But in this matter of flight it is the lazy drone that carries off the palm, having a wing-area of nearly twice (once and four-fifths) that of the worker. The tongue of the worker is more highly developed than that of queen or drone. As we shall see directly, the sense-endowment of the queen is in many respects inferior to that of the infertile female, while here again it is the drone that is the most highly developed.

In the matter of sense-organs we are met by serious difficulties of interpretation. As said the Danish naturalist Fabricius, nearly 100 years ago, "nothing in natural history is more abstruse and difficult than an accurate description of the senses of animals." And this abstruseness and difficulty is the more keenly felt in studying creatures so widely different from ourselves as the bee. Such an insect would seem at first sight to be about as susceptible to the delicacies of touch as an ancient armour-sheathed knight. Head, thorax, abdomen, limbs—all are ensheathed in chitinous armour. The bee has his skeleton outside. As an American gentleman once observed in my hearing, the main difference between an insect and a vertebrate is this: one is composed of flesh and bone, the other is composed of skin and squash. The question is, how can delicate impressions of touch be transmitted through the tough dense skin so as to affect the sensitive "squash" within. If you will examine one of the feelers of the bee, you will see that the surface is richly supplied with hairs. It is by means of such sense-hairs that the bee experiences a sensation of touch. Each touch-hair is hollow; and within it is a protoplasmic filament containing, it would seem, the delicate terminal threadlet of a nerve. A curious modification of the touch-hairs is found on the last joint of the antenna. They are here bent sharply at right angles so as to form rectangular hooklets.

That insects are possessed of a sense of taste cannot be doubted. Even if the caterpillars which refuse to eat all but one or two special herbs, or the races of blood-suckers which seem to have individual and special tastes, are guided

by other senses, there is much evidence which seems to admit
of no alternative explanation. Touch, for example, the feeler
of a cockroach with a solution of Epsom salts and watch him
suck it off; or repeat F. Will's experiments on bees, tempting
them with sugar, and then perfidiously substituting pounded
alum. The way these little creatures splutter and spit suggests
that, whatever may be the psychological effect, the physiological effect is analogous to that produced by an exceedingly
nasty taste. Lehmann, too, observed a fly begin to suck some
sugar that had been moistened with bitter decoction of worm-
wood. Directly it tasted the medicine it politely and dis-
creetly withdrew to a contiguous vase and endeavoured to
reject the nauseous drug. At the tip of the bee's tongue taste-
hairs, which do not project freely but are protected by other
longer hairs, have been described by F. Will; while Mr.
Cheshire states that the tongue of the bee has on each side,
near its root, thirty-two minute taste-papillæ.

Much has been written concerning the sense of smell in insects.
That they possess such a sense few will be disposed to doubt.
The classical observations of Huber seem to show that bees
are affected by the smell of honey, and that the penetrating
odour of fresh bee-poison will throw a whole hive into a state
of commotion. He was of opinion that the impunity with
which his assistant, Francis Burnens, performed his various
operations on bees was due to the gentleness of his motions,
and the habit of repressing his respiration, it being the odour
transmitted by the breath to which the bees objected. Bevan
mentions the case of M. de Hofer, who could handle bees
freely until struck down by fever, on his recovery from which
he was unable even to approach them without exciting their
anger. It is probable that humble-bees seek their mates by
the aid of smell.

The correct localization of the organ of smell has been a
matter of difficulty. Kirby and Spence localized it at the
extremity of the "nose," between it and the upper lip. That
the nose, they naively remark, corresponds with the so-named
part in mammalia, both from its situation and often from its
form, must be evident to every one who looks at an insect.
Lehmann, Cuvier, and others, misled by the fact that the organ
of smell is in us localized at the entrance of the air-track,
supposed that at or near the spiracles of insects were the
organs of smell. Modern research, however, tends more and

more clearly to localize the sense of smell in the feelers or antennæ. If the feelers of a cockroach be extirpated or coated with paraffin, he no longer rushes to food, and takes little notice of, and will sometimes even walk over, blotting-paper saturated with turpentine or benzolene, which a normal insect cannot approach without agitation. Carrion flies whose antennæ have been removed fail to discover putrid flesh; and E. Hasse has observed that male humble-bees, whose antennæ have been removed, cannot discover the females. The sensory elements are lodged in pits or cones, which may be filled with liquid, peculiar sensory rods being associated with the nerve-endings. Of these pits the queen bee has, according to Cheshire, 1600, the worker 2400, and the drone not less than 37,800.

The sense of smell is held by some observers to enable ants and bees to recognize each other. Sir John Lubbock's experiments seem to establish the fact that the recognition of ants is not personal and individual; and it occurred to Mr. McCook to test the olfactory hypothesis by endeavouring to ascertain whether, in presence of an overmastering scent, ants were unable to distinguish friend from foe. Selecting for experiment some pavement-ants who were engaged in a free fight, he introduced a pellet of paper saturated with *Eau de Cologne.* The effect was instantaneous; the ants showed no sign of pain, displeasure, or intoxication, but in a very few seconds the warriors had unclasped mandibles, relaxed their hold of enemy's legs, antennæ, and bodies, and, after a momentary confusion, began to burrow galleries in the earth with the utmost harmony. On carpenter-ants *Eau de Cologne* had no pacific influence.

From smell we pass to hearing. Sir John Lubbock failed to awaken any response in bees, though he played to them, shouted to them, and whistled to them. Perhaps had he been able to buz to them he would have been more successful. It is scarcely probable that they are deaf. Popular belief, at any rate, maintains that they are not insensitive to the soft melody that may be evoked by a door-key from a frying-pan; but here as Sir John has, I think, himself suggested, the bees may hear acute overtones inaudible to us. Mr. Cheshire is, however, clear about the fact of bees hearing such sounds as interest them. He regards certain hollows (differing from the smell hollows) in the antennæ as the seat of the auditory sense; but this must still be regarded as doubtful.

When we turn from hearing to sight we find that the difficulties take a new form, and concern, not the existence nor the nature of the recipient organ, but its mode of action. Sir John Lubbock has shown that bees are guided by a preference for certain colours ; while his experiments on ants bring out the still more interesting fact that these insects are sensitive to ultra-violet rays quite invisible to us.

Any one who will take the trouble to examine with a lens the head of a bee, will see on either side the large rounded compound eye, and on the forehead or vertex three bright little simple eyes. The latter are, as their name implies, comparatively simple in structure, each with a single lens. But the compound eyes have a complex structure. Externally the surface is seen to be divided up into a great number of hexagonal areas, each of which is called a facet, and forms a little lens. Of these the queen bee has on each side nearly 5000 ; the worker some 6000 ; and the drone upwards of 12,000. Beneath each facet is a crystalline cone, a so-called nerve-rod, and other structures, too complex to be here described, which pass inwards towards the brain.

It will be seen then that the so-called compound eye with its thousands of facets, its thousands of crystalline cones, its thousands of "nerve-rods" and other elements, is a structure of no little complexity. The question now arises, is it one structure or many ? Is it an eye, or an aggregate of eyes?

To this question the older naturalists answered confidently —an aggregate. And a simple experiment seems to warrant this conclusion. Puget, quoted in Goldsmith's 'Animated Nature,' adapted the facets of the eye of a fl—, pardon me, fair reader, of a minute aphanipterous insect of the genus Pulex—so as to see objects through it under the microscope. "A soldier who was thus seen, appeared like an army of pigmies ; for while it multiplied, it also diminished the object : the arch of a bridge exhibited a spectacle more magnificent than human skill could perform ; and the flame of a candle seemed the illumination of thousands of lamps." Although Cheshire, in his book on the bee, adopts this view and supports it by reference to a similar experiment, it numbers to-day but few supporters. One is tempted to marvel at the ability of the drone to co-ordinate 24,000 separate images into a single distinct object. Picture the confusion of images of one who had sipped too freely of the sweet but delusive dregs of the punch-bowl ! Under similar circumstances human-folk are reported to see double. Think of the appalling condition of an inebriate drone!

Those who believe the facetted eye to be one organ with many parts, contend that each facet and its underlying structures gives, not a complete image of the external object as a whole, but the image of a single point of that object. Thus there is formed, by the juxtaposition of contiguous points, a stippled image or an image in mosaic. Hence this view is known as Müller's mosaic hypothesis. Lowne has experimented with fine glass threads, arranged like the cones and nerve-rods of the bee's eye, and finds that (even when they are not surrounded by pigment, as are the elements in an insect's eye) all oblique rays are got rid of by numerous reflexions and the interference due to the different lengths of the rays. Some modification of the mosaic hypothesis is now generally adopted, and Dr. Hickson has recently worked out, with great care, the structure of the optic tract which lies between the crystalline cones and the brain.

Imperfect as our knowledge of the sensations of bees may be —and in a subject of such abstruseness and difficulty we must expect imperfection—we yet have no reason to suppose that this is due to any imperfection in their sensory endowments. There are three simple eyes for near vision, and a pair of large compound eyes for the ascertainment of space-relations. These facetted eyes are covered with delicate hairs which protect the facets from extraneous particles, and from which such particles may be removed by combs specially developed for that purpose on one of the joints of the fore-leg. There are organs of taste in the mouth, and tactile organs in various parts of the body. In the antennæ we have sense-organs of extreme delicacy which may perform other functions than those of smell and touch. Here again, as in the case of the eye, the bee is provided with a special apparatus for cleansing its antennæ. In the fore-leg, just at the hinge between two joints, there is in the outer joint a semi-circular notch into which the feeler neatly fits, its diameter, according to Cheshire, varying in queen, worker, and drone, in accordance with the diameter of the antennæ. Attached to the inner of the two joints is a little cap which, when the limb is bent, closes on to the antennæ and holds it in place in the semi-circular notch, which is provided with comb-like bristles that remove from the antennæ, as it is drawn through the notch, all extraneous particles. More primitive insects, like the cockroach,

suck their antennæ or clean them with their mouth-organs. But
the mouth-organs of the bee having been specially modified to
sip the nectar of flowers, a special antenna-comb has been
developed on the fore-limb. And the sensory importance of the
organ would seem fully to justify the care which the bee bestows
upon it. Huber's description of the distracted condition of a
queen whose antennæ had been cut off is quite heart-rending.

I have not by any means exhausted the points of interest
which my little friend presents. I have said scarce anything
about the tongue with which she sips the nectar of flowers ;
nothing of the manner in which this nectar is converted into
honey ; nothing of the beautiful petal-mouthed honey-sac. I
have scarcely alluded to the delicate hooks which serve to
connect the upper and under wings in flight, and have not
described the foot-pads and hooklets. I have left unnoticed the
pollen-baskets, and made no point of the sting. As to the
internal anatomy—the organization of the "squash "—I have
not had space to say aught of the delicate nerve-chain, the
many-chambered heart, or the air-tubes which ramify throughout the body and carry oxygen to every part. But perhaps I
have said enough to kindle (or rekindle) an interest in the honey-
bee, and may now leave the reader, if so he will, to seek fuller
information in the writings of Huber, Bevan, Lubbock ; in the
interesting volumes which Mr. Cheshire is now devoting to bees
and bee-keeping ; or, better still, by a study at first hand of the
honey-bee itself.

ON THE

BEAUTIES, HARMONIES, AND SUBLIMITIES

OF

NATURE.

ON THE

BEAUTIES, HARMONIES, AND SUBLIMITIES

OF

NATURE;

WITH

Notes, Commentaries, and Illustrations;

AND

OCCASIONAL REMARKS ON THE LAWS, CUSTOMS, HABITS, AND
MANNERS, OF VARIOUS NATIONS.

———————————— The sounding Cataract
Haunted me like a passion; the tall Rock,
The Mountain and the deep and gloomy Wood,
Their colours and their forms, have been to me
An appetite.   WORDSWORTH.

BY CHARLES BUCKE.

AUTHOR OF "THE BOOK OF HUMAN CHARACTER," &c.

IN THREE VOLUMES.

VOL. II.

A NEW EDITION, GREATLY ENLARGED.

LONDON:
PRINTED FOR THOMAS TEGG AND SON,
73, CHEAPSIDE.

1837.

LONDON:
BRADBURY AND EVANS, PRINTERS, WHITEFRIARS.

ONE branch of rural economy is, in the present age, but little attended to; though in France, in the time of Charlemagne, it formed a considerable article of profit, viz. the Culture of Bees:—insects which have been treated of, says Columella, "diligently by Hyginus, gracefully by Virgil, and elegantly by Celsus." Pliny was a lover of bees; and his Natural History contains all, that the ancients knew of their economy. Before his time there were only two practical writers: Aristomachus of Soli, who occupied himself entirely in the care of them; and Philiscus of Thasia, who lived all his life in forests, for the purpose of watching their manners and gathering their honey.

There are many passages in the Scriptures, commemorating the produce of this admirable insect. The sons of Jacob are described as taking Joseph, their brother, a little balm and a little honey for a present; and a curious and entertaining account of a trial of wisdom, between Solomon and the Queen of Sheba, which was decided by a swarm of bees, is related in the Talmud.

Galen says, that he had observed honey frequently upon trees and plants, in parts of the country, where no bees lived; and that the peasants, on those occasions, called out, "Jupiter has rained honey." Some writers have confused manna with dew; but manna was a round substance falling upon the dew, and as small as hoar frost [a]. When the sun waxed hot, it melted [b]; its colour resembled that of bdellium [c]; it resembled coriander seed; and its taste was like fresh oil; but if kept till the next day, it bred worms and stank [d]. Grinding it in mills, the Israelites made cakes of it, and baked it in pans; and for forty years lived almost entirely upon it [e]. St. Paul styles this food "spiritual meat [f];" David calls it "angel's food [g];" and Nehemiah [h] and St. John [i] give it the appellation of "bread from heaven [k]."

Burckhardt [l] says, that the Bedouins collect manna on Mount Djebel-Serbal, under the same circumstances, described by Moses. He says, that wherever the rain has been abundant, during the winter, it drops from the tamarisk tree, common in the deserts of Syria and Arabia [m], and in the valley of Ghor, near the Red Sea: but he is not aware, that it produces manna any where else.

In Ashantee [n] there is a cedar, the leaves of which exude a considerable quantity of liquid salt, which crystallizes during the day. There is, also, in Chili, a species of wild basil,

<hr>

[a] Numbers, xi. v. 9. [b] Exod. xvi. v. 14. 21. [c] Numbers xi. v. 7, 8.
[d] Exod. xvi. v. 20. [e] Joshua v. v. 12. [f] 1 Corinth. x. v. 8.
[g] Psalms, lxxviii. v. 24. [h] Neh. ix. v. 15. [i] Ch. vi. v. 13.

[k] Perhaps the writer of the following passage might allude to manna, when he speaks of honey:—"Bees derive their wax from the tears of trees; and their honey is that which falls from the air; especially during the rising of the stars, and when the rainbow is over the earth."

[l] Letter to the African Association, July 1, 1816.

[m] Travels in Nubia, p. 45.   [n] Bowdich's Mission, p. 175.

which is every morning covered with saline globules, resembling dew, which the natives use as salt.

Laudanum is procured in a curious manner, in some parts of the isle of Cyprus[a]. It is a species of dew, which falls during the evening and night upon plants, resembling sage, the flowers of which are like those of the eglantine. Before the sun rises, flocks of goats are driven into the field; and the laudanum fastens on their beards; whence it is taken. It is of a viscous nature; and collected in this manner is purer than that, which adheres to the plants; because those plants are subject to being covered with dust during the day.

Pliny mentions a mountain in Crete, where bees were never found; and yet which produced a considerable quantity of honey. It is, I believe, certain, that Pliny never was in that island; therefore, as in a multitude of other instances, he wrote from the testimony or imagination of others. It is, however, probable, that both Galen and Pliny may allude to what is familiarly called honey-dew; which, in certain climates, and under particular states of the atmosphere, may assume a consistency, not observed in other countries[b]. In certain seasons, there appears a species of manna on the leaves of trees in California[c]. This juice oxudes from the leaves like gum.

It is impossible not to be charmed with the manner, in which Marmontel speaks of the bee-garden of St. Thomas, and of its affectionate mistress. " I was never happier," says he, " than, when in the bee-garden of St. Thomas, I passed a fine day in reading the verses of Virgil on the industry and police of those laborious republics, that prospered so happily

[a] Abbé Mariti. Travel. I. p. 233.

[b] Vossius has some curious observations on a passage in Pomponius Mela, lib. viii. c. 7. " Ut in eo mella frondibus defluant," &c. &c. It is astonishing to observe, how little Nature some of the schollasts were masters of!

[c] Vid. Miguel Venega's Natural and Civil History of California, p. 51; ed. 1758.

under the care of my aunt. She had surrounded their little domain with fruit trees, and with those that flowered in early spring. She there had introduced a little stream of limpid water, that flowed on a bed of pebbles; and on its borders thyme, lavender, and marjoram; and in short the plants, that had the most charm for them, offered them the first fruits of summer. What passed under my eyes; what my aunt related to me; and what I read in Virgil, inspired me with such a lively interest in behalf of this little people, that I forgot myself whilst I observed them; and never quitted them without sensible regret [*]." I too, have taken delight in the management of bees! and I never reflect upon the days, which I passed in the garden of a farmer, in one of the most beautiful villages in Glamorganshire, where several bee-hives stood near the window, which commanded the neighbouring castle, the church bosomed in trees, and the small bay, which indented the sea-shore, without a sensible delight. In that garden there were three species of the orchis: one resembling a spider; another a wasp; and the third a bee:—and often have I meditated on the circumstance, that, as there are in some insects three bodies, as it were in one,—the caterpillar, the chrysalis, and the butterfly—the analogy might extend even to us: our body being only a temporary coat for the soul, which after a time may assume another, or exist without one.

The peasantry of this remote village were the most respectful I have ever seen. They were chiefly engaged in the lime quarries; where they gained a comfortable subsistence; most of them having a cottage, a pig, and a garden; and not a few possessed two cows and a horse. Every morning we bathed in the sea; and every evening, if the weather permitted, we visited the bees; not unfrequently lifting up the hive, to observe their numbers, or to ascertain in what pro-

[*] Mem. Marmontel, v. 1. p. 30.

portion each colony had increased the quantity of its honey-comb. " I delight," says Thallus to Pityistus, in one of the epistles of Alciphron, " I delight to see the fruits grow ripe ; it is a compensation for our labour: but, above all, I am charmed with taking the honey from the hives. I select a portion for the gods ; and then assign another portion for my friends. The combs are white; and drops of honey distil from them, equal to that produced in the Brilesian caves. I send you this for the present; but, next year, you shall receive some far better and more sweet."

No people are more employed in cultivating bees than the Ingushians and Circassians ; immense quantities of mead, busa, and bees-wax being prepared and sold, on the frontiers of the Caucasus, in exchange for salt. That, made in the province of the Abassincs [a], is said to have an intoxicating nature ; owing to its being chiefly extracted from the blossoms of the azalea pontica, and rhododendron.

The culture of bees was in much repute in Attica, and fresh honey from the hive is still in great request at Athens. The good quality of that on Mount Hymettus [b] is derived from two species of savory [c]. The peasants carry their bees in cane baskets up the hill in summer, and down the valleys in winter. They divide hives in spring [d] ; but do not permit the bees to swarm of themselves. Solon enacted a law, that every man's stock should be kept at a distance, not less than 300 feet, from that of his neighbours [e] ; and that the penalty of poisoning a hive was extremely severe among the Romans, we learn from the result of a trial, in which Quintilian accused a rich man of poisoning a poor man's bees with certain venomous flowers, that grow in his garden.

Ancient husbandmen frequently transported bees from field

---

[a] Pallas. South Russ. i. 386, 4to.

[b] There are said to be now on Mount Hymettus 3,000 hives; and in Attica 12,000.   [c] Satureja capitata.—Satureja thymbra.

[d] Denon, Sicily and Malta, 590, 8vo.   [e] Plutarch, in Vit. Solon.

to field for a more copious supply of flowers; particularly in autumn. The Greeks moved their hives every year from Achaia to Attica; and there is a wandering tribe, inhabiting the declivities of the Caucasus, who take their hives with them wherever they go; and the natives of Juliers, in Westphalia, move their bees according to the season. In some parts of France and Piedmont, there are floating apiaries of a hundred bee-hives; and similar republics once existed upon the Nilo.

The honey of the Brazils is chiefly used as a medicine[a]. The bees are black, small, and their sting comparatively painless. They have no hives; but deposit their wealth in hollows of trees; which are frequently cut down, for the sole purpose of getting their honey. Sullivan mentions a species of bee (the Tzulfalye), which has a poisonous sting, and is much dreaded by the Abyssinians[b]; and Strabo relates, that in Pontus the bees feed principally on hemlock and aconite; and that, in consequence, the honey was poisonous. This, however, has been contradicted by Lamberti, and more recent travellers; but that the honey of Corsica had a bitter flavour is certain:—hence the proverb—"Et thyma Cecropiæ Corsica ponis api."

In Caubul[c] bees are particularly attached to the sweet-scented yellow flowers of the bedeo mîshk: in the province of Pensa, in Russia, they fly, with the utmost eagerness, to the blossoms of the linden tree; which enable them to form honey of a greenish colour, and of a delicious flavour. When the linden tree sheds its blossoms, the peasants gather the honey. But the flower, which elicits the richest liquid is the nyctanthes (Arabian jasmine). The Hindoos believe, that bees sleep upon its blossoms every night; to

[a] Koster's Trav. Brazils, p. 319, 4to. Also in the isle of Timor, on the coast of New Guinea. Vid. Dampier, vol. iii. p. 74.

[b] Vol. iii. p. 287.]   [c] Elphinst. Introd. 41.

which Moore alludes, when describing the sounds of falling waters :

> —— —— Lulling as the song
> Of Indian bees, at sunset, when they throng
> Around the fragrant Nilica, and deep
> In its blue blossoms hum themselves to sleep.

No honey is more grateful to the palate than that, which is produced in Sicily, in Minorca, in the valley of Chamouni in the neighbourhood of Mont Blanc, in Moldavia and Wallachia, and in the fields round the town of Narbonne, abounding in rosemary [a].

The Guadaloupe bees lay their honey in bladders of wax, about as large as a pigeon's egg, and not in combs. They have no stings, are small, and of a black colour; producing honey of an oily consistency, that never hardens. The bees of Guadalaxara, in the same manner, have no stings [b], and thence derive the name of Angelitos, "little angels." In that province there are six kinds. The one, which is without a sting, makes fine clear honey, of an aromatic flavour, superior to any in the western world. It is taken from the hive every month. This honey, particularly that made from a fragrant flower, like the jasmine, used to be sent frequently as a present to the king of France.

So vast a multitude of bees once lived north of the Ister, that the country was said [c] to be possessed wholly by bees. Poland is still very abundant in those insects, and they are greatly cultivated in Lower Hungary [d]. In the province of Cagayan, in

[a] Of all flowers, the Cacalia suavolens gives the most honey to bees. Darwin relates, that he once saw a plant of this species so pregnant, that above two hundred butterflies, besides bees, were observed upon it at one time.—Econ. Veget. iv. L 1, in Notis.

[b] Some writers, however, insist that they have stings ; but seldom use them : the black bee of Ethiopia has no sting. There is a species of bee which have no neuters or modified females, called labourers. "In the genus Megachiles the *male serves for fecundation only*, while the business of nidification and providing for the larvæ is performed by a *solitary* female."—*Catalogue of Contents of Museum of R. College of Surgeons in London,* part iv. p. 131, 4to.

[c] Herodotus.

[d] See Bright's Travels, p. 304, &c. 4to.

the island of Manilla, there are such a number of bees, that
even the poor burn wax instead of oil. In the forest near
Lamas [a], where bees build in hollow trunks and branches, the
Peruvians decorticate the trees, split them in the middle, and
then seize the honey and wax, attached to their internal
sides. In Samar, the hives hang in the form of oblong
gourds from the branches of trees: beneath which float perfumes, arising from roses of China, and a fragrant species of
wild jasmine. In South Africa honeycombs suspend from
edges of rocks [b]. These nests are discovered by the Hottentots, who follow the flight of a little brown bird, called the
Indicator; which, on the discovery of a nest [c], flies in quest
of some person, to whom it may impart the discovery, which
it does by whistling and flying from ant-hill to ant-hill, till it
arrives at the spot, where the honeycomb suspends. There
it stops, and is silent ! The Hottentot then takes the chief
part of the honey, and the bird feasts upon the remainder.

In the Philippine islands [d], Mindano trades with Manilla,
exchanging tobacco, honey, and wax, for muslins, calico,
and China silk : while in Madagascar bees are exceedingly
abundant. The natives eat a great quantity of their honey,
and convert the rest into an intoxicating liquor, called Toack.
The best honey in Persia is collected from the orange groves
of Kauzeroon ; while that of Kireagah, near Pergamos, is
the best in Anatolia ; being collected from the cotton
that grows there ; and is of a snowy-white colour [e]. The
white honey of Lebadew is sent regularly to Constantinople,

[a] Present State of Peru, 4to, p. 421.

[b] In some parts of Africa the bees are exceedingly ferocious. A swarm had
nearly put an end to Park's second journey. Vid. p. 37.—An incident, too, is
related in the first ; 4to, p. 331.

[c] Barrow.   [d] Dampier's Voy. L. p. 333.

[e] Aristotle speaks of white bees in Pontus, which made honey twice in every
month ; and he mentions bees, near the river Thermodon, which made honey
in winter only ; and then chiefly from the flowers of the ivy which blossomed
at that season.

for the use of the Grand Seignior, and the ladies of his
seraglio.

When Gama arrived in the Bay of St. Helen's, on the
south-west coast of Africa [a], desirous of acquainting himself
with the manners and characters of the country, he desired
his crew to bring him the first native, they could procure,
either by persuasion or stratagem. They in consequence
seized one, as he was gathering honey, on the side of a
mountain. This man, as well as all his countrymen, showed
the utmost contempt for gold and fine clothes.

Bees are very prolific in the Uralian Forest; but there are
none in Siberia. The Scotch colonists at Karres, in the
Caucasus, have upwards of 500 hives [b]. Their honey is said
to have a fragrant smell, and a most agreeable flavour. Its
colour is a mixture of green and yellow. That of Guriel is
nearly as hard as sugar; and partakes of that intoxicating
nature [c], to which Xenophon alludes, in his history of the
retreat of the ten thousand Greeks [d]. The same quality has
been remarked in the honey of Paraguay [e]; and in that pro-

[a] The honey of Guinea is excellent. Bees are very numerous on the river
Gabon, near Cape Lopez, and in districts still more north in the Gulf of Guinea.
—Bosman, p. 260. Ed. 1721.

[b] The Tscherkessians of the Caucasus keep their hives in the villages till
midsummer, and then take them to the woods. They call the queen *Paheck*, or
prince. Vid. Klaproth, p. 327, 4to.

[c] The country round Trebizonde, in Amasia, produces a species of rock-
honey, so exceedingly luscious, that it is eaten with great caution.

[d] Colonel Rottiers relates, that, during his residence at Trebizonde, in 1816,
he visited the place from which the 10,000 Greeks under Xenophon beheld the
sea. He remarked the ruins of an ancient temple of the time of the Emperor
Adrian. The Rhododendrum ponticum grows there on all the mountains, and
the inhabitants assert that the bees extract a honey from it, which, mixed with
that of other flowers, is a kind of poison, causing stupor, in a greater or less
degree, according to the season of the year. M. Dupré, the consul of France,
who accompanied Colonel Rottiers, assured him that he had experienced this
effect himself. This, therefore, confirms what Xenophon says about this honey
in his " Anabasis." The inhabitants and the Turks call this honey *deli bol*,
or strong honey.—*Literary Gazette*.

[e] D'Azara's Travels in South America, ch. vii.

duced on the borders of the Ganges. Some honey, as we learn from Wedelius' Dissertation on Nectar and Ambrosia, was called Ambrosia; while the "pure virgin" received the appellation of Nectar: hence Linnæus called the repository in flowers the Nectarium[a]. The flavour of honey depends more on the quality of the flowers, on which the bees feed, than on the animals themselves. Hence the fine flavour of the honey of Derne, in the Tripoli States; which arises from the yellow blossoms of a plant, that blows during the principal part of the year.

It is singular that Malta, which is little more than a barren rock, should, in former times, have derived its name (Melita), from the abundance of its honey. With much less surprise we learn, that a district, in South Africa, derives its name, Anteniqua, "a man loaded with honey," from a similar cause;—this district being so beautiful, that some travellers call it an earthly paradise[b].

The uses of honey are various and important. The Susans were accustomed to comb their purple wool with it, to preserve its beauty and freshness[c]. The Greeks had a drink, called Hydrowel, which consisted of water and honey, boiled together, in which was infused a little old wine. Among the ancient Britons, mead (metheglin) was the principal, if not the sole, drink of luxury[d]. In the court of Hoel Dha[e], the mead-maker took precedence of the physician. In Ireland they have a drink made of honey and mulberries, which they call Morat.

The Spartans and Assyrians used honey for preserving the

<hr>

[a] Amœnitates Academicæ, vol. vi.

[b] "One cannot proceed a step here," says Vaillant, "without seeing a thousand swarms of bees. The flowers, on which they feed, spring up in myriads; the mixed odours which exhale from them yield a delightful gratification. Their colours, their variety, and the pure and cool air which one breathes, all engage your attention, and suspend your course. Nature has made these enchanting regions like a fairy land."—Trav. Afric. vol. i. p. 162, 3.

[c] Plut. in Vit. Alex.   [d] Diod. Sic. v. s. 26.

[e] Hoel Dha's Laws, b. i. c. 22, &c.

dead from putrefaction [a]. Hence Democritus formed the wish, that he might be buried in honey [b]. The body of Alexander was embalmed in that liquid. Then it was placed in a coffin of gold, which was inclosed in a sarcophagus, which some suppose to be one of those, preserved in the Egyptia Ggallery of the British Museum.

Honey was frequently used upon ancient altars : and in the ceremony of the Inferiæ, it was poured upon the tombs of virgins. Iphigenia, in Euripides, promises to pour upon the funeral flame of Orestes,

> " The flower-drawn nectar of the mountain bee."

In the Persians of Æschylus, too, Atopa prepares to pour, as libations over the tomb of his father,

> —— Delicious milk, that foams
> White from the sacred heifer ; liquid honey,
> Extract of flowers ; and from its virgin foant
> The running crystal.

Hence honey was considered an emblem of death : notwithstanding which, it was supposed to be the principal food in the golden age of the poets. It was used, too, in the burnt-offerings of the Persians ; but it was expressly forbidden by the Levitical law [c].

The honey of flowers tempts the bees to the corollas ; and they, in return, unconsciously waft upon their wings the fecundating dust to the styles of the females. When unable to reach the bottoms of the tubes of beans, they fly down to the calyx, perforate that and the corolla with their proboscis, and thereby extract the honey from the nectarium.

In medicine, honey is esteemed a purgative and aperient ; while it promotes expectoration, and dissolves glutinous juices. The wax is employed externally in unguents ; internally in

---

[a] Plin. xxii. c. 24.　　[b] Varro in Nonius, c. iii.　　[c] Levit. ch. ii. v. 2.

diarrhœas and dysenteries, mixed with oily substances; and, when dried and pulverized, bees were formerly believed to cure the alopecia. In fact, honey was once so much esteemed, that Horace frequently mixed it with his Falernian[a], declaring, that, of all medicines for the stomach, that and wine were the best. Epaminondas seldom took any thing but bread and honey[b]. The Bedas of Ceylon season their meat with it. Many of the disciples of Pythagoras[c] lived almost entirely upon it; also the modern Tartars; and Augustus, one day inquiring of an old man, who had attained the age of an hundred, how he had been able to arrive at such an advanced age, with so vigorous a body and so sound a mind, the veteran replied, that it was "by oil without and honey within." The same is reported of Democritus[d].

The Romans considered bees, in general, as favourable[e] omens. If, however, a swarm lighted on a temple, it was esteemed an omen of some great misfortune. This is alluded to by Juvenal[f]; and Livy[g] records an instance, also, in which they were supposed to predict calamity.

The peasants of Wales, and indeed of most countries, are extremely cautious of offending their bees; believing, if they do so, that some ill fortune will attend them. Some even go so far, as to imagine, that bees possess a portion of the

---

[a] Lib. II. sat. ii. 15.   [b] Athenæus, lib. II. c. 7.

[c] Philostratus gives a curious account of a tame lion, which refused all food but bread and honey. It afforded a good subject for ridicule to those who derided the doctrine of the metempsychosis. Vid. in Vit. Apoll. v. c. 43.

[d] Aristotle mentions a honey, gathered from the leaves of the box-trees, near Trapezond, which had the property of curing the epilepsy; and Nicl. of St. Fiorentino, discovered honey to be an excellent remedy for a burn. There is a curious disputation between an old and a young man, relative to the virtue of this concoction, in the Treasurie of Auncient and Moderne Times, collected from Pedro Mexico; and Ant. du Verdier, Lord of Vaupriaux, &c., booke iii. c. 13, p. 274.

[e] Plut. in Vit. Dion.   Val. Flac. lib. i. c. 5.   Virg. lib. xii. 64.

[f] Sat. xiii.   [g] Liv. xxi. c. 46.

Divino mind ; a belief so ancient, that even Virgil alludes
to it [a].   Others, however, extend their superstition only to
the length of granting to them a sacredness of character.
Even monarchs have respected them.   Thus bees were
wrought in the coronation robes of Charlemagne.   Pope
Urban VIII. too, chose three bees for his armorial bearings :
to which circumstance Casimir,—next to Piastus, the pride
and glory of his country,—has an elegant allusion [b].

Varro gravely asserts, that bees have their origin from the
putrified carcasses of oxen ; and M. Lemery that honey, by
virtue of its vegetable qualities, contains a portion of iron.
The last observation is assuredly true [c].   Virgil says, that

[a] " Esse in apibus partem divinæ mentis."

Pliny says, too, that they carry their dead out of their hives, and follow after
the manner of a funeral.   Vid. also Georg. iv. 256.   In some parts of Suffolk
the peasants believe, when any member of their family dies, that, unless the
bees are put into mourning, by placing a piece of black cloth, cotton, or silk,
on the top of the hives, the bees will either die or fly away.   In Lithuania,
when the master or mistress dies, one of the first duties performed is that of
giving notice to the bees, by rattling keys of the house at the doors of their
hives.   Unless this is done, the Lithuanians imagine the cattle will die ; the
bees themselves perish ; and the trees wither.

[b] Cives Hymetti, gratus Atticæ lepos,
Virgineæ volucres,
Flavæque Veris filiæ :
Gratum fluentis turba prædatrix thymi ;
Nectaris artifices,
Bonæque ruris hospitæ :
Laboriosis quod juvat volatibus
Crure tenus viridem
Perambulare patriam,
Si Barberino delicata principe
Secula melle fluunt ;
Parata vobis secula ?

[c] The presence of iron has been discovered by Dr. Clark in the petals of red
roses.   Mons. Geoffroy long since inquired whether there was any part of a
plant destitute of iron.   It has not yet been accurately determined whether the
iron, found in the analysis of plants, is produced by the vegetation itself, or from
the particles of iron taken up with their aliment.

been live seven years; and that they have many enemies besides man; but he is incorrect, when he asserts, that the insects, tinea, eat them; for they eat only the wax. He is equally incorrect in asserting, on Grecian authority, that the swallow has the same propensity. There is, however, a bird in Abyssinia, called the Moroc, which destroys them with the utmost wantonness; killing them, even after they have satisfied their hunger, and leaving them on the ground; and Clavigero informs us, that in Chaco, in South America, there is an animal, which sits upon the arms of trees to watch birds, and is fond of honey; hence the Spaniards call it " the honey-cat."

There is also an animal, inhabiting part of Africa, near the Cape, which though endued with a body, which emits a nauseous effluvia, subsists principally on honey. It is called the Ratel. The honey-guide cuckoo directs him to the nest of the bee; which, being frequently in a part of the tree, which it cannot reach, the Ratel signifies his rage, by biting its roots and trunk; which, being observed by the Hottentots, they know, in consequence, that the tree contains a bee's nest. The hide of this animal is so tough, that the sting of a bee cannot penetrate it.

Several persons have rendered themselves remarkable by their power over this little insect. The first account we have of this art occurs in Brue's[*] voyage. When that writer was at Senegal, (1698) he saw a man, who styled himself " the king of bees." It was not without some reason, that he did so; for he had acquired the art of attracting them to such perfection, that they would accompany him, wherever he pleased: not only singly, but by thousands. The same art

[*] Brue assumed the direction of the French African Company, on the Senegal, in 1697. For a more ample account of him, vid. Leyden's Hist. Acct. of Discov. and Trav. in Africa, edited by Hugh Murray, vol. I. 168.

has been practised by several persons in England and in Germany.

In Warder's Monarchy is a curious account of the affection, which the queen bee and her subjects have for each other. Reaumur gives a description of their architecture; while Smart, in his poem on the immensity of the Supreme Being, calls upon Vitruvius or Palladio to build, if they can, a cave for an ant, or a mansion for a bee.

A good hive contains a population of six thousand. Swammerdam gives the following account of a hive, he had the curiosity to open. It contained 1 female, 33 males, 5635 working bees, 45 eggs, and 150 worms. To accommodate this population, there were 3392 wax-cells, for the use of the working bees; 62 cells containing bee's bread; and 236 cells, in which honey had been laid up. Number of cells, 3690; population, 5864.

Bees bear an analogy to beavers, and to the genus in ornithology, called Crotophaga, which unite to form one nest, and labour for the general benefit of the whole tribe. One species of the orchis bears a strict resemblance, in point of external appearance, to our favourite insect; its flower, having a spot in its breast resembling a bee, sipping its honey. On this account it is called the bee-flower; and Langhorne thus alludes to it, in his fables of Flora :—

> See on that flower's velvet breast,
> How close the busy vagrant lies!
> His thin-wrought plume, his downy breast,
> Th' ambrosial gold, that swells his thighs!
> Perhaps his fragrant load may bind
> His limbs; we'll set the captive free:
> I sought the *living* bee to find,
> And found the *picture* of a bee.

The astronomers have also imagined its shape in the heavens; hence it has the honour of forming one of the southern constellations.

Bees are said to have placed honey on the lips of Plato; and Pausanias relates [a], that Pindar, on his way to Thesbia, fell asleep near the road, when bees flew to him as he lay asleep, and wrought honey on his lips. The poets are over happy to avail themselves of the Apian republic, in order to illustrate and embellish their subjects. Bees, therefore, are frequently important personages, in the odes of Anacreon, the Idyls of Theocritus, and the poems of Moschus and Bion [b]. Statius [c] has as fine a simile of bees, robbed of their honey, as any in Virgil. The Indian poets compare them to the quiver of the god of love [d]; and Euripides celebrates one of the valleys of Greece, because it was a haunt, sacred to " the murmuring bees." It is curious, that the first simile, in the Iliad, should refer to these insects: a passage successively imitated by Virgil, Tasso, and Milton. The ancient fathers, particularly St. Augustine, drew frequently from them; and

[a] Lib. ix. c. 23.

[b] Achilles Tatius affords the ground-work of an elegant poem :—" Portasse fortuna pridie ejus diei, circiter meridiem, Leucippe Citharam pulsabat, aderam vero et ipse, Clioque illi assidebat. Ibi dum me deambulante, apicula quædam, aliunde improviso advolans, Clionis manum pupugit," &c. &c., lib. ii. c. 5. Herrick has a poem, entitled the " Captive Bee," almost worthy the pen of Anacreon.   [c] Theb. x.

[d] NAGACESARA—To the botanical descriptions of this delightful plant, need only add, that the tree is one of the most beautiful on earth, and that the delicious odour of its blossoms justly gives them a place in the quiver of Camadéva [*]. In the poem, called Nalshadha, there is a wild, but elegant, couplet, where the poet compares the white of the Negacesara, from which the bees were scattering the pollen of the numerous gold-coloured anthers, to an alabaster wheel, on which Cáma was whetting his arrows, while sparks of fire were dispersed in every direction.—*Jones's Botan. Observ. on Select Indian Plants.*— A Javanese poet [†], describing the beauty of the wife of the king of Kurawa, says, " She is said to be exquisitely beautiful; even exceeding the beauties of Heaven; and containing more sweetness than a sea of honey." Warburton says, that bees were considered emblems of chastity in the Eleusinian mysteries. —Vid. Divine Legation of Moses, vol. i. p. 235.

[*] The Indian God of Love.   [†] Hist. Java, p. i. 428.

Milton gathers honey from the same vineyard: one of his amusements, before he laboured under a gutta serena, being to mark

> How Nature paints her colours; how the bee
> Sits on the bloom, extracting liquid sweet.

Howel compared the republic of Lucca (in 1621) to a hive; while Shakspeare, who left neither the depths of the heart nor the secrets of Nature unexplored, nor unexamined, compares them, after the example of Virgil, to a free and well-directed government[a]: and in the Persian anthology there is an apologue, showing how the imperial Jamshid borrowed several of his institutions from them.

Pantænus called one of his friends, "the Sicilian bee," because he selected sweets from various writers[b]; Macrobius, in his preface to the Saturnalia, compares himself to the insect, which imbibes the best juices of flowers, and works them into forms and orders, by a mixture of its own essence: while Boethius associates the stings of bees with those, which illegitimate pleasures leave behind.

> Honey's flowery sweets delight;—
> But soon they cloy the appetite.

---

[a] Marcus Antoninus illustrates the subject of legislation, by observing, with admirable precision, that what is not for the interest of the whole swarm, is not for the essential interest of a single bee, b. vi. c. liv. Shakspeare has illustrations, also: 2 Henry VI. act iii. sc. 2. Romeo and Juliet, act ii. sc. 6. Troilus and Cressida, act v. sc. 11. epilogue. There is a curious work in existence, by Samuel Purchas. It is entitled, "A Theatre of Politicall Flying Insects, wherein the nature, the worth, the work, the wonder, and the manner, of right ordering of the bee is discovered and described." 1657. The poem of Vaniere (*Prædium Rusticum*,) is very particular in respect to bees. His last canto (iv.) treats of the establishment in Paraguay, which, he says, was formed on that of bees.

[b] Seneca, too, Epist. 84. Of this Rollin has availed himself in precept and in practice. "An author," says he, "who draws honey from the nectarium of flowers, should convert the beauties, he finds in the ancient writers, into his own substance: thus making them his own, as bees do."—Belles Lettres, part ii. p. 2. See also p. 275. Mathew of Westminster was styled Florilegus, because he collected "the flowers" of former historians.

> Touch the bee,—the wrathful thing
> Quickly flees, but leaves a sting.
> Mark here the emblems, apt and true,
> Of the pleasures men pursue:
> Ah! they yield a fraudful joy!
> Soon they pall, and quick they fly;
> Quick they fly,—but leave a smart,
> Deep fermenting in the heart.

With what feeling does Thomson lament the destructive mode of obtaining the treasures of these intellectual insects! And—as I know the nobility of your nature,—I do not anticipate a smile of derision, when I confess, that I esteem Colonna more entitled to the honours of a monument, for having introduced the practice of obtaining honey, without destroying the bees*, into the Vale of Ffestiniog, than Field-Marshal Turenne. Turenne destroyed his thousands; Colonna has preserved his tens of thousands. Turenne's monument is of marble:—let that of Colonna be formed of honey-comb!

A curious custom prevails in Sicily. When a couple are married, the attendants place honey in the mouths of the bride and bridegroom; accompanied with an expression of hope, that their love may be as sweet to their souls, as that

---

* Bees are much attended to among the Himalayah Mountains. The natives keep them in earthen pots. When they rob them of honey, they drive them out by making a noise at the end; and taking the honey out at a back door, leave a little in the pots to recompense the bees, when they are permitted to return. Old honest Fuller, in tracing the ruin of the Templars, alludes to the destruction of bees in a manner that proves, he knew nothing of the method of preserving them. "The chief cause of their ruin," says he, "was their wealth. They were feared of many; envied of more; loved of none. As Naboth's vineyard was the chiefest ground for his blasphemy; and, as in England, Lord Pantope said, that not he, but his stately house at Ampthill in Bedfordshire, was guilty of high treason; so certainly their wealth was the principal evidence against them, and cause of their overthrow. It is quarrel and cause enough, to bring a sheep that is fat to the shambles. We may believe king Philip would never have taken their lives, if he might have taken their lands without putting them to death: but the mischief was, he could not get the honey, unless he burnt the bees."—Hist. Holy War, b. v. ch. 3.

honey is to their palate. Well might the ancients fable, that bees encompassed the cradles of Homer [a], Plato, Menander, and Simonides [b];—well might Sophocles glory in the title, which the sweetness of his diction had procured for him; and well might the Athenians take pleasure, in perpetuating the appellation, by erecting a bee-hive of marble over his grave!

The Greeks, not unfrequently, chose the form of a bee-hive for many of their erections. There was a temple of Apollo at Delphos, said to have been built by bees; no doubt, in allusion to its external form. This mode of building prevails, also, in New Caledonia [c]; in the Isle of Carniobar [d], and in Seal Island [e]. The Druids formed their houses [f], and not unfrequently their temples [g], in a similar manner. Sepulchres in Italy [h], too, are sometimes of an analogous shape.

The ancient Romans admitted into the number of their deities, Mellona; whom they styled the Goddess of Honey; while the Thessalians and Acarnanians offered bullocks to several species of insects, which indicated superior intelligence; such as bees and ants. In Monmouthshire, the peasantry entertain so great a veneration for their bees, that, some years since, they were accustomed to go to their hives, on Christmas eve, at twelve o'clock, in order to listen to their humming; which elicited, as they believed, a much more

[a] Homer, says Alexander Paphius, was suckled by a priestess of Isis, whose breasts distilled with honey: the first sounds, he uttered, were the notes of nine separate birds: and on the morning, after his birth, nine doves were found in his cradle, fondling and playing around him.

[b] Even the Hebrew writers describe honey, as being the first food of a Son, born of a Virgin; his name Imannuel; that he may know how to refuse the evil, and to choose the good.—Vide Isaiah, vii. 14.   [c] Cook's Voy. vol. iv. 112.

[d] Asiat. Researches, vol. ii.   [e] Vancouv. Voy. vol. l. 139.

[f] Strabo, v. 197.   [g] Plin. Nat. Hist. li. c. 2.

[h] Vide Descrizione e disegno dell' Emissario del Lago Albano. Tav. xlii. &c. fol.

agreeable music, than at any other period; since, at that time, they celebrated, in the best manner they could, the morning of Christ's nativity [*].

What a beautiful picture is that, presented by Virgil, in the Corycian swain! "I remember," says he, "an old Corycian, who lived under the lofty turrets of Obelai, on the banks of the Galesus. He cultivated a few acres of land, which, till they came into his possession, had been waste and neglected. The soil was too poor for the plough; not adapted to the keeping of flocks; nor was it well situated for the culture of vines. Yet, there, in a cottage, standing among bushes, he cultivated herbs, lilies, vervain, and poppies. He was the first to pluck the rose in spring; the first to gather fruits in autumn. In winter he employed the principal part of the day in attending to the shrubs and flowers, which were to furnish honey for his bees. In spring he fed them; in summer he watched their swarming; and in autumn gathered their honey. This was his sole employment, from year to year: and in this occupation, continues Virgil, being contented and happy, he was essentially richer, than all the kings of the earth.

Simonides, my dear Lelius, is well known to have written a satire upon women. In this celebrated poem he supposes, after the manner of Pythagoras, every woman to have had a pre-existent state; to have animated some body, or to have been composed out of some of the elements, which bear a similitude to the character, she supports in the present state of existence. This idea he carries on, in no very courteous terms, till he comes to the last species of women; the component parts of whom, he says, were made out of the bee. The qualities, by which this order was distinguished, were a faultless character and a blameless life. Orderly in her

[*] The music of bees has been reduced to a scale, vid. Butler's Treatise, 1645. c. 3.

household; loving and beloved by her husband; she is the mother of a virtuous and beautiful family:

> " And her whole course of living is a pattern,
> For chaste and virtuous women ᵃ ; "

forming almost as fine a picture of an admirable woman, as Lucian's portrait of the wife of Verus. Would you know more of her qualities, my Lelius? Consult the fascinating Hortensia; who has, like a jewel, hung "twenty years upon thy neck, and never lost her lustre." And as it was the wish of the Romans, upon the accession of a new emperor, that he might be more fortunate than Augustus ᵇ, and more admirable than Trajan, so, when Constance ᶜ has arrived at a marriageable age, may she possess the qualities of the bee; united to the grace and beauty of her mother! "A thousand graces sit, already, under the shade of her eyelids."

LOVERS OF NATURE ᵈ.

The Greeks were great lovers of Nature. CHIRON, whose fabulous history is the best criterion, by which may be judged the awful esteem, in which he was held, retired to a cavern at the foot of Mount Pelion, to qualify himself for the office of acting as tutor to many of the heroes, who afterwards distinguished themselves in the Trojan war. And we may judge of the impulses of PLATO by the skill, with which he adorned the academy; and by the pictures, he has exhibited in the opening and closing of his several dialogues. "If I had an-

---

ᵃ Massinger's Duke of Milan, act III. sc. 1.

ᵇ Pellcior . Avgosto . Melior . Trajano.—Eutrop. Brev. Hist. Rom. L. vili c. 5. —At Roman nuptials it was customary to wish the bridegroom as happy as Thalassius, who, in the reign of Romulus, having married a Sabine virgin, was esteemed the happiest of men.—Vide Livy, L. c. 9.

ᶜ O matre pulchrâ, filia pulchrior.

ᵈ *From Bees we ought now to proceed to Ants; but, owing to a mistake in the arrangement of copy, Ants are left to a future page. The error is of not much consequence; but it is right that it should be duly acknowledged.*

other world to stand upon," said ARCHIMEDES,—a man of stupendous sagacity[a], —I would move the globe, wherever I pleased." Secluded in his study, he was scarcely known to the general mass of Syracusans, till the attack of Marcellus: and then he was of more use in defending the city, than the whole population united. This profound genius was accustomed to say, that, next to the solution of a problem, was the pleasure of an evening walk in the suburbs of Syracuse.

The Greek tragic writers, too, were decided lovers of natural beauty. The tragedy of Philoctetes amply attests the descriptive talents of SOPHOCLES;—those of EURIPIDES are displayed in almost every tragedy, he has written; and the Prometheus and the Supplicants eloquently illustrate the descriptive genius of ÆSCHYLUS[b].

There are some men, whose love of Nature leads them too far in the regions of Hypothesis; but whose very errors teach us to think. Others there are, whose disregard to every thing unconnected with their interest is so great, that they would esteem any one idly employed, who was investigating a plant, even on the borders of paradise. The best method of viewing Nature is to unite poetry to science; and to enlist both in the pursuit of truth; in order that both may affect the heart, and purify the mind. " There is nothing so delightful in literature," says Cicero[c], " as that branch, which enables us to discern the immensity of Nature; and which, teaching us magnanimity, rescues the soul from obscurity." Thus, too, thought Mons. Necker.—For even amid the factions of Paris[d] he could recur to Nature's sublimities; and in age he still

---

[a] Vir stupendæ sagacitatis.— *Wallis.*

[b] " The Greeks were not blind to the beauties of rural scenery; but their descriptions of rural objects are almost always what may be called sensual descriptions, exhibiting circumstances of corporeal delight, such as breezes to fan the body, springs to cool the feet, grass to repose the limbs, or fruits to regale the taste and smell, rather than objects of contemplative pleasure to the eye and imagination."—*Campbell's Poets,* v. 215.

[c] Tusc. Quest. i. c. 26.   [d] Stael's Mem. p. 10.

Bees were not originally natives of New England. The
first planters never saw any : but the English having introduced
them to Boston, in 1670, they were carried over the Allo-
ghany mountains by a violent hurricane :—hence their propa-
gation on the western part of that continent ; where they have
multiplied beyond all power of calculation. There is no data
to prove, that bees are known in the South Sea Islands ; but in
Hammock, one of the Philippines, the chief subject for barter
is bees' wax. Bees were introduced to New South Wales in
1809. Two hives were taken from England ; but the bees were
suffocated by the melting of the wax, in crossing the Line.
Captain Wallis afterwards introduced four more hives in
1822, and the last time I heard of them, they were healthy
and increasing. They were introduced into Cuba by some
families, who, after the peace of Versailles, went from St.
Augustine's, only since 1784 : and yet in 1792, the settlers
exported not less than 20,000 arrobs of wax. In 1796, there
were 212 barrels of honey and 1854 arrobs of white wax
exported from the Havannah * to Buenos Ayres.

PROFITABLE BEE CULTURE

By

HERBERT S. SHORTHOUSE, F.C.S.

———

BIRMINGHAM
CORNISH BROTHERS LD.
37 NEW STREET
1903

PREFACE.

At the request of many friends, I have pleasure in publishing my lecture as it was delivered before the Midland Pharmaceutical Association, at the University, Birmingham, on November 27th, 1902.

I am but too cognisant of its many deficiencies, all of which, however, I hope to overcome in the larger work on which I am at present engaged. This will treat specially with Scientific Queen Culture, Fertilisation, and Diseases Natural to Bee Life and their Treatment, etc., and will, I trust, meet with the kind consideration of Apiculturists and Lovers of Bee Life.

47, PERSHORE ROAD,
    BIRMINGHAM.

          Jan., 1903.

INTRODUCTION.

Before the delivery of the lecture, SIR JAMES SAWYER, M.D., F.R.C.P., who was in the Chair, said :—Since I last spoke of honey I have extended my experiences concerning its remedial and other uses. We may be quite sure that honey is a demulcent, that is, that it has the property of softening and soothing the internal surfaces of the human body with which it may come in contact, and of protecting them against the hurtful action of acrid matters ; we may be quite sure that honey is an emollient, that is, that it has the property of softening and soothing irritated and irritable portions of the external surfaces of the body, when appropriately applied to them ; we may be quite sure that honey is a valuable nutrient, that is, that it possesses conspicuously the property of nourishing the human body when taken into the stomach as food. maintaining the muscular, nervous, and functional energies of the body, especially sustaining animal heat, and moreover, presenting its materials to the stomach in a condition of particular preparedness for assimilation ; and we may be quite sure that honey is an evacuant, that is, that it has the property of promoting the expulsion of refuse and noxious matters through the chief of the natural emunctories.

Profitable Bee Culture.

I FEEL that no apology is necessary for my deviating somewhat from the strict routine of pharmacy, and taking up a
subject which I hope to render as interesting as it is natural ;
and if it should be that at the close of my lecture I fail to
interest or even fascinate you with my choice, don't for one
moment harshly judge the subject, but rather fix the whole of
the responsibility on your speaker. I feel that I shall cause
disappointment in perhaps every direction, inasmuch as I shall
fail to pursue the detail necessary to satisfy the scientific
enthusiast. Possibly I may not dwell sufficiently on the
natural history to please the lover of that branch, and the
pharmacist by the omission of microscopical and polariscopical
observations so dear to his mind. I fully realise the magnitude
of my offence, and as an excuse would add that time alone
prevents my dwelling on each section as I would have wished ;
therefore I must ask you to content yourselves with a number
of slides, which, together with my remarks, will I hope illustrate the outlines of Apiculture as now universally adopted in
America, and which is already in its infancy in this country.
I realise a difficulty in choosing a starting point, as I would
gladly have wandered back through Grecian history, and have
drawn attention to the then important position of Apiculture,
when its supposed products accounted for the destruction of
Xenophon's army in his famous march through the Mephora-
dates ; and I might have followed it up with other various
interesting passages from later history ; but, as previously
mentioned, time forbids, so that with the exception of my

referring to the digging out of the cellars in Prussian Berlin in 1834 after the great Fire, when among a lot of rubbish and debris was found a vessel containing honey which had been preserved beneath the ruins for 500 years. Pharmacists and others, with sad experiences of tinned and bottled honey combined with heat and pressure, may smile incredulously at this, but history alone is my authority. But to trace Apiculture from its *debut* in history to the present day would be both tedious and in many cases disinteresting, so that I will refer back to the days of my own initiation into the arts and mysteries thereof, at which time I was three years old. This occurred in Sutton Park, then in the possession of Squire Chance, and my memory dates back as it were but yesterday, when I rendered an extremely doubtful assistance to the head gardener in suffocating a skep of bees with the smoking relics of a once hard-worked pair of corduroy trousers ; he or rather we, next removed the combs, and after wrapping them in a gauze or strainer of some description, suspended them from a meat jack in front of the kitchen fire. The honey was collected in what I should now think constituted the roasting pan ; and as a reward for my faithful services and labours I was treated to a supper of bread and hot honey. Whether or not mead or metheglim was brewed from the remaining relics, as was the country custom, I know not, but if such were the case it was imbibed at the hour when I enjoyed slumberland. In those days the straw skeps were almost if not entirely in vogue, or at least the frame hive was but in its infancy.

We will now, with your permission, pass over a few years, during which many developments have taken place, resulting in the practical abandonment of straw skeps and the establishment of the frame or bar hive which is now used throughout all well-conducted apiaries, especially if intended as a source of income, pleasure, and scientific observation.   Now having in our possession such a hive containing a stock of bees, meaning the queen with her (barren) female workers, we will assume that it reaches its garden destination in the middle of March, ready to take advantage of the coming spring flowers in all their perfumed splendour. At this time of the year on a sunny day we will carefully lift the blanket from the hive and observe its inmates with the object of seeing that they are in no danger from starvation, and should necessity demand, supply them with a cake of candy to satisfy their immediate requirements. This candy should consist of sugar, pea-meal, and honey, rendered edible by careful cooking, and serves to supply food and artificial pollen which enables our tiny servants to commence breeding, which they do instinctively so soon as food comes along. We now await the arrival of warmer weather to make a more complete examination of the hive. This time we lift out the frames one by one, not, please notice, with careless impetuosity like our friend the novice, who beside endangering the queen is also irritating the bees, but rather in the quiet and firm style of the expert, who believes in doing the maximum of work with the minimum of disturbance and fuss. We this time make certain that the queen has survived the winter, and to do this we must either obtain sight of her majesty or be assured of her presence by the finding of eggs, larvæ and young bees in the various stages of development. Assuming that all has gone well, we will in a week's time, weather permitting, again open the hive, when we should find that the queen has been very busy laying some few hundred eggs a day and taxing her capabilities generally in bringing the hive into a honey-getting condition.

[7]

Here I would mention that a prolific queen in her first
and second year will lay from 2,000 to 4,000 eggs daily irres-
pective of her other duties, and when we recollect that she has
to visit this number of cells for the purpose we shall be indisposed
to envy royalty her position. As just mentioned, the queen
is now rapidly laying, and her natural inclination is to do so
in the warmest part of the hive, so that we expect to find her
on the centre frames, or as we will term it, the " natural brood
nest." As this becomes filled with eggs she will gradually
work her way to the outer frames, leaving the eggs to be tended
and cared for by the young nurse bees, which they do by
clustering the frames, thus supplying the heat which
results in the hatching of the eggs and the after feeding
of the larvæ, and it is here that the apiarist renders the first
artificial aid by removing any pollen-clogged frames or surplus
storage and returning them empty unto the bees,
transferring outer frames containing few eggs to the centre
of the hive, by replacement, and perhaps in the centre of all
he will place an empty frame, in which the queen will rapidly
deposit eggs. By these means the young hatching brood is
constantly being distributed towards the outer frames of the hive,
consequently the queen lays more eggs and the stock is rapidly
getting into a strong condition ready to take advantage of the
first honey flow as it arrives ; and as we enter the orchard
on a sunny spring morning, when the blossom bursts forth,
we are attracted by the sight of these busy creatures flying to
and fro, each carrying out its special object, namely, the collection
of honey, pollen, or water, and providing the weather remains
favourable, breeding and honey-getting now sets in, in earnest ;
and if we open a hive at this season we should find a large
number of bees distinguished by their ragged wings and shabby

plumage, which constitute the honey-getting or field bees, and owe their ruffled appearance to many a hard flight in search of food. Noticeable amidst these by their youthful brilliancy and soft downy plumage, are the young bees, employed as nursemaids in the hatching of eggs and the feeding of larvæ. In the cells we shall see eggs and larvæ in every stage of development up to the young bees who are eating their way out of their hatching cells, and we shall notice that every cell not captured by the energy of the queen is promptly made use of as a storeroom for gathered honey or pollen. This proves the wisdom of offering every assistance to the queen in filling the brood chamber with eggs, for when no space remains for the deposit of honey the bees are naturally compelled to seek a further receptacle for the safe storage of their hard-gathered spoils. Here again science comes to their aid, for the observant bee-keeper quickly appreciates the condition of the hive and straightway offers them an upper storey, or super, rendered inaccessible to the queen, consequently her majesty reigns supremely in the lower or brood chamber, whilst the worker bees enjoy an uninterrupted career in the super, or upper chamber, which they more or less rapidly fill with honey, so that we find the super frames, which were originally a thin wax foundation, rapidly drawn out into beautiful combs and laden with honey awaiting the arrival of the bee-keeper. He comes along, drives his bees downstairs, either by the aid of a puff of smoke, or the fixing of the super clearer, by which means a bee passage-way downstairs is allowed, which prohibits a return to the upper storey. The capped honey is next taken to the extracting room, the cappings removed by means of a knife, such as a large bread knife, and the honey extracted by spinning the frames softly

in a centrifugal machine, from whence it is run through
a silk strainer into a vessel known as a " ripener," in which it
remains for a fortnight at a temperature of about 80 degrees
Fahr. : by which time it has become ripened and blended,
and developed a flavour sufficient to tempt the appetite of the
most fastidious. The combs are by this method undamaged
and are promptly replaced in the hive, again to be refilled
with honey. Here I would just note that it is possible by
judicious care to preserve the honey belonging to any particular
flower, as the full bloom of much honey-giving flowers,
rarely occurs at the same period, so that by having the frames
cleared at the moment of the full outburst of blossom, we can
secure the honey from that particular source. But I must
reluctantly forsake the blossom in all its splendour and direct
my attention more particularly to the bee itself. To appreciate
the important part the bee plays in out-door life we have
but to visit some of the large fruit farms in our eastern counties, which we shall find ably stocked with bees, their object
being the fertilisation of the blossom, consequently better
crops resulting therefrom, besides being a further source
of income in themselves.

It would be a grave omission on such an occasion as this
did I not refer all interested in natural history to the glorious
writing on the Bee and its Companion, by Sir John Lubbock,
but I particularly regret that the present opportunity forbids
my touching upon any of the interesting passages throughout
his works. Likewise has M. Maeterlinck gained a world-wide
reputation by the writing of his book " The Life of the Bee."
Again, that popular writer on Sunny or Butterfly Japan,
Sir Edwin Arnold, could not resist the tempting subject offered
by the honey bee. In one of his writings it is noted, that

time was, when the yearly looting of hives was a serious matter for these islands, for before the sugar cane was domesticated from the wild reed and other sources of sugar utilised, it was upon the bee the community relied for the indispensable sweetening. Out of honey it also brewed its heavy beverages of mead and metheglim, and a lump of sugar would have been as great a novelty to England's maiden Queen Elizabeth, as wireless telegraphy is to us to-day. In many countries the honeycomb of the wild bee in hollow tree trunk or rocky cliff is still the sugar-pot of tropical people, although they may live amid waving cane fields; and one can see how precious was considered that little waxen store so frequently mentioned in Holy Writ, for did it not refresh Absalom after fierce battle, as well as giving a famous riddle to Samson? For sugar the world must have, and in the early life of man the honey bee was one of his best friends.

The footing that Apiculture has gained in America is in itself a powerful argument why it should become an important industry in this country, and forms a strong incentive to anyone with the facilities and the desire to create a new source of wealth, a health-giving and pleasing pastime, besides offering such a field for exploration as is hardly attainable in any other form of life. For here I would mention that a hive of bees upon the death of her queen has the power to re-raise a queen, produce a drone or worker bee at their own free will, from any one egg of the many laid by their late queen. This is brought about by the after treatment of the eggs; thus for instance do they wish to raise a queen, they quickly erect round any particular egg the waxwork of a queen cell and we next find this egg or perhaps larvæ swimming in what we term " royal jelly." In a few days more we find this cell further elongated and capped, and we next find the young queen, having been cherished by the warmth of the hive, eating her way out of her cell, and we can only compare her, as she frisks about in her youthful coat of splendour, as agile as she is beautiful, queenly and graceful in every movement, with our own fair sex as they appear self-satisfied, flushed and glowing with the excitement of their first ball. But I would hastily dissociate all resemblance in their jealous natures, inasmuch as a queen only considers her rival royal sisters vanquished by death, which she herself personally carries out, whereas in woman it has been lightly suggested that milder but most intricate methods are practised for securing the impossible. It thus becomes necessary for the hatching up of queens to have such arrangements that the escape of a virgin queen is impossible. The means by which this is carried out I wish to dwell upon later when I refer particularly to the scientific breeding of queens. And in the near future it should be no uncommon thing to see the apiaries of experimentalists stocked with bees of different nationalities, all characterised by their beautiful colours, ranging from the most brilliant guinea-gold to the deep shining lustrous black. Here I would just speak of the peculiarities belonging to these different races, inasmuch as the most beautiful of all bees, namely the golden Palestines, have a peculiar habit of biting, besides which their temper is such, and their stinging capabilities so marked, that they would sorely tax the even and well-mannered temper of a pharmacist. A very able writer speaks most concisely when he describes them as being " Very beautiful but very hot." Again the Tunisian bees, which are of a coal-black colour, delight in the production of many queen cells, so that at the time of hatching of the royal subjects numerous swarms occur and battles result when any two royal subjects meet. Again, others, such as the Ligurians, are characterised by their gentleness. The honey bees I shall exhibit to-night are of two varieties only, the leather coloured Italian and the German, or what is known as the ordinary English bee. The more brilliantly coloured queens, from which of course the drones and workers get their special markings, are scarce, and consequently too valuable in this country to be deprived of life unnecessarily. This scarcity however will soon be a thing of the past, as the tendency to-day is to produce queens at a cheap rate, brilliant in colour, with prolific capabilities and longevity ; the bees resulting therefrom must be good comb builders, honey getters, strong enough to stand the climate of variable England, and to fight the various diseases and pests to which they are naturally subject. The methods by which we can obtain these results, have been the outcome of many years of steady and close observation by many able apiculturists, and are to-day unquestionably the summit of the apiculturist's art, and the means towards which he must look, would he hold a foremost position in scientific apiculture, and I venture to take this up as the most important feature of to-night's lecture, endeavouring to show both clearly and concisely how these results can be obtained. Before doing so however I think it only reasonable that I should briefly narrate the natural and artificial old-fashioned systems which have been adopted with more or less success, more or less inasmuch as queens have been found to be weak in many cases, their wings misshapen, to be of poor prolific capabilities and to live a life of short duration. This may have been the result of in-breeding, poor blood, poor food, partial starvation, weak stocks, consequently queens would be hatched at a low temperature or various other causes which to-day can, and are, fully remedied.

, All these and other causes of failure have, as previously mentioned, to be fully remedied before the production of high class queens is insured, and to accomplish this we must render scientific assistance wherever possible. This we can do by taking advantage of a hive preparing for swarming or by causing a hive of bees to commence to raise a queen so that it shall supply the necessary royal jelly which we purpose introducing into our artificially-made wax cups intended for queen cells. It is in each one of these that we deposit a recently hatched. larvæ obtained from the hive of our choicest queen (which is expressly kept on damaged combs, especially if much queen breeding is conducted).

This frame of prepared waxen cups we introduce into a strong queenless hive, containing sealed brood only, so that the bees shall have no uncapped larvæ to maintain. Likewise it leaves unto them no other way of re-queening themselves other than accepting the cells purposely introduced, consequently these cells should receive better attention and nourishment from the nurse bees than would otherwise be the case.

These cells, assuming that they are accepted, will be duly capped and matured and can be inserted on two frames and hatched out in nucleus hives, or hatched in either a lamp nursery or queen nursery contained in a hive. As an alternate method which is particularly adaptable to small apiaries where few queens are desired and it is the wish of the apiarist not to interfere with the general honey getting of the bees, he can, instead of rendering the hive queenless for the raising of queen cells take advantage of the upper or super chamber, which should preferably contain the deeper frames, and to do this he must insert two or more frames containing recently capped brood at a time when honey is rapidly being stored. A few days later, as the brood is hatching out, insert a frame of the previously mentioned prepared waxen cells containing the larvæ in royal jelly, when the bees, who have already realised their inability to re-raise further brood in this chamber, will as readily take to these cells as if the brood chamber of a queenless hive. By these means we raise queens in the upper chamber at a time when the bees are gathering honey. At the same time -the queen, as is the usual custom, is confined to her labours in the lower or brood chamber, and assuming that we allow one of the queens from the prepared cells to hatch out and escape in the upper chamber we have but to offer an outlet at the back of the hive, giving her an opportunity to escape, when in due course she will, under favourable circumstances, return fertilised and commence depositing eggs in the usual manner. We can then either allow these two queens to remain in the separate chambers of the same hive each to supply her own department with brood, separated only by means of a perforated zinc excluder, or we can remove same temporarily, when the recently hatched queen will descend, whence a battle unto death will ensue, in which the young queen is always victorious and will consequently reign alone, or by division of the super chamber, we can allow several queens to hatch out, and become fertilised in the manner already described. Again it would appear somewhat ludicrous to devote such care in the cultivation of these choice queens did we not consider the making thereof. This, as would be expected, has received the desirable attention, and in well-conducted apiaries hives are kept solely for the purpose of drone breeding for fertilisation purposes, likewise means are adopted to entrap drones from

undesirable hives. Further the experience of the apiculturist of Ontario College has clearly demonstrated that it
is possible to mate a queen with any particular drone in confinement (conducting his experiments in a glass bottle of some
twenty-gallon capacity). On this point I hope to make a
number of trials during the coming season. A hive recently
queened is in satisfactory condition for two years, as a queen
is in her best condition for that while, so that we only require
to supply this queen with sufficient frames to lay in and the
bees with frames for storing honey. Having now briefly,
and perhaps somewhat rapidly described the principles of
up-to-date queen culture, I would to some extent dwell upon
the eccentricities and peculiarities belonging to bee life. As
I have practically shown that queen breeding whether artificial
or by natural swarming commences as soon as honey comes in
freely, when male bees or drones as they are called are daily
hatching ready to mate with the virgin queens as they merge
from the hives, which takes place when they are five days
old, weather permitting. So long as swarming continues and
these queens are flying, drones are tolerated and allowed to live
their lives of idlenesss and debauchery in and about the hives,
for be it understood the drone, like savage man, be he Negro
or Hooligan, toils not, neither does he spin, but allows the
female bee to do the whole of the work, while he lives on his
life of pleasure. But we must not begrudge him these means
of ridding himself of his personality, for his life is not of long
duration ; for no sooner does swarming cease, which is usually
in July, when the drones are evicted by an army of irate
(lady) Amazons who, devoid of all compassion, animated by
their one desire to rid themselves of their useless mates, ruth-
lessly force them outside to die a lingering death of cold

starvation. M. Maeterlinck describes the drone as follows :—
Indelicate and wasteful, sleek and corpulent, fully content
with their idle existence as honorary lovers, they feast and
carouse, throng the alleys, obstruct the passages, and hinder
the work ; jostling and jostled, fatuously pompous, swelled
with foolish, good-natured contempt. The lady workers
finding themselves no longer hampered, again set to work
gathering in the final stores of honey, which in a favourable season
lasts until the beginning of September, when the queen
gradually ceases laying, so that no larvæ will have to be fed
during the winter months, which is the time when a bee econo-
mises food. The field bees now gradually die off and are cast
out of the hive by the ambulance corps to meet a grassy grave.
These bees have lived a life of perhaps six weeks, the first two
of which they spent in the hive as nurse bees. This work
is always carried out by the young bees, as they can eject a
jelly upon which the larvæ feed, a power they possess to a lesser
extent after becoming field bees or honey gatherers. The
queen is now left with a colony of more or less young bees,
and as the autumn sets in these are carefully examined and
the frames reduced to economise heat, fed if necessary by
syrup or candy, duly disinfected and carefully wrapped in
blankets to face the coming winter. Here they remain
nestled up together, living carefully on their stores, which
they uncap cell by cell.

Here I would point out the disadvantage in robbing bees
too closely of their honey, for if fed too largely upon sugar
food they frequently become attacked by the pest known
as the blind louse, which usually first infests the queen, and
unless remedied will prove the destruction of a hive. From
this fact it appears necessary that a bee should obtain nitro-

genous nutriment. Next did I not refer to pests belonging to
apiculture, which I am sorry to say are many, my remarks
would be incomplete. Under this heading I must class the
earwig, who in his crawly regions seeks the warmth and shelter
of the hive. The mouse too considers the upper storey as
a heaven-sent home for the winter. A queen wasp appreciates
the heat of a hive, as also does the wax moth, who deposits
her eggs to be hatched by its warmth, with the production
of larvæ which soon render themselves formidable by eating
their way through the combs, to the destruction of all bee
larvæ in their path. However all bees will not tolerate these
last intruders and so capture them, when they meet a hasty
death; especially is this so with Italian bees, which possess
in a marked degree the fiery nature of their nationality. Lastly
we have that most dreaded of all pests the bacillus alvei, or what
is commonly known as foul brood. This, unless remedied,
will promptly destroy the whole apiary, as it causes the whole
of the brood to become rotten and decomposed. The bees
lose their characteristic vitality, fall short in numbers and
ultimately die. This bacillus is extremely difficult to eradicate
as it becomes deposited among the waxen cells, which resist
the action of disinfectants, so that unless treated in its early
stages the burning of the hive and its occupants is the only
remedy.

And here I would conclude my remarks with the observations
and experiments of Sir John Lubbock and others, who have
clearly proved that although bees are peculiarly sensitive to
vibration they are absolutely incapable of hearing. This has
abolished a long cherished theory in apiculture, so that it
becomes necessary to establish a new one as to how bees
guide their co-workers to the freshly-found honey fields or

home. The fact that a bee creates what is known as the
" Merry Hum " must have been the origin of their having
been given credit for hearing. The careful observer (B.B.J.),
who pointed out that when creating this " Merry Hum," they
were actually working a dorsal gland from which a distinct odour
was emitted; which became scattered by the movement of the
wings, this suggests most reasonably that the sense of smell is the
guiding power, for the aldehydic odour produced on such
occasions is most marked to anyone trained in nasal observations. This, together with the fact that honey is naturally
preserved by bees, that they (too) have a means of ridding
themselves of the most virulent diseases by self-disinfection, and
that likewise the contents of the sting of the bee has been confirmed to contain much formic acid, these facts lead me to
suggest that formic aldehyde is the volatile perfume emitted,
also the preservative and disinfectant used.

This theory is one I volunteer personally, laying no claim
as to its absolute correctness, although I shall require much
convincing evidence to prove that formic aldehyde and acid
do not play an important part in bee economy, and I am
hoping to complete and publish a long series of experiments on
this all-important point, and if it should be that my assumptions
are correct it is at once apparent that formalin or formic
aldehyde is the disinfectant or bactericidal agent that should
become universal throughout apiculture; and it is a source
of gratification to know that it is this product that is being
recommended by the Board of Agriculture in those parts
of Ireland where foul brood is so prevalent. And too, I am
personally anticipating the recording of results made under
varying and exacting conditions in the near future with
this disinfectant.

Here I would bid my subject adieu. In my parting words I would again emphasise the desirability for cleanliness, judicious feeding and robbing of honey, gentle but thorough manipulation throughout the working season, the due application of warm covering and absence of any disturbance in cold weather, and finally, the habitual use of reliable disinfectants properly and systematically applied. These points are few among many others that are absolutely essential to attain success in apiculture. Lastly I would take advantage of this opportunity to express my indebtedness to Mr. George Franklin, the expert apiculturist for Warwickshire, from whom I received my initiation into Scientific Bee Culture, and to my dear friend, Mr. William Heming, of Littleton, Evesham, in whose apiary the whole of my experiments and observations have been conducted.